J. W. Orderson

Creoleana:

or,
Social and Domestic Scenes and Incidents
in Barbados in Days of Yore

and

The Fair Barbadian and Faithful Black;

or, A Cure for the Gout

Edited and with a new Introduction
by John Gilmore

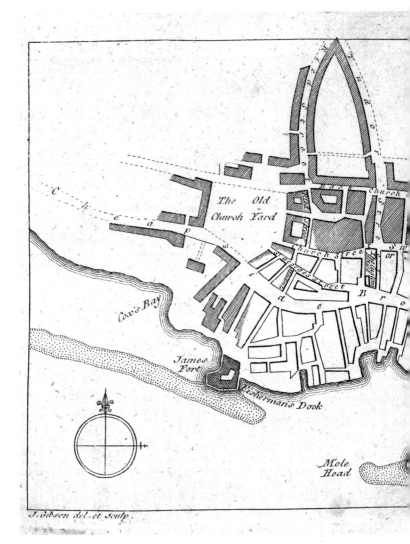

The Old
Church Yard

Church

Cox's Bay

James
Fort

Fisherman's Dock

Mole
Head

J. Gibson del. et Sculp.

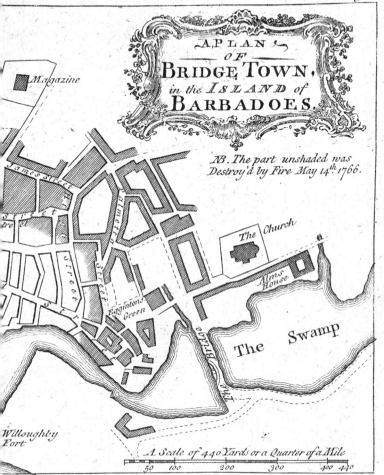

A PLAN
OF
BRIDGE TOWN,
in the ISLAND of
BARBADOES.

NB. The part unshaded was
Destroy'd by Fire May 14th. 1766.

Magazine

The Church

The Alms House

Eggintons Green

The Bridge

The Swamp

Willoughby Fort

A Scale of 440 Yards or a Quarter of a Mile

50   100   200   300   400 440

Macmillan Education
Between Towns Road, Oxford OX4 3PP
A division of Macmillan Publishers Limited
Companies and representatives throughout the world

www.macmillan-caribbean.com

ISBN 0 333 77606 2

Copyright Introduction and notes John Gilmore 2002
Design and illustration © Macmillan Publishers Limited 2002

First published 2002

Cover design by AC Design

Printed in Hong Kong

2006 2005 2004 2003 2002
10 9 8 7 6 5 4 3 2 1

CONTENTS

ACKNOWLEDGEMENTS

THE present edition draws on material which is the result of work done over many years in the Barbados Department of Archives, the library of the Barbados Museum and Historical Society, the British Library, the Cambridge University Library, the Lambeth Palace Library, and the libraries of the University of Warwick and the University of the West Indies (Cave Hill). I would like to acknowledge the unfailing courtesy and helpfulness of the staff of these institutions, and I am particularly grateful to Mr Ephraim Norville of the Barbados Department of Archives for checking an important reference for me. I am also grateful to the staff of the New York Public Library for the speed and efficiency with which they supplied a copy of Orderson's *Cursory Remarks* by post. Other useful resources have been provided over the years by various booksellers; among these, my friends Andy and Myrna Taitt of The Book Place, Bridgetown, deserve special mention for the constant enthusiasm and success with which they track down rare items of Barbadiana.

The LION – Literature Online – database has proved a useful addition to the traditional concordances and dictionaries of quotations in tracing a number of Orderson's more obscure quotations. Students on my Imperialism and Literature course at Warwick have made a number of suggestions about Orderson and other eighteenth- and early nineteenth-century Caribbean authors which I have drawn on in the preparation of this edition, while colleagues in the Centre for Caribbean Studies and the Centre for Translation and Comparative Cultural Studies at Warwick have provided constant support and encouragement without which this edition would not have been possible. My wife Marita, my father-in-law Grafton Browne, and my mother-in-law Vera Sandiford have all provided information on points of detail, while Marita and our children have displayed an extraordinary understanding and tolerance of my protracted disappearances into the chaos of my study.

Last, but certainly by no means least, I would like to express my thanks to Nick Gillard of Macmillan Caribbean for his faith in the idea of the Caribbean Classics series.

John Gilmore
Centre for Caribbean Studies
and
Centre for Translation and Comparative Cultural Studies
University of Warwick

A NOTE ON THE ILLUSTRATIONS

Front cover   "Rachel Pringle of Barbadoes"; etching by Thomas Rowlandson after a drawing by E. D. (whose identity remains unknown), published 1796. Reproduced courtesy of the Barbados Museum and Historical Society. Rachael herself is in the foreground. It has been suggested that the figures on the left may represent Lauder staring lasciviously at Rachael in her younger days, while the man in uniform is perhaps intended for Captain Pringle. The print is also known with the uniform coloured blue, which would be more in keeping with Pringle's being a naval officer. See Chapter IX of *Creoleana*.

pp. ii-iii   The first separately published map of Bridgetown, which appeared in the English periodical, the *Gentleman's Magazine*, in 1766. The unshaded part represents the section of the city destroyed by the fire of that year, which is referred to at the beginning of *Creoleana*.

p. 17   Cartoon by the well-known English artist James Gillray, first published in 1788, and satirising Prince William Henry's alleged interest in black women during his naval service in the Caribbean. The Wouski of the print's title was a black female character in the popular drama *Inkle and Yarico: An Opera*, by George Colman the Younger, which was first produced in 1787. See Chapter IX of *Creoleana*.

The title-pages on p. 19 and p. 157 reproduce the general appearance of the originals, but are not exact facsimiles.

INTRODUCTION

Sex, race, violence, and a happy ending: it sounds like a cynical recipe for how to write one of those inch-thick bestsellers which load the shelves of our local supermarkets and airport bookstalls. It's all there in the texts presented in this volume even though they were first published more than a hundred and fifty years ago, but, gentle reader, you will soon find that they are treated in a fashion very different from the latest historical bodice-ripper or sensational fictionalization of life in today's world of big business. While some things don't change – do we ever tire of reading about love's triumphs over adversity? – and these help to make *Creoleana* and *The Fair Barbadian* a 'good read', texts we can enjoy simply for the pleasure of the story, we are also reminded that, in L. P. Hartley's famous phrase, 'The past is a foreign country: they do things differently there.' Orderson is not a modern historian, describing and interpreting the Caribbean past for a twenty-first century audience, but someone who lived in the Barbados of the late eighteenth and early nineteenth centuries and who in his old age sought to give younger readers an impression of a time and place which he had known intimately but which had already vanished. Separated from it as they were by the great gap in historical continuity represented by the Emancipation Act, the Barbados of the era of the American War of Independence and the French Revolutionary Wars must have seemed almost as remote to the original readers of *Creoleana* as it does to us. Yet some of the legacies of slavery and the plantation system are still with us, and some of the other things which Orderson describes, such as the problems a small, island community faces as a result of its inevitable dependence on the outside world, will seem remarkably familiar – the food crisis Barbados faced in the 1770s as a result of the American War can be paralleled by the economic problems caused by the international oil crisis in the 1970s. Orderson's powers of observation and imagination allow us to get at least an idea of the attitudes and feelings, the everyday concerns of Barbadians of two hundred years ago – and not only those of his own class and race. Although Orderson endeavours to shape his material to support his conservative political and social position, he is not always successful, and he sometimes seems to reveal things without intending to do so – often it is precisely these things the modern reader will find most illuminating.

Orderson's texts are also important documents in the history of Caribbean culture. As Jerome Handler notes in the *Supplement* to his authoritative *Guide to Source Materials for the Study of Barbados History*, in *The Fair Barbadian* Orderson provides 'the lengthiest passages extant of black speech behaviour recorded by a Barbadian during the slave period.'[1] *Creoleana* is the first novel by a Barbadian, and perhaps the earliest novel of the Anglophone Caribbean to be written by somebody demonstrably a native of the region – it appeared twelve years before Maxwell Philip's *Emmanuel Appadoca*, which has recently been claimed as 'the first Anglo-Caribbean novel.'[2]

[1] Jerome S. Handler, *Supplement to A Guide to Source Materials for the Study of Barbados History, 1627–1834* (Providence, RI, 1991) pp. 41–42.
[2] See the Preface by Selwyn R. Cudjoe to his new edition of Maxwell Philip, *Emmanuel Appadoca; or, Blighted Life: A Tale of the boucaneers* (Amherst, MA, 1997) pp. xiii–xiv. The Trinidadian Maxwell Philip (1829–88) published *Emmanuel Appadoca* in London in 1854.

There were several earlier novels in English at least partly set in the region, but these appear to be all either anonymous or by authors born outside the Caribbean. Examples include *Hamel, The Obeah Man* (2 vols., London, 1827), which is by an author who is anonymous but who certainly appears to have had some first-hand knowledge of Jamaica, and *Tom Cringle's Log*, written by Michael Scott (1789–1835), a Scotsman who had lived in Jamaica for several years, which was first published in book form in 1833, and which remained immensely popular (at least with British readers) into the twentieth century.

✿ ✿ ✿ ✿ ✿ ✿

Although he appears on the title-pages of his publications as
'J. W. Orderson,' his full name was Isaac Williamson Orderson.
He was born in Barbados, 28 May 1767, and his baptism was
recorded as solemnized in the parish of St. Michael the following
day.[3] He was the grandson of a man who had been living in
Barbados at the time of the 1715 census, apparently the earliest
documented reference to the family in the island. His father, John
Orderson (d. 1798) had around 1772 become the proprietor of
the *Barbados Mercury*, and at various dates three of John
Orderson's sons were associated with the newspaper. Isaac
Williamson Orderson was one of the editors from 1787, and after
the death of his brother John Edward Orderson in 1795, became
sole proprietor and editor.[4]

   Of the early life and education of Isaac Williamson Orderson,
we know nothing. In 1800 he published (anonymously) a pamphlet entitled *Directions to young planters for the care and
management of a sugar plantation in Barbados*, which led
E. M. Shilstone (a later Barbadian antiquarian) to conclude that
he 'must have had some training and practical experience in
agriculture in Barbados.'

   He had married in England in 1798, but returned to Barbados
and continued as editor of the *Mercury*. In 1810 he and his wife
undertook a voyage to England for the sake of her health, but she
died at sea. Orderson himself returned to Barbados, but at the

---

[3] The baptismal record, which also gives his date of birth, is in the
St. Michael Register, RL1/4, p. 351, in the Barbados Department of
Archives. I am grateful to Mr. Ephraim Norville of the Department of
Archives for confirming this reference. Orderson's name and customary ini-
tials look like more of a discrepancy to us than they would have done to his
contemporaries: eighteenth- and early nineteenth-century practice regu-
larly treated I and J as the same letter.
[4] These and other biographical details are taken from E. M. Shilstone's article,
'Orderson Family Records,' *Journal of the Barbados Museum and Historical
Society*, XXV, 152–7 (August 1958); reprinted in James C. Brandow, comp.,
Genealogies of Barbados Families (Baltimore, 1983), pp. 427–432.

end of 1810 handed over control of the *Mercury* to William
Walker & Co. (presumably as the result of a sale), and in 1811 he
went to England again. He remarried there in 1812; his second
wife appears to have predeceased him at some uncertain date,
and there is no record of any children.

He seems to have remained in England for a protracted time.
In 1816 he published a pamphlet in London on the title-page of
which he was described as 'late of Barbadoes'.[5] However, he returned to the island. The rebuilding of the Molehead (as the pier
and breakwater on the southern side of the entrance to the
Careenage in Bridgetown was called) began in 1826, and
Orderson, as he later recalled in a letter in 1847, had 'the superin-
tendance of the work for many years'. He was nearly 59 when the
work started, and it is not surprising that eventually he was 'compelled from ill health to resign.' He also noted that he had 'many
years been a sworn Magistrate, and an Assistant Judge of the
Court of Common Pleas', a position which in this period in
Barbados did not require any specialist legal training.[6] In 1827 he
published a pamphlet, *Leisure Hours at the Pier; or, a treatise on
the poor of Barbados* for which he was thanked by the House of
Assembly.[7] His play, *The Fair Barbadian and Faithful Black; or, A
Cure for the Gout*, was performed in Barbados in 1832, and
printed in Liverpool in 1835, while his novel, *Creoleana: or, Social
and Domestic Scenes and Incidents in Barbados in Days of Yore*,
was published in London in 1842.

[5] This was his *Cursory remarks and plain facts connected with the question
produced by the proposed Slave Registry Bill* (London, 1816).
[6] These quotations are from an original letter of Orderson's to William Reid,
Governor of Barbados, dated 8 July 1847, and preserved in Shilstone
Notebook No. 2, Barbados Department of Archives. At this date Orderson was
living at No. 17, Spry Street, Bridgetown. He said he had been a magistrate and
assistant judge 'down to the time of consolidating those Courts under the present Chief Judge.' This appears to refer to the reform of the island's legal system under Sir Robert Bowcher Clarke, appointed as Chief Justice in 1841;see
the Note on *Creoleana*, p. 118. Page references are to the text in this edition.
[7] See the Notes on *Creoleana*, p. 22.

However, none of this appears to have brought him any lasting financial security. In the letter previously quoted, written when he was eighty and in the last year of his life, he refers to his 'fallen fortunes' and rather pathetically informed the then Governor of Barbados, William Reid, that he was 'still wishfull [sic] of active employment, not less from a desire of being useful than from the urgent calls of pecuniary necessity.' The governor's response was a note to his secretary scribbled on the letter: 'Acquaint Mr. Olderson [sic] that he is sorry that he is not aware of any public situation in which he could employ Mr. Olderson [sic].' Shilstone noted that there was no will of Orderson's on record, and presumed this meant that at the time of his death he 'had no estate of which to dispose.'

Orderson died 6 December 1847. In an obituary, *The Barbadian* newspaper said he was 'universally respected' and that his

> patriotic acts and intentions for the prosperity and welfare of his native country must be remembered with gratitude. For many years he was Editor and Proprietor of *The Barbados Mercury* which under his able superintendence obtained a circulation far exceeding any that colonial papers now enjoy. Many of our countrymen and friends who have gone before him experienced his liberality, benevolence and hospitality when he was in the days of his prosperity; and those who knew him in adversity highly appreciated his character and talents, and looked up to him with reverence and respect as one of the most patriotic men of his day. He was followed to his resting place in the Cathedral Churchyard by many of our most respectable citizens, by five of the clergy, and a large number of ladies, a circumstance unusual at the funeral of a gentleman, but it was his particular wish, for he always delighted in the Society of ladies.[8]

☞ ☞ ☞ ☞ ☞ ☞

---

[8] Quoted by Shilstone, 'Orderson Family Records.'

Although Orderson comments in his Preface to *Creoleana* that 'Barbados has contributed her share, with no unlavish hand' to what he calls 'West Indian Literature,' the only local work he specifically mentions in his novel is Griffith Hughes' *Natural History of Barbados* (1750). He had been a subscriber to the *History of Barbados* by John Poyer (1808) and may have used this to refresh his memory, but he does so in no very obvious manner. We might expect him to have been familiar with other earlier works by Barbadian writers, such as Nathaniel Weekes' *Barbados: A Poem* (London, 1754) or Matthew Chapman's *Barbadoes, and other poems* (London, 1833), or works from the wider English-speaking Caribbean, such as James Grainger's *The Sugar-Cane: A Poem* (London, 1764) or Bryan Edwards' *The History, Civil and Commercial, of the British West Indies* (first published 1793), but if this was the case, he seems to give no hint of it in either *The Fair Barbadian* or *Creoleana*. His identifiable literary references include a not very surprising preponderance of the King James Version of the Bible and Shakespeare, but also a range of British, Irish and European authors: the Anglican *Book of Common Prayer* and *The Whole Duty of Man*, Lord Byron, John Bunyan, Samuel Butler, Miguel de Cervantes (perhaps encountered in English translation), William Cowper, Thomas Gray, William Hone, Samuel Johnson, John Milton, Samuel Richardson, Richard Brinsley Sheridan, Laurence Sterne, Edward Young, and perhaps others, such as Richard Brome, John Hookham Frere, Charles Lamb, Nicholas Rowe and Robert Southey. Some of these are no more than mentioned by name, while some of Orderson's references or even quotations might have been acquired at second-hand; even if we assume that he had actually read significant parts of the works of all these writers, it would represent a relatively wide, but by no means unconventional selection by the standards of a fairly well educated English contemporary of Orderson's – those names in the list which are less well known today are still those of authors who enjoyed significant popularity in the early nineteenth century. One or two of Orderson's quotations have escaped identification altogether, even with the help of electronic databases, and there may be a few allusions I have missed, but these would probably not alter the overall impression significantly. It is noticeable that, with the exception of one well-worn cliché derived from Cicero, there is hardly a trace of the Greek and Roman authors of classical antiquity who provided the basic texts of a conventional education in Orderson's youth and for long after, though he is careful to have his hero, the young Jack Goldacre, remedy the defects in his own education by being taught by Mr. Cater, 'a man . . . of great classical attainment' who was to be found in Bridgetown.

The impression of a Eurocentric, indeed Anglocentric, cultural outlook which might be given by this survey of Orderson's reading is belied by an examination of his own work. While he refers to Barbados as 'Little England,' dedicates *Creoleana* to Lord Stanley, and refers to members of the British royal family in deferential terms, his writing is permeated with local references which must have been unintelligible except to Barbadian readers, such as 'St. Ann's' in *The Fair Barbadian* (p. 178), or 'Pilgrim gates' and 'our late patriotic Baronet' in *Creoleana* (pp. 30, 39). His treatment of Barbadian speech is, on the whole, quite realistic, and may be usefully contrasted with the approach of the anonymous author of the novel *Hamel, The Obeah Man*, set in Jamaica and published in London in 1827. In *Hamel*, the black Jamaican characters all speak Standard English, with only the occasional use of non-standard words or forms, and even then the author feels the need to tell his readers a word like 'gubna' means 'governor'; at one point he gives a song supposed to be sung in Jamaican English, but which he gives in Standard English prose, saying 'I regret much I must not give the story in its native simplicity, inasmuch as the lingo (I must not call it language) would be utterly unintelligible to all my uncreolized countrymen.'[9] While the author of *Hamel* does include a few Jamaican words without explanation, he clearly feels that the British readers for whom he seems to have

[9] Anon., *Hamel, The Obeah Man* (2 vols., London 1827), I, 244, 303.

intended his book could not be expected to understand anything
other than their own kind of English. Orderson, on the other hand,
has several sections of dialogue in Bajan, and while these are mostly
spoken by slave and free coloured characters it is noticeable that
some of his white characters also use words and turns of phrase
which are Bajan rather than English. Orderson provides little or no
explanation, and even in his narrative refers to things like bub and
cassava pone which would have puzzled a British readership. The
very title of his novel is programmatic: *Creoleana* suggests what he
refers to in his preface as 'the customs, manners, and habits of
Creolean society.' The slightly earlier writer William Dickson, who
had been private secretary to Edward Hay when he was governor of
Barbados (1773–9), had noted that in Britain the term Creole was
'often applied exclusively to mulattoes' though 'it really means a W.
Indian of any complexion.' Modern scholars often use 'creole society' to refer to the concept of a new society, with new habits, manners, institutions and modes of speech, created in the Caribbean by
the interaction of peoples from different parts of the world, especially the interaction of Africans and Europeans. This is what
Orderson means by 'Creolean,' and even though a large part of the
novel is set among the white creole society of Barbados, that society, like Barbados as a whole, is based on the various relationships
and interactions of both black and white people. Dickson claimed
that 'The W. Indian white people do not much like to be called cre-
oles,' but this is clearly not true of Orderson. While he hoped to appeal to 'the British public,' the title of his novel insisted that
Barbadians were different, that Barbados was not simply a 'Little
England,' and the whole of the work is an assertion that Barbadians
and their concerns are a fit subject for literary endeavour.[10]

[10] Dickson's comments on the term 'Creole' appear in a 'Glossary of Words
peculiar to the West Indies, or taken in peculiar senses' in his *Mitigation of
Slavery, in two parts [. . .]* (London, 1814; facsmile reprint, Miami, 1969),
pp. 526–8. The classic modern discussion of creolization is Edward [Kamau]
Brathwaite, *The Development of Creole Society in Jamaica, 1770–1820*
(Oxford, 1971). See also Karl Watson, *The Civilised Island, Barbados: A
Social History 1750–1816* (Barbados, 1979), and John Gilmore, *Faces of the
Caribbean* (London 2000).

✿ ✿ ✿ ✿ ✿ ✿

The action of *The Fair Barbadian* takes place just before
Emancipation, and all the characters are fictional. In *Creoleana*,
on the other hand, there are frequent references to both real individuals and to dateable events in Barbadian history (discussed
in more detail in the notes to this edition). In his Preface to the
novel, Orderson makes the claim 'that his materials are all (with
the exception of one incident) drawn from facts, which are as
closely adhered to as the nature of the subject would admit; but
the events, he must add, are not narrated in strict chronological
order.' The earliest event mentioned is the Bridgetown fire of
May 1766 (not 1776, as it is printed in the first edition of
Creoleana). Mr. Fairfield is said to have married 'about two years
previous to that event' (p. 24) and, in preparation for this, to have
manumitted the slave woman whom he had kept as a mistress and
made arrangements for the care of the child she had borne him,
who was then two (pp. 26-7). This child turns out to be Lucy, the
mulatto half-sister of Orderson's white heroine, Caroline
Fairfield. The great hurricane of 1780 is mentioned (p. 28), and
not long afterwards we are told (p. 33) that Lucy 'was now about
seventeen years of age' though this ought to be around 1779. Just
before, we are informed (p. 32) that Caroline, who is clearly at
least two or three years younger than Lucy, was 'now arrived at
this interesting approach to womanhood,' and within the next
page or so Caroline is already attracting the attention of potential
suitors, including the 'youth' Jack (or Johnny) Goldacre. By the
time 'Young Goldacre' has returned from his voyage to Bermuda,
having 'been about six months from home' (p. 49), Lucy had 'just
numbered her twentieth' year (p. 44) which would make Caroline
about seventeen or eighteen – a good marriageable age by the
standards of the period. This is the point at which what for
Orderson is the main part of the plot, young Goldacre's rather
inept wooing of Caroline, really gets going. Logically, we would
seem to be somewhere around 1782, which is consistent with the
fact that the departure of Governor Cunninghame has been

mentioned. The balloon episode which plays a significant part in the courtship can be dated to 1784. Yet while the courtship does not then seem to be all that drawn out, by the time the happy pair are married on the last page of the novel we have been told Caroline is 'now two-and-twenty' (p. 146) and the British, with Barbadian help, have captured Martinique, which took place in 1794. By this date, observance of 'strict chronological order' would have made Caroline almost thirty, virtually an old maid in the eyes of her contemporaries.

In spite of these and other inconsistencies, the setting of most of *Creoleana* is clearly the Barbados of the later 1780s and early 1790s. This was a period when the island was recovering from the problems caused by the American War and the hurricane of 1780; from the later 1780s until the very end of the 1790s, exports, prices and profits from sugar were all significantly higher than they had been in the later 1770s and early 1780s.[11] Orderson would have been in his teens or twenties during most of the events referred to in *Creoleana*, and one wonders if writing the novel in his old age was in part an exercise in nostalgia for the days of the author's prosperity.

The prosperity enjoyed by the upper classes of Barbados in this period, including that of those like the Ordersons, who belonged to the urban professional and mercantile group, was based on the plantation system. Most of the land in the island belonged to a fairly small group of planters, on whose estates sugar was produced for export by the labour of slaves. The master's power over his slaves was virtually absolute, and the social tensions inevitable in such an arrangement were heightened by the fact that, for complex historical reasons, slavery had come to be based on race. Most (though not all) slave-owners, in urban as well as plantation settings, were white, while all slaves were black or of mixed race (though by the 1780s the majority of slaves in Barbados were born in the island rather than brought from Africa). This was the great

[11] Otis P. Starkey, *The Economic Geography of Barbados: A study of the relationship between environmental variations and economic development* (New York, 1939; facsimile reprint, Westport, CI, 1971), pp. 107–8, and graph on p. 102.

defining fact of Barbadian society: the existence of significant numbers of 'poor whites' who owned little or no land, and of 'free coloureds' (persons of African descent who were not slaves, but whose freedom was limited by a number of civil disabilities) complicates the picture but does not greatly alter its overall pattern.[12]

This is the constant background to Orderson's work, though most of the time it is something taken for granted rather than explicitly referred to. The presence of the slave, Hampshire, in the very title of *The Fair Barbadian and Faithful Black* is an accurate indication of the important part he plays in the drama, but he is a favoured domestic. In *Creoleana*, Musso is Mr. Fairfield's 'confidential man,' while Amarillus is explicitly identified as a 'domestic.' Field-hands appear on stage in *The Fair Barbadian*, but they do not speak and are virtually part of the scenery. In the novel they appear in a similar capacity, for example at Judy Chrichton's funeral, where their 'vociferous lamentations' are referred to, but they are given no individuality. Sometimes they are referred to even more obliquely, as in the reference to Mr. Fairfield 'holing' his neighbours' fields. (See *Creoleana*, p. 25, and note on this passage).

Orderson does say that things were better after the slaves were emancipated in 1834: 'we now live not only in a *Christian* country – but are a *free people*,—and who does not rejoice at this happy

---

[12] At the end of the eighteenth century, cotton was a significant export from Barbados (though a long way behind sugar in importance) and was cultivated mainly on smaller estates. Note Orderson's reference in *Creoleana* (p. 50) to 'Cotton Coast' in Christ Church, a name no longer in use. There were also a number of minor exports, such as aloes, often cultivated by poor whites.

'Free coloureds' were sometimes divided according to their appearance into 'free blacks' and 'free mulattos' but there was no legal difference in their status. Their anomalous position provides illuminating insights into the attitudes and assumptions of Barbadian slave society: the classic study is Jerome S. Handler, *The Unappropriated People: Freedmen in the Slave Society of Barbados* (Baltimore and London, 1974). The most recent survey of Barbadian history as a whole is by Hilary Beckles, *A History of Barbados: From Amerindian settlement to nation-state* (Cambridge, 1990), while Karl Watson, *The Civilised Island* offers a more detailed social history of the period in which *Creoleana* is set.

change?' (pp. 44). The use of 'we' seems to imply the not implausible argument that Emancipation lifted a burden from the shoulders of the slave-owner as well as from those of the slave. However, his general outlook is certainly conservative: from *Cursory Remarks* through *The Fair Barbadian* to *Creoleana* he consistently endeavours to suggest that slavery, at least in Barbados, was not as bad as its critics (that is, British abolitionists) claimed. This appears not only in the explicit comparison of the condition of the slaves with the English labouring poor in *The Fair Barbadian*, but also in things like Hampshire's reluctance to accept manumission and the anecdote about the slave Prince in *Creoleana* (pp. 91-2).[13] While it can be argued that in the last half-century or so of slavery in Barbados the slaves were, at least in terms of physical conditions, fairly well treated and provided for, that conditions were certainly better than they had been before about 1780, and that Barbadian slaves were probably in some respects better off than those in some other Caribbean colonies, none of this altered the essential nature of slavery – that it placed one human being in the arbitrary power of another for life, with little hope of escape for either themselves or their children. That the arbitrary power of the slave-owner sometimes found expression in brutality or ill-treatment of one kind or another (such as Judge Errington beating Hampshire when his gout pains him) was less important than the fact that it always could do so. That a large number of Barbadian slaves felt that general good treatment was not enough to make slavery tolerable was shown by the rebellion of 1816 – which Orderson's choice of chronological setting for his play and novel allows him to ignore.[14]

[13] See also Orderson's chimney-sweep anecdote in *Cursory Remarks*, quoted in this edition's note on *Creoleana*, p. 22.
[14] The most important source is [Barbados House of Assembly], *The Report from a Select Committee of the House of Assembly, appointed to inquire into the Origin, Causes and Progress of the late Insurrection* (Barbados, n.d. [1818]), which, although a partisan document, does include some apparently authentic statements made by slaves involved in the rebellion. The rebellion has been extensively discussed by modern historians; see for example, Watson, *Civilised Island*, pp. 125–35; Beckles, *History of Barbados*, pp. 78–85.

Orderson disapproves of Tom Applebury's behaviour to Hampshire's daughter, and of Mac Flashby's seduction of Lucy, because the white man is behaving in an immoral manner, but in *Cursory Remarks* he made it clear he disapproved of sexual relations between black and white under any circumstances, stating explicitly that even Christian marriage between the races would be 'not only repugnant to my feelings, but contrary to my ideas of morals, religion, and policy.'[15] His discussions of obeah, black behaviour at funerals, and what he sees as the improvements brought about by the Christianizing activities of the Anglican Church suggest, if not a belief in white racial superiority, certainly a belief in the superiority of Eurocentric cultural norms.[16] While Emancipation was a major change in Barbadian society, it made little difference to who owned the land and who tilled it, and there is nothing in Orderson's writing to indicate that he thought that this should be otherwise. His view of what was right and desirable is shown by the eager willingness of the manumitted Hampshire to continue serving Judge Errington. The Judge emphasises that 'no society can exist without subordination,' and it would seem that for Orderson as well as his character, it was assumed that in Barbados blacks would continue to be subordinate to whites, even though as 'hired servants' rather than slaves, and that this was taken as part of the natural order of things. The Judge smoothly assures Hampshire that 'no human laws can counteract nature! – your condition in society is changed, but not your complexion; and though free and having rights and privileges conferred on you, you yet have *duties* to perform!'

The limitations of Orderson's position are obvious. From an aesthetic point of view, it leads him to make the main focus of *Creoleana* the somewhat insipid story of Jack and Caroline, the two white lovers, with its conventional happy ending where money marries money. The tragedy of Lucy, which for modern

[15] *Cursory Remarks*, p. 22.
[16] This can of course be paralleled in other writers of the period. Compare, for example, Sir Robert H. Schomburgk, History of Barbados (London, 1848; facsimile reprint, London, 1971), pp. 88–9.

readers is much more interesting, is relegated to a subplot. Nevertheless, perhaps because Orderson as a white Barbadian of his time takes certain things for granted, there are topics which he discusses with a frankness which non-Barbadians of the period (and perhaps even Barbadians of a younger generation) probably found disturbing. In his account of Mr. Fairfield's relations with Lucy's mother, in the story of Lucy herself, in the history of Lauder and Rachel Pringle, Orderson is quite open about the sexual exploitation of black women by white men which was a constant feature of Barbadian slave society, and about the temptation held out to black women to use such relationships as one of the very few ways open to them to improve their position in such a society where on every hand they faced the constraints imposed on them by race and class. When Lucy allows herself to be seduced by Mac Flashby in spite of her engagement to Pollard, this kind of relationship destroys her. In contrast, Rachael Pringle emerges from a series of similar situations as an independent and successful businesswoman. The English critic and essayist Leigh Hunt (1784–1859), who was the son of a Barbadian and who spent part of his childhood among other Barbadian relatives in London, came across *Creoleana* and noticed the account of Lauder and Rachael, but Hunt summarized it by saying that Lauder's behaviour was something 'which cannot be described.'[17] So perhaps it might have been for the drawing-rooms of Victorian Britain, but Orderson does describe it, in a manner which is quite explicit.

In *The Fair Barbadian* he also describes the remarkable encounter between Hampshire and Judge Errington. Hampshire is opposed to Tom Applebury's relationship with his daughter; we are not told quite how far this may have proceeded, but Hampshire is fearful that it will 'bring shame 'pon she' and says 'I no want my child for bring mulatto!' (p. 169). The Judge is equally opposed, but for a different reason: Applebury is his nephew and

[17] John Morpugo, ed., *The Autobiography of Leigh Hunt* (London, 1949), p. 5. See also notes on *Creoleana*, pp. 22, 75.

he feels 'contaminated by such a foul consanguinity.' He follows this up with a racist description of Hampshire's daughter. When Hampshire rebukes him 'With suppressed anger' saying 'Tho' we be black the same God who been make you – make we, too!', the Judge acknowledges the truth of this, and begs Hampshire's forgiveness (p. 197). The Judge appears to be sincerely concerned that he has upset his 'faithful black' – but this has not stopped him making the racist remarks in the first place. While all this fits in with Orderson's consistent hostility to miscegenation (previously discussed), it also shows that the ideological basis of slave society was not so much hypocrisy but a sort of Orwellian double-think – as a paternalist slave-owner, the Judge is able to sustain two mutually contradictory sets of beliefs and attitudes at the same time, and indeed has to do so if the system which maintains his position and power in Barbadian society is to continue to function. One can only wonder if Orderson intended this episode to be as revealing as it is, and what sort of effect it had when the play was actually produced on a Barbadian stage in 1832, when slavery was still a living reality.

There are other aspects of *The Fair Barbadian* and of *Creoleana* which call into question the established order of things. For many of Orderson's contemporaries, the assumption of white racial superiority did not mean that all whites were equal. In Barbados, poor whites were less equal than rich whites. While Orderson's devotion to his native island is beyond dispute, it is clear that Britain, as the colonial power, was of great importance in his mental world. He does not avowedly address himself to a Barbadian readership, but says in the Preface to the novel that 'It is with very humble pretensions that the Author brings the flickerings of his nearly exhausted lamp before the ordeal of the *British* public' (emphasis added). One is reminded of more recent generations of Caribbean writers for whom the realities of markets have meant that success with a European or North American readership continues to be what counts. The idealised view of the colonial relationship is given symbolic expression in Orderson's play by the way in which Captain Carlove, the British army officer, is portrayed as the perfect match for Emily, the 'fair Barbadian' of the title, in preference to her dissipated cousin Tom. Within Britain itself, and in British colonies, there was a tendency to accept the English assumption of their own superiority over the other nations of the British Isles (though this was certainly not accepted by all Scots, Welsh and Irish). Something of this perhaps appears in Orderson's pointing out (in accordance with historical fact) that the reprehensible Lauder was a Scot, and in his making the cowardly villain Mac Flashby an Irishman, though he does take some pains to suggest he does not consider all Irishmen to be like Mac Flashby. Barbados is honoured in the novel with the presence, however fleeting, of two princes of the British royal family, one of them a later king, no less – something which Orderson probably thought would increase the interest of the book where 'the British public' was concerned. Things are not as fawning as this might suggest, however. While the Barbadian official who has to greet Prince Edward is characterised as 'a half-witted, humble, uneducated man,' the Prince's response to him and the lieutenant-colonel who arrives on the scene later is shown as rude and boorish, 'his Royal Highness not being courteously disposed at the time' (pp. 140–1). The portrayal of the relations between the British Army and the Barbados Militia is not to the credit of the former. In the famous scene of Prince William Henry's visit to the Royal Naval Hotel, for which the novel is best remembered, the Prince is shown as what would now be called an upper-class twit of the worst order. His hostess, Rachael Pringle, on the other hand, is an almost perfect representative of Anansi, the West African trickster hero, part spider, part man, whose often unscrupulous use of his wits to survive against stronger and more powerful enemies made him a popular figure in Caribbean folklore. Like Anansi, Miss Rachael 'play fool fuh catch wise,' and there is no doubt that it is she who comes out best in the episode. Another character who can usefully be compared to Anansi is Ned Crosier, the poor white who, crippled and out of a job, is forced to

WOUSKI.

Free as the forest birds well pair together,
Without remembering who our fathers were;
And in soft murmurs interchange our souls.

Fray be the noise.
Of Kings & Crowds from us, whose gentle souls
Our tender fate have stood another way.

Pub.d Jan.y 23.d 1788 by H.Humphrey New Bond Str.

'cut and contrive'; his masquerade as 'Captain Kickero' is eventually found out and he gets his comeuppance, but he is treated with a degree of humour and tolerance not extended to Mac Flashby. Finally, the scene in which Miss Rachael scorns Mac Flashby would have been a challenge to any assumptions about white racial superiority which any of Orderson's original readers might have had.

No major British periodical appears to have given *Creoleana* any extended treatment. The *Gentleman's Magazine* recorded its appearance without comment in a list of new books under 'Travels and Topography.' *Tait's Edinburgh Magazine*, while getting its author's name wrong, condescended to say of the novel:

> It is homely enough; but evidently accurate and truthful in representation; and it is consequently possessed of more interest than many of those more ambitious attempts which depend only upon style and second-rate literary merit. The characters are felt to be literally taken from the life, and thus they please.[18]

Orderson does not seem to have received much of the recognition he seemed to have wanted for his novel in his own life-time. Nevertheless, it is hoped that this new edition will allow Orderson's writings, as he once hoped, to 'amuse and interest the general reader,' though of a very different era, in the Caribbean and elsewhere, who will find in them 'many little apertures [. . .] through which a discerning eye may catch a glimpse' of 'Barbados in days of yore.'

---

[18] *Gentleman's Magazine*, New Series, Vol. XVII, p. 527 (May 1842); *Tait's Edinburgh Magazine*, IX, 405 (June 1842). The *Gentleman's Magazine* noted that *Creoleana* was priced at six shillings. *Tait's* gave the author's name as 'John Ordeson' [sic]. In Barbados, the local paper the *Barbadian* carried an advertisement for *Creoleana* when it appeared in May 1842, and the paper's editor used this as a peg on which to hang some of his own reminiscences of Prince William Henry in Barbados – quoted by Neville Connell, 'Prince William Henry's visits to Barbados in 1786 & 1789,' *Journal of the Barbados Museum and Historical Society*, XXV, 157–64 (August 1958).

CREOLEANA:

OR,

SOCIAL AND DOMESTIC SCENES AND INCIDENTS

IN BARBADOS

IN DAYS OF YORE.

BY

J. W. ORDERSON,

Of Barbados.

LONDON:

SAUNDERS AND OTLEY,

CONDUIT-STREET.

1842.

RIGHT HON. LORD STANLEY, M. P.

&c. &c.

My Lord,

Influenced by an earnest desire of testifying my profound respect for your Lordship, I have presumed, unauthorized, to avail myself of the auspices of your Lordship's distinguished name, to place before the British Public the following political incidents and domestic anecdotes of my native country.

The present, my Lord, is the first favourable opportunity which has presented itself, and which I now gladly embrace, of acknowledging your Lordship's condescension in 1833, on an occasion, and under circumstances, which, perhaps, no other Minister of State would have felt himself called upon to notice.

Neither the lapse of time, nor change of position in which your Lordship now stands,* has lessened my sense of gratitude for so courteous a proof of your Lordship's zealous and indefatigable attention to even the minutest details of the high and important office over which your Lordship presided.

However pleasing the task, it would be arrogance in so humble an individual as myself, to attempt any panegyric on a Nobleman, whose eminent talents and high integrity render him so illustrious, both as a Statesman and as a Patriot. I therefore shall merely add, that if my humble literary offering be kindly received, and even one page thereof afford your Lordship a moment's amusement, I shall feel myself amply rewarded for the time and care I have bestowed on this unpretending little volume.

I have the honour to be, My Lord,

Your Lordship's

Most obedient humble Servant,

THE AUTHOR.

Saint Michael's Row,
Bridge Town, July 28th, 1841.

* Since this was written, there has been a change of Ministry, and his Lordship has again been appointed Colonial Secretary.

PREFACE

ALTHOUGH the Author of the following pages feels himself incompetent to decide on the extent or general merits of *West Indian Literature*, he yet ventures to affirm, from his own observation, that Barbados has contributed her share, with no unlavish hand. He does not, however, pretend that her sons have climbed the higher steeps of Parnassus, nor that they occupy any eminent station in the flowery paths of *Belles Lettres*. The streams of erudition, indeed, flow, as yet, but in gentle rills, but they are irrigating the intellectual soil, and coursing on with the general 'march of mind.' Yet, there are some of her children, who should not be considered as mere drones in the republic of letters; but rather as having contributed to enlarge the hive and dilate the comb; though their industry may not have infused much sweets into its cells.

With regard to the contents of the present volume, the Author conscientiously affirms, that his materials are all (with the exception of one incident) drawn from facts, which are as closely adhered to as the nature of the subject would admit; but the events, he must add, are not narrated in strict chronological order. He does not profess to give any extended view of the customs, manners, and habits of Creolean society; yet, in the progress of his tale, there will be found many little apertures (if he may so express himself) through which a discerning eye may catch a glimpse of each, as they existed in times of yore, rather than as they exist at present. The improvements which in later times have taken place in social order, in domestic life, in religion, and in education, have all tended to produce high influences, which, it may be hoped, will ultimately advance the happiness of the people.

It is with very humble pretensions that the Author brings the flickerings of his nearly exhausted lamp before the ordeal of the British public. But he feels assured, when it is considered, that *he* has, at an age at which most men are compelled to close *their* book, ventured to draw from the sources of his memory traductive events, and weave them into a volume, which he hopes may both amuse and interest the general reader; that he shall meet with that partial kindness which prompted that great and worthy philanthropist, the late *Mr. Wilberforce*, in quoting from a former publication of the author's, to speak of him as 'a humane and truly benevolent man,' and from which little work Mr Hone, extracting an anecdote, introduces it in his *Every Day Book*, as 'a specimen of pure feeling.'

His referring to these long gone-by notices of former literary attempts, no doubt savours of the vanity of authorship; but when to these flattering testimonies he adds that of his fellow countrymen, who, in their official capacity as 'representatives of the people,' unanimously voted him their 'Thanks' for his publication on the *Education of the Poor of Barbados*, he feels an honest pride in not having shrunk back from the employment of his feeble abilities whenever, through fiction or fact, they could be useful in the cause of religion and morality; and, under the influence of these impressions, the author, with all deference, deprecates the severity of criticism.

CHAPTER I

It was not long after that lamentable catastrophe which, in May 1766, reduced Bridge Town to almost one general heap of cinders and ashes, that Mr. Charles Fairfield, then an extensive merchant trading thence to the ports of Lancaster and Belfast, being actually 'burnt out of house and home,' retired from business, and took up his residence on a small property in the parish of St. George, which he had acquired as dower with his amiable wife. This gentleman suffered considerable loss, not only from his own stock and stores being consumed, but by the general calamity having rendered many respectable dealers, who were largely in his debt, penniless.

The merchants of Bridge Town at that time, and for many years subsequently, conducted their business upon principles very different from those which now generally prevail; no man, in fact, being ranked as a merchant who was not his own general importer. It was also an invariable rule among them not to engage in, or connive at, anything like retail traffic with the inferior dealers, their sales being always made on an extensive scale, thus creating a sort of middle-man, who purchasing in larger quantity, retailed them in smaller lots to the petty hucksters. Credit was very limited at this time, and almost exclusively confined to the accommodation of the planter, who in those days never thought of importing his plantation stores, or of shipping his crop, these being considered the exclusive rights of the merchant; and thus a reciprocal interest, as should ever be the case, was established between the landed and commercial interests.

Mr. Fairfield was a native merchant, and had received his education at Codrington College; and being of an adroit mind, he soon acquired great proficiency in all the learning of that seminary, and was esteemed in all his dealings an honest and honourable man; but from a too confiding nature, he deviated from the general practice of the times, and extending his credit among the small traders of the town, he consequently became a greater sufferer by the calamity which fell in common on them all.

Mr. Fairfield had about two years previous to that event married a Miss Wortly, a young lady who, educated under the immediate eye of truly virtuous and religious parents, was herself a bright example of prudence, circumspection and amiability. Female education in those days partook of none of those artificial embellishments which modern refinement renders so imperative, and it was then almost a phenomenon to hear of a young lady being sent to England for education. Miss Wortly, however, derived many advantages from the society in which her parents had moved, and being herself of an active, intelligent mind, and of a cheerful but unassuming temper, she was very generally respected, and had had many suitors before her choice fell on Mr. Fairfield.

Such were the parents of CAROLINE FAIRFIELD, who at the time of their retiring into the country, had just entered her third year, and was a fine blooming dimple-cheeked child, of lively disposition, and remarkable intelligence. Even at the early age of five, she had made much progress in her education, for she could read with great correctness, and recite with much pathos and precision many moral and religious poems; thus giving great promise of her future acquirements. Nor in this was there any after disappointment, for before she had attained her fifteenth year, she could write a fine Italian hand, had acquired a competent knowledge of arithmetic, could net, knit, and embroider, work her sampler with great neatness, play with some science on the harpsichord, dance with much grace, and was also skilled in all the domestic arts of a frugal housewife.

The property to which Mr. Fairfield and his family had now retired, consisted of seventeen acres of most fertile and productive land, with a comfortable dwelling house, comprising two good sitting and four airy bed-rooms; a neat gallery running round the whole, and a well proportioned porch projecting from the road front, having detached offices and storehouse in the rear. This little property, or 'place,' as such are usually termed, was called 'Staffords,' and was chiefly cultivated in grain, vegetables and ground provisions, which it yielded in great abundance. It had also a small field of canes sufficient to supply the family with sugar for their own consumption, and a very productive orchard. They reared a vast quantity of feathered stock, some sheep and pigs, with which they almost daily supplied the town-market, obtaining thereby sufficient means to enable the family to live in comfort and respectability. It should, however, be remembered that at that time the luxuries of the table, and especially of the bottle, bore no comparison with our present indulgences; and except on festive occasions, such as Christmas time, or on weddings, christenings and birthdays, wine was rarely introduced, and even then was confined to honest Madeira and humble Port – Champagne being altogether unknown; the industrious and independent planter being content to regale himself and his friends with improved punch and falernum, and make an evening's finish with bub or black-strap.

It was by means of this fertile 'place,' cultivated with indefatigable industry, and occasionally 'holing' his neighbours' fields, together with the general economy of his family, that Mr. Fairfield in the course of a few years was not only enabled to overcome all his difficulties, but to enlarge his property to more than double its original extent, and thus convert his 'place' into an 'estate.' It must not be forgotten, however, that from his punctuality and general integrity in business, his English and Irish friends most liberally relinquished all claims upon him at the time of the calamitous fire, before mentioned.

Thus far has the reader, with somewhat of anticipation, been made acquainted with this interesting family, the heiress of which is the heroine of our tale. There is, however, another member of it of whom we have yet to speak, as being deeply, and in some measure criminally, involved in its progress.

CHAPTER II

MR. FAIRFIELD, during the early part of his commercial pursuits, had led the life of a bachelor; but he conducted himself with such circumspection and decorum, that whatever were his peccadillos, his general attachment to religion and virtue secured him from the brazen tongue of scandal, and the gossip of those who see all the faults of others, but none of their own; or, as the Scriptures better express it, 'see the mote in their brother's eye, but discern not the beam in their own.' It is not, however, to be dissembled that during this period, giving way to the influences of robust health and a warm constitution, he fell into the commission of that frailty which 'a certain Levite' of old did 'in those days when there was no king in Israel.' The result of this unhallowed connexion was a daughter possessed of tolerably fair complexion, regular features, and all those endearing witcheries which sparkling eyes, dimpled cheeks, and an ever-smiling face render so fascinating in the innocence of infancy.

Endued with a mind naturally sensitive, and alive to all the charities of a benevolent heart, Mr. Fairfield felt whenever he beheld this child, as it daily waxed stronger, all the parent stirring within him; but from a conviction of the moral turpitude of his conduct, experienced much compunction mingling with his better feelings at having given birth to a child whose future life seemed bounded by the wretched prospect of inevitable prostitution, which consequently would bring shame and disgrace on himself.

About this period, Mr. Fairfield began to entertain serious thoughts of changing his condition of life, and became more than ever anxious to enter into the matrimonial state; he therefore determined to shake off his illicit connexion. In conformity with this decision, his first care was to manumit his paramour, securing to her £6 per annum, in addition to the interest on the deposit he had made, according to law, in the parochial funds. He then put her away, but by a willing consent on her part, took the child, now two years old, under his own protection, placing it under the care of a respectable matron, who became its foster-mother, and who faithfully discharged her duty towards it while under her care.

Before further pursuing the narrative of domestic events we are here recording, it will not altogether be uninteresting to the general reader to take a retrospect of the extraordinary circumstances of the times we are speaking of – a period in which a more melancholy or calamitous series of events never perhaps afflicted any country, striking terror and dismay through the land.

Bridge Town, which had not then such an extent of boundary or so dense a population as at present, was scarcely resuscitated from its ashes before a general drought prevailed that rendered the land almost sterile, and even the little vegetation it yielded was nearly all destroyed by vermin of every description which infested the island. The borer, a grub peculiar to the sugar cane, made such general ravage, that for several years the average crop did not exceed 7000 hogsheads of sugar, and that of very inferior quality to what is now manufactured. The supplies of various grain and other esculent plants and roots with which the town-market had hitherto always abounded, were then only to be had in very limited quantities, and at considerably increased prices. The supplies from America had also at that time greatly diminished and become very precarious – the unhappy differences between that country and the parent state having arrived at open hostility; and thus the distresses of the island were considerably heightened.

It will give a clearer idea of the miserable condition of the times by stating the price of some of the necessary articles of life at that period. Flour was from forty to forty-eight dollars a barrel, and families were compelled to club together to purchase even a single one; salted beef and pork were from forty to fifty dollars a barrel; neither dry, salted, nor pickled fish were to be had; of native produce, such as yams, potatoes, and eddoes, with which the

market had before been abundantly supplied, the prices were
from two to three pounds for the bit; peas one pint per bit; eggs
three for two bits, and could not be bought in less quantity.
Butcher's meat and poultry were proportionately dear and very
scarce, both of Pharaoh's lean kine, and such was the poverty of
the times that no butcher would venture to slay his beast until he
had carried round his list to ascertain what quantity was likely to
be wanted.

Among other calamities which at this time afflicted the island,
was a plague of ants, which actually overran the country; not
merely the fields and public roads, but even the streets and
dwellings swarmed with them; they gave general annoyance and
in many instances were fatal to infants. The destruction these ants
made was incalculable – cattle in their pens, sheep in their fold,
pigs in their sty, and poultry on their roost, had their eyes eaten
out, and their heads and bodies, as it were, scarified by the tor-
menting bites of these little insects.

But the sufferings of the island did not cease here; other and
severer ills awaited it; an influenza and dysentery attacking the inhabitants made great ravages, especially among the poorer classes
and slaves, and it proved equally fatal to the seamen in His
Majesty's service and to those in merchant vessels.

Another – yet another phial of wrath, was to be poured out on
our devoted country. That pestilent disease – the small pox – now
burst forth, as if the very air had been impregnated with its loath-
some virus, and it made such ravages, as struck despair in every
breast! the town becoming as it were one continuous lazaretto.
These afflicting visitations occurred between the years 1772 and
1779; and were followed in 1780, by one of the most severe and
pitiless hurricanes that ever desolated a country. That of 1831
bears no analogy to it, either in duration or destruction of life, although in loss of property it far exceeded it. This may readily be
accounted for, from the increased extent of the town at the latter
period; in the improved state of society, which had introduced an
extravagance of living, a taste for costly articles of furniture, splen-

did equipages, and other embellishments of life, unknown to our forefathers.

Amidst these physical ills which thus desolated the Island, the inhabitants had to contend with various political evils which created schism in her councils, and party feuds among the people. About five months previous to the hurricane briefly noticed above, the government of the Island was conferred on Major General C—— whose arrival here was harbingered by the most favourable reports of his friendly disposition, and who professed his intentions to render the country prosperous, and the people happy. These expectations, however, were not realized – but whether the disappointment arose from a natural cupidity and thirst of gain on his part – or from the offensive slight – if not insult – of a too parsimonious economy, on the part of the popular branch of the Legislature in their bill of settlement, we will not here inquire; but it is worthy remark, that while at this time the public revenue was most wantonly wasted by the expenditure of the Mole Head funds in firing salutes from our forts and batteries on the most trivial occasions, the Assembly commenced the work of retrenchment by reducing the means of the Executive for supporting the dignity of his station. He however sought to indemnify himself by the most arbitrary impositions and exactions on every occasion where his seal or signature was to be affixed; and he carried his cupidity so far, – that because the Jews (then a very numerous, respectable, and wealthy body) had withheld from him their hitherto accustomed present of a *pie* to each Governor on his arrival – he seized upon their synagogue and had it run out, intending it for barracks; the 89th regiment, then on this station, having their quarters in Old Bridge Street, comprising the whole extent of the west side of it, from the present cabinet-maker's shop at the corner, to the foot of the bridge. Thus it might be said that his Excellency had stirred up the whole community against himself – ladies and all, for he laid an exorbitant fee on marriage licences. But his rapacity was frustrated – the people at large evaded his exactions – the fair sex even preferring to be 'asked in church' rather than submit to an imposition on their 'intended,' and the Jews, knowing they were under the protection of British laws and not governed at the caprice of an arbitrary Governor, still withheld their unleavened pie – composed neither of apples nor pigeons – but a simple crust covering a pretty round sum in the current gold coin of the day. His Excellency therefore, after a few days, relinquished his possession to the rightful owners but otherwise he relaxed none of his arbitrary measures – and what is most extraordinary the Council greatly countenanced his unconstitutional proceedings. But at length, on the humble memorial of the people and their representatives, his Majesty was graciously pleased to recall this oppressor of his loyal colony, and our obnoxious Governor privately embarked without the least notice to the legislature, and remained three days on shipboard previous to his sailing – seeing the town, each successive night while he remained in the Bay, brilliantly illuminated on account of his dismissal – a sight which embittered his feelings, and, as it is said, caused him to shed many a bitter tear.

It is hardly within the scope, even of conjecture, what would be the feelings and opinions of that gone-by generation of which we have been speaking, could they be told that the annual public expenditure of the Island is at present over £100,000!!! What would that frugal President say to this? he who, to set an example of retrenchment and economy, when the whole charge of the Government was under £12,000 per annum, announced to the Legislature that he had ordered the discontinuance of the lamps usually lighted at Pilgrim gates! If this was not a saving of 'cheese parings and candle ends,' it at any rate was that of 'a ball of cotton wick and a jug of oil.'

One of those severe visitations of Divine wrath, of which we have taken a hasty retrospect, ultimately proved highly beneficial to the country, for the violence of the hurricane swept away all those noxious reptiles and vermin which had so fatally destroyed the vegetation of the land, and was no less efficacious in purifying the air from its pestilent vapours; so that in due time 'Little

England' once more became the Montpellier of the West Indies. And by the removal of the Governor, peace and concord were restored to the people – whose losses and privations were mitigated by the munificent donation of the British Parliament and people.

CHAPTER III

REVERTING now to the fair object of our tale, whom our digression has given time to arrive at an interesting age of adolescence, we find Miss Fairfield equally elegant in person as in mind, and in full possession of all those accomplishments which she derived from the system of education then prevalent, and of which her more juvenile years had given such promise. Her countenance was the true index of a soul replete with intelligence, benevolence, and tenderness; her complexion of the most transparent whiteness tinged with a delicate roseate hue; her teeth like rows of pearl peeping between twin rosebuds pouting to be kissed, while her expressive dark blue eyes were like crystals illumined with rays of day-spring light. There was yet that diffidence and unobtrusiveness in her whole deportment, blending with the grace of unaffected gentility, that rendered her an object of irresistible attraction, captivating alike the heart and the understanding, by the loveliness of her person, the purity of her mind, and the fascination of her conversation. But a faint idea can be given of the joy and delight of the parents of this lovely girl,— which however was best manifested by those pious orisons, which they daily poured forth to the Author of every good gift in gratitude for so inestimable a treasure.

Caroline having now arrived at this interesting approach to womanhood, her mother deemed it advisable that she should be supplied with sufficient means to place her in some measure independent of the ordinary routine of their domestic arrangements, which, however, united a liberal provision and every social comfort with that strict circumspection and decorum that constitute a well regulated and happy family; she therefore suggested to her husband the propriety of making their daughter a yearly allowance of pocket-money, and of providing her with a female of exemplary character, to attend exclusively on her as a lady's maid. Mr. Fairfield readily assented to this proposal; and it occurred to him, as it were instinctively, that the illicit offspring of his early amour might thus be placed in better security from evil temptation, while from the moral education he had given her, and the useful instruction she had acquired, she could without impropriety be introduced in that capacity into his family; the rather too, as he supposed, that neither his wife nor his daughter knew of the existence of such a being, the girl herself being entirely ignorant of the relation in which she stood to them. She, however, was sensible of great obligation to him, for she considered him as her guardian, and as the particular friend of her deceased father, who had died in America. This girl, who had been early baptized by the name of *Lucy*, and whose mother (of whom she had no recollection) had been carried off by rapid consumption soon after her emancipation, was now about seventeen years of age;— possessed of a natural archness of manner, blended with great good humour, her countenance gave an expression of mirth and simplicity to all she said. With much levity she united a warm frankness of heart and a willing disposition to please; and she possessed a lively feeling of gratitude. The great error of her conduct, and which required correction, was that of too much flippancy of manner and a habit of familiarity unbecoming her situation: upon the whole, however, she conducted herself on most occasions with much deference, and before she had been three months in the family, so ingratiated herself in their good opinion and esteem that she became a general favourite with them all, and won the entire confidence of her young mistress; being also regarded with kindness and good will by every friend and visitor at the house.

The accomplishments of Miss Fairfield, or rather, the grace and elegance of her person and manners, did not fail to attract the attention and admiration of the whole circle of young men of any consequence or respectability in the parish, and of all who knew her. Indeed it was no unusual thing on Sundays to see genteel young men from the neighbouring parishes, and many from

Bridge Town, congregated in the church porch merely for the gratification of seeing her – evidently, not for devotion, as it too often happened that many of them lingered without for a further gratification of their curiosity, but never (to their shame be it spoken) entering to join in the service. Among these her admirers there was one, however, who was not less devout in his religious duties than ardent in his admiration, although diffident in manifesting it.

This youth was the son of wealthy, but humble parents, who had acquired by unremitting industry and exertion a fortune, which might have given to a suitor fair pretensions to the hand of Caroline Fairfield, had money been all that was necessary to win her heart; but the parents not having received any education brought up their son in almost the same state of ignorance as themselves. He, however, being of a strong mind and possessing good natural abilities, readily acquired all the instruction to be derived from the humblest of country schoolmasters. His father, Mr. *Goldacre*, although ignorant himself, was not insensible to the disadvantages under which his son laboured, and would often lament to his wife that 'Johnny had not had a little more *book learning.*' This she always met with a triumphant reply, that 'their Johnny was as handsome a young fellow as any in the parish, and had a fortune ready cut and dried for him, that put him upon a footing with the best of them.' Johnny, as they termed him, was really a personable youth, of manly form and stature, and had proper culture been bestowed on him, he might have been an intelligent gentlemanly youth; but was now timid, shy and bashful. The old man saw all this, and daily upbraided himself that 'after he had begun to pick up a few scrupes, he had not sent him to Bridge Town and placed him under Parson Hebson,' who was at that time classical master of Harrison's Grammar School. 'And what's the good of all that grammar, Latin, (tauntingly would ask his wife) and outlandish gibberish they make such a fuss about? It won't buy the hair of a nigger, nor an acre of land; for look at Tom Cleavelan, who all the world cries up as a non-such of learning –

didn't old Cleavelan (as proud as Lucifer) spend pounds of money on his son's learning, instead of paying his own debts? – and see what's come of it! Han't the pro'-marshal broke up the Estates, and neither he nor his son has got a moidore to bless themselves with.'

It must be observed here, that about the time this conversation is supposed to have passed, such was the general distress of the landed proprietors that there were more sugar plantations and other extensive places 'broken up' than had ever been known before, and, we may add, than has taken place since. This arose chiefly from the shameful procrastination of Chancery suits, it being as improbable at that time that a suitor would live to see his cause terminated, as he who planted an acorn should fell it a hundred years hence, a sturdy gnarled oak. The provost-marshal, therefore, generally settled these matters in a more summary way – not always partaking of that benevolent consideration for the unfortunate debtor which at the present time we see exercised by the gentleman filling that office, and without violating the justice due to the creditor. It was no unusual practice in these times, when doubts arose as to the priority of executions in the office, for the provost-marshal to decide the question by a foot-race from the clerk's office to his own; the parties interested procuring the fleetest runners they could get, the whole starting together by signal, and the classification was then made according as each runner arrived at the office and handed in the execution with which he had been entrusted. Many ludicrous scenes occurred on these occasions, and it did not unfrequently happen, that during the contest one half the runners were laid sprawling in the mud, while the others continued the struggle by vigorous attacks on each other, as chance or skill brought them near, and often many arrived at the goal half stripped of their garments. Curiosity, sometimes blended with interest, seldom failed to collect great crowds in those streets through which the 'racers' had to pass, and much betting was made among the sportsmen. We have often felt the impulse in the course of our narrative, although we are but yet on the threshold, to exclaim, *O tempora! O mores!* but, thank God, we have arrived at better times and better manners.

The arguments used by Mrs. Goldacre to satisfy her husband on the score of their son's want of 'book learning' were, as he used to say, 'knock-down blows'; but still their impression led him to wish 'that he could see Jack make a figure in the world,' and he would sometimes add, 'then we might hope to see him married to that nice young woman at Staffords.' 'Leave that to me,' would reply the thrifty dame, 'I'll bring it about all in good time.' With a view to this, or as she used to say, 'of paving the way,' she would occasionally send over little presents of various articles, that served also to show her own notability and domestic skill; and not unfrequently would she add, 'give our love, and say, that if the family's not engaged, Mr. Goldacre, and I, and Johnny will come over this afternoon and drink coffee with them.' This mode of social intercourse was not peculiar in Mrs. Goldacre. Families then dined at two o'clock; even the most ceremonious parties never made it later than three; and domestic hospitality being a prominent trait in the West Indian character, a reciprocity of feeling among neighbours induced this social habit of self-invitation. In this way, it sometimes happened that three or four families would accidentally find themselves together under the same roof, and this chance assembly would, as it were, instinctively couple themselves off, and keep up the merry dance by the aid of a violin, pipe and tabor, half the night through.

Upon occasion of one of these self-invited parties, when for the first time Mr. and Mrs. Goldacre had succeeded in persuading Johnny to accompany them, no sooner had they reached the avenue leading to the dwelling-house, than our poor youth was seized with an invincible fit of bashfulness, and suddenly turning on his heel, vowed 'by blingers I can't go,' and in spite of every effort to persuade or encourage him to proceed, he left his parents to make their visit without him, whistling his way home like a simple clown.

The family at Staffords were ever ready to exercise the rites of hospitality, and having a kindly feeling towards their neighbour, would encourage these visits, and occasionally return them in the same spirit of familiarity and ease, and thus enhance the pleasure their company gave. When these visits were made the Fairfields seldom saw the young man, who if he caught sight of them in their approach would slip away and conceal himself until their departure. On one occasion, however, it so happened that the little party from Staffords entered the mansion of Silverdale before 'Mas. Jack' was aware of their approach, and he was thus obliged to join the family circle. His diffidence, however, rendered him a mere cypher; and notwithstanding every effort of his mother to 'bring him out,' which rather heightened his embarrassment, he sat silent, and as it were, stupid. But our youth's mind was not so great a blank as it seemed to be – it was a soil pure and fertile, but barren for want of cultivation; and at the very time of which we are speaking, he was reflecting in bitterness of heart on his own sad lot in having been reared in ignorance, considering his own deficiencies rather than those of his parents. He was at one moment on the point of giving way to an excited irritability in consequence of his mother having said (in the simplicity of her heart) 'What a pity it was that Johnny should be so bashful, for he is a smartish looking young fellow but for that;' and then turning to Miss Fairfield, continued, 'don't you think so, Miss Caroline? and you know he'll have such a handsome fortune too; for who else have we to give the plantation to, and all that money we've got out; and it's 'pon best security too!' Mr. Fairfield saw his daughter's embarrassment on these observations being so pointedly addressed to her – her mother saw it too, but with more provoked feeling – he palliating it in consideration of the old lady's ignorance, and she viewing it as an indication of 'great presumption.' With a kindly feeling towards the young man, and to relieve his daughter's agitation, Mr. Fairfield attempted to draw him into conversation, and so far succeeded as to divert his attention from what had just been said by his mother;

and in a few minutes something like general conversation ensued, while our hostess prepared the coffee and poan for the
ladies, and the gentlemen enjoyed their bub and roasted corn.
Mr. Fairfield kept our young hero in chat for some time, and by a
happy tact in arguing with him, elicited many observations that
gave proof of a rich but uncultivated mind. The kindness of this
gentleman never failed to leave our untutored youth depressed
and gloomy; for he was not slow in attributing this kindness to
some latent motives corresponding with his own bosom-feelings.
When in these reveries, his mother, in the warmth of affection,
would endeavour to rouse and encourage him by 'the prospect
she saw before him, of his adding Staffords and its fine gang to
Silverdale.' Jack, however, affected never to understand her allusions; but a tear would sometimes bedew his cheek when too
closely pressed by her, and he would occasionally exclaim, 'la,
mother, how can you think such things!' and would precipitately
leave her. The fact is, this youth had in silence sipped deep of the
nectarious sweets distilled from the fascinating charms of this
lovely fair one, and had 'let concealment, like a worm in the bud,
feed on' – his pining heart.

As he approached his majority, he felt more keenly the defects,
or rather the neglect, of his education; he daily became melancholy, unsocial and recluse, until at length his health began evidently to be impaired, and he was recommended by Dr. Seawick
(an eminent physician of that day) to take a trip to Bermuda. At
the period of which we are speaking, a voyage to England was a
matter of more serious consideration than to be lightly undertaken as at present, when a young man of spirit will step on board
with his portmanteau, and make the voyage upon as slight a pretext, as if he went merely to have his hair cut in the newest mode,
or his cravat adjusted in the most fashionable taste.

Generally speaking, the intercourse, indeed between the West
Indies and Great Britain, except by monthly packets, was then little more than annual, nor had we at that time any regular trade
with Liverpool (now become the emporium of our supplies) until

the establishment of that eminent and celebrated house, which, baffling all the casualities and difficulties of transatlantic commerce, continues to this day under the firm of Higginson, Deane and Stott, occupying the same premises, but greatly extended, in which William Barton and Co., originally embarked in colonial trade, more than half a century ago! There are at present, however, several other Liverpool houses here which bear a fair rivalry with them. With the Bermudas there was then frequent intercourse, and we were constantly exchanging with them our rum, sugar and molasses, for their cedar posts, sawed stones, ducks and onions; and although we no longer obtain any of these precious articles from them, our Bermudian friends have not lost sight of us; but, adopting a more personal intercourse, have founded several commercial establishments, and have amalgamated themselves by marriage, as well as by trade, with our countrymen and fellow citizens.

CHAPTER IV

With all the solicitude and anxiety that a mother's care and tenderness could devise, or a father's circumspection and prudence effect, Jack was speedily equipped for his voyage; but a pensive melancholy hung over him, that baffled all the efforts of his friends to awaken in him that lively curiosity generally excited in the youthful mind by the idea of travel, especially on a first voyage. Many a day had his parents earnestly but fruitlessly importuned him to go with them to bid adieu to their friendly neighbours at Staffords; but now all things being in readiness for his voyage, and it being moreover the evening previous to his departure, it occurred to him that it would be very ungrateful were he to quit the island without taking leave of Mr. Fairfield. Thus influenced, and unknown to his parents, he set out by a by-road to pay this visit, wishing particularly to elude his mother, and secretly intending, if he could catch the opportunity, to whisper some soft things in the ear of Miss Fairfield. Poor love-stricken youth! the very thought of such a daring unnerved him, and when he had 'screwed himself up to the very point of sentimentality,' utterance was denied him.

The family at Staffords were ready and just on the point of going over to Silverdale, when Jack entered. They gave him that kind and hearty reception, which at once put him at ease. He felt satisfied that their friendly and obliging expressions for his recovery, were the result of partiality; and especially as Mr. Fairfield offered him much good advice, both as to his general conduct, as well as to the care of his health. Nor, indeed, was the good lady of the house backward in her counsel, but she was rather more reserved than her spouse; and as to Miss Fairfield, she sat all the while exceedingly mute. Whether this arose from the mere respiration of suppressed breathing or sprang from any latent feeling struggling to be relieved, we will let those young ladies decide

who have been similarly circumstanced, but as faithful chroni-
clers, we state the fact, that Caroline's taciturnity was suddenly
broken by — a deep sigh!— It seemed to electrify our invalid, who
hurriedly rising from his seat, and trembling with agitation, took a
formal leave of Mr. and Mrs. Fairfield, and then with increased
excitement, approached the young lady, and taking her hand, (the
first time he had ever been in such contact with her) said in a
tremulous faltering accent, 'God bless you! Miss Ca— r——!' He
would have said 'Caroline'; but though the name hung like honied
dew on his lips, he could not give it utterance. Hastily dropping
her hand, he precipitately quitted the house, leaving the family in
consternation at this strange conduct. An interchange of looks –
often more expressive than words – passed from one to the other;
but none spoke, and Caroline at length left the room. Her parents retired into the porch, when a long conversation ensued between them, criminatory on the part of Mrs. Fairfield towards
her husband, on the score of his attentions to the young man,
which she alleged had put 'wild notions' into his head; and defensive on Mr. Fairfield's part, who contended that his attentions
sprang from a friendly consideration towards a harmless and
unassuming youth, who, he added, 'wanted only education and
society to make him a bright man.' The young lady, however, was
the object of her parents' displeasure, and was censured by both
for having privately cherished an ignoble flame; when, in fact, she
had felt only, for the first time, an evanescent spark transiently flit
across her mind.

Mr. and Mrs. Goldacre missing their son, had gone over to
Staffords, suspecting that he might be there.— They reached the
house just at the moment after he had so precipitately fled; and
he, taking the same by-road by which he came, was missed altogether. Anxious for 'dear Johnny,' they could not be prevailed on
to rest themselves, but instantly returned, leaving the elder
Fairfields yet undetermined whether the youth's conduct proceeded from aberration of mind, or a mere temporary excitement
from contemplating the new position in which he would shortly

be placed by being separated from his family, and embarked for the first time on the 'vasty deep.'

Miss Fairfield, however, did now begin to have some surmises as to the young man's pretensions, and thought with her father, that a little polishing would make a bright man of him; and being of an ingenuous and unsophisticated mind, spoke freely of him to her mother, who taunting her with 'thinking more of the booby than he was worth,' demanded in rather harsher terms than she was wont in general to use, 'What if he was to pay his addresses to you, Miss?'— 'Poor man, I pity him,' was all the reply. 'Pity indeed!' echoed her mamma, and pettishly left the room. Her indignation had not subsided when joining Mr. Fairfield in the back gallery, which he was pacing up and down in rather moody silence, she explained all that had just passed between herself and Caroline, throwing out in angry terms, 'that she feared their daughter had lost her pride.' 'Had she any (replied he) It were well that she did lose it; for the more we see of it the more are we convinced of its emptiness, self-sufficiency and folly. (do we not behold; exclaimed he in an angry tone) 'that from this evil source springs all the vexations and disappointments of life?'—'But, would you have your daughter marry such an ignorant young man?' angrily rejoined she. All, however, that the good lady could urge, elicited nothing further from him, than that he trusted Caroline would in due time make a prudent choice, for that he was determined not to interpose his authority unless he saw a palpable impropriety in her selection. Thus was Mrs. Fairfield left to draw her own conclusions of her husband's and daughter's opinions on a subject that had stirred her anger, and for the first time created dissension in this happy family.

Leaving this first ebullition of domestic disquietude to subside, and the family to settle down into its wonted tranquillity – merely following our voyager to his embarkation, and seeing him fairly put to sea in the well-found schooner Fame;— his parents brooding in melancholy and dejection over the thousand

and one dangers they had conjured up, which their son must encounter – and withdrawing themselves even from neighbourly intercourse with the family at Staffords; – who, each in his or her
own way, having reconciled themselves to the 'presumption' of
the young man, were still disposed to exercise friendly offices
towards his parents. We now turn to the giddy and wild Lucy,
whom we before mentioned as an inmate of the Fairfield family, and who from prudential motives had been rendered less
prominent than her own natural inclination would willingly
have conceded. She, however, in her regular attendance at
church, whither she constantly accompanied the family, had
not failed to attract the notice of those few coloured persons
who then joined in Christian devotion.— The diabolical super-
stitions and witchcraft of *Obi*, prevailed at that time throughout
the Island among all the sons and daughters of Africa and their
descendants; and having its nucleus in Bridge Town, it was no
unusual thing to see, as each Sunday returned, hundreds – nay,
thousands of these poor deluded creatures 'throwing victuals,'
and with drumming, dancing and riot practising frenzied incantations over the graves of their deceased relatives and friends!
These orgies were chiefly carried on at Fontabelle (situated to the
north-west of the town) and Lightfoots-ground (to the north of it),
both sites being since covered either with spacious mansions or
neat cottages, thus obliterating the scene of those abominations,
and of one, at the former place, yet *more abominable*, of which we
shudder to think. The desecration of the Sabbath, however,
ceased not here, for to our shame be it recorded, that day was then
our chief market day, and almost every street converted into a
market place, the town presented on those occasions but one continuous scene of riot, drunkenness and heathenism! 'A better
order of things' now happily prevails throughout the island; and so
long as we constitute a part of 'Christ's church militant' we must
hail the establishment of an Episcopal head amongst us, as giving
an hallowed tone to the exertions of our clergy, and an awakened
spirit of piety in the people. The question, however, is not alto-

gether 'what absolute improvement has been made in religion and morals? but, how much of blasphemy and vice have been dispelled?' But it must nevertheless be admitted that our *first* Bishop has (if we may be allowed so homely a metaphor) not only macadamized the way for his successor, but laid down railroads and adjusted locomotive engines to them, that must facilitate his labours whenever so unwished-for a time may arrive. Thanks to the ameliorating spirit of the times! we now live not only in a *Christian* country – but are a *free people,* – and who does not rejoice at this happy change?

Lucy, as we have said, had attracted the attention of the few coloured men who then attended at church, but there was one among them, who by the uniform correctness of his conduct, and honest industry as a mill carpenter and wheelwright, had not only gained the esteem and encouragement of the gentry and proprietary body of the parish, but had also realized sufficient wealth to enable him to purchase five acres of land with a neat cottage, and three or four slaves. It will not much retard the progress of our tale, here at once to remark, that this man, *Joe Pollard*, to the end of his life (which numbered eighty-two years) maintained so exemplary a character, that when he died he was borne to his grave by twelve of the most respectable gentlemen of the parish, among them a member of Council and two of the Assembly; the venerable rector of St. George's performing the funeral service. This was a most unusual occurrence in those days, but it serves to show that even then, neither complexion nor descent precluded the virtuous and just man from respect and attention. Would to God this were ever the criterion for bestowing honours and rewards!

Pollard, at the time of this love affair with Lucy, had been a widower about two years, if the loss of a 'help-mate' to whom he had not been united by the rites of the church (marriage being not much in vogue then among coloured people) could give him that title, and he was now near forty years of age, while his innamorato had but just numbered her twentieth; but this disparity was met by a healthy constitution and athletic form, which with his general good character, gave encouragement to his pretensions. He had at different times found opportunity to whisper 'soft things' in her ear, (she being 'nothing loath' to hear his tender tale,) and now flattered himself that he had won her partiality, from her having accepted some trifles with which he had occasionally presented her; but as often as he attempted to obtain a definite answer, she eluded his importunity with great coquetry and flirtation; Joe, from the frequency of this trifling on the part of his Dulcinea, at length began to grow restive, but being really enamoured of the girl, and knowing that he stood well with the family, hoped that by their interest she might be brought to a speedy decision in his favour. He therefore broached the subject to Mr. Fairfield, stating his intentions, if Lucy would accept him, of making her his lawful wedded wife (a thing very rare in the then state of morals among that class of persons, although a more solemn feature is now given to an union between the sexes;) but Mr. Fairfield, after expressing his good opinion of the suitor, and his approbation of the suitableness of the match, referred him to Mrs. Fairfield. This lady, although she also expressed her approbation of his views, would not interfere, but referred him to her daughter, as having the more ostensible control over the girl; and Miss Caroline not choosing to influence her maid in a matter on which she thought herself incompetent to decide, though approving of his pretensions, considered it best to refer him to Lucy herself. Thus poor Joe was thrown back, as it were, upon himself: – and to this imprudent indecision and neglect of a due and temperate exercise of domestic authority might be attributed in great measure the unfortunate errors of the girl; which, although we may censure, we yet must pity. Pollard had now no other alternative than that of prosecuting his suit with redoubled ardour, or of giving it up altogether; but he still hoped for success, for notwithstanding the family had declined positive interference, he knew from *Amarillus* (an old domestic) that each in turn, as occasion presented itself, spoke to Lucy on the subject, and gave her most kindly advice to close with Joe's proposal; but nothing could be drawn from her further than that 'she did not wish to marry yet, and would prefer waiting on her young mistress.' – Here, however, we must for a time leave the affairs of these swarthy lovers, and introduce another personage, who will make no small figure in our domestic history.

CHAPTER V

MR. FAIRFIELD had, some months previous to the circumstances above stated, received an intimation from his old mercantile friends at Belfast, that it was their intention to found a branch establishment of their house at Barbados, under the management of a junior of their firm; and they solicited his patronage and interest towards it. The vessel with the investment for this establishment, and the chargé d'affaires for conducting it had for some weeks past arrived; and Mr. Fairfield, anxious to show every attention to the request of his former friends, had invited the young merchant, while his stores were getting in readiness and the landing of the cargo was going on, (there being then no such facilities in these matters as at present,) to recruit himself at Staffords; and he had already been an inmate there for eight or ten days when Pollard's overtures had been submitted to the family.

Mr. *Robert Mac Flashby* (such was the name of our young Hibernian) was a characteristic specimen of his countrymen in all those traits which distinguish them for warmth of heart, gaiety of temper, and, when well educated, gentlemanly manners. In person he was what even the most fastidious would call 'fine looking' – he possessed great volubility of speech and a rich fund of humour, but was given, perhaps too much, to practical jokes. He sang with pleasing effect, played on the flute with much skill, at chess with some science, told a story with much humour, and altogether was a most lively and agreeable companion – especially among the ladies!

The Fairfields seemed to vie with each other in their efforts to make his sojourn agreeable; still Mrs. Fairfield would sometimes with a little impatience privately inquire of her husband, when that madcap Irishman was to open his store? Miss Caroline, however, now thought less frequently of the family of Silverdale, and

scarcely at all of our Bermudian voyager, of whom she had sometimes wondered what had become of him! Even Lucy was ambi-
tious of contributing to the comfort of their guest, who although
in the background, had been much delighted with his light humour and thoughtless gaiety.

The time, however, at length arrived for Mr. Mac Flashby to
enter on more serious pursuits, and to commence the man of
business; a friendly adieu was therefore given by all parties;
Mr. Fairfield at the same time kindly inviting his departing guest,
as a relaxation after the business of the week, to spend his Sundays
at Staffords – an invitation he thankfully accepted.

Mac Flashby, although full of fun and frolic, was no idler when
business claimed his attention, and we find him, immediately on
his return to town, actively engaged in mercantile affairs – his establishment occupying extensive stores near the landing place, ju-
diciously arranged. At that time there were no commodiously
constructed wharfs as at present – the whole line of the carenage
being then one continuous sloping bank of slime and mud, from
which a fetid miasma continually exhaled, which rendered the
town unhealthy, and doubtless was the primary cause of that
wretched disease, *fever and ague*, with its unsightly elephantiasis,
that then greatly prevailed, but which now is scarcely known
amongst us. Over this filthy puddle two or three jetties some forty
or fifty feet long and about twenty wide, projected into the stream,
and afforded the only means for landing our supplies and shipping
our produce.

We here leave our friend of the Emerald Isle, for six days of the
week zealously giving all due attention to business, and passing
the seventh in domestic quietude mingled with becoming religious observances (for he was a Protestant) with the family at
Staffords; and shall now revert to our, as it might seem, neglected
friends of Silverdale.

Since the departure of their son, Mr. and Mrs. Goldacre had
seldom gone over to their neighbour Fairfield's, nor had much intercourse taken place between the families, since Mac Flashby's

intimacy there; the old lady often declaring with more ingenuousness than discretion that 'she did not like that outlandish chatterbox,' as she termed him. In truth, he once very unpolitely attempted a joke upon her, by inquiring 'if she could tell him how many pigs' tails it would take to reach from the mill door to the moon?' to which she promptly retorted, 'Yes! just as many as it would take of saucy Irishmen's tongues, if they were the same length as the pigtails;' thus throwing back upon Flashby (to the no small satisfaction of Mrs. Fairfield) the laugh he would have excited at Mrs. Goldacre's expense.

Young Goldacre had at this time been about six months from home; but, to let the reader into a secret that must not yet be divulged to the parents, scarcely more than twice as many weeks from the Island. His health, however, even in that short period, had greatly benefited by his trip; and as he carried with him to Bermuda several letters of introduction, he received the kindest attentions from the hospitable inhabitants of those rocky regions. The change of scene as well as of society, had not only improved his health, but awakened new ideas in him, and had given an impetus to his mind, that rendered him restless and impatient to obtain free scope for the display of his intellect; as he daily became more sensible that it wanted but cultivation, to befit him for that station in society to which the fortune he must ultimately inherit gave him a just claim. He therefore resolved to return to Barbados, with the fixed determination of placing himself under competent instructors, until he should have surmounted the difficulties under which he then laboured. Nor indeed was he without other motives for this step, as he had often dwelt with fond recollection on Caroline's involuntary sigh, which he interpreted into a full betrayal of the emotion of her heart; and thence fondly cherished the hope of realizing his youthful dreams of happiness.

As soon as this young man had returned to Barbados, which he did under the assumed name of *Brushwood*, he had an interview with his father's town agents, Messrs. Littledale and Makewell, eminent merchants of that day; and consulted with them on his project of improving himself by education, and of mixing in society, as far as practicable, without the risk of discovery by his parents or their friends, before his return to the parental roof. These gentlemen highly approving of his scheme, with great kindness and alacrity made such arrangements as at once placed him out of public observation, and secured him the able assistance of Mr. Cater, a man of unimpeachable morals, and of great classical attainment; and of Mr. Donohugh, a celebrated mathematician. A residence in a very healthy situation was obtained for him with a respectable family at Cotton Coast, about a mile and a half from town, but long since converted into Government property, and now covered by extensive and stately barracks, hospitals, and other military quarters and depot; besides a splendid and spacious parade ground.

Mr. Brushwood (as for a time we must designate him) applied himself with all earnestness and application to his studies, seldom leaving the boundaries of his residence but at early dawn or evening tide, for horse exercise; and although mental cultivation was the chief object of our good gentleman, he also took private lessons in dancing and fencing, in both of which he soon became an adept. The former simplicity of his mind now ripened into activity and intelligence; and his awkwardness and diffidence, into gracefulness and self-possession. Though gifted with a temper most amiable and conciliating, he was yet sensitive and tenacious of all those decorums and courtesies which distinguish civilised society. A little incident introduced here which occurred between him and his mathematical teacher, may give some illustration of his feelings on this point. He had been several hours working at a problem, without making any great progress in its solution, when Mr. Donohugh (the kindest of men, but of a most irritable temper) impatient at the delay, seized Brushwood by one of his ears, and well wringing it exclaimed in the strong accents of his country— 'Ah! you stupid dog! don't you see it is –' but before he could add another word, he was levelled to the floor by the powerful arm of his pupil. Brushwood had, however, no sooner thus avenged himself for the indignity offered him, than every feeling of resentment instantly subsided, and he ran to the assistance of the fallen pedagogue, to whom, after raising him from the floor and brushing the dust from his clothes, he expressed much regret at what he had done, and his hopes that he was not hurt. Poor Donohugh! I remember the good old man well; and have not unfrequently witnessed similar scenes between him and some of his full grown pupils!— 'Rat ye! Gad rat you, sarrah! (exclaimed he when he found himself again raised to the perpendicular) I didn't mean to harm ye – no more than ye meant to harm me! – Betsey! rat ye Betsey! (calling for his housemaid, who was his factotum upon all occasions) Betsey! bring the punch! and mind ye put a wee drop more rum in it.' Thus all differences between master and pupil were adjusted, and their studies resumed in perfect good humour.

While our student was thus laudably occupied, with a view to qualify himself for mingling with better society than that to which the humble habits and contracted sphere of his parents had hitherto confined him; he occasionally fulfilled his epistolary duties by writing them letters expressive of affection and tenderness, (which he really felt,) at the same time giving gratifying accounts of his amended health. He promised to give timely notice of his return, which he added he did not immediately contemplate, as he was much pleased with the attention of the inhabitants, and delighted with the wild rocky scenery of the country. These letters were carefully forwarded through his father's town agents, who strictly preserved the secret confided to them, and who were the only medium of communication between the parties. These gentlemen interested themselves much in the young man's welfare, and introduced him to many of their particular friends, and into general society as occasion offered. Our hero took much pleasure in visiting at Mr. Littledale's, whose elegant and accomplished daughter (a clear brunette with brilliant sparkling eyes) might possibly have obliterated the recollection of Caroline Fairfield from his thoughts, had not that memorable sigh upon parting (which he pertinaciously attributed to a feeling sympathizing with his own,) constantly played round his heart like a will o' the wisp; but we must not admit this, as we are not bound to betray the young lady's secret.

Leaving matters for a time in this state, and progressing with our story, we now find Mr. Mac Flashby further availing himself of the hospitality of Mr. Fairfield, by making his visits at Staffords, if not of more frequency, at least of greater duration; for instead of going there on Sunday morning in time to join the family in their regular attendance at Church, and return to town at night, he would now leave town on Saturday evening and not return until Monday morning.

It must not be dissembled, that Caroline had begun to feel more pleasure in his company, than she was at first conscious of (so insidious are the approaches of the little god!) but as Mac Flashby's visits were prolonged, she became more sensible of certain inexplicable feelings which caused a palpitation of her heart, that she either could not, or was not over anxious to define, but which occasionally betrayed her into an involuntary, 'pshaw!' uttered when by chance her 'pity' for poor Goldacre came across her mind. Few young ladies indeed, we must allow, could have remained insensible to the fascinating wiles of our designing young Hibernian, who applied himself diligently to bring all the artillery of his native confidence to bear on the citadel of her too susceptible heart; while, like a skilful engineer (to use a military phrase) he was undermining the out-works.— But in this affair, there was great want of moral judgment;— for let the chivalrous gallant ever bear in mind, that the weapons of warfare to be used against the stern god of the sword and buckler differ materially from those to be applied in our hostilities with the mild god of the bow and quiver!— Lucy had at this time so far ingratiated herself into the confidence of her mistress (who with all her circumspection and prudence was not proof against her wiles – a salutary caution to young ladies in general, not to repose confidence in their menials) that she con-

fessed to her that 'she thought **Mr. Mac Flashby** a charming man!'
This was quite sufficient for the intriguing maid, who playing a
double game, communicated to each what she had heard from the
other, too often embellished by the fertility of her own imagination – and she thus fanned a latent spark into a glowing flame.

CHAPTER VI

MR. AND MRS. FAIRFIELD now began to have some 'inklings' of what had long been the parish gossip; and the old lady especially, saw with much concern, that their daughter was not inimical to the advances of her gay and insinuating admirer. She strongly pressed the subject on the attention of her husband, and would urgently remonstrate with him on the impropriety of facilitating Mac Flashby's intercourse with their daughter; of whom she would often declare that 'she would rather see her married to the booby at Silverdale than to that "wild Irishman" '— as she sometimes called him. Mr. Fairfield, however, could not see any cause to apprehend the consequences his wife predicted; and to pacify her, would say that 'It would be high time to start objections when the young man made proposals.' This reasoning served but the more to irritate his better-half, who had imbibed a strong prejudice against the young man, arising from some suspicions of his moral character, little however imagining that his intrigues were so nearly connected with her, as will in due time appear. The scrutinizing eye of maternal solicitude is ever more prompt in detecting such indiscretions, than that of a father, although he himself be more prone to fall into them:— she, however, did not show her usual sagacity on this occasion.

It was about this time that Lucy began to make her appearance in some articles of dress and ornament, of better quality and taste than she had hitherto been accustomed to. This alteration in her attire did not fail to attract the observation of Mrs. Fairfield, who however, on investigating the matter, was made to believe that it arose from Pollard's liberality; but on the girl's pertinaciously persisting in rejecting him as a husband, Mrs. Fairfield peremptorily prohibited her acceptance of any further gift from him: determin-

ing also to bring the affair without further delay to a final conclusion. On their next meeting, which took place in the presence of
our cautious matron, Joe so effectually pressed his suit (for he was
really enamoured of the girl,) that Lucy at length yielded, and
promised to take him, 'for better for worse,' as her lawful wedded
lord. She insisted, however, on some delay, to which the old lady
would not have conceded, had not Pollard (although reluctantly)
assented to it.

Lucy had, as it appears, found many sly opportunities of meeting Mr. Mac Flashby, and having overheard much of the discussion between her old master and mistress (as she called Mr. and
Mrs. Fairfield) respecting Caroline and her lover, whispered it
into his willing ear, together with many additions her own inventive genius so readily supplied; he therefore resolved without further delay to address the young lady. An opportunity of doing so
soon presented itself, – indeed what earnest lover, having made
up his mind to hazard the issue, but will always find opportunity?
Availing himself therefore of the casual mention of a young couple who had been recently married, he 'pop't the question;' – but
as we were not present on the occasion, and have not the inventive
talent of Lucy, we can give no particulars of what passed, and shall
therefore decline making a speech for either; leaving to all gentle
beaux and sentimental belles to adopt the language most pleasing
to themselves and the most appropriate to their own particular
case. Suffice it here to say, that they returned from the garden,
where this interview had taken place, nothing displeased with
each other; although Caroline seemed to labour under some nervous excitement, as she and this 'gay Lothario' entered the house
and met her mother. A few hours after, Mr. and Mrs. Fairfield had
the whole secret divulged to them by Mac Flashby, (Caroline in
the mean time being seated pensively in her room, listlessly occupied in altering a dozen times over the trimmings of her bonnet,)
who, with all a lover's flowery protestations and honied promises
of making their daughter happy, solicited their approbation as in-
dispensable to his happiness! The wary mother heard him with

impatience, and almost lost her usual urbanity of manners, for she presently left the room sarcastically exclaiming, 'Sir, I shall leave this affair to the discretion of my husband, who, I dare say, knows best how to treat such matters!' Mr. Fairfield, however, being in some measure influenced by feelings of regard for his old friends at Belfast, a connexion with whom through an alliance of his daughter with a junior of the firm, he could see no objection to, gave a patient hearing to our professing lover; and after entering into much discussion, and requiring many explanations which terminated to his satisfaction, he referred the enraptured youth, whose elasticity of spirits was rendered more buoyant than ever, to his too confiding daughter.— After what has been before stated, the sagacious reader will not look for further explanation of Caroline's conduct on this momentous occasion – our fair readers, especially, whose own sensitive bosoms will best inform them, need not be told how her heart palpitated, when her lover approached to communicate the result of his interview with her parents:— much, to say truth, was glossed over of what passed between him and her mother; but all that her father said was decked out in glowing colours; and yet it could not be concealed, that whatever internal satisfaction Caroline felt, still a dark and heavy gloom overspread her countenance that perplexed both her father and her lover; while her mother's displeasure, approaching to indignation, ran so high that she disregarded the anguish evidently preying on her daughter's mind. Poor dear Caroline! Her heart had been left too much exposed to the crafty wiles of an insinuating gallant – she knew not its weakness; and while she thought she was treasuring up her young love for the absent, she by degrees surrendered her heart to his rival!

There were at the period of these occurrences, a series of six balls, given in Bridge Town at the British Coffee-house, as those extensive premises near the South Bridge, at present occupied as an ironmongery at one end, and a saddlery at the other, were then called. This house was kept by a Mrs. Rebecca Hill, (a perfect

hostess Quickly) and the balls were given in aid of a recently established institution called the 'Barbados General Dispensary' for
supplying the sick and maimed poor with medicine and advice
gratis.° These balls were conducted by twenty-four gentlemen –
four in rotation bearing the entire expense of each evening, (the
refreshments consisting of tea, coffee, light sandwiches and
negus.) Tickets were limited to one hundred and fifty for each
evening – the price for ladies being one dollar each, and two dollars for gentlemen. This admission money formed the fund for
the support of the Dispensary; – at the head of which were all
the principal medical and chirurgical practitioners of the Island,
who rendered their services gratis – the only stipendiaries being
a visiting and a house apothecary and two porters. The premises
now occupied by the 'Literary Society' for their library was the
property of this institution, and appropriated as their
Dispensary.

To one of these balls, Mr. Mac Flashby, as the recognized lover
of Miss Fairfield, prevailed on her father (against the opinion of
his lady) to allow him to chaperon her, in company with three or
four other young ladies, whom Mr. Fairfield had promised to take
under his care. He was himself an advocate of such amusements,
which he considered not only agreeable, conducive to health and
suitable to the vivacity of youth, but also desirable by giving young
people opportunities by juxtaposition during the dance, of displaying much grace and elegance, blended with that decorum
necessary to be observed in so numerous an assembly, and which,
while it heightened the enjoyment, not unfrequently awakened a
reciprocity of feeling that ultimately terminated in wedded love.
It so happened that on this same evening, Mr. Littledale had invited Mr. Goldacre, under his assumed name of Brushwood, to
accompany him and his daughter (the beautiful and elegantly

° We regret to have to record that this institution, like many others from
time to time among us, – whose seeds falling on stony places spring up and
flourish for a season, but having no depth of earth soon wither and decay –
was but of a year or two's duration.

formed brunette) to the ball. Both she and Brushwood attracted
general attention; Miss Littledale, in consequence of her recent
arrival from England; and he, not only from having absented himself from society since his return from Bermuda, but from the
grace, ease, and polish of his manners, and the peculiar elegance
of his person.

At this period, quadrilles, waltzes, and galopades were unknown, dancing being confined to the graceful minuet and social
country dance. It was customary for the stewards of the evening to
arrange the order of the minuets, and to select the parties who
were to dance them, always studiously choosing the most elegant,
graceful and showy to commence with, that greater eclat might be
given to the exhibition. It was left to the gentlemen's own choice
to select partners for the country dances, or the stewards introduced them, as occasion might require.

Miss Caroline Fairfield, on this occasion, was the first lady
handed out to 'open the ball' (as it was termed) and in order that a
young lady so generally admired might have a suitable partner to do justice to her graceful movement in the minuet,
Mr. Brushwood, as chance would have it, or as that 'wanton boy
who delights in love's gambols' decreed, was selected to the pleasing duty. The minuet was performed to the admiration and ap-
plause of all present, testified by an enthusiastic clapping of hands
(no unusual practice at that time on such occasions)— while the
almost petrified Caroline was handed to her seat by her scarcely
less astounded partner; both having at the same instant, in concluding the figure, interchanged looks of confused and doubtful
recognition. After presenting the lady with a glass of negus, of
which he stood in as much need as herself, Mr. Brushwood, apol-
ogising to Miss Littledale and her father, precipitately quitted the
assembly, leaving the whole circle anxiously inquiring 'Who is he?
where did he come from? who knows him? is he a native?' and
many other like questions – all however agreeing that he was 'a
handsome, fine looking fellow.' But at length, having recourse to
Mr. Littledale, they learnt that his name was Brushwood, and that

he was a particular friend of his. Mac Flashby, who had witnessed with jaundiced eye the performance of the minuet, was the first to announce to Miss Fairfield, the (supposed) name of her partner; designating him with some warmth a 'conceited coxcomb!' thus evidently betraying to her that he was piqued at being thus eclipsed.

It was about this period that his Royal Highness Prince William Henry (subsequently William the Fourth) third son of our late venerated but unhappy Monarch, George III. arrived in this Island, and set all its gaieties and hospitalities in full play: an event we are led here to mention, in allusion to an incident connected with the little history of our heroine. At one of those balls given in honour of the Prince, at Pilgrim House (the seat of Government, and in days of yore celebrated for its hospitality and festivities; and where the fair daughters of our isle were wont to delight in going) both Miss Fairfield and Miss Littledale were present;— the Prince honoured the former with his hand in the country dance; while our late patriotic Baronet (then speaker of the Colonial Parliament) led down the latter. The Prince and his lovely partner had scarcely reached the bottom of the set, and finished the figure, when the Baronet and his interesting partner followed close upon them, Miss Littledale laughing in high glee at some incident that had attracted her notice, and which her cavalier was urging her to explain to him. This lively colloquy engaging the attention of His Royal Highness, he lustily called out— 'Baronet, kiss her, kiss her, till she tells you!' which the Baronet, never deficient in acts of gallantry or loyalty, instantly did, saying that 'he could not do less than obey the command of the son of his Sovereign.' 'Nor can I (instantly replied the Prince) do less than follow so gallant an example,' and he also kissed Miss Littledale; then turning to his own partner exclaimed, 'Upon my word, Miss Fairfield, so fair a lady must not be made jealous,' and throwing his arm round her waist, kissed her before she could possibly resist, had she even been so inclined!

We leave to the historian of our Isle to record the general events connected with the Prince's visit here, it being sufficient for our purpose to 'set down' this little anecdote of royal gallantry – the main features of which are correct, but the veritable names of the two ladies have not been given to the reader.

CHAPTER VII

WE now turn to circumstances involving the sequel of our tale. And first, we have to record a great change in Lucy, whom we find in a delicate state of health, complaining of frequent headaches, and other nervous affections bearing hard upon her spirits, producing depression and languor unusual with her: her lover (like all true lovers) daily growing more impatient for the consummation of his wishes, and with careful solicitude preparing his cottage for her reception. The whole family at Staffords evinced much interest in providing for the comfort of the bride and bridegroom elect, and Mr. Fairfield generously added five acres to Pollard's little 'place.' On the other hand, we find Mr. Mac Flashby, with glowing feelings of delight, producing for the perusal of Mr. and Mrs. Fairfield letters from his parents and friends at Belfast, expressive of the highest approbation of his engagement to Caroline, for which interesting young lady, his parents at the same time had forwarded some pleasing tokens of their goodwill and kindness.

Mrs. Fairfield had, some time before this period, become acquainted with the secret of Lucy's parentage; but like a prudent wife, not willing to give uneasiness to her husband, or bring unhappiness on herself by taking cognizance of an event which occurred long before she possessed an exclusive right to Mr. Fairfield's affection, determined for the foregoing reasons not to let the secret transpire. The good lady was nevertheless somewhat piqued at the girl's being brought in so near association with the legitimate heiress; but she kept her resolution not to notice the circumstance, but which induced her the more urgently to press Lucy to contract the period she had stipulated for the postponement of her marriage. In the meantime Pollard, like an ardent lover, was pressing on the measure, and by his urgent and incessant entreaties the reluctant Lucy at length yielded, and the happy day was fixed upon. All things necessary and appropriate for this momentous event were put in active requisition, and the preparations then going on seemed but the prelude to those important ones contemplated for crowning the felicity of the ever dear Caroline!

At this critical time, when, but a moment before as it were, we had seen Pollard, with all the impatience of an enraptured lover, wooing the reluctant fair one to hasten his happiness, and who at length had triumphed over her coyness and scruples; – while yet beholding the festive preparations making for the consummation of his fondest hopes – preparations that might have excited the frigid heart of an old bachelor to corresponding hopes! while witnessing all this, and just at this momentous period, the rational, sober, and love-stricken Joe Pollard was nowhere to be found!

The family were all lost in amazement, apprehension, and perplexity! Mr. Fairfield, solicitous for Lucy's happiness, did all he could to tranquillize her agitated mind and re–assure her. To accomplish this he set inquiries on foot in all directions and Mrs. Fairfield, with most kindly feelings, seconded all his efforts. Caroline, whose sympathising heart would have deeply felt for poor Lucy, was spared the anguish of the scene, as she was from home on a visit in a distant part of the country to two elderly but most amiable ladies, who were sisters. No clue could be found, no tidings gained, tending in the slightest degree to unravel this mysterious flight. But at length, after nearly a fortnight's suspense, during which time Lucy had fallen into a state of reserve and melancholy, that threw her on a bed of sickness, a letter was found placed under a stone in the porch at Staffords, and although this missive removed all apprehension for Pollard's safety, it rather heightened the anxiety as to the cause of his disappearance. The letter was addressed to Mr. Fairfield and ran thus:—

HONOURED SIR,

When you come to know how I come, to leave home, the cause of it will show you that bad as it now looks in me doing so, I couldn't do no otherwise under such a heavy affliction as I see coming on me. Believe me, honoured Sir, I love Lucy too dearly to be ever so base as to ever give her unhappiness, but if she thought fit to bring it on herself I'm not to blame, and nobody will blame me that I won't involve myself in the shame of another. My love for Lucy makes me pity her, and it can't be thought that I wou'd say any thing to add to her unhappiness; but I hope, honoured Sir, that under all her badness to me, and the disgrace she has put upon you and your worthy lady, you may both of you forgive her. It is a shocking thing, honoured Sir, that a certain person who you have been so kind to, should make a whole family so miserable. But it is my hope that before it is too late you will, honoured Sir, put a stop to its going further. No more at present from, honoured Sir, your dutiful servant at command,

JOE POLLARD.

N.B.   As young Misses an't at home, better not let her know nothing about it.

P.S.   I hope to be home soon, as I shall go back soon as I hear you and your worthy family are again restored to peace and comfort.

J. P.

The consternation and conjectures to which this letter gave rise may be better imagined than described. No one could be found who was able to explain by whom the letter had been deposited, or where Pollard had secreted himself. Search and inquiry were diligently set on foot, and every effort made to gain further information as to his absence and the mysterious purport of his letter; but all without effect. Ambiguous, however, as was the letter, it awakened some painful suspicions in the breast of Mrs. Fairfield, which from delicacy she feared either to charge Lucy with, or communicate to her husband. The whole matter, however, was soon after developed, as we shall presently see, by a most unexpected event, terminating in wretchedness and anguish on the one hand, and indelible disgrace on the other.

CHAPTER VIII

WHILE these domestic disquietudes were passing within the hitherto peaceful walls of Staffords, the fair daughter of the mansion
(as we have seen) was from home, on a visit to the Misses
Chrichton, of Whiston Hall. These ladies, although each had
numbered forty and five years of 'single blessedness,' still possessed all the cheerfulness of blooming twenty; and had, when not
yet arrived at that captivating age, lost both their parents, who
were carried off by the small pox, to the ravages of which dreadful
disease they also had nearly fallen victims. The elder sister still exhibited in her face those sad marks which so often disfigure the
countenance, but which in this lady had not tended in the least to
diminish the natural softness of expression, that well contrasted
with her dark hazel eyes; and in her manner she was rather precise
and retiring; but upon the whole, after a little intimacy, she became cheerful and social. Her sister, but one year her junior, was
striking both in her figure and address, and possessed a rare combination of archness with ingenuousness – waggery with sincerity
– and a playfulness of wit, that greatly amused without ever giving
offence. She was godmother to Caroline, of whom both the sisters
were extremely fond, while Caroline took much delight in visiting
them. It would seem (according to Sterne) that there is some fa-
talism in names, and hence it might have arisen that neither of
these ladies ever changed their single state, although they had
many suitors, and each of them once in their life approached, as it
were, to the very foot of the hymeneal altar!

Miss Deb, (whose more lengthy name of Deborah had for
brevity's sake been curtailed of two of its syllables,) was the elder,
and had been addressed by a young Cockney, who insinuated
himself into her good graces by the promptitude with which he
conducted the town business of the estate (a very extensive and

valuable property called Whiston, of which the sisters were co-heiresses) as chief clerk and expectant partner of the house of Fisher and Ewing, their agents; but who, after having won the lady's heart, betrayed her confidence, as well as that of his employers, and made off with a thousand pounds of their money with which he had been intrusted.

Miss Judy (otherwise Judith) the younger, goodnaturedly joined in the laugh against herself, whenever the tale of her 'love-stricken' heart was told, and she would often amuse her god-daughter with the story, that it might be, as she would say, 'a warning to her how she trusted the treacherous sex!'

Stop, my dear young lady! Don't be so impatient; you shall hear the particulars of this adventure directly. It may be a warning to you and all other Misses from adolescent fifteen, when the heart, first impatient of restraint, begins to palpitate and flutter, it scarce knows why, to mature twenty-five, when the feelings are softened down by prudence and circumspection, and the heart knows how to love.

Know then, that— One rainy day in the month of November, (some sixty years ago), the heiresses of Whiston Hall were seated together on the sofa, employed in weaving some furniture fringe, when a person in military costume rode dashingly up to the block through the falling shower, and throwing himself from his horse, called out in a stentorian voice to a servant whom he saw standing within the mill door, for shelter, 'Hoy! hoy! my man! come here, my fine fellow – take this horse – take care of him until the rain is over – I'll not forget you, mark me, when you bring him up!' All this was said with an ease and confidence that gave great weight to his commands. The ladies, mean time, were on the *qui vive*, and had sent a servant to ask the gentleman to walk in. He entered, and approaching in the most confident manner, apologized for his intrusion and the unsightly trim the rain had put him in, was persuaded they would not deny shelter to a war-worn soldier (at the same time raising the stump of his amputated arm, and with the fore finger of his right hand tracing the scar on his left cheek) and turning to the servant, begged for a towel to wipe the wet from his clothes. The ladies were all courtesy, gave him a hearty welcome, and were much struck with his '*officer-like*' elegance; felt it a great pity that there should be such a barbarous thing as war, and that war should so cruelly cut up such fine looking men. This introduction, unceremonious as it was, led to many subsequent visits from our veteran campaigner, who often interested his fair, but artless entertainers with an account of his daring exploits and gallant achievements. He had served in the East Indies, under General Gage, and had taken two nabobs prisoner with his own hands at the storming of Mexico; was the first man that entered Russion, when they attacked the Castle of Ceylon; and marched from thence, a distance of fifty miles, directly on the Cape of Good Hope, where he himself applied the match to the bomb that blew up the Moro-Castle. He was presented with a company for this service; and had immediately after to march his brigade against Constantinople, which he took with 500 men, whom he put in ambush before Cadiz; but had the misfortune here to lose his arm, and was no sooner recovered, than he had to face a whole regiment of wild Indians that had been bribed by the Queen of Hungary to plunder and burn the town of Denmark; and there had his check laid open by a tomahawk. He was compelled by his wounds to get leave of absence and return to England, but as soon as he got better, the King wanting his services, he was ordered out to Barbados to assist the Governor in placing the Island in a state of defence; for (said he in a lower tone of voice) to let you into a secret, we have positive information that the Count D'Grasse is preparing an expedition at Martinique, against us; but for this, he should have been long ago made a general; but he was sure his promotion was not far off. He would thus, as from time to time he renewed his visits, interest and delight these credulous ladies with the account of battles and sieges, never before heard of – confusing and mis-calling places, persons, and things in one heterogeneous chaos, that neither they nor himself could understand.

It must be borne in mind, that these ladies had never studied geography, and knew merely that there was such a place as the East Indies – they had of course heard of France, and believed England to be the best country in the world; and that London was bigger than Bridge Town (where they had never been half a dozen times in their lives.) Upright, honest and simple hearted women!— their reading had not extended beyond that of the Bible, the 'Whole Duty of Man', and the 'Pilgrim's Progress' except indeed they had dipped into 'Sir Charles Grandison' and 'Pamela, or Virtue Rewarded.' No wonder then, that these warlike exploits, and a hundred others equally ridiculous, but astonishing to the credulous ears of his fair auditors, should have deluded their unsuspecting natures, and actually made captive Miss Judy's sensitive heart.— Like the fair Desdemona, she loved him for the very dangers he had encountered— for the hair-breadth escapes he had had! She, however, was too prudent to 'surrender at discretion.' A parley was to be had, a reference made, and a friend consulted. Unfortunate boaster!— Thou bastard son of Mars! O vile impostor! He was served like all such rascals in red – who disgrace their Sovereign's uniform, and tarnish the epaulette which should be their honourable distinction, by basely betraying confiding innocence and virtue – ought ever to be served; that is, by being stripped of his false plumage, and exposed in all his native insignificance to the scorn and contempt of these ladies, and left to the ridicule of the whole community.

Mr. Walmsly, the old friend whom the ladies desired to consult (Miss Deb feeling great interest in her sister's happiness) attended their summons; came most opportunely, most happily, and like their guardian angel, to expose the presumptuous impostor, and frustrate his daring scheme. Captain Kickero (for such was the assumed rank and name of this hero) was, notwithstanding the loss of an arm, and the scar on his cheek, rather a good looking, sturdy, rough, off-hand, plausible fellow; he was seated with the ladies, urging the decision for the 'happy day,' when they gave him to understand that they were momentarily expecting the

friend whom they were desirous of consulting. Instantly he rose –
protested he had urgent business – was to meet the Governor on
a consultation of great importance – had already overstayed his
time – begged the servant to hasten his horse – exchanged a parting adieu, and rode off in great haste. The ladies, it must be con-
fessed, were a little surprised at this sudden movement; they went
to the door, and looked after him with doubtful mind; but as he
was in the act of turning the angle of the road which would have
hid him from their view, they saw their friend Mr. Walmsly encounter him – the gentlemen drew up together on the road side—
had a few minutes' chat, and separated, each pursuing his des-
tined course— the Captain driving furiously and our friend gently proceeding to the mansion. He was warmly greeted by the
ladies, and being seated, 'Well,' said Miss Deb, 'we are glad to find
that you are acquainted with Captain Kickero.' 'Captain Kickero!'
exclaimed their friend, 'pray who is he?' 'Bless me!' said Miss
Judy, 'why the gentleman you met and conversed with at the corner of the road.' 'Ha, ha, ha!' roared Mr. Walmsly, 'Captain
Kickero, forsooth! Why that chap to whom I spoke coming along
the road, is Ned Crosier; as plausible a fellow as ever wielded a
cow-skin.' 'Surely,' said Miss Deb, 'you don't mean the gentleman
with one arm?' 'But surely I do,' replied their friend, 'and he has
also a great gash on his cheek!' 'Tell us then, we pray, who and
what he is,' rejoined the sisters in breathless attention. 'About five
or six years ago,' said Mr. Walmsly, with great solemnity, 'Crosier
was book-keeper on the Pool Estate, where playing some of his
mad pranks in the boiling-house, (for he was ever a mad-cap sort
of a chap,) he slipped from the rack over the taches, and falling on
the edge of the cooler, shattered his arm so shockingly as to render instant amputation necessary, and he received at the same
time a desperate wound in the cheek.' 'Ha, ha, ha!' laughed Miss
Judy. 'Ha, ha, ha!' echoed Miss Deb. 'Ha, ha, ha!' joined in the
chorus Mr. Walmsly; and the laugh went round and round again,
until Miss Judy exhibiting some slight hysterical symptoms, their
friend put a stop to it by thus finishing the history of our military

impostor. 'Colonel Græm,' said he, 'adjutant-general of the militia and owner of the Pool, was a benevolent and kind-hearted man, and in consideration of the loss of Crosier's arm and his other sufferings, settled twenty-five pounds a year on him; and upon his going to England, gave him his half worn uniform and other cast-off clothes; with which this redoubtable Captain has been making a figure ever since; declining all business, and palming himself off for a gentleman!' This adventure, in conjunction with Miss Deb's former one, decided these ladies in their determination never to surrender their liberty, nor again to trust the faithless sex! and with true sisterly affection they have dwelt together; dispensing with liberal hand, succour and assistance to the poor in their neighbourhood. Neddy Crosier ended his career in Demerara, then under the government of the Stadtholder of Holland, and it was said not in the most honourable manner, the Fiscal having consigned him to the penal gang for having made too free with property not his own.

Caroline's visit to Whiston Hall was greatly protracted by the occurrences at Staffords; where, since her absence, Mr. Mac Flashby had but seldom made his appearance; and her parents had found some reason for advising her to be more distant in her conduct towards him, than she was wont to be. Indeed this gentleman had of late much fallen off in his attentions to her, and in many points seemed a strangely altered man, having fallen into much dissipated society. He was at this time engaged with a party of young, gay, light-hearted sons of Mars, who were making a frolicsome excursion through the country, and among other feats, had engaged for a bet of one hundred guineas, to send a horse safely down into the 'Animal Flower Cave.' So extraordinary a bet did not fail to excite the curiosity of sportsmen far and near; and that some idea may be formed of this hazardous exploit, we shall here introduce a brief description of the place, as given by Hughes in his History of Barbados. He says: 'It is a cave near the bottom of a high rocky cliff facing the sea, in the north part of the island, in the parish of Saint Lucy; the descent to it is very steep and dangerous, being in some places almost perpendicular, and what adds a horror to this dreadful situation, is, that the waves from below almost incessantly break upon the cliff, and sometimes reach its highest summit.' An adequate idea cannot be formed of it, without visiting its locality. The track along this awful declivity is so narrow, that looking down its precipitous and craggy side, it can scarcely be discerned, and the head becoming dizzy at the sight of the dashing surge rushing along its broken and rocky base, is sufficient to unnerve the most hardy adventurer. Think then, what must have been the sensation of the poor little animal when launched over the cliff and placed on the track which he must either follow, or by missing his footing for a single step, be inevitably plunged amidst the foaming billows below, and lost in an overwhelming sea! I think, even now, I see the 'little pony' trembling at his perilous situation – first casting a wistful look on the eager throng above, then eyeing the melancholy track before him – and having no alternative but quickly trotting down without one moment's pause, and reaching the cave in safety! He was brought up by block and tackle, rigged on a projecting pole, and received the caresses of most of those who witnessed the achievement.

These military gentlemen (of whom we are speaking) were of a regiment who had relieved the 89th: and for whose better accommodation a spacious barrack had been recently erected at Constitution Hill, stretching along the lawn of the King's House, diagonally from the present West Gate of the enclosure to within about twenty feet of the front portico of that building. This regiment had but just arrived from Ireland, where they had left a fame that showed they had not altogether contented themselves with empty parade and drill discipline; and they brought with them here a full share of that mischievous spirit which tends to generate broils and strife. There was at the same time another regiment here, under Major W—, of Buenos Ayres notoriety, the officers of which, by the contagion of bad example, soon became adepts in row-making. As to the *men*, the character given them by their *gallant* commander, in a caution to the inhabitants through the public press, was such as would no doubt in these times bring an officer for such a degradation of his corps to a court-martial!

The officers of both these regiments (especially the former) were much caressed by the inhabitants, and found at all times ready access into our domestic society, which at that period was hospitable and generous. Notwithstanding this, it was a general practice among these parade sons of Mars, as they then deserved to be called, to indulge themselves in a levity of conduct very offensive to a peaceable and friendly community. Among other freaks, they would walk through the streets of an evening, forming with united oustretched arms, a link from one side to the other, impeding the passing of passengers, and causing thereby broils and disturbances. These gentlemen sought also to burlesque the character of our Militia, by calling to each other as they passed through the streets, in derision of the rank by which our civilians were accustomed to address each other at their monthly mess (to which many of these military were frequently invited) —'Colonel, your health,' 'Thank you, Major.' 'Captain, I'll take wine with you,' 'With pleasure, Lieutenant.' 'A bumper to the Adjutant, for his skill in the field to-day!' and then would 'hip hip, and huzza,' as they proceeded on; 'Rachael's' generally bringing them up to make a finish of the evening; but frequently, not until they had otherwise indulged themselves by offending the inhabitants. Such conduct often produced 'an affair of honour' between the parties – and so frequent had this at one time become, that it was as natural to ask among the early inquiries of the morning, 'What duel?' as 'what arrival?' – And we are thus led to the recital of the fatal termination of one of these miscalled 'affairs of honour.'

In those days, it was usual with the candidates for a seat in our Colonial Parliament, to give at their election what was called a 'freeholders' feast.' It was a meeting that occasioned much riot and drunkenness; and too frequently tended to increase the calendar of the Grand Session – a practice, therefore, now 'more honoured in the breach than in the observance' – but yet the discontinuance of it has destroyed much kind intercourse be-

tween the upper and lower classes of society. However, at the period of which we are speaking, the candidates for St.——'s parish
had prepared the festive board, at which not only the electors and
numerous other guests were welcomed; but to give variety and hilarity to the entertainment, music was provided, and ladies invited
to form the 'merry, merry dance.' It was a just observation of the
Governor's lady on this occasion, that 'a ball should never succeed
a dinner, for when men are flushed with wine they are not
befitting companions for ladies,' and so it unhappily proved
here.— Among the guests were several military men, one of
these, Lieutenant C——, was as fine a looking soldier-like youth
as ever drew a sword or wore an epaulet. Practical jokes are ever
considered by well-bred men as the wit of the low and vulgar; and
indeed, no man of sense will ever adopt or countenance them; but
at this merry-making many present indulged in such pleasantries.
Ah, fatal folly! Mr. F——, one of the gentlemen there, received a
sly blow while amusing himself by looking at the dancers, and in
order to retort the joke in kind and without a tincture of hostile
feeling, he promptly turned on the person nearest him, and
played off a corresponding 'witticism.' Would that it had ended
here!— but no!— the joke fell upon a gentleman who, though he
could revel in fun and frolic himself was too sensitive to be joked
with in like manner by others. It was Lieutanant C——. What? a
soldier receive a blow! Much discussion and confusion ensued –
no regard was paid to the ladies – some scuffling followed, and a
magistrate being at hand, the parties were bound over to keep the
peace for twelve months, a period (one might have thought) quite
sufficient to have cooled the blood and dispel the ire of a Turkish
pasha or a Russian autocrat!

It is a fact that our civilian, notwithstanding the constitutional
warmth of his blood, soon regained a tranquil mind, and conceiving the affair to have been finally adjusted by the interposition of
the law, thought no more of the occurrence. Think, therefore,
what must have been his consternation when he was called upon
by Lieutenant B——, on the part of C——, to remind him of the

day on which their bonds would cease! 'Twas a week distant and the only alternative was, 'pistols or apology.' F——, conscious of no premeditated insult, disdained an apology, and placed his cause in the hands of his friend Mr. W——, who with B—— soon made arrangements for the meeting. It took place near the Hermitage, then an old-fashioned small red painted building in a secluded spot, but now a spacious cottage ornée situate in a populous neighbourhood. The distance measured, the parties took their stand. 'I'll give you the first fire,' tauntingly said C——; 'Pop away.' W——forbad this, and it was agreed between him and B——, that the combatants should fire together, and the word to be given by the latter. 'One, two, three, fire,' said B——. Oh, fatal shot! C—— fell to the earth, a lifeless corpse! and the king lost a soldier of as stately a mien as ever marched with a company of grenadiers. The body was speedily conveyed to a house in Quakers' Meeting-street, and the same evening was interred at St. Michael's church, with military honours, and other impressive and affecting ceremonies. Alas! what a warning! Oh! may it make due impression alike on the civil and the military broiler, and check that false honour which would sacrifice a fellow-creature's life to avenge an inadvertent offence!

It was about six months after this lamentable affair that W—— was walking with a friend on the parade adjoining the King's House (at that time a general promenade of the inhabitants of the town) when he met two young militaires arm in arm. One of them, Ensign ——, said to his companion in a deliberate manner as he approached W——, at the same time pointing towards him, 'There goes one of poor C——'s murderers.' Stung to the quick by this wanton insult, W——was on the point of striking him with a cane he carried in his hand, but being prevented by his companion, said in a firm but agitated manner, 'By ——, I will slap your face the first time I meet you off your own dunghill; and passed on. About ten days after this, our young soldier in company with the same brother officer, passing down Suttle-street, was recognised by W—— from his father's balcony—he instantly ran down, and getting to the door just as the others came opposite, with more impetuosity than prudence, he seized him by the shoulder, and wheeling him round, inflicted with his open hand a blow on his cheek. 'Run him through!' energetically cried his companion – and well would such brutal temerity have deserved it – but our young Ensign was content to draw his sword but half way from its sheath— and then returning it to the hilt, and applying his hand to the part smarting under the blow, said 'Oh, mine Got! I never taut to see tis day!' and walked on — his companion in disgust taking another road. Both these gentlemen had leave to return to Europe, and sailed the same evening to join a transport at St. Vincent, homeward bound. The one who received the blow was of foreign extraction, and related to Lord ——.

CHAPTER IX

AMONGST those led by curiosity to witness the 'neck or nothing' exploit detailed in a former page, was Mr. Brushwood, who at the time happened to be on a visit in the neighbourhood. Having witnessed the feat, he was quietly returning to 'Cadogans,' whence he had set out, and was gently walking his horse, musing on the way, not so much on the merit or success of the undertaking as on the cruelty of jeopardizing the life of the pony. Whilst thus wrapped in thought he was suddenly overtaken by three or four officers, who were followed by a gentleman in 'mufti,' all rapidly passing him; and as soon as the latter came near to Mr. Brushwood he called out, 'Ge-up, ge-up, my hearty,' and laid his whip across Brushwood's horse with a violence to which the animal was unaccustomed, and being a high mettled steed, and already much excited by the rapid galloping of the other horses, set off at full speed with his rider, who although a skilful and dexterous horseman, and possessing much nerve, was unable to draw him up until he had proceeded in his angry career nearly two miles. Although it had been his intention to return to the estate whence he had set out, his feelings, however, being aroused by the insult he had received, he resolved to proceed homeward; but when he reached town he felt fatigued from his 'Gilpin' like race, and it being late, he turned into the 'Royal Naval hotel,' purposing to rest there for the night, in order that he might have an early opportunity the next morning of ascertaining by whom he had been thus shamelessly assailed.

Rachael Polgreen then kept this Hotel; which indeed she had built, and she conferred on it its distinguished name, in consequence of *His Royal Highness Prince William Henry*, who then commanded the *Pegasus* frigate, having made this hotel his temporary abode when on shore. It will not lead us far from our

subject, if whilst Mr. Brushwood refreshes himself, we here introduce our readers to the celebrated hostess of this hotel, and give a
short sketch of her remarkable history.

'Miss Rachael,' as *par excellence* she was called (the prefix being
then rarely given to black or coloured women,) was the daughter
and slave of the notorious William Lauder, a Scotch schoolmaster,
who with equal effrontery and ingenuity had represented Milton as
a plagiary; and this he did with such success, as to induce great Dr.
Johnson to write a preface to the work, exposing the supposed literary dishonesty of our immortal bard! Detection, however, of this
gross imposition was not long delayed, and the exposure of the unworthy pedagogue immediately ensued. His friends disgusted, and
the literary world incensed, he was compelled to quit his country,
and he sought shelter in Barbados. For a short time he kept a grammar school, but not succeeding therein, he opened a huckster's
shop in the Roebuck, which he conducted with the aid of an African
woman whom he had purchased, and by whom he had our celebrated hostess of the 'Royal Naval Hotel.' Lauder's conduct to his
offspring, is a damning proof how debasing to the human mind is
the power given us over our fellow creatures by holding them in
bondage! The ties of consanguinity were all merged in the authority of the master, and he saw but the slave in his own daughter! She
was not a very fair mulatto, but had rather wiry than woolly hair, and
in her juvenile days was a remarkably well made, good looking girl,
possessing altogether charms that touched not the heart, but awakened the libidinous desires of her disgraceful and sinful parent; who
made many – but to her eternal honour be it spoken – unsuccessful
attempts on her chastity. This vulgar, unnatural and wretched
brute, irritated and enraged at her repulses, ordered the unhappy
Rachael into the hands of the 'Jumper.' Poor girl! We here see *the
accursed thing,'* Tlavery, blighting and uprooting every Christian
principle that teaches us 'to do unto others as we would they should
do unto us;' but we also see here the timely interposition of Divine
mercy rescuing an innocent and helpless victim from the hands of
oppression! She was already 'tucked up,' in the indecorous manner

of those days, and the brutal hand of the mercenary whipper, armed with the fatal 'cowskin,' stretched forth to lay on the unpitying merciless lash, when a British tar! a gallant seaman! rushed on the relentless executioner, seized the whip from his grasp, and rescuing his panting victim, carried her off in triumph amidst the cheers of a thronging multitude! And who was this British tar?— this gallant seaman? None other — no less a person than that celebrated hero!— *Captain Pringle* of the *Centaur!* who not many years after, by as singular an interposition of Divine Providence, was rescued from shipwreck!

Lauder, irritated and provoked that his victim had thus escaped, and viewing her but as a slave, sought redress of the Captain, by arresting him on the 'detinue act;' but our hero's benevolence and generosity did not cease here— Captain Pringle, to satisfy the demands of this mercenary wretch, purchased the girl at an extortionate price, and satisfying the claims of the law, emancipated her. It may perhaps be considered but as a venial error, for which he may be excused, that his 'protection' of this young interesting creature (not then eighteen) did not cease here! He established her in a small house at the lower end of the town, which by her industry was afterwards enlarged, and ultimately became the celebrated hotel of which we have spoken, and the temporary residence of a British prince who subsequently became sovereign of the United Kingdom. Not a vestige of this hotel now remains! We now return to Rachael, who dropped the hateful name of Lauder, – who, we may as well add here, died some few years after the above event, in wretchedness and contempt — a striking admonition, we hope, to some yet equally criminal wretches! – and took that of Pringle; but unfortunately for her reputation, being too anxious to strengthen her influence over her benefactor, she contrived to deceive him by assuming the appearance of that 'state which ladies who love their lords like to be in,' and went so far as to present him, on one of his returns from a cruize, with a smiling 'little cherub' as the offspring of their loves! Unluckily however for Rachael's scheme, the real mother of the infant, feel-

ing those yearnings which nature has so deeply implanted in the
maternal breast, demanded back her child, and made such clam-
our and uproar, that the imposition coming to the Captain's ears,
the child was restored to its rightful parent, and he consequently
broke off all further intercourse with the faithless Rachael. Soon
after this, Captain Pringle sailed for Jamaica, and it was on his
homeward bound voyage from that Island, that the *Centaur*
foundered at sea, and her gallant commander, with eight or nine
of his surviving crew, after encountering unparalleled sufferings
in the long boat, at length reached England in safety. The volatile
Rachael, however, was not long without a 'protector;' a gentleman
of the name of Polgreen succeeded to the possession of her
charms, and gave that addition to her cognomen, which distinguished her ever after as 'Rachael Pringle Polgreen.' She had
'now about' (as Moore says in his almanack) given those symptoms
of *en bon point* that progressively *ballooned* to those dimensions
which in due time so amply filled her great arm-chair — and
which many among us must at this time well remember!

We cannot here resist giving an anecdote of the Prince and
Rachael, which will furnish some speculation on the character of
both. His Royal Highness had dined with the mess of the 49th regiment, then on this station, and returning to the hotel in the
evening, *more* than 'half seas o'er,' accompanied by some of the
choice *spirits* of the corps, he commenced a royal frolic by break-
ing the furniture, &c., and with the aid of his boon companions
carried on the sport with such activity, that in a couple of hours
every article was completely demolished — the very beds cut up,
and their contents emptied into the street, and the whole neighbourhood strewed with the feathers, representing a mimic snow
storm! Crack went the pier glasses, pictures, chandeliers and
lamps; smash went the decanters, goblets, wine glasses, porcelain
and crockery, all, all went in the general havoc, while the sly and
cunning Rachael sat quite passive in her great arm-chair at the entrance door of the hotel. Servant after servant came running to announce to her the destruction that was going on, but the stoical

hostess moved not! It was all the same to her, and there she sat unruffled, and as if glued to the huge chair! She would, as each fresh communication was made, reply with perfect nonchalance, 'Go, go long man, da' no King's son! If he no do wha' he please, who d'en can do'um? Let he lone! lay he muse heself – da no King's son! Bless he heart! Da' no King's son,' and with many other like expressions of indifference at what was going on, kept her seat as unconcernedly as if her house was in perfect tranquillity. It was, however, now time for the Prince to return on board, and as he had literally (in nautical phrase) 'cleared the decks,' he was 'taking his departure,' when encountering Rachael still occupying the 'gang way,' he bid her 'good night,' and to crown his sport, upset her and chair together, leaving her unwieldy body sprawling in the street, to the ineffable amusement of the laughing crowd. Rachael showed no ire even at this — but calling out in her sweetest dulcet tones, 'Mas Prince! Mas Prince; you come ma-morning, to see wha' mischief you been do!' — and after a little floundering and much assistance, she was reseated.

The morrow came – Rachael soon heard that the Prince was to sail in the evening for Saint Vincent. A clerk was here – a servant there – friends everywhere throughout the house, taking an inventory of the overnight's destruction; the good dame reserving to herself the privilege of valuing the articles; and before the sun's altitude had been taken on board the *Pegasus*, one of the satellites of the hotel was on her deck with 'a full, true and particular account,' of the loss, destruction and havoc, of the preceding evening – accompanied with an humble petition for indemnity – the losses being stated at the trifling sum of £700 sterling! Our generous-hearted Tar, with a magnanimity as conspicuous in him after he became sovereign, as at this juvenile and sailor-like period of his life, made no question of the correctness of the account, but sent her an order for the amount on Firebrace and Co., (merchants of the town,) which was duly paid, and 'Miss Rachael' thereby enabled to furnish the 'Royal Naval Hotel,' with more splendour than ever!

CHAPTER X

BUT now to return to Mr. Brushwood. Before he retired to rest he ordered a *petit-souper* to make up for his loss of dinner, and while he was partaking of this he heard a jovial party in an adjoining room, enjoying themselves and making merry over a similar repast. It was the very party of officers who had passed him on the road, and they were all in high glee recapitulating the events of the day. Mirth and good humour seemed to prevail amongst them. After a hearty laugh at something which had just been said, one of the party asked, 'MacFlashby, do you know who the gentleman was?' 'I! No, not I,' said the other, 'but I have given him a lesson in horsemanship for which he ought to thank me.' 'And I'll warrant you,' added a third, 'that he'll not be ungrateful, and that you'll receive from him such thanks as neither your horse nor yourself will much like.' 'It was very improper conduct, let me tell you, Mr. Mac Flashby,' said another of the party, in a very stern and sonorous voice; at which the whole rose from table and departed.

Brushwood's first impulse was to follow them and take instant vengeance on the aggressor—but a moment's reflection determined him to act otherwise, so calling for a light he retired to bed; but ere he wooed sweet sleep he resolved on the line of conduct he would pursue the next morning. He rose at seven, breakfasted at eight, and amused himself in chat with his hostess until ten — he then sauntered forth, bending his way towards the wharf. Before he could inquire for Mr. Mac Flashby's residence, he recognised that individual at the door of his store. — The recognition was mutual, but not the feelings arising in the bosom of each. Mac Flashby slunk into his store – Brushwood quickened his pace – in an instant they were in collision; the latter laying his whip over the shoulders of Mac Flashby with a degree of energy and activity that made him writhe under the chastisement;— this 'manual exercise' being over, and his resentment with it, Brushwood withdrew with as much deliberation as though he had been making a friendly call; leaving Mac Flashby to 'chew the cud,' after this flagellation, and reconcile himself to the disgrace in the best manner he could.

We all know with what facility a mob is collected in Bridge Town, even now that we have the guardianship of an extensive police — what it must have been on this occasion, when we had not even the semblance of such an establishment beyond a few constables, may readily be imagined. Had the 'Irish Giant,' just landed and taken refuge in Mr. Mac Flashby's store; or a 'dancing bear' been led from the wharf to Broad-street, a more eager curiosity could not have been excited than was produced by this affair. Poor Mac Flashby was actually blockaded on the one hand; and Brushwood beset on the other, as he passed along to Messrs. Littledale and Marwell's; — hootings and hissing assailing the former, plaudits and huzzas greeting the latter! – both viewed as 'Lions' of exquisite rarity, but of unequal merit!

We, for a moment, again break the thread of our story, to notice a very different species of Irish cowardice to that just detailed, and which occurred here not long ago: — we do this merely to show, that however justly the sons of Erin are universally esteemed for generosity and bravery, there are exceptions which disgrace the individual. In the instance alluded to, the assailant was an Irishman – not one of the brave and generous – but one who with a drayman's strength, and merciless blows, tanned the hide of a poor pigmy incapable of resisting him!

Mr. Brushwood remained some time at his friends' store in Broad-street, occasionally showing himself at the door; but when the crowd that had followed him was dispersed, he quietly walked down to the hotel, where he dined and remained until five, when he took horse and leisurely rode home to 'Cotton Coast.' Mac Flashby at dusk of evening went to his countrymen in High-street, Messrs. Branker and Weatherhead, two gentlemen from Dublin who had long been established in the Island as provision mer-

chants, and were highly respected; Mr. Branker having the command of a company of 'cadets,' consisting of young gentlemen not
yet qualified by age to join the regular militia, and whose duty it
was to attend on the Governor on state and other occasions when
required by his Excellency. When qualified, they generally received commissions in the militia.

Mr. Mac Flashby being on terms of great intimacy with these
gentlemen, no sooner reached their house, than he walked up
sans ceremonie, into the drawing room, where Mr. Branker was
alone reading, who hearing footsteps, turned towards the door,
and seeing Mac Flashby, hastily rose, and in no very courteous
manner demanded, 'Who are you, Sir? What has brought you
here?' To which the other, in a drawling deferential tone replied,
''Tis me, Branker' — 'And, Sir,' said Mr. Branker, with some degree of asperity, 'what has brought you here, after your disgrace of
the morning?' 'I've come to consult you as a friend! — what would
you advise me to do?' 'Advise you to do! Go, Sir, and consult your
tailor.' 'Tailor! — consult my tailor! — Why consult my tailor?'
'Because,' replied Mr. Branker, 'he can pad your coat, and may
save your shoulders from the effect of the next horsewhipping you
get.' 'Poh, poh!' cried the other, 'no man alive shall ever again
serve me after that fashion with impunity.' 'Then, Sir,' said Mr.
Branker in a firm and commanding tone, 'go, prepare yourself
with the courage of a true Irishman, to repel the insults that will
be continually heaped on you, for every shop-boy will henceforth
despise you. Go, go to —— and never let me see you here again –
you are a disgrace to your country!' 'Poh, poh,' repeated Mac
Flashby, and walked off.

Poor fellow! — thus disconcerted, and knowing not what to do
with himself, he sauntered down to Miss Rachael's, and there
found the wary landlady seated, as usual, at her hotel door. As
soon as he drew near, and without waiting his salutation, she addressed him in a tone and manner that quite astounded him, exclaiming — 'Whau! whau dis! what you come here for? You tink
gentleman go have any ting for say to you? Go! you better go

home! Go, go hide youself!' Wretched man! — the darkness of the night enabled him to get home unobserved; and we will here leave him to ruminate over the events of the day, while we direct our attention to other scenes to which they gave birth, yet more lamentable, and as in due time will be seen, more disgraceful.

CHAPTER XI

IT so happened that on the same day that the occurrences which have just been stated took place, Mr. Fairfield despatched his confidential man, Musso, to town, to bring down a supply of negro clothing and provision, which had been ordered from the town agent; and Musso, having, like all his class, an inventive mind and fertile imagination, knew every particular of what had occurred, as circumstantially as if he had been present throughout the whole transaction; although, in fact, he had not reached town until an hour or two after the disgraceful occurrence had taken place. Having accomplished the object of his errand, he proceeded home with his well-laden wagon, and arrived just after sunset, full of agitation and bustle; and looking like one overcharged with some weighty matter, of which he was anxious to disburden himself, he hastened into the dwelling-house, where he found his master and mistress seated in the entrance-hall. Without ceremony or preface, he began to tell them 'all about it.' 'Law, law, Sir! they most kill he with beat – they gee he a meal of licks! He been most mudder with blows.' And thus he ran on, regardless of the frequent commands of his irritated master and impatient mistress to be more explicit in what he had to relate. 'Sirrah,' petulantly demanded Mr. Fairfield, 'who has been killed? who has been murdered?' 'Yes, Sir, I tell you "all bout um." ' 'Say, at once, sirrah, who has been killed,' sternly urged his incensed master. 'Mister MacFlashby, Sir!' tremblingly uttered Musso. But here the attention of the whole party was arrested by an awful and sudden scream, followed by Amarillus's shrill cry for help! Another, and another shriek, more piercing than the first, succeeded, before Mrs. Fairfield could sufficiently collect herself to attend to Amarillus;— recovered from her fright, she now rushed into the room where Lucy lay, and where she had been confined for some days with cold and headache; the windows closed, and the patient left in almost total darkness. The thrifty Amarillus (an old but intriguing servant) had been in constant attendance upon her, and was now at her bedside, chafing her temples and using other restoratives. When Mrs. Fairfield, all anxiety and tremor, entered the room, Amarillus, with greatly excited feelings and alarm, begged her mistress to send for the 'great doctor.' 'Lay, um run for he! she too bad, fait um be!' And thus were removed from the good lady's mind those doubts and fears with which her bosom had been so long tormented, but which, from the kindest, tenderest considerations, she revealed not to her husband, knowing the pain and mortification Lucy's disgrace would occasion him. Indeed, such were her feelings of delicacy towards the poor girl, that until Pollard's ambiguous letter, she never even thought of charging her with any dereliction from the paths of virtue; and even then such was the pertinacity of Lucy in denying the truth of the charge, that Mrs. Fairfield willingly suffered her fears to be lulled; and thus this too confiding gentlewoman was thrown off her guard; and became negligent of those attentions she would otherwise have exercised towards the guilty girl.

Lucy continued in a succession of fits until the 'great doctor' (so the negroes called the physician or surgeon) arrived, who came but just in time to assist at the birth of a still-born infant! We will not attempt to describe the perturbation of mind or outraged feelings of Mr. Fairfield; for, though Lucy was the child of his early irregularities, the paternal love he bore her had only a secondary place in his bosom's affection. He had fondly hoped to see her respectably established in a manner becoming her sphere of life, and he looked forward to her marriage with Pollard as an event which would accomplish that end. That worthy man (for so Joe really was) had, about the time he so mysteriously quitted home, accidentally seen Lucy in amorous dalliance seated on the knee of her paramour, and though he never before suspected her chastity, this sight roused in him a jealousy amounting almost to frenzy, and he was on the point of avenging himself on them both, with a carpenter's adze he then had in his hand, when Amarillus (at whose door it happened) rushed on him, and fortunately frustrated his purpose. This treacherous woman had long connived at their intrigue, and the family of Staffords being on one of their friendly visits to their neighbours at Silverdale, (Miss Fairfield being still with her godmother,) the lovers were more unguarded in the soft hours of their dalliance, and it was thus that Pollard came so unexpectedly upon them. This detection by him caused much confusion to the parties, and Amarillus was made the medium of negotiation between them and Joe, who was induced by the tears and intreaties of his faithless fair, to promise never to divulge what he had seen; but when it was afterwards proposed to the wronged and irritated man, that he should still marry Lucy, and that upon his compliance her seducer would give him three hundred pounds, he indignantly thrust the treacherous mediatrix from him, saying, 'What! am I a dog, that I should do this thing?' and thereupon quitting the scene which had so disgusted him, hastily set off, he scarce knew whither. It was shortly after this occurrence, that he got Amarillus (who told him more than he even then suspected) to place his letter where it was subsequently found.

Lucy, from her unhappy and dangerous situation, now engrossed the most solicitous attention and care of Mr. and Mrs. Fairfield. Her health daily became more critical, and her danger was aggravated by constant delirium, during which her incessant cry was on Caroline to forgive, to pardon her! And she would, for hours together, bewail her own unhappy state, until at last, completely exhausted, she would fall into an almost lifeless swoon. Her malady, at length, assumed a fearful madness, when, in one of her maniac ravings, resisting all restraint, she rushed from her bed-room into the back gallery, denouncing, in wild frantic accents, curses and vengeance on the head of her vile seducer. At this critical moment, Pollard (who having heard of her illness, and lamenting her misfortune, had cast off all resentment) ran into the gallery, breathless and agitated, and seizing hold of the poor creature, prevented her further egress; but, alas! it was the last act of affection and kindness he was ever to administer to her living! Uttering a fearful yell, as if terrified at his presence, she fell from his grasp, a lifeless corpse! Ah! poor deluded, wretched girl! thus has thy melancholy and untimely fate illustrated that maxim of the wise king, which saith, 'Better is it to have no children, and to have virtue; for children begotten *of unlawful beds* are witnesses against their parents!' Hear this, ye revellers in adulterous joys, and hear further what Solomon also saith, 'That the multiplying brood of *fornicators* shall not thrive, nor take deep root from bastard slips.' What think ye!

The reader's imagination will depict to itself the unhappiness which now prevailed throughout Staffords. It might truly be said to be the abode of wretchedness and sorrow; but it is such occasions, however, that present us the best opportunities of exerting our strength of mind; and it was now that Mrs. Fairfield eminently displayed that fortitude for which her sex is so justly celebrated. She had not only to combat with her own lacerated feelings, but to sustain the accumulated weight of her husband's 'wounded spirits.' Their neighbours at Silverdale did all that their kind and benevolent hearts would naturally suggest, to soothe and mitigate the sufferings of Mr. and Mrs. Fairfield; and the disappointed and deeply-afflicted Joe Pollard, regardless of his own feelings, undertook the whole arrangement of those last sad offices which are so well adapted to testify our regard for a departed friend!

It is with Christian satisfaction here added, that the *solemnity* of these occasions has become more decorous now than it was at that time, and that the hilarity which formerly amounted to little less than revelry and debauch, created by the profuse introduction of 'burnt wine' and 'sangaree,' is happily exploded.

The remains of this will-fated girl, who thus early fell a sacrifice, as much to her own levity as to the treacherous wiles of a vile seducer, were interred the following evening in the parish churchyard, and were attended to the grave by a solemn procession of all the most respectable negroes and mulattoes of Staffords and the neighbouring estates, Pollard officiating as chief mourner.

Amarillus, who, for sordid lucre, had basely lent herself to this poor girl's downfall, now gave way to all that elaborate lamentation and wailing so habitual amongst those people at that time, but which has since given place to a more decent sadness, expressive of Christian resignation, which may also be classed among the fruits of our bishop's zealous care.

The sagacious reader need scarcely be told who was the criminal author of all this disgrace and anguish heaped on a family, by one who ought rather to have interposed his every effort to save them pain and sorrow; but we will, nevertheless, leave to Amarillus the explanation of the fatal mystery. On the morrow after the interment of poor Lucy, Mr. Fairfield called up this treacherous domestic (in whom the family had too long placed so much confidence) to explain what she knew of the circumstances that had thus led to so melancholy a catastrophe; and she, with characteristic duplicity, palliating her own participation in the guilt she had promoted, related to him scenes of intrigue and assignation which seemed to his unsuspecting nature almost incredible. She, at length, brought down her recital to the evening of Musso's return from town, with his overcharged account of the occurrence between Mr. Mac Flashby and his indignant assailant, and thus proceeded: 'Massa! when titty Lucy been yerry uncle Musso tell you ' bout'um, she rise up in she bed fa listen to wha he say – and when he tell you they somebody been kill, she ' top she breath fa yerry all ' bout'um. So when he say, deem be Mr. Mac Flashby they been kill, she fall back in she bed and had all dem fits that make she go dead!'

CHAPTER XII

MISS FAIRFIELD, as the reader is aware, was, during the whole of these melancholy transactions, absent from home. It was at that cheerful period generally denominated 'crop time,' when the proprietors and managers feel more generous and sociable, and in which the slaves also, perhaps, from kindlier treatment, look more sleek and comely, are more happy and healthy, that this young lady, who being a great favourite among all her acquaintances, was sure to be 'where'er the merry dance was trip't among.' Mr. Mac Flashby, as her recognized lover, had been generally of her party; but, at times, he conducted himself with so little decorum, that he greatly disgusted Caroline, and gave much offence to other of the ladies present; in a word, he would become so intoxicated even in the early part of the evening, as to be incapable of participating in the rational amusements which all besides were enjoying. From the character of Miss Fairfield, it will create no surprise that she should have peremptorily 'desired Mr. Mac Flashby to discontinue his attentions to her!' but when it is added that he vulgarly attempted to kiss her in the presence of several of her young associates, we need scarcely ask whether any lady of sentiment and delicacy, under analogous circumstances, would have acted otherwise than the lovely heiress of Staffords.

Mr. Mac Flashby, from the new associations he had formed, had now so degenerated from those habits and manners which distinguish a well-bred Irishman (who in general possesses the pleasing art of insinuating himself into the good graces of the ladies,) that it might be said he no longer resembled his former self. He had run through all the gradations of whist and billiards, to the debasing practice of hazard, gambling, and cock-fighting, – amusements, if they be such, now happily abandoned to the lowest ranks of society, and he had also imbibed such a propensity for intoxicating liquors, as totally to disqualify him either for genteel society, or the proper management of his mercantile affairs. This may appear to have been the consequence of his dismissal by Miss Fairfield; but Mac Flashby's sensibilities were not of that delicate texture. Besides, the young lady had given him his dismissal with such gentleness of manner, as would have spared him much pain even had the cause been less justifiable.

Caroline's parents had studiously guarded against all communication to her that might shock her feelings either in regard to Lucy's illness, or the lamentable cause that ultimately led to her untimely death; nor had she been made acquainted with any of the particulars of the collision between Mac Flashby and Brushwood; what, however, she had heard of the latter circumstance mortified her on the one hand on account of her lover's disgrace, and perplexed her on the other from a vague recollection of the name of the gentleman she had once 'moved in a minuet' with, and in whom she thought she recognized the son of her father's neighbour. These circumstances greatly broke in upon her innocent pleasures, especially when she heard of Lucy's death, which deeply affected her, and induced her to provide habiliments suitable to that unhappy event. She now again expressed to her parents her wish of returning home; and as there no longer existed any cause for her absence, this matter was left to her own option, and in a few days Staffords joyfully greeted her return, although a gloom still hung over it which marked the sadness of its inmates.

We must here, for a time, leave the sorrowing and disappointed family of the Fairfields to congratulate themselves on Caroline's fortunate escape from a union that could only have produced vexation and wretchedness, while we dispose of the degenerate author of their sufferings, who had now, from the effects of a mind cankered by its own folly, and a heart vitiated by gross indulgence, fallen into the lowest species of debauchery and vice. Mr. Branker, whom we have before mentioned, and Mr. Thompson, (another eminent Irish merchant,) having some connexion with the principal of Mac Flashby's establishment, jointly took his affairs into their hands, and, after much persuasion, induced him to return to his friends at Belfast. He, however, did not quit the island without committing himself by the egregious folly of 'calling out' Mr. Brushwood. This gentleman treated the matter (now broached for the first time after the lapse of nearly twelve months) with the contempt it deserved, by 'assuring Mr. Mac Flashby that, having no longer any resentment against him for once jeopardising his life, he saw no reason for his now wantonly putting it in his power to take it, and begged that all further communication between them might cease, and wished him a safe voyage', and here the matter ended, Mr. Branker having timely interposed to frustrate a treacherous design Mac Flashby had formed of avenging himself on Brushwood the night previous to his departure.

There is a remarkable circumstance connected with the mercantile speculations of this Mr. Thompson, of whom we have spoken above, which will afford some clue that may lead to a fair estimate of the difference between an African's civilization, after a few years' residence in a West India colony, and that in which he exists in his own country, even under the advantages of court etiquette, if we may venture to use such a term when speaking of a savage nation. This gentleman, who in former times was a very eminent merchant here, had in his service a young African, whom he had purchased when not more than ten or twelve years of age; a smart shrewd lad, of an active mind and docile manners, and who constantly affirmed himself to be a king's son, and who gave many amusing accounts of his father's wealth and grandeur, from which circumstance he obtained the cognomen of Prince.

About the year 1782 or 1783, Mr. Thompson fitted out a large brig for a slaving voyage to Africa, and proposed to Prince, then about eighteen years old, to take the opportunity of visiting his royal sire, giving Prince full permission to remain, if he should so choose; and instructions to this effect were given to the captain of the vessel, whose name was Ashfield. Prince was duly equipped for the voyage, and furnished with various presents for his parents and friends, and he made no mean figure on the occasion among his comrades and friends here. The voyage was made to the Gold Coast; and on the vessel's arrival, Ashfield found, upon pursuing the directions of Prince, that the young African's father was actually sovereign or chief of Dahome, a warlike prince, inimical to the slave-trade, but carrying on great traffic in ivory, palm oil, and gold dust, with which articles he assisted Captain Ashfield in freighting the brig, which made a very successful voyage, although she did not bring more than one half the number of slaves expected. To the surprise of Mr. Thompson and of all who knew the circumstances of the voyage, Prince returned in the vessel, and cheerfully resumed his former occupations. It appears, by Ashfield's account, that great importunity was used to detain Prince; and such, it seems, was his fear of being forcibly detained, that he absconded from his family, and travelled upwards of sixty miles to regain the party from the vessel. The unexpected and welcome visitor had been much caressed, and treated with great distinction: he showed off in his best clothes, and delighted the whole court by his manners and address. He carried some articles of finery for presents, which would have been considered elegant even at Bartholomew Fair; but it was remarkable that, while with his family and friends, he ate very sparingly, and never drank any thing but water. His father was very aged, and there were two or three brothers much older than himself. He gave as a reason for returning, that 'he liked the white people's ways, and their victuals and dress, and all that something in backara country, which he no have in he own.' About five years after his return here, Prince, then about twenty-six or twenty-seven years of age, caught the smallpox, and died. We recommend these circumstances, of whose main facts the writer has a perfect recollection, to the consideration of the Anti-slavery Society, and generally to the friends of the African race.

CHAPTER XIII

WE have no longer to speak of young Goldacre as Mr. Brushwood; for this gentleman, having completed his studies, and acquired that polish of manners which a well-informed and intelligent mind will ever gain by application and diligence, now resolved to resume his proper name, and return to the parental roof. In order that the family at Silverdale might be prepared for his presence, Mr. Littledale wrote to apprise them that their son was shortly expected from Bermuda, where the honest, simple-hearted folks thought he had been ever since his departure from home. A few days after, another letter was dispatched to them announcing his arrival, and that he was following close upon the heels of the messenger. The whole plantation was instantly thrown into commotion; the fond and anxious parents, all agitation and delight at the idea of again beholding their beloved son, watched impatiently for his approach. At length a spruce cavalier is seen in the distance – anon galloping and hurrying near; – now he's at the gate! – jumps from his saddle, and the next moment sees him extending his arms to embrace his parents; but *they*, all amazement, stand aloof and gaze with doubtful and unrecognising eye; until at length his father, with awakened recollection, exclaims, ''Tis my son Jack!' and, throwing his arms round the young man's neck, presses him fondly to his bosom, and gives him a truly paternal welcome. Meantime, the good old lady, overcome by her feelings, sinks on the sofa, dissolved in tears! Soon, however, she also receives his fond and dutiful embrace, and the hall of Silverdale resounds with joy and gladness! 'Mas Jack's come!' was echoed along every field and through every gang; and whether from joy of heart on the occasion, or mere pretext for a holiday, the labourers struck work, and, hastening to the mansion, expressed their hearty welcome by loud and clamorous huzzas. It was, upon the whole, a trying moment to the sensitive feelings of our young heir; he was deeply affected by the overflowings of affection and tenderness of his parents, and greatly overcome by the boisterous greetings of the negroes, among whom he had always been a great favourite. To heighten this general domestic joy, the delighted proprietor, while celebrating his son's return by sumptuous feasting within, took care that there should be no lack of rum and molasses, with an extra allowance of corn and fish, to cheer the hearts of those without.

All who have been for any length of time absent from home, know with what eagerness and delight our family and friends relate to us, on our return, every incident, even to the veriest trifle, that has occurred during our absence, dilated on, and embellished as the feelings or fancy of the reciter desires either to interest or amuse. So, on this occasion, our returned heir had a budget opened to him; but he had to listen with the 'dull ear of a drowsy man to a twice-told tale,' for he already knew all that they had to relate. Hence it was that, to the disappointment of his loquacious parents, he betrayed so little curiosity or emotion at what he now heard from his father – then from his mother – anon from both together, as if they would outrun each other in the grateful task of giving him delight. But they, nothing discouraged by his too palpable absence of mind, pressed especially on his attention those occurrences in which he himself had been the chief actor. The whole history of Mac Flashby's love affair with Miss Fairfield – then his degeneracy and dismissal – the excitement at the Dispensary ball, from the appearance of a stranger who danced with Caroline – the gallantry of the Prince at the Pilgrim ball – all appeared alike indifferent to him; but when they intimated that the young lady had a new lover, he hastily rose from his seat, and, ejaculating an emphatic 'Ah!' he exclaimed breathlessly, 'Who is he? what's his name?' and, pacing up and down the room, left the good old folks puzzling themselves to recollect the name, but all in vain!

At this critical moment, while his parents were still taxing their memory for the name of the new lover, their neighbour Fairfield arrived on a friendly call of congratulation on the return of their son. This gentleman seemed almost as much surprised at the fine, manly, and self-possessed appearance of the young man as were his parents on his first arrival; but what astonished Mr. Fairfield most was his recognising in the person of young Goldacre the individual who had been his daughter's partner in a minuet at the ball. An explanation took place between them, which threw the honest, simple-minded old folks into much perplexity, as they could not understand how their son, when in Bermuda, could dance with a young lady in Barbados! But when, in the course of relating the circumstances, the name of Brushwood was mentioned, the old lady, in the simplicity of her nature, exclaimed, 'Ah, Jack, that's he that horsewhipped Miss Caroline's sweetheart; and now they say he's in love with her himself!' Jack was much confused, Mr. Fairfield bit his lip, and old Goldacre looked stupid – he knew not why! An embarrassing silence of some minutes ensued; and after a little commonplace chat, our visitor took his leave. When he returned home, Mr. Fairfield informed his lady of all that had passed at Silverdale, and gave such a glowing portrait of young Goldacre's person and manners as made her involuntarily 'wish Caroline was at home.'

That young lady was then on a visit to Mrs. Plumberry, both being under an engagement to accompany Mrs. Parry, the Governor's lady, to witness the ascent of a balloon, which, after being duly inflated, she was to set at liberty for its aërial voyage. Balloons at that time were novel experiments even in England; in Barbados, therefore, such an experiment was both difficult and expensive, there being but few persons in the island who either had any knowledge of aërostation, or who took any interest in scientific pursuits: the materials, also, for this balloon were both costly and scarce. The exertions and influence, however, of Mr. Jordan, (an eminent lawyer of that day,) whose philosophical

and liberal mind originated the project, overcame all difficulties, and subscriptions were soon obtained to defray the necessary
expenses. Our young hero entered with spirit into the proceedings of the day, and was appointed, in conjunction with Mr. Jordan
and Mr. Græm, to receive the Governor's lady and her party, his
Excellency being prevented by indisposition from attending. The
ascent was to take place from an extensive enclosure running from
the gaol-wall to the corner of James-street, lately the site of a splendid theatre, destroyed in the hurricane of 1831; the two houses now
at the corner formerly comprising one building, and appropriated
to public exhibitions, but antecedently made use of as a place of
confinement for American prisoners of war. Mrs. Parry and her
friends arrived at eleven o'clock, that they might witness the
process of inflation, &c., and were handed from their carriage –
the Governor's lady by Mr. Jordan, Mrs. Plumberry by Mr. Græm,
and (as the elfish imps who delight to tamper with fair maidens'
hearts would have it) Mr. Goldacre gave his arm to Miss Fairfield.
We leave our readers to imagine the surprise and embarrassment
occasioned by this unexpected rencontre, especially on the part of
our heroine, who dreamed not of Goldacre's return to the island.
Caroline naturally felt much confused when she found herself
resting a second time on the arm of him whom she had recognised
as the once simple son of her father's neighbour; for whose sake,
too, she had been rebuked by her mother for having once suffered
an involuntary sigh and an expression of 'pity,' to escape her; poor
girl! she was so much agitated that the gentle tints of roseate hue
which were wont to give a charm to her features, entirely fled her
cheeks, and her limbs trembled to such an excess as to render her
quite unequal to the exertions of following her party. Goldacre,
dreadfully confused and flushed, and ready to sink into the earth,
scarcely knew whither he led the fair one, until he found himself
under the portico of the theatre, where he seated his trembling
charge. Indeed, it was well for them both that they there found an
asylum, for the young lady felt herself quite unequal to join the
cheerful throng in the garden, and stood much in need of some

restorative; while he – but all who have hearts will know what his feelings were, without any description, we therefore merely add, that with a trembling hand and in silence he applied the vinaigrette, and afterwards persuaded her to sip a little refreshing lemonade. It was not long, however, before they recovered their self-possession; but still, as either caught the glance of the other, there seemed some secret thought, some silent wish, to flit through the mind of each; and they were mutually desirous, no doubt, to be relieved from the prying observation of those anxious friends, who kindly tendered their services to the young lady; when most opportunely the first signal gun announced that the preparatory arrangements of inflating the balloon were completed. All were instantly in motion, and rushing towards the main object of curiosity; when young Goldacre, presenting his arm to Miss Fairfield, said, with a warmth which showed that his blood flowed again through its proper channel, 'Permit me, Miss Fairfield, to hand you to your party.' Rising and taking his arm, she replied, 'Thank you, Mr. Brushwood.' Oh! what a look! what an indescribable look he gave, when turning his dark blue eyes on her and nearly dropping her arm, he repeated in faltering, tremulous accent, 'Mr. Brushwood.' But it was no time for explanation – they had arrived at what was the magnet of attraction to all but themselves, and Mr. Jordan and his associates were busily employed in the last process for letting off this gaseous orb. Mrs. Parry was at hand to perform the part she had undertaken, but some little delay arose in consequence of a pigeon having been placed in a small car suspended to the balloon, a procedure that lady's sensibility would not permit, and she objected to the sacrifice of the feathered innocent, (which she anticipated from its aërial voyage,) and had it removed. All now being quite ready, Mrs. Parry, with much grace and a smiling countenance, put forth her fair hand, and severed the last detaining cord. Up rose with inflated majesty the gaseous globe, amidst the enraptured acclamations of the wonder-stricken gazers! – mounting slowly at first, as if lingering that the beholders might the better be gratified – then varying its course from the westward, it then with increased velocity took a northern direction and a greater elevation, until in the course of half an hour it was for ever lost to human sight. This balloon was ten feet high, and about seven feet in its greatest diameter; made of light fawn-coloured silk well varnished, and the gas was generated from steel filings and vitriolic acid, and it cost between two and three hundred pounds; and was never after heard of. Thus we see that in those days there were in the West Indies men of science and of experimental enterprise.

The Governor's lady, with her two fair attendants, were soon after handed to their carriage, and drove off, and in a short time the whole company dispersed, leaving one solitary being behind, walking to and fro in the garden 'like one forlorn, crazied with care, or crossed in hopeless love!' Our readers will readily recognise in this individual the faltering, trembling echoer of the word 'Brushwood,' but who was none other than the now disconcerted and sensitive 'Goldacre.'

There was given that same evening at Pilgrim (sweet, humble name) one of those tasteful and social parties with which Mrs. Parry was so wont to enliven society; and which, indeed, under most of our Governors, distinguished the hospitality of that mansion, and was the delightful rendezvous of the élite of both sexes. Miss Fairfield was already there, and young Goldacre was among the earliest guests; but when he arrived he had scarcely yet recovered from his mortified feelings of the morning – still musing on those grating words, 'Thank you, Mr. Brushwood,' – unmindful of the agitation he had himself occasioned. It was, however, his first care, after making his obeisance to the lady hostess, and his Excellency, to seek out Miss Fairfield, and, 'as in duty bound,' (for he never lost sight of that politeness which is a real characteristic of the gentleman) inquired anxiously how she felt after the morning's exertion – cautiously abstaining from all allusion to the embarrassment which they had both experienced. There was a smile of complacency on the young lady's countenance when she replied to his inquiries, which for a time acted like a lullaby to his perturbed mind; but yet, he could not altogether divest himself of the idea that she still harboured some resentment against him on the score of the ren-contre between himself and her former lover. These reflections made him feel but ill at ease, and he thought that her addressing him in the morning by the assumed name under which his assault on Mac Flashby had taken place, was proof of her angry feelings; and therefore, in some measure to put this to the test, he re-quested Colonel Southrell (one of the Governor's aides-de-camp, with whom he was intimate) to introduce him by his real name, and by way of ceremony, to Miss Fairfield. Unfortunately for his peace of mind, as well as for the dignity of his pride, he gained nothing by this manœuvre, for at the moment that his friend was about taking him to the lady, she, unpropitiously for him, was in the act of rising from her seat, handed by Colonel Blagdon, to join in the favourite country dance of 'the soldier's joy.' 'The ranks and file' were already formed, so that the young lady really had no other opportunity of noticing the introduction than simply by a hasty curtsey, accompanied by a familar nod and flattering smile. Piqued at the moment, he neither perceived the nod nor the smile, which to so susceptible and captious a mind as his, was as galling as if she had premeditatedly repulsed him. He could no longer remain where it seemed to him as if he were an object of derision to all present, his wild imagination concentrat-ing in one, one only being, all else seemed a blank to his jaun-diced vision. Impatient and restless, he left the scene of his vexation, and hastening into the courtyard, threw himself into his chaise and drove home to Silverdale.

We cannot follow either party through all their 'sayings and do-ings' during the remainder of the evening; but we must here state, that Miss Fairfield, after she had returned to her seat, sought with searching and wistful glances for some object which from time to time seemed flitting before her, but which in no tangible form could be identified among the cheerful throng. She thought it strange – 'twas passing strange – that now she was at leisure to return his salutation, he should not renew it. But no; the object she sought was now far away—tossing restlessly on his bed, and 'cursing his stars' that he had so precipitately left a party where all were so gay, and all seemed so happy!

When young Goldacre reached home, the family had all retired to rest, and were sound asleep; they therefore heard nothing of him until morning, when his mother (ever stirring with the dawn) heard from his servant man, Sam Tom, that 'his young Massa came home sick.' The good old creature with anxious care got ready the warm exhilarating coffee, and herself hastened with it to his bedside; her entrance disturbed him in his first gentle slumber, and rousing himself, he with unfilial petulance refused the refreshing beverage; but his kind mother still pressed it on him, saying ''twill do you good, my son.' Think what were the feelings of this affectionate parent, when her son testily replied to her urgent entreaties, 'I beg you'll not teaze me.' His impatience was too much for her maternal feelings! She gently placed the cup by his bedside, adjusted the frill round her mob-cap, drew down her stomacher, and, smoothing the folds of her apron, silently left the chamber. Her son, smitten with remorse, instantly rose from his bed, and hastily dressing himself sought his insulted mother. As soon as she heard his footsteps, she hastened to meet him, and oh! what a meeting! He could scarcely articulate – his respiration was short and hurried – all that he could utter was, 'Mother, I am sorry that I have offended you.' She could only reply, 'My son, I am not angry!' They fell upon each other's neck. And here, let those giddy, thoughtless, and incorrigible youths, who regard not the anguish of a parent's heart, pause and reflect, before they give way to rudeness, ingratitude, and undutifulness! How sweet is reconciliation between those whose hearts glow with affection and tenderness! But it were ever better to avoid all contention and strife.

The old lady's heart again at ease, she was all joy and delight when she saw her son mount his horse to join his father in the field, where he was engaged in superintending the labourers, then

busily preparing the soil for the ensuing crop. It was not long ere
they returned together, and formed a happy circle round the
sumptuously spread breakfast table, so characteristic of that
primitive hospitality which was then so prominent a feature of
West Indian society. It would afford but little interest to the
reader were we to relate all that was said at this social and domestic repast; suffice it to observe, that from a unanimity of sentiment
on some subject broached by the old lady, Mr. Goldacre, senior,
soon after they rose from table, ordered his horse, and rode over
to Staffords to invite Mr. Fairfield, who was alone, to come over at
noon and partake of a fat turkey preparing for dinner, Mrs.
Fairfield having left home early for town, for the double purpose
of shopping and bringing Caroline home in the evening. This
neighbourly invitation was as kindly received as it was given, and
they passed a pleasant and social day together. The only mention
made of the young lady was by her father, who incidentally remarked, 'Caroline returns with her mother this evening, and I
hope she will now give us more of her company than we have
lately enjoyed.' The good old dame was on the point of making
some reply, when her son, fearing she might commit herself and
embarrass him also, gave her a sly nod, which she perfectly understood and was silent.

Mrs. Fairfield and her daughter reached home in the twilight
of evening, accompanied by a gentleman who gaily rode by the
side of the chaise, engaged in lively chat with them while they
were passing the broad avenue leading towards the mansion of
Silverdale. This did not fail to attract the notice of young
Goldacre, whose mind, as we have seen, was easily excited by
the most trivial incident relating to the young lady; but when a
messenger soon after came over from Staffords to inform Mr.
Fairfield that Colonel Blagdon was there, and that Mrs.
Fairfield requested he would return, a cold chill ran through
every vein of the youth, which his anxious mother perceiving, exclaimed with great agitation, 'Jack, are you ill, my son?' and thus
was his embarrassment not only heightened, but betrayed when

he most wished to conceal his feelings; for Mr. Fairfield saw Jack's perturbation, but being a man of feeling, as well as discernment, he apologized for his hasty departure, withdrew, and returned home.

We may be quite certain that young Goldacre would not have yielded to that nervous irritability, had he known that the Colonel's visit was purely accidental; he having overtaken the ladies on the road in one of his accustomed evening rides. The worthy Colonel then proceeded home with them, and was well disposed to pass an hour in their cheerful society, as he had often done before, being a great favourite of Miss Fairfield, and indeed a general favourite with all the ladies, although fallen into 'the sear and yellow leaf.' He was also a man of gallantry, or, as we may more correctly say, of all well-bred military men, a gentleman!—we mean not of that spurious kind which, puffed up by self-impor-tance, derives its pretensions from mere fortuitous circum-stances; but of that genuine stamp, which conveys to the mind an assemblage of virtues, and an union of manners, at once pleasing and commanding respect. There is indeed, as we have often seen, a constitutional tendency in some men, spite of advanced age and bodily infirmity, to be in love all their lives; and from the Colonel's attention and occasional visits at Staffords (for he had long known the family,) it had been whispered by the gossips of the parish that 'he was courting Miss Caroline Fairfield!' True, this gentleman was a widower, but he had a daughter in England as old as Caroline, and it might be that the thoughts of that daughter, whom he tenderly loved, made him the more pleased with this young lady, who looked upon him with reverence and respect.

Mr. Fairfield asked young Goldacre to accompany him home, but he declined the invitation, and soon after his friend's depar-ture, retired to rest; but, alas! he was doomed to pass another sleepless night.

CHAPTER XIV

OUR 'love-stricken' youth seemed at times to be the sport of his own peevish mind; and circumstances, the most trivial in themselves, were imbued by his too sensitive feelings with a hue and colouring, the wild conceits of a lover's impassioned mind alone could give. His father and himself rode the next day to see the family at Staffords; when they arrived there, Mr. Fairfield was out, overlooking the cultivation of his lands; Mrs. Fairfield, seeing the approach of visitors, ran to her toilet to remove some ordinary garment she usually wore when about her domestic concerns, and Miss Caroline – but we will not leave our neighbours, who had alighted, standing in the porch, for they had been shown by a servant into the parlour, where, being seated, they were for a time left alone. 'Was not that Miss Fairfield,' said the young man to his father, in a tone of doubtful inquiry, 'who so hastily left the room as we reached the door?' to which, without thought or reflection, the father replied, 'Yes, I think it was;' and this reply was sufficient to throw his son into a feverish impatience, and to induce him to attribute the non-appearance of the family to intentional slight; and had the father been as petulant as the son, and as much in love, both would have instantly quitted the house. Fortunately, however, at this moment Mrs. Fairfield entered, and with her accustomed benignity and cheerfulness, shook them heartily by the hand, and requested they would be again seated, and this gave a tone of more softness to the young man's feelings, and was no less satisfactory to the father.

A messenger had been dispatched to apprize Mr. Fairfield of the friendly visit of his neighbours, and he soon made his appearance; but it was not until after the 'punch and mandram' had been handed round, that any mention was made of Miss

Caroline, when our lover, impatient at her absence, inquired
for her, saying that 'he had called to pay his respects to her, and
to inquire how she felt after the fatigue she had lately undergone in her attendance on Mrs. Parry.' Mrs. Fairfield apologized in the politest terms for her daughter's absence, alleging
that she had taken cold the previous evening, and was unable to
leave her room. This explanation, however, but indifferently
satisfied the suspicious mind of our lover, piqued as he was by
the idea that he had seen her retire on his appearance. Thus he
became more peevish, from a combination of many little incidents of disappointment following so closely upon each other,
and which, to his distempered imagination, were 'confirmation
strong' that the young lady despised his passion, a passion never
yet avowed!

Our visitors now took their leave, and had proceeded in silence
nearly half-way home, when the young man, as if disturbed in his
musings, suddenly exclaimed, ' 'Tis all folly of me! I'll no longer
pursue an *ignis fatuus* that constantly eludes me;' and putting
spurs to his horse, would soon have left his father behind, had not
the affectionate old man rapidly followed him. It was a cheerless
day to the parents; for these kindhearted people deeply sympa-
thized with their unhappy son; without venturing to reason with
him, lest they should aggravate his malady, for such, indeed, had
his passion become. His father and himself went out for an afternoon's ride, and in their absence, the anxious mother took a 'turn
over' to Staffords, being determined (as she resolved in her own
mind) to see whether the young lady was indisposed. When she
got there, she found the family under much anxiety and alarm, for
Caroline's cold having been attended with high fever, she was
much worse, and her parents' solicitude greatly increased. Under
these circumstances, the old lady's visit was protracted to a late
hour, feeling, as she did, much sympathy with the family on the indisposition of their child, and a no less lively anxiety for her son's
peace of mind. Having much experience, too, in domestic phar-
macy, she rendered great service both in the recommendation of

remedies, and in assistance in their application; and before she took her leave, the good dame was gratified by seeing her interesting patient sink into a profound sleep.

On Mr. Goldacre's return, she merely observed in the presence of her son that Miss Fairfield had a slight cold and headache, and that she was sure the young lady had been confined to her room for the day; but when alone with her husband, she frankly explained to him how seriously ill she thought her to be, and it was agreed between them that their son should be made acquainted in the morning with the true state of Caroline's health. In this purpose they were nearly disappointed, in consequence of the young man's having risen earlier than usual, with the intention of going to town on an errand that stamps his character with caprice and fickleness, and which was eminently calculated to have cut off for ever all chance of marrying his 'first love.' Our thoughtless, impassioned hero had actually formed the intention of sueing for the hand of Miss Littledale, and of obtaining the father's acquiescence to an immediate union with his daughter – 'calculating without his host,' as if 'the bill of costs' (as the lawyers say) was all under his own control. We see by these intentions, that Goldacre, like all other young men, had his full share of vanity, and which would have met its just reward had he broached the delicate subject; for Miss Littledale (unknown to him) and with her father's approbation, was already engaged to a young countryman, then studying the law at one of the inns of court, in London, and who was shortly expected out to practise at the Barbados bar.

Young Goldacre was in the act of mounting his horse in the pursuit of this chivalrous enterprise, when the good dame, his mother, as luck would have it, encountered him. With an affected indifference, ill according with the state of her mind, she said to him, 'I wish, my son, while you are out, you would ride towards Staffords, and if you see any of the family stirring, you would just inquire how Miss Caroline is this morning, for when I left her last night, I thought her extremely ill.' — 'Ah! ill, do you say? ill!' repeated he, drawing his foot from the stirrup. 'Yes,' replied his mother, 'she was very ill, she had high fever, and was very restless.' He now dropped the reins—turned into the house—again was at the door—mounted the block, paused, patted his horse, and adjusted the reins, as if intending to mount, but then suddenly dropping them, ordered the servant to take the horse to the stable; but, no sooner was he moving off with the animal, than his master countermanded the order—then again rebuked the man for being so tardy in putting up the horse. All this while, his ever anxious mother looked on in silence; but at length said to him in a low soothing tone, 'John, as your horse is saddled, suppose you let Sam Tom ride as far as Staffords, and inquire after Miss Caroline.'—'Sam! Sam Tom!' shouted he, 'here, take a message from my mother – do as she bids you – be quick. Mind that you bring back a correct answer – why don't you set off?' 'I wait, Sir, fau yerry whau Missee say.' The message was given – the servant rode off – mother and son returned into the house; she to her domestic concerns, and he into the parlour, throwing himself on the sofa. There he sat, one moment tattooing with his fingers on the table, then taking a book and turning over the leaves, as if searching for some particular passage – anon throwing the book from him, then, again, drumming on the table – humming a tune – whistling, and altogether doing so many idle things, that at last, getting tired, he rose and paced the room. This brought his mother in to him. He instantly approached her, and with deferential tenderness, taking her hand, addressed her: 'Mother,' said he, 'I fear I give you and my father much uneasiness;' and overcome by his emotion, he burst into tears! Oh, ye affectionate mothers! whose hearts responsive to our tears, sympathize in all our sorrows, – by whose side we grow up under the gentlest sway, and from whom we receive the first lessons of tenderness and love – how keenly ye must feel for this unhappy son! for this tender, anxious parent!

Sam returned from his errand, and was about entering the parlour when his mistress beckoned him back; but in a few minutes after the worthy father, accompanied by the servant, entered the room, and in a tone of cheerfulness, addressing his wife, said, 'Sam brings us good news from our neighbour; Miss Fairfield has had a refreshing night's rest, and is quite hearty this morning!' These words fell on the ear of our anxious lover like 'the dew of Hermon,' and as one just awakened from a pleasing dream, he instantly rose from his mother's side, and taking her by one hand, and his father by the other, 'Come,' said he, 'let us take breakfast.' They all sat down cheerfully; the good old folks delighted to see their son in such high spirits, and making a hearty meal. 'Did you not,' said he to his mother, 'promise Mrs. Fairfield to go over this morning?' The old lady readily took the hint, and replied, 'Yes, and I have ordered the chaise; won't you drive me over, John? and after you have set me down, you can take a drive further, and return in time to take me home.' It was an arrangement quite congenial to the young man's feelings, and they soon after set off.

On arriving at Staffords, Mr. Fairfield received them with joyous countenance, and a welcome most flattering, and he then insisted on young Goldacre's alighting and sitting with him, while the old lady visited 'her patient,' as he designated his daughter, in grateful recollection of the attention and kindness she had received from Mrs. Goldacre the preceding evening. The old lady was soon shown into the convalescent's chamber, and she felt no small share in the satisfaction of the family at the evidently favourable change in Caroline's health. Mrs. Fairfield taking her by the hand, and placing it in that of her daughter, said, 'My dear Caroline, under the mercy of God, we owe your speedy recovery to this our kind neighbour, whom, I am sure, you will thank as you ought.' Much recovered as Caroline evidently was, there yet remained much feebleness and debility, and her countenance exhibited a paleness and languor, that created an interest sufficient to have awakened a misanthrope to tenderness and love. 'I thank you, my dearest' – here her voice failed: but affectionately kissing the old lady's hand, she made another effort to speak; when again overcome by her sensibility, she could only repeat 'I thank you' – the good old lady kissing her cheek.

While our two friendly matrons were holding a consultation at the bed-side of our interesting invalid, the two gentlemen whom we left in the parlour were engaged in scarcely less important discussion, as incidentally leading to a disclosure of circumstances highly important to the happiness of the same fair object.

Neither of these gentlemen was much accustomed to confine himself in conversation to the ever-engrossing subjects of the 'want of rain' and the 'price of sugar;' for both being of intelligent minds and enlarged views, they readily found occasions for the interchange of opinions and sentiments on whatever subjects presented themselves during their friendly chat. Soon after they were seated, Mr. Fairfield observed to the young man, that he supposed his father was very busy to-day planting corn, as there had been fine showers during the night. 'My father,' replied the other, 'has the whole care of the plantation thrown upon his hands today, having given the overseer leave of absence, that he may attend the wedding of one of his friends.' 'Then, I suppose,' said Mr. Fairfield, 'your overseer is to be bridesman to my under-manager, Ben Crowfoot, who is to be married to-day to the daughter of one of my tenants; but how, with a salary of forty pounds a year, he is to support a family, which in all likelihood he will have, is what I fear he has never for a moment thought of.'—'It is a thoughtless propensity among our lower classes,' said Goldacre, 'to entangle themselves with a family before they have the prospect of providing for one; but yet I conceive there is much good arising from it, as it preserves the moral relations of society among them, and induces habits of virtue.' To which the other replied, that he feared that we could not always be assured of that; 'but,' continued he, 'I am not inimical to these marriages, and have given some assistance to the young couple on this occasion; for although the benefit to the party is very doubtful, yet to society at large it is more evident, for it has a great tendency to keep up our white population – a feature in our little country which gives it an ascendancy over our neighbouring colonies.'—'But,' said Goldacre, 'do we not, by countenancing marriage among them, encourage pauperism? and is it not lamentable to see their laziness and indolence, arising from ignorance and pride of caste?'—'There is another cause of their degradation,' said Mr. Fairfield, 'which, from your inexperience, is not so evident to you, but for which we have much to answer – I mean *neglect*! for there was a time when our tenantry were a valuable portion of our population.' Young Goldacre here remarked that he had often heard his father express the same opinion, and acknowledge, with honest pride, that his career in life commenced as a tenant. 'Yes, yes,' rejoined the other, 'but your father has been an industrious man through life, and has had the countenance and encouragement of a liberal landlord, who, like some others still to be found amongst us, consider their tenantry as part of their family, or, at any rate, as objects demanding their encouragement and consideration.'—'I have heard my father attribute much of the comforts and consequence given to the tenantry of his early day to the enactments of the old militia law.'— 'And well he might,' said Mr. Fairfield, 'for our militia law was justly called "the poor man's friend." Your father, let me also add, did not marry with that haste now so common to our young men, but first made some progress in life, and then sought a befitting partner, in whom I have often heard him say he has found a second "right hand." 'Tis a pity he did not marry sooner.'—'Marriage, no doubt, is that state of life,' said Goldacre, 'to which every man looks forward with an instinctive longing.'—'Unless,' said Mr. Fairfield, hastily interrupting him, 'he has rendered himself unworthy of that happiness which is only to be found in matrimony.' From the manner in which Goldacre had been interrupted, he conceived the observations of Mr. Fairfield as intended to convey some censure on himself; he therefore replied with his accustomed asperity when he felt himself offended. 'Sir, although I may have often done wrong, acted absurdly, nay, even presumptuously, I have never yet committed a base nor a servile action.' Mr. Fairfield was at once struck with the apparent application to

Goldacre of what he had said; but not intending any reflection on the character of that high-minded and sensitive youth, he took him kindly by the hand, observing, in a deliberate and softened tone, 'My young friend, I am willing to view your warmth as the offspring of your virtues, and as a testimony of a good conscience; and I am quite certain that no man will ever be respected who has not a becoming respect for himself. From my long observation, too, of your conduct, I have reason to infer that you are yet happily untainted with the vices of the world; but I must add that, in some instances, your temper has given way to the impulses of harsh resentment.' 'Resentment,' replied he in a firm, manly tone, 'has been given us by Nature as a safeguard against wanton aggression: by retaliation the offender is made to smart for his unjust acts, or to repent them. I know that my feelings are easily ignited, but I feel that I am not vindictive.' Mr. Fairfield saw that his young companion was excited; he therefore mildly replied, 'I cannot but admire the noble sincerity of your mind.'—'Then, my dear Sir, how much I wish that you would permit me to unbosom myself to you!'—'Speak out freely,—it is confidence between man and man that advances the moral principle of society, – speak honestly, and I will give ear to what you have to say,' said Mr. Fairfield. To which the other, with an energy of expression and an agitation of feeling that lovers may understand, but the feeble nerve of old age cannot describe, replied, 'Then, Sir, I honestly tell you, I love your daughter! She has long been the ascendant spirit that has influenced my every thought, and given tone to my every feeling.' Mr. Fairfield was about to reply, but at this interesting moment to the impassioned and ardent mind of young Goldacre, the two elderly ladies, who had been in friendly chat and congratulating each other on the convalescence of the invalid, entered the parlour, and thereby suspended for the present all further discussion between the two gentlemen on the subject so full of importance.

They were both disconcerted at this unexpected interruption, and the young man, scarcely knowing what he did, in a fit of disappointment, seized his hat, and rushed out of the house. His mother called after him in vain; Mr. Fairfield followed some little way in quest of the madman, but succeeded no better; he therefore returned, and to quiet the old lady's agitation immediately ordered her chaise to be brought up, and drove her home, having greatly pacified the poor creature on the way, by assuring her that he would do all in his power to contribute to her son's happiness. This she did not fail to interpret in a manner most congenial to her own wishes; but before she could utter a suitable reply, which she was preparing in her mind, and which would have explained in no unequivocal terms her acceptation of the nature of his promise, when the chaise halted, and to their equal surprise and delight, young Goldacre came out to the portico to receive them. Handing his mother into the house, he then turned to Mr. Fairfield, whom taking by the arm, and leading aside, he addressed with a feeling much subdued, in the following words: 'Forgive me, my dear Sir, I am quite ashamed of the impetuosity – the inconsistency – the impropriety of my conduct. I fear it must disgust my friends, and I see that it renders my parents unhappy. My spirits are now sobered – I am awakened to a sense of my folly.' Mr. Fairfield was greatly affected by the young man's manner, as well as by his expressions; and feeling an interest in his welfare, replied,—'My young friend, cherish your present composure—keep your mind tranquil, and at some future period' – Here they were interrupted by the appearance of the senior Goldacre, who returning from the field, had rode up to the door, and alighting, joined his neighbour and son where they were in chat. He congratulated the former on the improvement of his daughter's health, and with a hearty shake of the hand, pressed him to stay dinner; but as Mr. Fairfield knew that the absence of the under-manager had diverted Goldacre's attention from the business of the estate, and that it consequently required a little additional superintendence, he very considerately excused himself, and being furnished with a horse, took his leave and rode home.

It may readily be conceived what was the nature of the discussion that took place in the course of the day in both families. We shall only remark that at Staffords, although every circumstance that had occurred and all the conversation that had passed between Mr. Fairfield and young Goldacre, were deliberately discussed between Mr. and Mrs. Fairfield, not one word of the matter was communicated to Caroline; nor could the quickest ear listening at the keyhole have gathered from their conversation what were their intentions, should the young man make overtures in a more formal and consistent manner.

At Silverdale, the good old folks were rejoiced at their son's tranquil manner and social chat. He related to them much of the conversation that had passed between Mr. Fairfield and himself on the subject of the tenantry, and stated the opinions which they had both given respecting marriages among the poor. 'And John,' said his father, 'why shouldn't the poor marry as well as the rich? A poor man's house without a woman in her proper place in it, has none of those comforts which decorum gives, and without which he will never be looked upon as respectable.'—'Besides,' added the mother, 'a single man always living alone, must be a miserable being, and more likely to fall into vice.'—'True,' replied the son, 'but all that we objected to, was their imprudently marrying without a prospect of supporting a family; for to multiply human beings without improving their condition, is to create either a burden on themselves, or to throw an increased number of paupers on the parish.'—'Matrimony, my dear son,' replied his father, 'is a part of the religion of a virtuous poor man, and however poor he may be, it is to that state to which he looks for happiness here; and my old woman can tell you what true felicity it gives when real affection unites husband and wife—when their hearts beat with but one feeling either of sorrow or joy.'—'The aspirations of man towards happiness,' observed the young man, 'are the most active and enduring of all his feelings; and when he seeks it in marriage, his sensibilities become a duty, for conjugal love is the tie which binds the present life to the future.'—'Ay, ay, John,' said the father, 'when we know what leads to happiness, why don't we embrace it?'—'There, there now,' said the mother, 'why don't you go and attack Miss Caroline?'—'Heaven bless you, my dear parents! I fear I have hitherto caused you more sorrow than joy; but henceforth the affection of a dutiful son shall increase your happiness,' said the young man, warmly shaking each of them by the hand.

The tear of tenderness will ever flow when awakened by the influence of sympathy, and it was a tear of tenderness that bedewed the cheeks of each. 'What can add to my happiness?' exclaimed the honest old father in a burst of irrepressible rapture: 'I am in good health—out of debt—have a competent fortune—a clear conscience— a kind wife—a dutiful son!'—'Why Johnny! to see that son married!' said the warm-hearted dame, shaking her apron and hastening to the pantry to see after dinner. Meantime the father went to his writing desk, and the son took up his flute. And here ends this chapter.

CHAPTER XV

THE day after the events which are so circumstantially related in the foregoing chapter, young Goldacre, sensible of having, in the impulse of an ardent feeling, committed himself by an abrupt declaration of his passion to the parent of the young lady, (to whom, in obedience to the conventional laws of love, he ought in the first instance to have told the tender tale,) went over to Staffords with an intention of—But we need not say of what, convinced as we are that there is not a pretty little Miss possessed of one particle of sentiment, in this our hymeneally addicted isle, but will instinctively know why he went – whom he saw – what he said – and all that passed. Let them, however, not be too certain of having rightly guessed, except indeed as to his purpose in going; but as to his sayings and doings, why he neither said any thing nor did any thing, but like—

> The king of France, with twenty thousand men,
> Marched up the hill, and then – marched down again.

When he reached Staffords, Mrs. Fairfield was piously engaged in religious duties with her daughter, and would not be seen. Mr. Fairfield had gone to town on public duty, and could not be seen; and thus, as had frequently happened before, another disappointment chilled the hopes of our too ardent lover. But how altered was our hero! and how stoically he bore the present disappointment! for, leaving his inquiries and compliments with a servant, he took a short airing, and returned home as calm and passive as heart could desire.

Mr. Fairfield, as has been said, had gone to town on 'public duty;' and as the domestic occurrences of the week in neither family supplied anything further respecting our hero and heroine, except that Mrs. Goldacre daily saw the young lady, and marked with satisfaction the progressive improvement of her health;

while at Silverdale all was tranquillity and peace, the son joining
his provident father in all his agricultural occupations; we shall
briefly state, that Mr. Fairfield being 'turned down' to serve on the
grand jury of the court of session commenced that day, caused his
absence from home. And as a novelty to all those who have not yet
passed that climacteric which places ladies on the list of old maids,
and gentlemen on that of old bachelors (we leave it to them both
to settle the period to their own fancy,) we will give the pro-
gramme now before us of the procession of the chief justice to the
parish church, preparatory to his opening his commission at the
Town-hall:—

Two constables with their staves of office.
A band of music,
(consisting of a pair of kettle-drums, four French horns,
two trumpets, four hautboys, and two fifes).
A body of constables with staves, two and two.
Gentlemen summoned as jurors, and others attending in
compliment to the judge.
Attorneys at law, two and two.
Barristers in their robes, two and two.
Clerk of the crown in his robes.
Attorney and solicitor-general in their robes.
Clergy in their robes, two and two.
Provost marshal, wearing his sword.
Members of council, two and two.
The clergyman who was to preach, in his robes.
The chief justice,
dressed in a full suit of black silk, wearing a bag-wig
and a court sword.
A deputy marshal,
Livery servants.

In this order the procession moved at twelve o'clock, from the
British Coffee House, (where the chief justice had provided a
sumptuous breakfast to regale the party,) to St. Michael's church,
the bells ringing, and the streets lined on either side by the militia,
who presented arms as the judge passed, the officers saluting with

their swords, and dropping the colours, drums rolling; the whole *cortège*, on arriving at the church gate, opening to the right and left for the judge to pass through, the others then following in inverted order. The Rev. Mr. Sair read the desk service, and Dr. Wharton preached from the following text, 'When the righteous are in authority, the people rejoice.' After the whole was concluded, the procession proceeded in the same order to the Town-hall where the flank companies of the militia had previously arrived to receive the judge; a company daily attending there in manifestation of the union and mutual dependence of the civil and military establishments of the island upon each other.

What a sad contrast this dignity of ceremony and parade furnishes to that of more modern times on the same occasion! We have seen a chief justice, with some five or six followers, rambling to the church, and thence to the Town-hall, as if they had lost their way! We have beheld another, regardless of all etiquette and ceremony, driving in his phaeton from his town-house to church, attended only by his groom, leaving those who list following in his wake to church and court as they thought fit! We have seen the *magnates* of the land fill this high office with dignity and distinction; and we have seen—

'But, my good sir,' cries Miss Eleanora Letitia Elvira Fretfull, 'what is become of the lovers?'—Why, Miss, there's poor dear Caroline, who has been these two days past, like the modest primrose – pale, yet lovely – sighing, yet smiling – wishing, yet not anxious – expecting, yet not impatient – with feeble voice and languid eye, all meekness and innocence—

As pure as the consecrated snow
That lies in Dian's lap,

with none but her affectionate and tender mother in companionship, seated in the corner of the parlour sofa.

And there, in yon back parlour, with palpitating heart and tremulous hand, with perplexity of thought and indecision of purpose, sits young Goldacre. He takes the pen – writes – blots – transposes – interlines – erases, and suddenly rising from his seat, tears sheet after sheet, and scatters them to the winds. 'Dear me!' says Miss Eleanora Letitia Elvira, 'how I should like to have seen them before they were torn!' All that I can tell you, Miss, about them is, that the gardener, in sweeping the walk under the back parlour window, which looks into the garden, picked up a slip of paper, from which, with much difficulty, the following only could be deciphered, and which we take for granted was part of one of those sheets thus destroyed: 'Madam!'—'That's a very cold ad-dress for a love-letter,' says Miss Eleanora. But we are not writing for him, Miss; so if you wish to hear what we are able to collect from the scattered fragments, you must give attention and not in-terrupt us. 'Mum,' says she.

'Madam – If a passion which has been the dream of my youth, and is now the deliberate conviction of my manho'—'Oh dear! what a pity he should have torn it. I dare say it would have been very pretty, if he had finished it. I'm sure, if it had been addressed to me, I should have' – and here Miss Eleanora blushed.

It appears, from some other fragments, that Goldacre had first addressed Mr. Fairfield – then Caroline; again her father, and once more the young lady; but not succeeding to his satisfaction, he destroyed at least three sheets of fine gilt-edged paper, saying, as he threw them from the window, ''Twill be better to wait until Monday. Mr. Fairfield, by that time, will have recovered from the fatigue of attending the sessions, and we can then talk over the matter together.' His mother overheard this soliloquy as she en-tered the room; and sagaciously concluding that it referred to Caroline, said to him, 'My dear John, you should speak to the *gal* first. You know them there sort of young ladies is mighty particu-lar in those sort of matters.'—'Yes, yes, my dear mother, I'll walk over with you this afternoon. I should have first spoken to Caroline, 'tis true: but'—'But never mind, John' replied the old lady, 'we'll go over and drink coffee with them, and you can then catch an opportunity to speak to Caroline; she is quite brave now, and sits below.' Five o'clock came, and off go the heart-gladdened mother and her love-stricken son. It was not ten minutes' walk across the fields; and the crop having been reaped, it was no unpleasant ramble; but ere they reached Staffords, the son had exhorted his mother more than once not to utter a word on the subject, lest she should spoil all, and make the remainder of his life miserable.

Well! there they are in the porch, heartily welcomed into the hall by Mrs. Fairfield, joined in a few minutes after by Mr. Fairfield; when the two worthy matrons leave the gentlemen and proceed to the parlour, where our interesting convalescent is seen reclining on the sofa. She had heard the footsteps of the friendly visitors, and recognized a voice that thrilled through her frame and gave a quickened pulsation to her heart! O divine instinct of love! with what genuine expression of a sympathizing feeling, yet with delicately shrinking grace, did she put forth her hand to receive that of her benign neighbour's. 'My son,' said Mrs. Goldacre, 'desires his'—But here Mrs. Goldacre checked herself, and left her meaning to be guessed at. Caroline's feeling spoke in no equivocal smile, and her cheeks were for a moment flushed by an evanescent glow that rendered the succeeding paleness yet more pale. The agitation of the young lady was too evident to both the matrons, and her mother with much solicitude applied some restorative, which speedily had the desired effect; a gentle flow of the spirits now animated the languid form of our heroine, and gave to her pallid cheeks and feeble voice an interesting loveliness that endeared her the more to the maternity of the two elderly ladies.

During the absence of the two friendly matrons, Mr. Fairfield gave some account to his young companion of the proceedings of the court, at which he had been so recently engaged; he made many pointed observations on our judicial system, and censured the mode of appointing the chief justice; 'for,' said he, 'however fortunate we have been in always having had men of probity and integrity to hold the office, we cannot compliment them on their

forensic knowledge or legal acquirements; it may, therefore, be
said that the lawyers preside both on the bench and at the bar. Yet
while our laws are equitably administered, we need not much
complain.'—'And while our taxes are light, we have no cause to
murmur,' said Goldacre. 'True,' rejoined Mr. Fairfield, 'but if our
rulers once begin to weigh us down with heavy imposts, the people, fearing they may be stripped of their hard earnings, will resist,
and, which Heaven avert, anarchy and confusion be spread
through the land.'—'Our resources mainly depend on agricultural industry,' observed the young man, 'and my mind is impressed with the belief, that he who cultivates the soil with
diligence, acquires a greater stock of religious merit than he could
gain by fasting and penance.'—'But you will admit,' replied Mr.
Fairfield, 'that *religion* has ever been the most effectual support
of civil institutions; and to the lower classes, the fountain from
which they acquire civilization; instilling into them, when virtuous, an innocence and humility that give them a stronger claim
upon the benevolence and kindness of the wealthy and great.'
'The true relation between the rich and poor,' said Goldacre, 'I
hold to be that of kind, just, and benevolent superiors; and honest,
humble, and industrious inferiors. We, however, too often find a
repulsive *hauteur* in the former, discouraging even to the most
virtuous; and, in the latter, an overweening presumption that frus-
trates the most anxious care for their welfare.' 'Presumption,'
replied Mr. Fairfield, 'is the offspring of ignorance in all classes;
no wonder, then, that when men of eminent fortune and transcendent talent withdraw from public duties, that the mean and
base should aspire to honours and distinctions; for, though ambi-
tion is natural to man, and is often associated with true nobility of
soul, yet should it, in all cases, be tempered by the fear of God and
a due regard for ancient institutions; and never be encouraged to
the subversion of the natural order of society.'

During the time of this conversation, a servant had twice
handed to the gentlemen the cauliflower-cap't tankard of
nectareous bub, and as they chatted they occasionally nibbled

the ear of roasted young corn; but young Goldacre, ever and anon, cast a wistful look at the parlour door, hoping to be invited in; but, alas! no invitation came. At length, every hope of seeing the fair object of his desires vanished by the entrance of a servant, whom his mother had sent to inquire if he was ready to return. There was no alternative – 'he was quite ready.' Ah, poor fellow! he was nigh relapsing into one of his former fits of impetuosity when the two elderly ladies entered. Mrs. Fairfield apologized in very kind terms for not having asked him in to see her daughter; and his mother, with that genuine expression of feeling which sprang from the simplicity of a heart overflowing with as much tenderness for the fair invalid as for her son, said, 'Never mind, John, the next time we come you'll see her – she's quite flurried now, and says'—Here Mrs. Fairfield hastily took her by the arm, looked up at her and deprecatingly observed, 'Oh, my dear Mrs. Goldacre;' which checked the old lady's volubility, though it did not much relieve her son's anxiety.

There is a willing homage in the heart of man towards the woman he loves, which subdues his most violent impulses; and it was this homage which checked the ebullition of our lover under his present disappointment, and made him regard what his mother had said, as coming from the lips of Mrs. Fairfield; under this illusion he took that lady's hand, and in a softened sentimental tone, said to her, 'I beg, Madam, my best regards to your daughter. It will give me the greatest happiness to be admitted to her presence on my next visit; and I hope you will permit it to be soon.' A courteous smile was her only reply, with which he seemed well satisfied; and he and his mother, taking a cordial leave, proceeded homeward.

Our lover was half disposed to be sulky on the way, but after humming the air of 'Hope told a flattering tale,' his spirits seemed to revive, and he asked his mother, in rather an insinuating and coaxing tone, 'what was it that Caroline said, which you were about to repeat when her mother so hastily interrupted you?' 'Oh,' said Mrs. Goldacre, 'it was – dear me, I quite forget – some-

thing about – but indeed, Johnny, I quite forget.' Her son was an-
noyed at this evasive answer; but there was ever a deference in his
conduct towards his parents that repressed all expression of anger,
and he merely replied, 'Mother, I do not wish you to betray the secret, if you consider it one.' Now I'd wager there are many little
misses – aye, and some full grown young ladies too, who would
sadly like to know what that secret was. But no, though we must
confess that Miss Caroline did unguardedly commit herself by saying that – but we will not be so ungallant as to betray her; for young
men are vain; and had Goldacre come to the knowledge of all that
was said, ten to one he would have thought, 'his market made.' His
simple hearted mother, who had been enjoined to secrecy by Mrs.
Fairfield, inviolably kept her promise; and her son, whether from
pique or a more worthy feeling, never after alluded to the subject,
and accompanied his mother home in perfect good humour. Thus
peace and harmony were re-established throughout the mansion of
Silverdale.

At Staffords, meanwhile, a discussion took place between the
trio, that elicited from Caroline more than she had ever before expressed to her parents respecting her lover; and when Mrs.
Fairfield informed her husband what Caroline had said, and how
Mrs. Goldacre had been prevented from repeating their daughter's words; they rallied the invalid for having betrayed her feelings to the simple-hearted dame. 'But,' said Caroline, 'he must
not build too much upon an inadvertent expression, which had
reference to one particular occurrence. Besides,' continued she,
'Mrs. Goldacre promised you, mother, not to mention it to her
son.' And here rests this mighty secret for the present.

CHAPTER XVI

THE parents of Caroline had for some time closely watched the conduct of young Goldacre towards their daughter, and they frequently spoke of those unreserved expressions of attachment which had escaped him in a moment of uncontrolled feeling. They had also exercised much circumspection in order to ascertain Caroline's sentiments towards Goldacre, which, after frequent and protracted discussion, resulted in a conviction that a mutual attachment did exist; the worthy parents therefore determined to request their child to be candid, and fearlessly open her mind to them, her natural guardians. 'If it appear,' said they, 'that we have not formed a wrong estimate of her opinion and feelings towards the youth, we will give him a fair opportunity of explaining himself fully to her; and we will then act according to circumstances.'—'And I think,' said Mrs. Fairfield, 'that whatever be her sentiments towards him, it will be most proper that the affair be at once brought to a conclusion.'— 'Not with precipitancy,' replied the gentleman, 'for after all, we may have wrongly read Caroline's heart, and should she have any objections to the union, time and a more intimate acquaintance with Goldacre might tend to remove them.'—'Then,' said the old lady, 'I will lose no time in speaking to Caroline on the subject.'

Conformably to this arrangement, made with the tenderest solicitude towards Caroline's future happiness, Mrs. Fairfield sought her daughter, with the intention of eliciting her real sentiments towards Goldacre, (now her avowed lover;) but the young lady, strange, capricious, coquettish, as it must necessarily appear, actually endeavoured at first to evade the subject, but at last she hinted that her feelings towards him had changed. Her mother, who was a sensible and discreet woman, naturally felt much surprised at her conduct, so inexplicable to her, and she attempted to draw an explanation from Caroline, who replying somewhat pettishly, gave umbrage to her good mother, and the old lady left the room angrily. On Mrs. Fairfield's communicating to her husband what had just passed, he participated in his wife's displeasure, and suggested to her the propriety of refraining from again mentioning the subject to their daughter. The displeasure, however, of her parents was evident to Caroline, from the marked coolness of their manners; and she became painfully convinced that her conduct in withholding from them the ground of her objection to Goldacre, was both injudicious and undutiful, and that she had thereby deprived herself of that blessed solace which a child derives from making a parent's bosom the sanctuary of the most hidden thoughts. These circumstances affected Caroline's spirits, and threatened seriously to injure her health. Her anxious parents perceiving this, determined, notwithstanding their previous resolution, to speak to her again on the important subject, and to elicit from her, if possible, the true cause of that sudden and unexpected change in her sentiments towards an object whom they had for some time considered agreeable to her, and to whose pretensions they themselves were favourable.

These kind and affectionate parents, therefore, whose every thought and wish centred in their daughter's happiness, and who were naturally most anxious for the consistency of her conduct, renewed this discussion with a delicacy and tenderness that greatly affected Caroline's sensibility, and showed that, if women are not made of finer clay than men, there has certainly been more of the dew of heaven employed in tempering it. This line of conduct on their part, induced her at once to unbosom herself without reserve; and thus all unhappiness was dispelled. It is greatly to be lamented that in a family of such affection and unanimity, any discontent should have ever arisen; but unfortunately, there are too often found persons ever ready to infuse into the cup of our happiness, the poison of their own vitiated minds, and who take a malicious pleasure in sapping that peace and joy of heart to which their own are strangers. By similar arts had Caroline been tampered with, by one of those toad-eating intruders who foist themselves into families, and who, under the character of a humble friend, insinuate themselves into the confidence of the inmates, and then circulate from house to house, with additions and embellishments not a few, the gossip they have heard, or the secret they have wormed out of some domestic. Miss Auberry, (who, by the by, ought long ago to have taken the brevet rank of Mistress,) was one of those dealers in that convenient phrase, '*they do say,*' which serves so often to conceal the propagator of a falsehood. This person had whispered this 'they do say' so often into Caroline's ears, and appended to it so much scandal against young Goldacre, that the poor girl began to fear a second version of her former misplaced affections. Now, what added greatly to Caroline's chagrin was, the fear that that ardent expression uttered at the time her mother applauded Goldacre's conduct in his rencontre with Mac Flashby, might transpire; for this expression contained the memorable avowal that 'she loved him for horsewhipping the imposter.' And here is explained that conduct which at the first blush seemed so capricious; but which in fact arose from a too sensitive apprehension of her having acted derogatory to the dignity of her sex.

Mrs. Fairfield, anxious to remove every false impression from her daughter's mind, gave her the fullest assurance of the high opinion she entertained of her lover's conduct; and her father also passed high commendations on his character and good sense. They then expressed their united and anxious desire to promote her happiness to the full extent of their power, and left to Caroline's own judgment and decision the line of conduct that should be pursued in future towards Goldacre; for Mr. Fairfield thought it due to themselves, as well as to the young man, after his impassioned declaration, that the matter should be brought to a close without further delay. Caroline deeply felt this kind and tender solicitude of her parents, thanked them for the deference paid to her feelings, and submitted herself entirely to their guidance; and it was thereupon agreed that the family of Silverdale should be invited to spend the next evening.

Scarcely had the servant been despatched with this neighbourly invitation, than the family at Staffords were thrown into agitation and alarm by the appearance of a well mounted black, hastily riding up to the door, and delivering, in panting anxiety, a letter addressed to the fair daughter of the house. Placing the missive in Caroline's hands, they soon perceived, by her suddenly altered countenance and agitated frame, that it bore melancholy tidings, and in a few minutes she informed them, with quivering lips and faltering voice, that her worthy and affectionate god-mother, the junior Miss Chrichton, lay at the point of death. The last words of this lady, just before paralysis had impeded her artic-ulation, expressed a wish that Caroline should be sent for; and this ever affectionate and sympathising girl, with a heart warmed by gratitude for the kindnesses she had experienced from these ami-able sisters, was all anxiety to proceed on this melancholy duty. Her parents, equally desirous that she should attend to the dying request of her friend, the chaise was instantly ordered; and, ac-companied by her mother, they set off, attended by the trusty and indefatigable Joe Pollard, who, regardless of former disappoint-ment and sufferings, still remained faithfully attached to the Fairfield family, and was ever a willing attendant at their call.

The hurry and anxiety with which Mrs. Fairfield and her daugh-ter had left home, added to the neglect of the servant who was sent over to Silverdale, in not delivering an answer on his return, drove from Mr. Fairfield's mind all recollection of the invitation that had been given to the family there, nor did it recur to him until he saw the good old folks and their dutiful son sauntering hand in hand up the avenue to Staffords. He, however, greeted them with the most hos-pitable welcome, and as soon as they were seated, explained the cause of his wife and daughter's absence, and apologized for not hav-ing sent to inform them of it. During the whole of this communica-tion, he perceived an evident mistrust in the mind of the young man, who betrayed much restlessness and discontent; and Mr. Fairfield, weighing all the circumstances in his own mind, perceived the causes which gave birth to that suspicion which he was now anxious to dispel; he therefore took the young man most kindly by the hand, saying, 'I see, my friend, the state of your feelings, and as a punish-ment for your ungenerous surmises, I award, as an appropriate penalty, that you proceed with the morning's dawn to Whiston Hall, to make inquiries after the inmates, and bring me back a true and circumstantial account of Miss Chrichton's health; I will leave to your gallantry to make such other inquiry as may seem necessary.' By this conciliatory badinage, Mr. Fairfield, who in every thing he said and did indicated a benevolent heart, placed young Goldacre quite at his ease; who, with vivid feelings of delight, expressed his willingness to undertake so pleasing a mission, and said, 'he would enter upon it with equal pleasure as it regarded either his own feelings or that of inquiring after the health of the lady.'

This visit, as may naturally be supposed, was not characterised by that cheerfulness which generally pervaded the intercourse between these friendly neighbours, but yet there was no want of hospitality, nor of social chat, though no inconsiderable part of their conversation turned on the melancholy state of the family at Whistons. Under these circumstances the visitors took an earlier leave than usual; and upon parting, Mr. Fairfield reminded young Goldacre of his mission for the following morning, who, with visible pleasure in his countenance, cheerfully promised that all should be fulfilled.

It is scarcely necessary to say that our hero was punctual to his engagement, for this was an errand in which his spirit rejoiced; and he had already, ere well seated in his saddle, conned over a thousand pretty 'sayings and doings,' which were to be played off in his interview with Caroline. The journey in those days was a fatiguing one of nine miles, over roads impassable but by the perseverance of a native accustomed to hill and dale, to crag and precipice;— but since the year 1803, when a spirited example was set by Mr. Grasett and Mr. Barrow, of Saint Philip's parish, which these gentlemen then represented in our Colonial Parliament, and who were subsequently called up to the Council; from that time our roads have been considerably improved, and generally macadamized. In later times, indeed, they have been kept in pretty good order, and except in width, and when not cut up by those torrents occasionally produced by tropical rains, might vie with those of the mother country. But no true lover will ever find an impediment in that road which leads him to the abode of his heart's best treasure; and as our hero was, in every sense, an ardent and impassioned lover, he accomplished his journey in little more than two hours, which brought him at nine o'clock to the stately portico of Whiston Hall, a large,

massive, dull building, as gloomy without as within. It is thought
that Caroline saw his approach from a window of the paralytic's
bedroom; for just as he alighted, she was seen to whisper to her
mother, who, in a tone sufficiently audible to be heard by the nurse,
(from whom it was reverberated to us,) said, 'Go down to him, my
dear; you see I can't move at present without disturbing our poor
friend;'—who at that time, almost insensible, was resting on Mrs.
Fairfield's shoulder. Goldacre had, in the mean time, entered the
hall, and quietly seated himself in one of those high-backed leather-
bottomed chairs, so fashionable in those days in the mansions of the
wealthy. A servant left the room to announce him, but to whom
Goldacre had not told her, for he was unconscious of the existence
of any other person in the house, save that of one all-engrossing object, she, who was then lingering on the stairs, one minute advancing—then receding, she scarce knew why; while he, all anxiety, was
flapping his gloves across his knees, adjusting the frill of his shirt,
drawing down its ruffles, and casting a wistful look towards the
three arched doors which led into the hall—his ear catching the
sound of every footstep; at length, the trembling, agitated fair one
entered. He rose, and went forward to meet her; with diffidence
and perturbation he took her hand – she curtseyed – 'twas an embarrassing silence – they stood as if planet-struck: but a stanza of a
little song by the late celebrated R.B. Sheridan, so well describes
her position at this moment, that we will here quote it:—

When a tender maid
Is first essayed
By some admiring swain,
How her blushes rise
If she meets his eyes,
While he unfolds his pain!
If he takes her hand, she trembles quite!
Touch her lips,– and she swoons outright!
While with a pit-a-pat – pit-a-pat
Her heart owns her fright!

They truly were *both* frightened – confused – overcome! There
is always a delicate, shrinking grace in virtue, that cannot stand the

first electric shock between two sympathizing hearts. Her eyes, her languid look – that thrill which shot through her frame – all betrayed the emotion with which *she* was struggling. *He*, suffused by a crimson flush – hesitating, faltering, and not less agitated than herself – attempted to address her. 'If,' said he, 'the ardour of my passion has not led me to mistake'– here further utterance was denied, and a momentary pause ensued. Recovering himself, he resumed, 'If, Miss Fairfield, if I have not been preparing a disappointment for myself'– but such was his agitation, such the absence of all self-possession, that the power of speech was again denied him. Their eyes now met; it was

> That glance that took
> The thoughts each of the other at a single look.

It spoke that language of the heart, which is felt when the lips move not—it held that discourse with the eye which is more eloquent than speech. They both felt the full force of this noiseless rhetoric, and Caroline shrunk back from this development of her feeling as if conscious of some undefined culpability of conduct, something bordering on unfeminine temerity. Goldacre, emboldened by a confidence which quickened every pulsation, and which sent the blood with redoubled force back to his heart, grasped her hand with uncontrolled vehemence, and throwing himself at her feet, passionately exclaimed, 'Caroline, I adore, I love thee! it is no new-born love, Caroline, but one which entered early into my bosom! it clings to my very soul, and will live there till I cease to breathe! May I then, Caroline – dare I hope?' Here his emotion paralyzed all power of utterance; but how shall we describe the increased agitation of his ardent mind, and the intensity of his feelings, when Caroline, making a slight effort with her feeble arm, to raise him, acknowledged, in faltering, tremulous accents, but with all the innocence of a pure and unsophisticated mind, that his love was returned! This confession of a reciprocal passion, which, in the warmth of her heart, and excitement of the moment, unguardedly escaped her lips, mantled her cheeks with blushes, and Caroline hastily left the room. If we may be allowed to paraphrase the language of the simple squire of that redoubtable knight, whose chivalrous spirit has immortalized him as the champion of the fair sex, we will here say— 'God bless the woman that first *invented* love!' It winds round one like a garland of sweetest scented flowers, distilling into the heart a golden elixir of heavenly joys that make of man a hero!

Goldacre, as if roused from some vision, stood in motionless bewilderment, like a half-crazed man, watching the receding steps of some mysterious figure; nor was he conscious where he actually was, till Pollard entered and invited him into the parlour to take some refreshment. Mrs. Fairfield received him in the parlour with her usual urbanity; and though they sat *tête-à-tête* for some time, nothing of importance passed between them, except an attempt on his part to disclose his passion for her daughter, which the mother evaded, by saying, 'that her mind was so engrossed by the unhappy state of the family, as to preclude her consideration of any other subject for the present,' and being soon after opportunely summoned to the sick chamber, she apologized and left the room. Goldacre was a little disconcerted at this apparent coolness; but from the gloomy stillness of the house, as well as from an evident melancholy which shrouded the benignant features of Mrs. Fairfield, he brought his mind to yield a reluctant acquiescence as to the propriety of her conduct.

Having no expectation of seeing Caroline again, during this visit, and being anxious to follow up the encouragement he had received, which he estimated not a little, he obtained the necessary materials, and hastily penned the following pithy, but laconic note:—

CAROLINE,

The long cherished hopes of my heart have become a portion of my existence. These hopes were the dreams of my youth, and are now the realities of my manhood. I have through life venerated the divinity of love, and thou hast ever been the goddess of my adoration! Encourage my hopes, or you drive me to despair.

Yours truly–truly yours,

J. G.

This note was confided to Pollard, and was in a few minutes placed in Caroline's hands. Her eyes became dimmed with tears, and her pulse quickened as she read it; and with the sincerity of an upright mind she answered with a pencil on a slip of paper, and with even greater laconism than he had employed,

Be calm and tranquil; let not hope deferred create despair.

CAROLINE.

Oh! with what vehemence of impassioned delight he read, kissed, re-read, and kissed again and again, the heart-inspiring, the soul-subduing note! Pollard seeing his agitation, approached him, and gently laying a hand on his arm said to him in humble and meek accent, 'Mas John, Miss Judy's so ill she can't last long! shall I order your horse? You won't see any of the family again, they all in the room with her!' The horse was soon at the door; in an instant Goldacre mounted and rode off. The animal was a docile, sure-footed creature, and seemed to enter into the rider's impatience by the facility with which it scrambled over the broken and craggy way; still Goldacre did not reach Silverdale until night-fall, having been obliged to halt twice from the drenching, pitiless rain which had assailed him. Wet and lowering as it was, he hastened over to Staffords, but not to answer the anxious inquiries for which Mr. Fairfield was waiting, for, strange to say, he brought him not a particle of information as to the state of the paralytic patient. Such were the glow and impetuosity of Goldacre's feelings, that one endeared object alone engrossed his every thought; so that when Mr. Fairfield made inquiries after the invalid, Goldacre conceiving the inquiry to relate to Caroline, took her father by the arm with unusual familiarity, and with a gaiety and delight that quite astonished him, answered, 'Oh, my dear friend, she's most charming! more lovely than ever! a personification of innocence adorned with meekness and grace! She is'—'But,' said Mr. Fairfield, interrupting his rhapsody, 'how is Miss Chrichton? How did you find her? are there any hopes of her recovery? What account did Mrs. Fairfield give you of her? What was the state of the family when you left Whiston?' During the whole of this inquiry, springing from the benevolent warmth and sympathy of Mr. Fairfield's feelings towards his old friends, the young man stood aghast; his mouth half opened, his eyes fixed in vacant stare, and himself as if transfixed to the very floor. But on Mr. Fairfield again asking, 'How was Miss Chrichton?' he started from his reverie as one just receiving an electric shock, or awakened to a new consciousness of existence. He then, with a humiliation of manner which sensibly touched Mr. Fairfield's sensitive mind, replied, 'I confess to you, my dear sir, with shame and regret, that absorbed by my own selfish feelings, I totally lost sight of the melancholy mission with which you entrusted me; and heard not – saw not – and thought not but of one dear and all-engrossing object on whom my peace, my happiness, my life depends! I can therefore give you no tidings relating to the patient!' 'Did you see my wife?' asked Mr. Fairfield. 'I think,' replied Goldacre, 'I think I did; but, no, no, it was Pollard I sent;' but checking himself, he continued, 'aye, aye, I recollect I did see your kind lady – I breakfasted with her.' Then after a short pause, and taking Mr. Fairfield's hand in a more gentle and respectful manner, he added, 'My dear sir, I have been labouring during the whole day, under such a torrent of contending emotions, that I am not altogether myself! From my earliest youth I have respected virtue, cultivated reason, and endeavoured to regulate my conduct by my understanding, but unhappily I have now to confess an aberration of mind wrought by the intensity of my feelings! Need I say that I idolize your daughter, and that my admiration is unbounded.' 'But,' said Mr. Fairfield, 'regulate your enthusiasm by your reason, and act like a man of sense as well as of feeling. For the present I recommend you to return home and compose yourself; a refreshing night's rest will put all to right; and when we meet again we shall be able to converse more coherently.' The young man took this kind advice, returned home, and after taking some refreshment with his parents, retired to rest.

CHAPTER XVII

Mr. Fairfield being anxious respecting the state of Miss Judy Chrichton's health, and not having heard any further tidings of her than what had been communicated by his wife through the medium of a verbal message, determined to proceed himself on this painfully interesting inquiry; and next morning, as soon as he had arranged some domestic concerns, and had given some necessary orders to the manager, he set off for Whiston Hall. When within half a mile of that mansion, he was not a little surprised on turning the angle of a cane field bordering the road, at suddenly meeting the heir of Silverdale. During the previous night young Goldacre, it seems, reflected deeply on the delirium of his conduct during the day, and how completely he had disregarded the mission on which he had been employed by Mr. Fairfield, resolved to atone as well as he could for his former neglect. We will not be certain that he was not instigated by other feelings than those arising from a desire to make the *amende honorable*; however, he did proceed at sunrise on the self-imposed task; but the journey being protracted in consequence of the horse casting a shoe on the road, gave time to Mr. Fairfield to overtake him when thus near Whiston Hall. Goldacre frankly explained the object and cause of his journey, at least so far as was connected with the inquiry after Miss Chrichton's health; what other motive he may have had, is left to float in the regions of conjecture; but it was no small gratification to him, that Mr. Fairfield applauded his attention, and expressed no unwillingness that they should now proceed together. On their arrival, they had the happiness to find the family in a state of more comparative ease and tranquillity than either of them had contemplated, and they were greeted by Mrs. Fairfield with a cheerfulness which gave evident indication that the patient's malady had taken a favourable turn.

It appears that during the early part of the night, paralysis had greatly abated, and in a few hours the unfortunate sufferer was so generally relieved that she was able to express, in feeble, broken words, her consciousness of the presence of her friends. As morning approached she gained a trifling more strength, and at the time the two gentlemen arrived, she appeared to be so much recovered as to be able to sit up and receive the medicine which had been previously ordered. It was from these circumstances, which proved so fallacious in the end, that a general satisfaction had been diffused through the family. After a time Mr. Fairfield was shown into the invalid's room, and he was instantly recognised by her; she put forth her hand to welcome him, and in a faltering voice and feeble tone she desired a chair to be placed by her bed-side, and that he would be seated. Mr. Fairfield spoke to her with great tenderness on the alarming situation she had been in, and he expressed much satisfaction at seeing the present improved state of her health, encouraging the poor invalid to hope for speedy and permanent restoration. 'I have, indeed, my friend,' said she, 'been on the brink of the grave, and feel myself still tottering on its verge; but thank Heaven, death has no terrors for me, for the God whom I serve is a merciful God!' Her friend replied that it made him happy to find her in such a peaceful state of mind, to see that the consolations of the Christian religion were so deeply impressed on her feelings; and that he yet hoped shortly to see her perfectly recovered. 'That,' answered she, 'is what I do not expect, and I only desire it, in as far as it may be consonant to the Divine will. I am not unimpressed with the awful change which awaits me, but I shall never shrink from that death which leads me to my God.' Mr. Fairfield mentioned the sure and certain hopes held out to us of a future state, through the atoning sacrifice of Christ. 'Ay!' said she, raising her languid eyes as if contemplating some heavenly vision, 'it is on that rock all our hopes are built! He is the God of peace, of goodness, and of forgiveness; and which of us needs not forgiveness?' 'True,' said Mr. Fairfield, 'and even the worst of sinners may have hope in that forgiveness, if sought with true faith and repentant hearts,

believing in the redemption through the sufferings of that great
Mediator.' 'I am not,' rejoined our invalid, 'oppressed by an accusing conscience, yet as a peccable mortal, can there be a doubt
that I have much to atone for, both of commission and omission.'
Here her articulation became interrupted by the increased
difficulty of her breathing; and her sister, who had been much affected during this solemn conversation, said, 'My dearest Judy,
the humble and pious life we have led saves us from all grievous
and bitter reflections; and among the joys and consolations of that
religion which we have made the rule of our conduct, there is
none I more devoutly cherish than the hope of a personal recognition in another world of those whom we have loved in this. This
hope clings to my bosom, and I am therefore the more reconciled
to the thought of our present separation, feeling, as I before said,
a presentiment that though the grave may soon divide us, our immortal spirits will soon meet in the abode of endless bliss!' Having
with great emotion thus spoken to her dying sister, she fell on Mrs.
Fairfield's bosom in an hysterical swoon, and was taken to her own
chamber. Meantime poor Caroline, in whom affection was part of
her nature, watching with anxious solicitude the alternate
changes in the countenance of her godmother, was overwhelmed
with grief, when she saw her attacked with fresh paroxysms and
sinking rapidly into the arms of death. 'It is my body,' said the almost exhausted patient, 'and not my mind, that is disordered; I
feel as it were a celestial wind wafting me to other regions – yes,
Caroline, I feel my approaching end; see then, my beloved child,
in what tranquillity a Christian can die!' Here her speech again
failed her, a difficulty of breathing ensued, a marble paleness fell
on her face, a glossy film covered her eyes, she sank back on the
bed, and expired without groan or sigh! Thus, in holy, calm resignation she closed her saint-like life – a life of pure and undefiled
religion – a life that had been exercised, in conjunction with her
sister, in visiting the sick, the fatherless, and the widow in clothing
the naked and feeding the hungry, and in giving employment to
the industrious. Such scenes awaken afresh in my mind the hal-

lowed recollection of former sorrows, and even now, after more than thirty years, renew the sigh for *her* whom I then lost – the light of my soul, the partner of my heart's best affection – her, who rendered my then prosperity more brilliant, and who, had God spared her, would have lessened the anguish of present adversity, and been a sweet solace to me in the cheerless winter of old age. But what folly to open our hearts to the world! Such a death presents the most forcible argument against infidelity—it drives the atheist from his dark and slippery hold, and the deist sinks under the terror of his own corrupt heart; while the true Christian, with his humble and pious faith in revelation, embraces in joyful hope, the cross of Christ.

During these melancholy occurrences, young Goldacre sat below in lonely meditation, from which he was occasionally aroused as Pollard entered to inform him of the fluctuating changes in the appearance of the invalid; but at length the sudden gust of grief which broke forth among the domestics, warned him, that the poor patient was beyond all mortal suffering. Mr. Fairfield now joined him, and their united judgment and advice were employed in making those arrangements which the last sad offices of humanity have to fulfil, and which so powerfully awaken our feelings. Mrs. Fairfield's attention was engrossed by the surviving sister, who, as we have seen, had been removed in a state of great suffering and anguish from the bed-side of the deceased.

It would lead us into too minute a relation were we to describe all the subsequent events – Caroline might be said to have been dumbfounded – she neither sighed, spoke, nor wept; the poor girl's sufferings were pent up in a heart too full for utterance. Miss Chrichton lay in a state of apathy, uttering some incoherent expressions; but at length she succeeded, more by signs than words, to make herself intelligible to Mrs. Fairfield, to whom she signified that there was a paper of some consequence in a private drawer to which she pointed, and which she desired might be acted on in case of her death, of whose near approach she seemed not only conscious, but even to court.

The funeral of the deceased took place on the following day, and was conducted in the most solemn and impressive manner. The corpse was first taken to the parish church of St. Thomas, where the funeral service was impressively performed by the Rev. William Duke, the then venerable incumbent; the melancholy cortege then returned to Whiston Hall, where the corpse was deposited in the ancient vault of the family, under a shady arbour of overhanging bamboos. This last ceremony called forth from the negroes of the plantation, one of those vociferous lamentations by which that class of persons was formerly so accustomed to display their feelings, but all this loud wailing was merely lip-deep, and came not from the fountain of genuine grief. This thrilling, piercing cry, however, had such an effect upon the already shattered nerves of the grief-stricken Miss Chrichton as to hasten that catastrophe which was but too evidently approaching; and when Mrs. Fairfield returned into the room, she was dismayed and horror struck at finding that during her absence from the chamber, her pious and worthy friend had sunk into the haven of eternal rest and happiness; while the composed and placid smile that overspread her countenance showed how tranquil had been her last moments! The careless nurse, it seems, who had been left in charge of the invalid, having been amusing herself with watching from the window the crowd retiring from the vault, was quite unaware of the melancholy event which had taken place.

As for poor Caroline, who was already overwhelmed with sorrow, she was now by this second shock thrown into a state of mind that greatly alarmed her mother. It was that grief which, shunning all observation steals into the heart, and is there treasured as a sacred memento of those we venerate and love!

The same ceremonies were observed on this melancholy occasion as on the former one, with this difference only, that Mr. and Mrs. Fairfield now followed as chief mourners; whereas Caroline and her father had on the former occasion acted in that capacity. On the present occasion she was attended by young Goldacre, who, with the utmost delicacy and tenderness, refrained from in-

truding on her sorrow in the slightest degree; he never once broke
in upon that silence in which she sat by his side, as if unconscious
of his presence, and he conducted her through the solemn ceremony, displaying in every word and look how truly he sympa-
thized with her in her affliction. At the request of Mrs. Fairfield,
the whole family of Silverdale, who had attended both funerals,
remained at Whiston the two following days, and that kind moth-
erly old lady, Mrs. Goldacre, obligingly stopped several days
longer, that she might afford her maternal assistance in nursing
and attending on poor Caroline.

But we must now, for a while, leave these affecting scenes, and
without invading the rights of the historian, take a short notice of
an invasion of another kind – one more interesting to the patriot,
than pleasing to our fair readers, should our humble pages be honoured by them with a perusal.

CHAPTER XVIII

AT the period to which our domestic occurrences are brought down, the republican '*dogs of war,*' deluging the throne with blood, had overthrown the monarchy of France, and were crying 'havoc' throughout Europe. England had been compelled to interpose her mighty arm, and although she could not then stay the 'battled pestilence,' she maintained the integrity of her own dominions, and ultimately chained the imperial eagle to a solitary rock!

The pernicious spirit of republicanism which prevailed in France, was not long in reaching the shores of her Atlantic possessions, and Martinique soon felt all the horrors of intestine commotion. A strong party, however, favourable to royalty, still existed there; but as it daily became more and more endangered by the increasing anarchy, those loyal men, in the hope of saving their country from utter ruin and themselves and families from destruction, sent a deputation to the naval and military commanders at Barbados advising an attack on Martinique, and promising the co-operation of a powerful party, that would render conquest easy. Allured by these suggestions, General Bruce and Admiral Gardner promptly assembled all the disposable force under their command, and sailed from Carlisle Bay on this enterprise. On their arrival off St. Pierre, a partial landing in that neighbourhood was easily achieved, but the defensive preparations on the part of the enemy with their immense force left no hopes of success to so slender an armament. Under these trying circumstances, it was determined, with that magnanimous humanity so characteristic of British officers, to forbear all useless and wanton aggression; the troops thereupon were re-embarked without loss of time, bringing off about 2,000 of the loyalists, who were thus rescued from the democratic violence they so much dreaded. These fugitives were brought to Barbados, and received from the inhabitants all that hospitality, benevolence, and sympathy could dictate, many of them remaining there until the subsequent reduction of Martinique.

Scarcely more than six months, however, had elapsed after this failure, than a more powerful armament was assembled in the same bay, under Sir Charles Grey and Sir John Jervis. At this time there was no other barrack than that situated on the brow of the hill at St. Ann's, and it became therefore necessary to lodge a portion of the men under tents; and a novel and pleasing scene was thus presented to the eye, by a regular encampment of about 1,000 men on either side the road at Constitution Hill, and nearly up to Pilgrim. As soon as these veteran commanders had completed their arrangements, in the furtherance of which President Bishop, who then administered the government, had lent the most zealous assistance, they proceeded with their truly formidable force to Martinique, leaving all the women and children behind, and about forty or fifty invalid soldiers under charge of Lieut. Colonel B——m, D. Q., B. M. G. These poor women were left almost in a state of destitution; but the president was not wanting in the rights of humanity, and perhaps influenced by that cordiality and good feeling subsisting between himself and the two commanders of the expedition, he promptly raised by subscription a sum sufficient to supply the wants of these poor creatures till they were permitted to join their husbands. In addition to this subscription, and while the siege was carrying on, the President also raised by voluntary contribution a considerable supply of poultry and other live stock and vegetables, which he sent to the commanders for the use of the forces. Such was the good understanding between these parties, that the President regularly received from them a detail of their proceedings throughout the whole of the expedition, and for the information of the public he had them inserted in the official paper of the day.

Shortly after the expedition had sailed, and while it was actively prosecuting the attack, and several minor positions had been

carried, His Royal Highness Prince Edward, bearing the rank of
major-general, arrived in Carlisle Bay, from Halifax, to join the
forces. Our soldier Prince, possessing all the ardour and courage
of his royal line, was not a little disappointed and mortified at
finding that the armament had left a few days before his arrival,
for he was most anxious to be at the first brunt of the embattled
field. His illustrious daughter, we may here observe, now wields
the British sceptre, a premature death having cut off her illustrious sire from the hereditary succession, which would have raised
him to the throne on the demise of our old royal sailor-friend,
whose memory is still revered in the island.

The arrival of Prince Edward (afterwards Duke of Kent) was as
unexpected, as inauspicious to the display of the loyal feelings of
our countrymen, who are ever most anxious to do honour to the
throne, whether in the person of the sovereign or his son. On the
present occasion there was no opportunity afforded to either
President or people to testify their loyalty to the young Prince, for
the frigate in which he arrived was not only in the bay, but had
despatched her boats to the shore for a supply of water, before
even the captain of the port had made his appearance alongside.
At length, this important officer, in the person of Andrew Miller, a
half-witted, humble, uneducated man, but zealous in his duty,
made his appearance. His blue coat, with red cuffs and collar, his
epaulette and sword, augured some official importance, and he
was courteously received by the lieutenant of the watch, from
whom he first learned that the Prince was on board; and, that august person being pointed out to him, Miller unhesitatingly presented himself as the President's messenger to greet his Royal
Highness, at the same time assuring the Prince that 'his honour
would be happy to see him, and begged that he would go up to
Pilgrim,' adding 'that he (Miller) would immediately send to let
his honour know of the arrival of his Royal Highness.' The Prince
listened to Miller's address (of which we have given the mere sub-
stance) with ineffable kindness, though he was evidently piqued
at what appeared to him so neglectful on the part of the authori-

ties; and he asked, 'where was the President?' Poor Miller, in all the artlessness of his nature, adopting the vulgar designation given to the estate (Hethersal's) where the President then was on a visit, replied, 'at Hogsty!'—'Hog-sty! Hog-sty!' ejaculated the Prince, 'that's a very inappropriate place for my royal father's representative!' Miller bowing, replied, 'I'll get ashore as quick as I can, and fire a royal salute at Pilgrim,* in honour of your Royal Highness, and that will let *everybody* know you're here.' And, so saying, he took his departure, leaving the Prince much amused with the simplicity of his manners, but giving him no high opinion of the officials of the island. The promptness of Miller in getting to Pilgrim and firing this salute, is really inconceivable; and it was the first notification to the public that another son of our venerated sovereign had approached our shores. Lieutenant Colonel B—— (who had been left in charge of the stores, &c.) upon hearing the salute, immediately hastened on board, but, on being introduced to the Prince, his reception was marked with that stern demeanour which always threw the 'fortiter in re' of a soldier around his Royal Highness. The colonel, who was of mild, gentlemanly manners, apologized for the delay in the best way he could; but his Royal Highness not being courteously disposed at the time, briefly replied, 'As I suppose, Colonel, the President was occupied in "shearing the hog," and yourself in "hunting the boar," I will not be so inconsiderate as to interrupt either of you in your sports;' and he then fairly bowed the colonel off the quarter-deck. The frigate directly after made sail, and proceeded to her destination. The Prince arrived in Martinique yet in time to exercise his martial prowess. His Royal Highness was immediately placed in command of the British encampment at La Coste; but, soon after, the commanders resolved on a combined attack of the naval and military forces on the fortifications and town of

* A platform of brass cannon was then there for the purpose of complimenting distinguished personages.

Fort Royal, directing that the siege of Fort Bourbon should, at the same time, be more vigorously pressed. The former was carried most gallantly, by assault; the latter, compelled to surrender by capitulation; and our gallant Prince, at the head of three brigades of grenadiers, and one of light infantry, took possession of the gates of that extensive and important fortress; after which, receiving the submission of General Rochembeau, the conquest was completed. Fort Bourbon was called Fort George, after that Third George, whose posterity still adorn the British throne and nation; and Fort Royal was named Fort Edward, after the heroic progenitor of our present Most Gracious Queen,—whom God preserve! As a little P.S. to this achievement, we will here note, that when the armament sailed from Barbados, President Bishop presented the military commander with a full-sized British union flag, wrought by the hands of his fair daughters, which the veteran general, with great gallantry, had hoisted at Fort George, on its being so named.

But, a truce to all this war and doings! England and France now dwell in neighbourly amity and peace; and long, long may their united arms be the safeguard of Europe and of the world!

CHAPTER XIX

WE left our heroine, and indeed, the whole family of the Fairfields, and the good old dame of Silverdale, at Whistons; we now, however, find them all returned to their respective homes. Caroline's health was much amended, but she still remained in seclusion; nor had her lover seen her since he attended at the funeral. Her spirits continued much depressed, and she was much enfeebled by the shock she had undergone from the death of two such kind and affectionate friends as the Chrichtons had uniformly been to her. She felt anxious to pay some tribute to their memory; and, therefore, proposed to have an obelisk erected near the family vault, with this inscription on its pedestal:—

To the MEMORY of DEBORAH and JUDITH CHRICHTON,
SISTERS!
Who lived in the bonds of peace, and died in unity of spirit,
But were dying all – it were grief indeed!
And better far He'd ne'er been born to bleed
On Calvary, who there so freely gave
Himself – a sinful world to save!
Whence, in dying, we are *born again*.
For 'tis through death's short transitory pain
We rise *immortal*, and new life attain.

It will be remembered that the elder of these ladies, just before her death, had pointed out to Mrs. Fairfield a drawer, containing a paper, which she gave her to understand was of much consequence, and which she desired might be acted on immediately after her decease. On examining this document, it was found to be a deed, executed several years ago by the two sisters, conveying (with the exception of about two thousand pounds, in charitable donations, among their tenantry and the poor of the parish) the whole of the Whiston estate, and all other their property, in trust, to Mr. Fairfield, for the sole use of his daughter during her minority, and, in fee simple, to her and to her heirs, upon her coming of age. Caroline was now two-and-twenty, her right therefore was complete; but it became a question between her parents whether she should be informed at present of so great and immediate an acquisition of fortune as had fallen to her. From some prudential motives respecting young Goldacre, it was decided that no communication of it should yet be made, and Caroline was only told, in general terms, that the Misses Chrichton had been very liberal to her in the disposal of their property.

Although no decisive arrangement had taken place between the young folks, nor any final settlement been urged upon the elder party by the lover, Mr. and Mrs. Fairfield were too honest to dissemble in a matter so intimately connected with their daughter's happiness, seeing as they evidently did, her growing predilection in favour of Goldacre. Under these circumstances, they thought it best for the present to withhold the deed from her, not wishing that either she or her lover should in any respect be influenced by it. In this state things remained for some days, when Mr. Goldacre, senior, made his appearance at Staffords, requesting an interview with Mr. Fairfield. 'I am come,' said he, in all the blunt honesty of his nature, 'to see if I can bring matters about between your daughter and my son – John is taking the matter to heart very much, and makes my old woman and me quite unhappy – and so as he's gone to town about some business, his mother thinks it would be better for me at once to tell you what I intends doing for John upon his marriage, but you know every thing will be his at our death.' Mr. Fairfield was greatly embarrassed at this unexpected, ingenuous and simple address, and scarcely knew how to reply, being fearful of committing himself on so delicate a subject. He earnestly wished, but hardly expected, that his neighbour would not further pursue the conversation; however, after a little hesitation he said, 'My good friend, in our anxiety to witness our children's happiness we must not lose sight of propriety, and talk of arrangements connected with an event not yet decided on. It is true, that your son, in no very coherent language, did mention to me his passion for my daughter, and I believe the young folks have had some conversation on the subject of a satisfactory nature, but I am not in possession of sufficient information to authorize my entering into any final arrangement with you for the present.' 'You know, Mr. Fairfield,' said the other, 'I am out of debt—have one of the best plantations in the island, and that I can give Jack £12,000 cash upon his marriage; besides which I will make over to him one half the crop, while I and my old woman live, and at our death it will all be his; I asks nothing about what you mean to do for your daughter – John says she's treasure enough for him without a farthing; so I begs, Sir, you'll come to the point, and say at once if you'll give your consent to the match.' 'I cannot enter into any discussion with you at present,' replied Mr. Fairfield. 'In a day or two I hope Caroline will be able to see her friends, and if your son will then come over, he may probably have an opportunity of ascertaining her sentiments, upon which only can I be guided in this important affair.' 'Why,' said Goldacre, 'you've left me as far off the mark as ever; yet I dare say, Sir, 'twill be best after all to leave it to be settled by the young folks first. John,' continued he, 'is fallen away very much, and grown so melancholy, that we fret to see it. But when he meets Miss Caroline, I suppose he will be able to bring the matter to his mind; for, between you and I, I really thinks she has a liking to him, and every thing will then go on smooth and easy.' Mr. Fairfield took him kindly by the hand, saying, 'I cannot interfere till I know my daughter's opinion,' and being then joined by his wife, some general conversation ensued, and in a few minutes Mr Goldacre took his leave. His return home was greeted with much delight by his wife, and upon the whole they both seemed satisfied with the prospect of their son's ultimate success.

Young Goldacre returned from town in the evening; but as the father's visit to Staffords had been undertaken without the son's knowledge, he was merely told in general terms by him, that he had been there; but the old lady, ever anxious to soothe her son's feelings, whose late depression of spirits had caused her much solicitude, quickly added with much warmth and animation, 'and, John, Mr. Fairfield said, that he hoped you would soon come over and see Miss Caroline.' Scarcely had she given this version of what Mr. Fairfield had said, than her husband ejaculated, 'No, no, Molly! No, he only said that he hoped his daughter would soon be able to see her friends, and that you,' addressing his son, 'might then have an opportunity of freely communicating your thoughts, and thus finally arrange all matters.' 'And did he, father, really say this? are you quite sure of it, father?' energetically asked the young man. 'Ay, ay, John,' replied he, 'As sure as I stand here alive he said it; you'll never catch old John Goldacre fibbing.' The young man, full of ecstacy and bliss, affectionately seized his father's hand and shook it most heartily; the good old dame embraced her son with all that glow and warmth which springs from the bosom of maternity; John's eyes sparkled with true delight, and his countenance was a galaxy of joy! And this affectionate trio, the sunshine of whose hearts was the brighter from a kind of reflective happiness, spent a more cheerful evening together than they had done since their return from Whiston Hall.

A day or two after, our lover learnt from his mother that Caroline had resumed her seat in the parlour. It was this information no doubt, that made him soon after dinner on the following day select one of his best handkerchiefs from his wardrobe, scent it with 'best double distilled,' pass the powder-puff afresh over his hair, and otherwise adjust his dress with the utmost neatness and precision, and no doubt in that ridiculous and fantastic costume which distinguished a man of fashion in those days. From dinner time (the *élite* even then dined at two o'clock) till five appeared to our impatient hero as if the sun and moon had for a second time been stayed in their course; but the long wished for hour at which friendly visits were generally made at length arrived. Goldacre mounted his horse, adjusted the reins with more than usual care, and strode his saddle with as noble a bearing as ever did the great Duke on entering that famed city which his valour, for a second time, subdued. With what pride of heart, with what joy of countenance and innate delight, the good old dame and honest old father saw him ride off!

Mr. Fairfield was from home, and it was shrewdly suspected that he had designedly absented himself. His lady, however, gave our hero a cordial reception; and upon his inquiring, a few minutes after, how Miss Fairfield was, the mother replied, 'I am glad to tell you that Caroline's health is daily improving. She is now able to join us at table, and is at present in the parlour; will you walk in and see her?'

Pray, young lady, were you ever in love? or you, Sir? Mark me – I do not inquire of that simpering miss who sits listening to that youth dangling at the back of her chair and whispering soft nonsense in her ear. These scarcely yet know that they have a heart, and will hereafter laugh at each other for their past folly. Such as these it is who mistake the light buoyancy of adolescence, and the quick pulsation of newly awakened feelings, for that genuine passion which filled the bosom of our hero and heroine. We appeal not to these very young misses and masters, but to you, Miss Georgiana! and to you ***** whose devotions at church seem heightened by the perception of each other's presence, and by being mutually engaged in the same spiritual duty.—By the by, I have always remarked, that that love which receives its first germ at church, is generally blessed with connubial happiness. But to proceed with our tale.—Well, when our lover entered the parlour, Caroline's pale cheek became flushed, and her bewitching confusion indicated more than need here be expressed. Goldacre was hardly less agitated: which of them was most embarrassed, I will not say!—She – but wherefore, Miss Georgiana, should I account for feelings which you already so well understand?—Or explain to you, my old friend ***** that of which you are already master in all its phases? It was some minutes before either Goldacre or Caroline could speak, but as he approached the sofa on which she was reclining, she presented him her white taper-fingered hand with an ease and grace, which, added to her delicate appearance, and her attire of a long loose robe of snowy whiteness, made her look the personification of angelic purity. Goldacre received her hand most gently, and pressed it to his lips with all the fervency of a lover. Mrs. Fairfield saw the agitated feelings of both, and was not unmindful of the injury her daughter's health might sustain by a protracted interview; she therefore, after engaging them in some light general conversation, smilingly said, addressing the young man, 'We must have compassion, and not intrude too long on our invalid.' Goldacre readily interpreted the mother's meaning, and gently taking Caroline by the hand, whispered in a tone soft as Apollo's lute, 'May I hope soon to have an opportunity of –' the last few words were uttered in a voice so feeble and indistinct, that we can but guess at them; but be they what they may, Caroline evidently assented to his wish, if we may judge by that gentle nod and fascinating smile. Oh, that smile of assentation! What witchery did it embody!

Speaking of first impressions at church, brings to my mind a ludicrous circumstance that happened some fifty or sixty years ago at ***** Church. The Rector, though a man of profound learning and a great theologian, was of such eccentric habits as often to create a doubt among the vulgar whether he was at all times *compos mentis*. Having remarked, for several successive Sundays, a gentleman who was no parishioner, invariably usurp a seat in a pew next to that in which a young widow lady had her sitting, he intently eyed them, and at one time detected the gentleman slyly draw the lady's glove from off the back of the pew, where she was accustomed to place it (her hand and arm were

delicately fair!) and place in it a small neatly folded note. By and
by the lady's prayer book fell, of course accidentally, from the
ledge of her pew into the gentleman's; he picked it up, found a
leaf turned down, and he hastily scanned a passage which evidently caused a smile of complacency. Our minister saw all their
sly proceedings, and continued to watch them with scrutinizing
eye for two successive Sundays. On the third, as soon as the col-
lects were read, and while the beadle yet obsequiously waited to
attend him to the chancel, our eccentric pastor, in a strong and
distinct voice, said, 'I publish the banns of marriage between M
and N, (deliberately pronouncing the names of the parties,) if
any of you know cause,' &c., &c., &c. The eyes of the whole congregation were turned on the widow and our gay Lothario—the
lady suffused with blushes, and the gentleman crimsoned with
anger; she fanning herself with vehemence, and he opening and
shutting the pew-door with rage and violence; the minister
meanwhile proceeding through his accustomed duties with the
same decorum and ease, as if perfectly innocent of the agitation
he had excited. The sermon preached and the service ended,
away to the vestry rush the party at the heels of the pastor. 'Who
authorized you, Sir, to make such a publication of banns?' demanded they both in a breath. 'Authorized me!' said he, with a
stare that heightened their confusion. 'Yes, Sir, who authorized
you?' demanded the gentleman. 'Oh!' said the minister, with a
sly glance alternately at each, 'if you don't approve of it, I'll for-
bid the banns next Sunday.' 'Sir,' said the lady, 'you have been
too officious already – nobody requested you to do any such
thing – you had better mind your own business!' 'Why, my pretty
dear,' said he, patting her on the cheek, 'what I have done has
been all in the way of business, and if you do not like to wait for
three publications, I advise you, Sir,' turning to the gentleman,
'to procure the licence, the ring, and—the fee—and then the
whole matter may be settled as soon as to–morrow.' 'Well!'
replied the gentleman, addressing the widow, 'with your permission, I *will* get them, and we may be married in a day or two.'

'Oh! you may both do as you please,' pettishly, yet nothing loathingly replied the lady. It was but a day or two after that the licence was procured, the parson received his fee, the bride-groom his bride, and the widow, for the last time, threw her gloves over the back of her pew; and it was afterwards said, that all parties were satisfied with their gains.

CHAPTER XX

Young Goldacre began to feel more confident than ever in his aspirations after the lovely fair one, and he now resolved to come to a final understanding with all parties, and not let his doom float longer in the mist of uncertainty. Impelled by this determination, the gentleman, in a few days after the interview we have described, (postponing his visits that the young lady might the better recover her strength,) took horse and rode over to Staffords a little before noon. The light of the sun is never so propitious to lovers as the beams of the soft moon, or the gentle twinkling of the stars on a still balmy evening. Whether Mrs. Fairfield was aware of this we will not positively say, but we do assert that she made an excuse for the non-appearance of Caroline, saying she was engaged with some of the tenants' daughters whom she had kindly undertaken to instruct in reading, and to say the catechism properly. 'Mr. Fairfield,' concluded the dame, 'will be at home in the evening, and perhaps, Sir, you will come over and sit with him.' Goldacre had no alternative, and although his object in calling was thus frustrated, he returned home in no dissatisfied humour.

> True as the dial to the sun,
> Though 'tis not shone upon.

Precisely at five o'clock our lover rode over to Staffords. Mr. Fairfield was in the act of mounting his horse to take a ride along the fields with his manager, to see the progress of the work then going on. 'Alight,' said he to the young man, 'you'll find my wife and daughter in the parlour; I will soon be back,' and off he rode. A few minutes after Goldacre had entered the parlour, Mrs. Fairfield thought proper to retire. Goldacre then drew his chair nearer the sofa – a little nearer – nearer yet, till at length he brought himself in close proximity to Caroline's seat. Oh! happy, thrice happy man! thus to be seated for the first time by the side of her whom he so truly loved! With palpitating heart he took her hand, while the warm blood flowed with more than usual rapidity through every vein. But think not that the lover's feelings found no vent in words; no, no; there were 'lovers' vows,' and soft sayings, and tender sighs, fervid protestations, eternal promises, and – but it were a flat, profitless tale to repeat all that was said, for though to the lovers' ears each word fell with harp-like tones of softest melody, yet a repetition of them by vulgar lips would almost seem a mockery. Notwithstanding all this, Goldacre was not quite happy, for Caroline would come to no positive decision until she had consulted with her parents. Her father, though he had left the young people an opportunity for this interview, had strictly enjoined his daughter not to give a final answer, until he had communicated to her the particulars of the Misses Chrichton's bequest, the old gentleman wishing that her lover might solicit her hand previously to his or her knowledge of such an acquisition of fortune. This reserve on the part of Caroline was no less mysterious than perplexing to Goldacre; but submit he did, for the lady was inflexible.

Mr. Fairfield returned home at twilight, and he and his wife joined the lovers in the parlour. Now, thought Goldacre, is the 'glorious golden opportunity' to decide my fate; and he was on the point of 'putting the hazard on the die,' when Caroline said with ineffable sweetness, 'I prohibit all violation, Mr. Goldacre, of my father's injunction; he wills that nothing further shall be said, until he has conversed with me, relative to our late interview, and I am all obedience.' Silence ensued, except that father and daughter were earnestly conversing in an under tone; but in a few minutes a lively chitchat followed, and cheerfulness and good humour prevailed until the hour arrived for parting, when our lover rode off with a mind as happy and a heart as gay as the hopes of requited love could make him.

The following morning, Mr. Fairfield placed in his daughter's hands, the deeds and other documents by which the Whiston estate and upwards of ten thousand pounds in the hands of the agent, were conveyed to her. ''Tis for this cause,' said he, 'that I have prohibited your decision, lest any after feelings arising from such an acquisition of wealth might induce regret at an engagement you could not with honour retract; you will now decide for yourself.' 'O my dearest father!' exclaimed she, 'where my heart is, there let my treasure be!' and she burst into tears. When Caroline was sufficiently composed, she opened the documents and casting her eyes over the writings, saw at one view the extent of her acquisition, and we may truly aver, that she was scarcely less affected at this liberality, than she had been overwhelmed with grief at the death of her benefactress. Such exuberant kindness renewed afresh all her former sufferings, and seemed 'e'en to touch the nerve where agony was born.' Her anguish again required all the soothings of a mother's tender care and a father's fond solicitude. For some days it was requisite to keep her quiet and secluded; during which time her lover was left in that painful anxiety which none but lovers feel; and although the good old dame his mother renewed her zealous care of the young lady, she could not divine the cause of her sudden indisposition, and all remained a chaos of conjecture to herself and son.

In this state, an anxious week passed away; during which Caroline's parents became fully acquainted, not merely with the partiality of her feelings, but with the true state of her heart! and they therefore came to the decision that Goldacre should be spoken to unreservedly, and that all matters should now be finally arranged. With this view, Caroline being sufficiently recovered, the whole of the Silverdale family were invited to Staffords to take their Easter dinner, which in those times always included the following day, and, although but three days intervened, it seemed an age to our impatient lover.

Mr. Fairfield had made up his mind that, during his neighbour's visit, he himself would make the communication fraught with so much interest, but that nothing should be said on the subject on

the Sunday. The happy day came, and all were at Staffords –
Monday – and there they are all again; and what a day of unalloyed
cheerfulness! Our lovers were all life and spirit. Caroline, though
yet pale and languid, was as lively and vivacious as any. Dinner
over, and cloth removed, after a few introductory words,
Mr. Fairfield said, 'Come, let us take a bumper to the heiress of
Whiston Hall – here's to Caroline Fairfield!' Who can describe the
agitated feelings of young Goldacre? A thousand conflicting
thoughts rushed into his mind. At one moment he saw Caroline
too wealthy for his hopes, the next moment showed him some elevated mercenary favoured with her smiles! All the liberal and
considerate arrangements by which he was to have testified his
devotion and secured her a handsome settlement, all the castle-
built schemes by which he was to have made her home a perfect
paradise – all, all were in a moment dispelled, as if some evil spell
had struck him, and all his prospects in life had suddenly vanished. But, how in an instant he was roused from all these jealous
and gloomy thoughts, by the affectionate and warm-hearted
Caroline! 'You will all,' said she, 'join me, I hope, in wishing that
while the heiress of Whiston shall ever gratefully cherish the
memory of her munificent friends, and faithfully fulfil her duties
to her parents, she may never feel the inflation of pride or be estranged from those old friends she' – 'loves,' warmly ejaculated
Mrs. Goldacre, her feelings at the same time bringing a tear to her
eyes; 'there's a girl for you,' continued she in breathless rapidity,
'there's a girl – bless, bless her heart! Jack, did you hear her?' Poor
fellow! astounded and confused no less by the sweet words of
Caroline, than by his mother's abrupt interruption and embarrassing appeal to him, he was prevented from making that pretty
sentimental speech he was on the point of uttering, expressive of
the tone and complexion of his feelings; all he could do was merely
to express his warm participation in Mr. Fairfield's parental approbation of Caroline's sentiments. The ladies soon after rose
from table – anon the gentlemen followed, and the two elder indulged themselves cosily (it being holiday time) in the corner of

the gallery, with a pipe. Mrs. Fairfield had some domestic arrangements to make, on which she wished to consult the judgment of her neighbour; and as it was a cool evening, there being a delightful sea breeze, Goldacre and Caroline strolled into the orchard. To see them there in the full flush of health, revelling in the soft rosy delights of pure love, would make even an old man's heart expand with joy, and awaken the remembrance of those sweet affections, once the inmates of his own bosom! And surely, the hoary-headed man, whose feelings are not quite withered by the chill blast of time, may be indulged in the fond reminiscences of those virtuous joys and sanctified affections, which, though long gone by, once gladdened his existence and made him the happiest of the happy! for such transcendent bliss he cannot but pour forth his thanks to the all-fruitful source of every terrestrial good!

At the little wicket at the entrance to the orchard they met the watchman, who, trusty guardian, suffered no one to pilfer but himself, and who bore in his hand a calabash full of choice fruit. This, in the hopes of removing suspicions of his dishonest practices, he presented smilingly, and begged they would select what best pleased them. Our gallant lover, with eyes sparkling with delight, selected a *pomme rose*, and presenting it playfully to Caroline, said, 'Accept the homage of my adoration, Miss Fairfield, in this apt emblem of those bright charms and soft affections which so richly adorn you, and whose faithful image has so long been enshrined in the depths of my heart!' Caroline's laughing eye beamed with pleasure, and never face that wore a sunny smile blushed more maidenly than hers, when snatching a *cashew apple* from the same calabash she presented it to her lover, observing, with sweetest intonation of voice and manner truly fascinating,

> 'Sweet as noyeau, and as mustard tart –
> Soft as melon, and as radish smart.

You will find *this*, Mr. Goldacre, no inapt emblem of yourself. 'Tis pleasing to the eye, sir, and no less sweet within; the nut is

pungent and warm, and its combined qualities not very unlike
Mr. Goldacre's head and heart!' 'You little siren,' exclaimed
Goldacre, fondly embracing her, 'I must confess that you have
drawn a true picture, but I fear 'tis a little flattered; still, my sweet
Caroline, if you will but venture to sip the noyeau and taste the
melon, I faithfully promise that neither mustard nor radish, nor
any other bitter or tart ingredient shall intermingle in the sweets
of our wedded life; nor shall aught unpleasant interpose to disturb
our halcyon days of peace, of joy, and happiness!' and here again
he passionately kissed the fair object who kindled all this glowing
rapture. Long as our lovers had been rambling in the orchard, still
when they were summoned to supper, they were astonished at the
fleetness of time – never knew it fly so swiftly – had not the least
idea 'twas so late – surely the old people had mistaken the hour;
but as Caroline was 'all obedience,' she could not keep her parents
waiting, and so, with tardy reluctant step, but not without *another*
last kiss, she and Goldacre returned to the house. The conclusion
of our tale is easily told.

Behold these lovers in the fulness of happiness, and with reflective joys warming the hearts of their respective parents! The marriage took place at Staffords. The honey-moon was past at
Silverdale. In a month after, the happy couple sailed for England.

THE FAIR BARBADIAN

AND FAITHFUL BLACK;

OR,

A CURE FOR THE GOUT.

A Comedy in Three Acts.

————————

BY J. W. ORDERSON:

OF BARBADOES.

AS PERFORMED THERE IN 1832.

————————

LIVERPOOL:

PRINTED BY ROSS AND NIGHTINGALE,

CHRONICLE-OFFICE, LORD-STREET.

————

1835.

DEDICATION

The following Dramatic attempt, the first of its Author, and at a time when his 'lamp of life' being nearly exhausted, it may be considered as the 'Song of the Swan,' is most respectfully DEDICATED TO THE LADIES OF BARBADOES, as an homage to their domestic virtues, amiable manners, personal attractions, and purity of heart, (which have exemplified the union of many a fair EMILY and gallant CARLOVE!) by their

Very sincere,

And devoted servant,

THE AUTHOR.

ADVERTISEMENT

THE Author of the following Dramatic attempt, after a lapse of two years since its appearance on the Barbadoes stage, ventures to commit his feeble production, in its present form, to the ordeal of the British public. Conscious of its many defects, he not merely deprecates the severity of criticism, but would anxiously propitiate its favourable reception under the humble pretentions to which alone it aspires – that of recording (through some incidents of fiction and others of fact) the real existing relations between Master and Slave, previous to the new principle of connection just established between them.

Without exaggeration, he has shown the former acting under the combined influence of climate and disease, excited to momentary acts of tyranny that instantly yield to a more amicable nature; while in the latter, a true delineation is given of unshaken fidelity and forbearance, which is of fair promise of the confidence that may henceforth be mutually reposed by each in the other.

As a general trait of West India character, it will not (except as regards the fair sex) throughout apply; but as a sketch of individual dissipation and laxity of manners, the picture is true to nature – not altogether, perhaps, as NOW existing under an improved state of religious and moral feeling, but certainly we need not go half a century back to find the original of the outline here sketched. Upon this change he exclaims with father Paul, 'Esta perpetua!'

BRIDGE TOWN, 1835.

DRAMATIS PERSONÆ

JUDGE ERRINGTON, a wealthy Planter.

TOM APPLEBURY, his nephew.

SAM SHADOCK, companion to Tom.

CAPTAIN CARLOVE, an officer, fellow passenger with Emily, come out to join his regiment.

MAJOR CHIDER, a brother officer more recently arrived.

HAMPSHIRE, confidential black servant to the judge.

WOMEN

EMILY, the Judge's daughter, affianced in marriage to Tom Applebury.

ALICE, aunt to Emily.

PLANTATION SLAVES, &c.

SCENE LAID IN BARBADOS.

THE
FAIR BARBADIAN AND FAITHFUL BLACK

———

ACT I

SCENE I – *An apartment in the* JUDGE'S *House; the Curtain rises and discovers the* JUDGE *seated in an armed chair, affected with the gout; one leg on the stool, a stick resting by his side;* HAMPSHIRE *on a window seat dozing.*

JUDGE Oh! O lack! O lack! (*As in pain.*)

HAMPSHIRE Sir! Yaur I be, Sir! (*Hurried as just waking.*)

JUDGE Sir, here you are, Sir; who wants you, Sir? (*Angrily.*)

HAMPSHIRE I bin tink you bin call, Sir. (*Submissively.*)

JUDGE Call! Why I have been calling and bawling this half hour for you, but you are never in the way. – No, Sir, I may as well not own a Negro, as never to be able to get one near me – want him ever so much. (*Angrily.*)

HAMPSHIRE Oh! Massa! no bex, Sir, me quite sorry; me no yerry you; no bex, Sir. (*With tenderness, and goes to adjust the Judge's leg on the stool.*)

JUDGE Oh! oh, dear! oh, dear! – What are you at, sir? I didn't tell you to touch my foot; confound you! – He has done it on purpose! What do you mean, sir? (*Under great apprehension of pain.*)

HAMPSHIRE Oh! massa! me beg you pardon; me no mean for hurt you.

JUDGE Who said you did, sir? – I did not say you had hurt me. I told
   you go and call my sister, – but I may as well talk to the Moon! I
   am worried off my life with you!

HAMPSHIRE Tan massa – me go call she, sir. (*Going.*)

JUDGE Where are you going now, sirrah? – Do you mean me to sit
   here all day? You know I cannot stir without your help, and that
   is why you leave me. (*Pettishly.*)

HAMPSHIRE No, sir! danna you sen me faw call Miss Alice?

JUDGE No! I don't want her: I don't want any body! I'll care as little for them all as they do for me. There's Emily, too, cares no
   more for me than – than – than you do, sir! (*Pettishly.*)

HAMPSHIRE Oh! massa! Miss Emily no care for you? Cui!
   Hampshire no care for you? Ah! God know we heart! aye, and
   massa know, too!

JUDGE Know! I know nothing, sir! – confound this gout – oh! oh!
                              [*Rises from his seat and hobbles.*

Enter MISS ALICE

ALICE What now, Hampshire? What have you been about? Why
   your poor master is worried off his life with you. I never saw
   such a Negro! from morning till night you do nothing but tease
   my poor brother.

JUDGE Why, what has the poor man done now? you didn't hear me
   complain of him – poor fellow! If it wasn't for him I don't know
   what I should do. – I might sit down from morning till night,
   and never have a soul to speak to. – Hampshire!

HAMPSHIRE Sir!

JUDGE Where's Emily?

ALICE She's at the piano, according to custom – strum – strum. I
   am sure for the good of her company to me, she might as well
   have remained in England! It is nothing but strum, strum, all
   the morning; and then when the girl might be working me a
   frill, or making me a cap, or so, the rest of the day is wasted in
   drawing or *studying*, as she calls it. In truth, I don't know what's
   the good of your English education, not I, except it be to send a

girl back to her parents with her head filled with maps and globes, and French gibberish – her fingers with pianos and paint-brushes – and her feet with waltzes and quadrilles. For my part –

JUDGE Hold! I pray you, sister, hold! or you'll bring on a fresh fit of the gout. Hampshire, go call me Emily.

HAMPSHIRE Yes, sir. (*Running out.*)

JUDGE Hampshire! you Hampshire! where are you going?

HAMPSHIRE [*Returning.*] Me go call Miss Emily, sir.

JUDGE I don't want her, sir! – I didn't send you to call her. You only want to get away from me. It is as much as I can do to keep you a minute with me.

HAMPSHIRE Oh, massa, me no been go no way! I bin tink you been send me for call my nyung missy: – I no bin go no way.

ALICE Hampshire, how can you be so bold as to contradict my brother? How can you say you were not going away when there was such hallooing and bawling to bring you back?

JUDGE Bawling! – hallooing, and bawling? – There's for you! who has been bawling? who has said a word but yourself for this half hour? Why, I shan't be able to speak a word in my own house soon, without being set upon for hallooing and bawling.

ALICE Well, Mr. Errington, if this is the way you choose to treat me, merely for speaking to your favourite man there, because he was not paying proper attention to you, I must be content to sit down in one corner of your house, like a mere cypher. It is no wonder the negroes pay me no attention, when their master encourages them in their impudence to me!

JUDGE Insolent to you, eh? – How dare you, sir, be insolent to my sister? I'll break every bone in your skin, you scoundrel! (*strikes him.*) – You dare to be impudent to my sister, eh? (*strikes him again.*)

HAMPSHIRE I didn't bin rude to Miss Alice, sir. – I yent say nothing to she!

ALICE Brother! why brother! what is it you strike the man for? He hasn't done any thing to deserve it. – Poor fellow; it's a shame!

JUDGE Hampshire! What – what did I strike you for? You hav'nt offended me! you never offend me; you – you never offend any body! – why did I strike you? I am sorry for it. I am sorry that I struck you! Why will you make me strike you? (*With great agitation and sorrow.*)

HAMPSHIRE Oh Massa! no bex! It's no me make you trike me! It's no you bin trike Hampshire! Ums da dam sonting in you foot make you trike me! No bex! Massa!

JUDGE True, Hampshire! – true my good man! – you know I regard you – you know I would not harm a hair of your head. Here, here, carry my stick into the kitchen – order them to burn it – I'm too fond of using the cursed stick! Zounds! to think that I should strike Hampshire! Poor Hampshire! (*With feeling and regret.*)

HAMPSHIRE (*Refusing the stick*) – No! no, Massa! no burn um! bin-bye when you want for go walk, you want um again – No burn um, Massa!

JUDGE True, true, Hampshire! but keep out of the way when you see me angry – Keep out of the way when I'm in a passion.

ALICE And do you, brother, restrain your passion! Don't give way to so much ill temper! I'm sure if I were not the best temper in the world, there would be no living in the house among you all. (*Exit in a pet.*)

HAMPSHIRE Cui! Miss Alice good temper! Massa nago! (*Aside, with a half suppressed laugh.*)

JUDGE And if I were not the most patient and forbearing – damn this gout.   (*Throws down his stick and hobbles out.*)

HAMPSHIRE (*Taking up the stick*) – Oh, Massa, Judge! – Heart too good – hand too quick! For all you gee Hampshire hard knock some time, you very good to he!   (*Exit, following the Judge.*)

SCENE II – *Another apartment in Judge Errington's house; table and chairs therein.*

EMILY (*Sola.*) (*Sighing.*) I resort to every thing that I think of for amusement – but alas! all are equally tiresome. I have lost my taste for French, for with whom can I converse? My piano has no attraction – the music is all sad and monotonous, the same to-day as it was yesterday, and alas! will be the same again to-morrow – My very paints have lost their mellowness, and my pencils become as hard as bristles. (*Sighs.*) My aunt is so peevish – my father! my poor dear father, so worn out with the gout: – The solemn pledge given to my lost, ever dear mother. In short – But here comes my aunt – (*takes up a drawing from the table.*) My dear aunt, I was just coming in search of you.

Enter MISS ALICE

ALICE Were you indeed, Miss Errington? – I'm greatly honoured. I hope you have sufficiently amused yourself at your music and your studies. I suppose I am to consider it a great condescension you intended me? (*Sarcastically.*)

EMILY My dear aunt, I was in hopes that whilst I was at the piano, I was amusing you as well as myself, but when I found you had left the room, I then went to my drawing, to finish this sketch I had taken of the King's House. I have brought it to ask your opinion of it. (*Showing the drawing.*)

ALICE I am no judge of these refinements that you young ladies are now-a-days brought up to – in my time, girls were taught more useful occupations, by being made capable of managing the domestic affairs of a family – (*looking at the drawing*)— however, I think the picture is like enough to the place, too; and this, I suppose, – (*pointing to a part of the drawing*) is the General's Aid de Camp at the gate? Yes, sure, I thought the house would be nothing without the Aid de Camp! Did Captain Carlove sit for the likeness, my dear? (*Sarcastically.*)

EMILY I don't understand your insinuations, aunt, concerning Captain Carlove, but the figure you see there, is the sentinel on duty.

ALICE Insinuation! Let me tell you, Miss Errington, if you knew your duty, you would not insult your late mother's sister with such an expression. Insinuations, indeed! I tell you what, Miss! since it has come to this – blind as your father may be to the gallant Captain's frequent inquiries after *his* health, your aunt can plainly see that these calls are more intended to the heiress of *Hickford Plantation* than to its present old gouty owner. Tell me nothing, Miss, I'm not so dull as not to know how natural it was that a young officer, fellow-passenger for six weeks on ship board with a smart young lady fresh from a boarding-school, should exchange an occasional sigh, or reciprocate a tender sentiment, even three months after their arrival.

EMILY I do not know, aunt, what constructions you may choose to place on Captain Carlove's polite attentions to my father; but certainly you have had no opportunity of judging of that gentleman's attentions toward me, nor of my reception of them, for I have not seen him in either of his last three or four visits.

ALICE Yes, thanks to my regard for your late mother's wishes, and your father's property!

EMILY I am quite ignorant what connection there can be between my late excellent mother's wishes, or my father's property, and the visits of Captain Carlove.

ALICE No, indeed! not when you well know that it was her dying wish that you should marry your cousin! And I believe you will not deny that there are many captains who would have no objection to an heiress of eighteen, with such a plantation as Hickford's.

EMILY I do not know which afflicts me most! my late dear mother's inconsiderate wishes, or my aunt's illiberal insinuations (*aside*). I shall confide, my dear aunt, in my father's affections both as regards his disposal of myself, and of his property, whenever the time shall arrive for him to decide upon those measures.

ALICE And care not, I suppose, how soon he may give the gallant Captain the one, and your amiable self the other; but it shall not be my fault if the plantation goes out of the family. [*Exit.*

EMILY (*Sola.*) Well! And so my aunt's penetration has discovered what I have scarce yet dared to trust myself with a thought of – and I fear her prejudices will not be wanting to frustrate what

I must e'en confess I would hope were possible. My heart, certainly, is not insensible to Captain Carlove's attentions, nor can I persuade myself that I am indifferent to him; surely after his flattering assiduities during the whole passage, and his continued attentions since our arrival, I may be forgiven this vanity. Indeed, I am persuaded that a girl runs more risk of losing her heart in a voyage of six weeks across the Atlantic with an agreeable companion, than the merchant does of his ship either from piratical cruisers or equinoxial storms or winds.

Enter TOM APPLEBURY

TOM Storms and winds! why my pretty cousin, not yet got rid of your fears of equinoxial storms and winds? Why, I declare you are as pale as if you had just had a fresh attack of sea-sickness! Are you ill?

EMILY (*Hesitative and confused.*) Yes – no – at least – (*aside*) – I hope he has not overheard me! I am – I feel very ill. Excuse me, cousin Tom, I must – [*Exit.*

TOM What the devil ails the girl now! This is a touch beyond bashfulness. Faith I should have been better pleased, if when the old folks had been making up a match betwixt us, they had been contented to keep the girl in her native country, and taught her to mend stockings and hem cravats! The girl does not even know a guinea fowl from a turkey; and as to fattening stock or rearing pigs, she's as ignorant as a goose! All this comes of immuring a girl in an English boarding-school for eight or ten years, where her head has been filled with nothing but romantic sentiments and supercilious airs. (*Conceitedly.*) It might, perhaps, have done well enough to have given her a few months' polish t'other side the water when she had grown a little into womanhood; but to send a mere child to be kept in England only to forget the customs and manners of her own country! damme it's a humbug! Gad! look at me – see what three months in London has done for me! Bond-street for ever! Damme that's your sort! (*Struts affectedly.*)

Enter SAM SHADOCK

SAM Monstrous! Capital – capital, Tom! *Bow*-street for ever; eh! That's your sort!

TOM Pshaw! Bow-street! (*Contemptuously.*)

SAM True as a gun! I have been hunting for you, Tom, this half-hour, but I suppose you have been detained by my cousin; eh, Tom?

TOM My cousin! Yes, Sam; but I am, it seems, to metamorphose this fair cousin of mine into my wife; yet how or when, damme if I know, except I bring old Surplice in souce upon her, and tie the knot at once. I never can keep the girl five minutes together in conversation: yet, as my dear aunt, her late mother, and old square-toes, her father, had settled the matter between them that *we* should marry, – and with all, I have no objection to a smart girl with a fortune, – I'll slyly get the licence, and settle the hash at once. Eh, Sam?

SAM Monstrous! That's the way to clinch the nail, my boy! and, I say, Tom – when you've got spliced to your cousin, you may turn over – I say, Tom, you take! eh, you take?

TOM Thank you for nothing, good Sir! But come, let's have no more of this joking! If my cousin expects that when I take her to wife, I'm to be always dangling on her arm like a showy reticule; t'wont be the first mistake of her pretty innocence!

Enter MISS ALICE (*Hurriedly and angered.*)

ALICE I tell you what, Tom, this goings on won't do! I will acquaint your uncle of your conduct, that I will, sir! 'Tis shameful! – abominable, sir; you are not contented to play your pranks on the plantation, but you must bring your vices even into the very house with your uncle and aunt; and before the young woman, too, you are to marry! Shame on you, sir, I'll not bear with it! (*Enraged.*)

TOM (*Hypocritically.*) My dear Aunt, what do you mean? I scarce saw my cousin a minute; she complained of being ill! I did not say half a dozen words to her. I don't know what you mean!

ALICE (*With indignation.*) You know well enough, sir, what I mean: you know, sir, I am not speaking of your Cousin, but of your rude conduct to that innocent black girl, poor Hampshire's daughter!

Enter HAMPSHIRE, (*hurried and distressed.*)

HAMPSHIRE Oh, Mas Tom! Mas Tom! You want for bruck me heart? I sooner you da kill me pick'nee than you go make she bring shame upon me face this time o'day.

SAM Tom! I say, you've got it my boy! monstrous! eh!

TOM What the devil's all this? Aunt! Hampshire! what's all this? (*Affectedly and with surprise.*)

HAMPSHIRE Mas Tom, I beg you no go trouble me child! no trouble my poor pick'nee! (*Grieved and distressed.*)

ALICE What have you to say now, sir? Where is now your hypocritical wonder? What have you to say to this poor man? Because his skin is black, has he less affection for his child – less parental feeling? Thou graceless spark, your Uncle shall know of your conduct. Out upon you, sirrah!   [*Exit indignantly.*

TOM What the devil's piece of work have you been making here, you old scamp? What have I to do with your frizzle-head child? Do you think that I want to eat her, eh?

HAMPSHIRE No, you want for bring shame 'pon she. My poor child tan you, do Miss Alice work – wait upon nyung Missy; neber do wrong; and now you want for make she wicked! I no want my child for bring mulatto! Oh Mass Tom, Mass Tom! You bruck poor Hampshire's heart. (*Sobs.*)

TOM Devil take the fellow's snivelling! (*Aside.*) I tell you what, Master Hampshire, (*sneeringly.*) if my Aunt goes with any tales to my uncle about me, damme sir, I'll break your head!

SAM O, come along, Tom. Don't mind the old fellow! give him a dollar, and say no more about it.

HAMPSHIRE What! Gie me dollar! Gie me dollar! Wha you tink I make off! I no flesh and blood as well as you? No hab feeling? Ah, God Almighty, da'na top! God Almighty, da'na bottom! He no love ugly! Mass Tom, if you go trouble me child, so help me,

I tell Massa Judge, and make you little before Miss Emily. (*With great emphasis.*)

TOM You will, will you? Take that, you old scoundrel. (*Strikes him.*)

Enter JUDGE ERRINGTON

JUDGE What! what's this I see? (*Closing in great anger upon Tom.*) You dare to strike that man? What! strike my poor Hampshire! you young scoundrel! did you ever see me strike him! Sir, sir, I'll never forgive you for it! My poor Hampshire! what is the matter, Hampshire? (*Tom makes signs to Hampshire of apology, and not to betray him.*)

SAM Monstrous! it's time I should be off, lest I get into the scrape.   [*Exit.*

JUDGE Tell me, Hampshire, why has he used you thus?

HAMPSHIRE (*Tom all the while making signs of entreaty.*) Sir, I bin tell Mass Tom – I – I bin – I bin rude to he, sir – so – so he cuff me, sir. (*Hesitatingly and confused.*)

JUDGE And cuff't you! and cuff't you well, I hope! You rude to my Nephew, sir? You dare to be rude to my Nephew! Take that, sir. (*Strikes him.*)

TOM Yes, sir, I assure you, his insolence was beyond bearing; he provoked me without measure.

JUDGE You did, did you? Take that again, sirrah! (*Strikes him again.*)

HAMPSHIRE Law, law! what I go do? So poor negro get beat for nutting. What I go do? (*Greatly perplexed.*)

Enter MISS ALICE.

ALICE I am glad, Brother, that I have found you here! there's such goings on in the house; it is shameful; it is indecent! (*Tom makes signs of deep contrition and apology to his Aunt with earnest entreaty.*) I don't know what the neighbours will think of us all. Here's your nephew on the point of being married to your daughter, and – (*Tom continues by signs to entreat.*)

JUDGE Hey day! What now? What is the meaning of all this?

ALICE What? what indeed? you ought to be ashamed of yourself. From morning till night you're beating that poor man. His life is worried out of him, poor fellow! What with watching and waiting and attending upon you; what with cuffs, and blows, and abuse, the poor man is worn to a skeleton.

HAMPSHIRE (*With astonishment.*) Kelleton! Cui! me tan like kelleton! Me who hab belly full eb'ry day; hab plenty of bittle and drink; hab half dollar in my pocket ebery week; me tan like kelleton! Massa nago! You call me kelleton!

JUDGE Hampshire! speak, sir! Do I treat you ill? Do I abuse you, do I cuff and kick you?

HAMPSHIRE No, sir! Whau you call buse? whe'y I get bittle? whe'y I get money? whe'y I get jacket and trousers, if dan'na you give me? and you call that buse? Massa nago. (*Indignant and vexed.*)

JUDGE Bless my heart! Is it to be endured that I should be accused of ill treating this man, who, although he is my slave, I am under the greatest obligations to? Whose attentions to me deprive him of rest and of every recreation which negroes are fond of? Shall I! Bless my heart! (*With agitated feelings.*)

TOM True, sir; only look at the man! Does he look as if he was abused? My aunt said so, only to –

ALICE To what, sir? Eh! To what –?

Enter CAPTAIN CARLOVE.

(*The whole party are thrown into confusion and surprise.*)

CARLOVE Your pardon, Judge! My impatience has led me into the impoliteness of entering without being announced; and I fear I have intruded on your family circle!

JUDGE No, my good friend, always welcome! and welcome to make one among us.

CARLOVE That, sir, would be the greatest pleasure of –

ALICE Sir! Sir! Mr. Errington does not mean – Brother! do you know what you're saying? My brother only means, sir –

JUDGE Why zounds! – what should I mean? (*Then turning to Carlove.*) Captain, will you stay and take pot-luck with us today? You have been rather a stranger of late, and I feared you had given up your fellow-traveller as an old acquaintance.

ALICE There – there again! Did you ever see such a man! (*Aside.*)

CARLOVE It has been the happiest incident of my life that I had the honour of so amiable and interesting a companion of my voyage! – and –

JUDGE Well, well – you'll stay and take dinner with us, then?

CARLOVE Most willingly, had I not received the commands of the General to attend him to-day.

ALICE (*Aside.*) I'm glad of that! (*Then seeing Hampshire going out hurriedly to him.*) Hampshire! Where are you going, Hampshire? Do you mean to leave your master here without any body to wait upon him?

JUDGE Why, what have you to do with the man's going?

(*Exit Hampshire.*)

ALICE I know what he's going for. I see his art! (*Aside.*) Well, let him go, I don't hinder him.(*Pettishly.*)

CARLOVE Your niece, I hope, madam, has continued well since I last had the honour of seeing her?

ALICE Not very well, I believe, sir, as she confines herself much to her room – (*then seeing Emily and Hampshire entering*) – Didn't I say so! I knew his art!

Enter EMILY *and* HAMPSHIRE.

CARLOVE (*Respectfully approaching*) – I am ever happy to see Miss Errington! but doubly so at present, having been unprepared, by her aunt's report, to see her look so charmingly.

JUDGE Aye, yes. Emily looks well enough! – You see, Captain, she still wears the English bloom on her cheeks!

EMILY I am much indebted to Captain Carlove for his kind attentions, but have had no cause of late to complain of ill health, although my aunt's solicitude might have induced her to think me indisposed.

ALICE (*Pettishly.*) – Your aunt did not go about *reporting* that you were ill, Miss Errington. I only said I *supposed* you were not quite well, as you confined yourself so much.

JUDGE (*Aside.*) – Pooh, sister! Well, but Captain, when are we to make our long-promised visit to the plantation? The crop will be all got in except you make it soon.

CARLOVE Thank you, Judge! It shall be tomorrow, if agreeable to yourself, for I have made this call to arrange it with you, as I shall then be on leave.

JUDGE Aye, you military men are under as much subordination as our negroes; and yet you rail at slavery as if there was any difference in authority whether exercised over a red coat or a black skin.

CARLOVE But surely, sir, you can draw no analogy between the necessary discipline of an army of free men engaged in a loyal defence of their king and country, and the compulsory labour of the African, forced into slavery.

JUDGE There now! 'Tis that cursed *word* which raises every prejudice against us; for while by your military law you may give the soldier a thousand lashes – it is but *discipline*; if we inflict at the most, but thirty-nine on the slave – it is *cruelty and oppression.*

EMILY But is there not, my dear father, an otherwise too great power usurped over the slave that too often counteracts the natural benevolence of our hearts?

ALICE It is not very becoming of you, Miss Errington, to take part against your father! and I wonder how you'd get the plantation cultivated, if the manager hadn't authority over the Negroes?

JUDGE But my good sister, if his authority was not controlled by mine over him, how do we know what abuses might be committed? – for as manager, he has not that self interest in a temperate exercise of his power, which the right of property induces in me.

CARLOVE Nay, sir, – is there not a moral feeling of more influence than self-interest, that should restrain the abuse of our casual power? and which –

EMILY Actuates my father in the performance of every duty he owes to society and morals, as a man and a Christian!

JUDGE And how I perform those of a master, you will better judge when you visit the plantation, for if you will examine into the whole system of our management, you will find throughout, that though the slave may sometimes suffer from a wicked, or even, a passionate master – la, damn this gout! – he is by no means habitually ill used or systematically oppressed; but by his labour is rather a copartner with his owner in the product of the soil, than a debased bondsman.

CARLOVE We should, however, consider them, sir, as our humble partners in creation! and born, as the natural consequence of slavery, to an inheritance of labour, their morals should be founded in *industry*; for human wants are the first, and with the slave the only stimulants to exertion.

EMILY Industry will, no doubt, with them, be a powerful incentive to virtue; but unless we persevere in disseminating true principles of religion among them, I fear their morality will be but a selfish feeling.

JUDGE Yes, but progressive amendment is all that we can at present aim at; therefore, the first lesson that should be given them is – that disgrace is not in the *punishment* but in the *commission* of crime. This, however, I fear will now become more difficult to teach, since they have lately seen successful crime and daring profligacy favoured and flattered by the undue exercise of a false philanthropy!

EMILY There has, however, been given to the greater portion of the rising generation of their class, a moral elevation by religious instruction, that neither time nor accident, it is to be hoped, will deprive them of.

CARLOVE I accord most heartily in your sentiments. But, Judge, I fear if our discussion is further pursued it will lead into too wide a range for my present convenience; I must, therefore, however reluctantly, beg to take my leave.

JUDGE But you will keep in mind your engagement for to-morrow, and take any friends you please, along with you. *We* shall set off by times in the morning.

CARLOVE Until when, I bid you, ladies – Judge – adieu.   [*Exit.*

JUDGE What an example for Tom, if he would follow it – Emily, under your tuition, much may be effected.

ALICE (*Aside*) – Tom's not the pupil after her mind.

HAMPSHIRE Sur, 'ums dinner time.   [*Exeunt severally.*

SCENE III – *An apartment in the King's House. Enter* MAJOR CHIDER *and* CAPTAIN CARLOVE, *as in familiar conversation*.

CARLOVE True, my dear Major, but without women, society can be neither agreeable nor interesting.

CHIDER But there are some women, you must allow, whose conversation and manners are neither pleasing nor agreeable.

CARLOVE Granted! but my observation presupposes that their minds have been formed by morality and religion, and their manners cultivated and refined by education and society; otherwise we can only expect from them a tiresome prattle of mere words, and an insipid affectation of gentility.

CHIDER And those high qualities which form the chief merit of the sex, and you so much admire in them, not being to be found in your own country-women, you have crossed the Atlantic in quest of them among the ladies of Barbados? (*Sarcastically.*)

CARLOVE This observation, my dear Major, would seem to have some allusion to a particular object; but when I assure you that I have spoken only in reference to the whole sex, you will exonerate me, I trust, from all dissimulation.

CHIDER Not altogether, my dear Carlove; – and if I speak more explicitly on the subject, attribute it, I pray you, only to my anxiety for the feelings and wishes of a fond father, the venerable Dean! and as taking an interest in your own welfare.

CARLOVE I am, Major, so fully persuaded of your kind feelings towards my worthy father, and your warm friendship towards myself, that I should deem it unpardonable were I to dissemble with you; – and –

CHIDER You therefore admit that your late fair fellow-traveller has made such an impression on your sensibilities as may lead to a result that may ultimately disappoint the hopes of your friends?

CARLOVE Warmly interested, as I am free to confess, I have felt myself in Miss Errington's welfare, and attentive as I was to her every word and action throughout our voyage, not an expression, I assure you, has ever escaped my lips that could indicate any other sentiment than that of profound respect.

CHIDER Yet, Carlove, you will admit that she must be the veriest simpleton of her sex, if she is insensible how dear she must be to you, that this *'profound respect'* should be unremitted months after the voyage is over.

CARLOVE (*Taking Chider kindly by the arm, as if to interest his sympathy.*) – Major, I have, at times, indeed, thought that I had created an interest in her heart, – though perhaps, she herself, as I would fain hope, is unconscious of it, for there is an innocency and simplicity in all her thoughts and actions that seem to realize that purity of soul which we are taught to believe angels only possess.

CHIDER And this fair Barbadian, then you destine to be the guardian angel of your future fortunes! – Carlove! beware how you precipitately form an alliance that may blight the hopes of your venerable parent; or by basely trifling with the feelings and affections of an artless girl, dishonour the profession you have embraced! By the one you may break the heart of a father! by the other, for ever destroy the peace and happiness of an unsuspecting woman! – and in either case render yourself despicable and contemptible!

CARLOVE O, my kind friend! – think not so unworthily of me! Whatever may be my feelings and wishes towards this interesting girl, I stand pledged on my duty as a son, and on my honour as a soldier, not to adopt any measure without consulting you –

CHIDER And obtaining the consent of your father?

CARLOVE Decidedly.

CHIDER Then, Carlove, you shall introduce me to this young lady.

CARLOVE An occasion offers most opportune for it. To-morrow, I am to make an excursion to the family estate; and you, Major, shall accompany me. The Judge is a true personification of West India hospitality; and you will find his heart, like the doors of his mansion, ever open to receive a guest!

CHIDER Agreed!   [*Exeunt, Chider taking Carlove's arm.*

[END OF THE FIRST ACT]

ACT II

SCENE I – *An apartment in the Mansion-house, on the plantation. Enter* JUDGE ERRINGTON, EMILY, ALICE *and* SAM SHADOCK.

JUDGE (*To Sam.*) Where's your friend? Tom's a thoughtless boy. – You must excuse his leaving you thus, and make yourself at home among us.

SAM (*Bowing affectedly.*) Yes, sir – thank you sir, – quite at home, thank you sir! – (*then eying Emily*) – What a charming young woman! I wish I was her cousin!

JUDGE (*To Alice.*) Where's Tom?

ALICE Where, indeed! – where he ought not to be, I'll warrant you!

JUDGE Hampshire, I fear, has led our friends a tiresome jaunt – it is time they had returned: – but yet, I wish they should be fully gratified, by seeing the whole of the plantation.

ALICE See what they will, they, no doubt, will have fault enough to find.

JUDGE Don't let us be illiberal – while we expect honesty and truth from others, we should practice them ourselves.

ALICE Aye – here comes Squire Schanco, and the two Knights of St. Ann's; but, if I don't clip the wings of one of them, before this visit's over, it shall be no fault of mine. (*Aside.*)

Enter MAJOR CHIDER, CAPTAIN CARLOVE, *and* HAMPSHIRE; *Chider and Carlove bow to the ladies, then approach the Judge – Hampshire retires to the back scene.*

JUDGE Welcome, gentlemen, from your ramble – I hope your guide has gratified you without imposing too much fatigue. As a gouty subject, I claim an excuse for not having proceeded with you beyond the buildings.

CHIDER We are alike indebted to you for your hospitality and indulgence; and, I assure you, we found our guide both intelligent and kind, for while he has gratified our curiosity, he has been equally anxious for our comfort and ease.

JUDGE (*Taking each by the hand.*) Captain, you must show your friend here, how to be at ease amongst us; and I beg you will both make yourselves at home.

ALICE Aye, I warrant you they'll do that – and let that cock-sparrow alone, and he'll soon turn us all out of house and home: – but I'll keep a good eye on him! (*Aside.*)

CHIDER Thanks, worthy sir, for your kind indulgence.

CARLOVE And to the ladies, equally, for the courtesy of theirs.

JUDGE Your ramble, my friends, I hope, has whetted your appetites, for you made but a poor breakfast; – my good friend, the manager, with his usual attention to all my concerns, has set out a lunch for us in the adjoining room.

CARLOVE And it will form an agreeable prelude to the further gratification we expect in witnessing the festivity of your slaves – for I will remind you of your promise, Judge, that they should have a holiday making on the occasion of this visit. (*Distant sound of Negro music.*)

ALICE (*Pettishly.*) My brother needn't, I assure you, sir, be reminded of that: – and, as to holidays – it's nothing now but holiday with them half the year round.

JUDGE Aye, Captain, and they have been more alert in entering on their pastime, than we in witnessing it. Does not that sound of music warn you of it?

CARLOVE Then, the sooner we dispatch our lunch, the sooner shall we enjoy the happy scene.

JUDGE Emily, you shall lead the way. – Gentlemen, I'll follow. (*Chider gives Emily his arm.*)   [*Exeunt, except Alice.*

ALICE I'm glad of that! I wish I could make the young spark jealous of him, my poor sister's son might then get the girl, and *Hickford's* be kept in the family. But Tom's a sad lad – he's a sad lad!   [*Exit.*

SCENE II   *View of the works on a sugar estate; Negro cottages in the back-ground: – Negroes pass to and fro with animation and cheerfulness, on the back of the stage. Sound of Negro music increases; – great merriment and uproarious mirth heard behind the scenes, as among the Negroes: – groups of them, for a time, continue to pass to and fro – Tom occasionally mixes among them. A band of them, then halt on the back of the stage. Enter* JUDGE ERRINGTON, EMILY, MISS ALICE, CHIDER, CARLOVE *and* HAMPSHIRE. *Slaves come forward, and half encircle the party.*

Then together. God bless Massa! *Huzza!* God bless nyung Misse. *Huzza!* Good crops and good prices, that Massa may live as well as his Negroes! *Huzza!*

HAMPSHIRE (*Advancing.*) God bless Mass Captain and he Major! —(*all*) *Huzza!*

JUDGE Well thought on, Hampshire! Our friends are most welcome to our rural feast; and we freely give them our blessing.
>   *HAMPSHIRE advances further in front, and sings:—*
>> Massa Judge – Massa Judge! You very good to me!
>>> Tiddle dum, diddle dum, tiddle dee!   (*Chorus by all.*
>> Miss Emily, – Miss Emily, we all of we lub dee!
>>> Tiddle dum, &c. &c.
>> And we wish, – and we wish you happy married be!
>>> Tiddle dum, &c. &c.   (*Exeunt Negroes.*

CHIDER But Judge, where are your field slaves? – your working chain gangs?

JUDGE (*With surprise and asperity.*) Working chain gangs! What, sir, do you mean? – What chain gangs? Search throughout *Hickford's* – nay, sir, search throughout this calumniated land, and see if chain gangs exist but in the malevolence, falsehood and spleen of anti-slavery societies, and fanatical Quakers.

CARLOVE The Major, my dear Judge, has expressed to me, that he suspects all this gaiety and apparent happiness has been got up for this occasion; and he owns that he left England with impressions most unfavourable as to the condition of the slave; – but although much prejudice has already been removed, he is still sceptical as to the reality of that happiness he has everywhere witnessed among them, since his arrival.

JUDGE If the prejudices of the Major's mind have not too far perverted his understanding – let him, now that he has an opportunity of forming a fair opinion and an honest judgment, determine whether West India slaves do not possess more actual comfort and personal liberty than the unhappy, gagged, maimed and deformed white children of the factory mills of Leeds and Manchester; or the inhumed miners of Cumberland and Cornwall!

ALICE Yes! people will talk of things they know nothing about! – but then those that know the truth, should speak out! and I hope, sir, you'll be honest enough to do so after what you have seen.

CHIDER It were too trite an observation, Madam, merely to say that our own experience leads to a correcter judgment than the report or opinion of others of less information than ourselves; I will, therefore, now in honest candour confess, that I have been, like thousands of others, so deceived by the artifices and false philanthropy of Aldermanbury, as to be brought to believe that I should only see in West India slavery a race of half-starved, ill-clothed, miserable-looking, lacerated and degraded Africans.

ALICE Whoever this *Alderman Bury* is, tell him from me, sir, that our Negroes want none of his turtle or venison: – and that it were better that the wives and daughters of him and his whole fraternity of Aldermen, keep their tears and sympathy for, and give their, charity pence to, the miserable poor of Ireland, and the wretched objects at their own doors; and not to meddle with a people four thousand miles off, who would be contented and happy but for the mischief and false notions put into their heads! – Tell him that! – that from me, sir!   [*Exit.*

JUDGE You must, Major, forgive the warmth of my sister's feelings. – She's a true West Indian, and can never repress her indignation when speaking of the falsehoods and calumny heaped upon us by the enemies of the colonies!

CHIDER She stands justified, and needs no apology! I am a convert
to your cause! – Slavery, however, I yet must own, is a term
which bears no toleration in this liberal age, and must daily
grow of less repute.

EMILY But yet our persecutors at home should bear in mind that it
implies a very different state in different countries.

JUDGE And that here, in the West Indies – where it is confined to
one particular race of people, it scarcely bears the name of vas-
salage; while in England, though the very name of slavery is
held in detestation, its effects predominate through a system of
manufacturing competition that debases a large portion of the
population into brute animals, or mere machines.

CARLOVE We are taught, however, that we should 'love our
enemies!' If they be such, let us yet hope, that when they are better informed as to the real condition of slavery in the colonies,
they will become your friends – and embrace you as such!

JUDGE And that this may be speedy, we will toast in our first
bumper after dinner – for which we will now retire and prepare
ourselves.

CHIDER And as the day is already fast closing in, we will beg your
permission to depart as soon as it is over; our duty requiring that
we return to the garrison to-night.

JUDGE Be it so – for the greater freedom with which you may
depart, the more cheerfully you will return.   [*Exeunt.*

SCENE III – *An apartment in the Judge's house (same as
opening scene of 1st Act.) Enter two Negro men, one with a
portmanteau and a bundle of sugar canes, the other with a trav-
elling bag and a small jar of new sugar: – they obliquely cross
the stage to the upper wing, where they deposit their articles.*

1ST NEGRO Old Massa travel home last night so late, he'll well cry
for he foot bumby.

2ND NEGRO Pshaw! um's no travel late gee he gout, um's the old
wine he drink, and da sunting dey call Sampain.

1ST NEGRO Ah, ah! Den he'll hab um well – dem officer baccara make he soak um nuff, na'sa he no bring nyung misse home in de moonshine.

2ND NEGRO Aye! And buddo Hampshire will feel he tick soon as he begin hollow fau he foot. Come, come along!   [*Exeunt.*

Enter JUDGE ERRINGTON (*fatigued*) *followed by Hampshire.*

JUDGE My sister's right – there's no good, now a-days in sending these young fellows to England for education. We send them to study men and manners, and they return with a knowledge only of –

HAMPSHIRE Women, Massa!

JUDGE True, sirrah! – yet strangers to the deep and lasting sentiment of the heart, which a virtuous woman ought ever to inspire!

HAMPSHIRE Mass Tom too fond of we colour! um's Mass Captain know how for love Miss Emily!

JUDGE (*With amazement and agitation.*) – Who! eh, love who? – love Emily? – (*with increased agitation.*) Where's my sister? Where's Tom? Where's Emily? What's this I hear! Treason! rebellion! insurrection! I'm betrayed, deceived – I'm – I'm – eh! eh! – (*agitated and confused.*)

Enter MISS ALICE, EMILY, *and servants*

HAMPSHIRE I didn't been say so nyung Missy! I no say so, Massa – I yent been say so, Miss Alice – Faite! Miss Emily, I no been say so. (*In great anxiety and distress, alternately addressing each.*)

ALICE I knew it was you – you devil's bird, that had been worrying your master. What is the matter, brother? What has this man been doing? What is the cause of all this hubbub and to do?

EMILY My father! my dearest father! (*Approaching him with great anxiety and tenderness.*)

JUDGE (*Sternly repulsing her*)– So, Miss! – So, Miss Errington!

EMILY My father! – Miss Errington? oh! my father! am I not your Emily? your own dear Emily! your beloved daughter! – In what have I offended? (*With great agitation and distress.*)

JUDGE My plague; – my torment; – my – my – (*With indignation.*)

EMILY Your dutiful and affectionate child! – your loving and obedient daughter – and when I forfeit that character, O, may I forfeit the love and esteem of –

JUDGE Capt. Carlove! Yes, it is thus you shew your duty – your affection – your love – your obedience to a fond, foolish, dotard of a father! It is thus you acquiesce in the last dying wishes of a tender mother! It is thus you requite all my anxious care! Oh! my heart! it will burst! – my head – my feet – my gout – my gout! oh! – (*Hurriedly and distractedly.*)

ALICE There, there Miss! – see what all your fine doings have brought your poor father to! And as to you (*seizing hold of Hampshire and shaking him*) – you shall be hanged!

EMILY My father! oh, my – (*Fainting, falls on Hampshire's shoulder.*)

HAMPSHIRE Help – help! O, la! O, la! Help!

ALICE Help – help! – She's dying! (*Both greatly agitated and alarmed; the Judge in distracted anxiety.*)

JUDGE My daughter! my child! my Emily! my own dear Emily! (*With affectionate tenderness.*)

EMILY (*Reviving.*) Where am I? – where's my father? – did I not hear him call his Emily? – his own dear – (*Throws herself on her father's bosom; he embraces her tenderly.*)

JUDGE Emily! – O, my child! why have you deceived me? why dealt treacherously with me?

EMILY No, no, my father! Never! – never! (*With great emotion.*)

JUDGE What! have you not clandestinely received the addresses of Captain Carlove? Has not his tinseled shoulder-knots – his red coat – his military air, estranged your affections from the object I would have you place them on, and seduced you from the duty you owe a father's wishes?

EMILY By all the tenderest affections of a dutiful daughter, I have in no instance, as far as I have been able to control the impulses of my heart, violated your commands, or my lost lov'd mother's wishes! and I am at this moment as free and ready to yield to your commands as ever.

ALICE Aye, but have you not encouraged the young fop to make love to you? – Answer that! – Hav'nt you? (*With vehemence.*)

JUDGE Sic boy – sic boy! (*clapping his hands as if setting on a dog*) that's always your way! But it is to *me*, that she's to answer.

ALICE Yes! – and answer for *yourself*! – Hav'nt *you* encouraged the young coxcomb to come after her, by inviting him to your house, and welcoming him to make one of your family?

JUDGE What? – who? – me? – I, I, – (*Distractedly.*)

EMILY Do not agitate yourself, my dearest parent! You shall find me ever obedient to your will! Ever ready to meet your wishes!

JUDGE Come then, my child! we will retire; and when you are more composed, I will reason with you, and shall expect that obedience you have promised.

EMILY And you shall find me ever ready to confirm it.

[*Exeunt Judge and Emily.*

ALICE (*To Hampshire*) You! 'tis, 'tis you – you –(*Menacingly.*)

Enter TOM APPLEBURY.

TOM What's all this kickup about, dear aunt? I suppose this black scamp has again been worrying my poor dear uncle. – What with the Negroes and the gout, he is worried off his life! (*Hypocritically.*)

ALICE You scape grace! – It is you – you dissipated, incorrigible young rake, that causes all your uncle's unhappiness: – that disgraces his family, and makes every virtuous female in the house blush at your conduct. (*With asperity.*)

TOM Dear aunt, what have I done? The moment I heard that my uncle was ill I hastened to see what was the matter; and that I might not delay a moment in my affectionate duty to him, I left all my books and papers in disorder and confusion.

HAMPSHIRE Hey! – Book and paper! Lau, mas Tom! where you get book and paper in nego-house? You know dis minute –

TOM You old scamp! 'Tis you makes all the mischief in the family. (*Strikes him.*)

ALICE And you, sirrah! what is it you make of the family? Are you not suffering your cousin to slip through your fingers, and the plantation to go out of the family!

TOM My cousin to slip through my fingers! – The plantation to go out of the family! – What does all this mean? (*With surprise and deliberation.*) A'nt I ready to marry my cousin as soon as my uncle pleases, and won't *Hickford's* then belong to me?

ALICE Marry your cousin! And *Hickford's* belong to you! (*With indignation.*) Ask the gallant Captain that! and see if he has not set up a claim to both, that will baulk your pretensions, and disappoint the plans of the family!

TOM What! who! – Captain Carlove! – I'll call him out! By the powers, I'll call him out! I'll shoot him! – If he has a hundred lives I'd kill him!

HAMPSHIRE Ha ta'ca tho' he don't shoot you! You better no go play fool wid he! – He know how for shoot, as well as you. (*Sarcastically.*)

ALICE You old traitor! It is you that carry on the intrigue between them.

TOM You scamp – you snake in the grass! I'll – I'll send you to the treadmill. I'll ship you off! I'll hang you.(*They both beset him – he shifts about to escape them.*)

Enter SAM SHADOCK

SAM Good sport this! At him again. (*Joins in besetting Hampshire, who continues to shift about to avoid them. Then exit, followed by Alice*)

TOM Sam! you're the very man I want! I've a damn'd job upon my hands! – An affair of 'onor!

SAM Of horror! Why, what the devil ails you? – The night mare, I suppose.

TOM Tut! No! – no nonsense, man; – an affair of *honor*! I must pink that red breasted robin; or, by the powers he'll march off with my cousin; and I shall lose not only a pretty girl, but a fine estate into the bargain.

SAM What! is the girl smitten with him! – No wonder though, for he's a fine dashy fellow!

TOM But dash me, if I don't make him meat for worms before he shall have her! You must therefore get me pistols, and carry him a challenge.

SAM That's your sort, my boy! never flinch – I'm up to the thing – and mind me, – six paces! – bang! bang! – sure to hit him: – Down he falls – kicks up his heels, and – dam'me, we are off! I'll fetch you pistols in a minute.   [*Exit.*

TOM (*Solus, musing*) Why, as to the matter of that – I don't much care about fighting for the girl! – but then, indeed, my aunt seems to expect that I should! – umph! as old Hampshire says, he can shoot as well as I – and dang it, I shouldn't like to be shot – killed outright! Why, what then would be the good of the plantation? But, damn it, I'm no coward! – I'm a true Barbadian! – and there never yet was one drop of coward's blood in a Barbadian's veins. I'll take the consequences – and damn me, I'll shoot him – if I can!

Enter SAM *with pistols.*

SAM That's your sort! – hair triggers! – flash a single grain in the pan! – never miss! Whiz! (*Presenting one, as if discharging it.*)

TOM Let me see! (*Takes one of the pistols, makes six paces counting*) – one, two, three, four, five, six! (*briskly turns round and levels the pistol towards Sam, who, in great apprehension, dodges.*)

SAM No, damn it, man! No, none of that fun! It might go off, and then I should cut a pretty figure, to be sure, with my brains blown out!

Enter MISS ALICE, *agitated, followed by Hampshire.*

ALICE. (*Shrieks.*) Murder! – suicide! – assassination! (*Lays hold of the pistols, takes them away, and gives them to Hampshire; then seizes hold of Tom with one hand, and Sam with the other, shakes them, and alternately addresses each.*) Graceless birds – wicked murderers – cut-throats – vile wretches! – you–you – oh! (*Agitated and breathless – the young men looking in consternation at each other.*)

TOM Aunt! – my dear aunt!

SAM O, pray, Ma'm, do not be so alarmed!

TOM We were only in fun – no harm was meant – not a –

ALICE Not a what, sirrah! Weren't you plotting to shoot Captain Carlove? Hasn't this man, whom you all so barbarously use, overheard all? Yes, this poor, good, worthy man, has saved you both from being *hanged!* And you, you good-for-nothing chap! you brought the pistols! – but I'll pistol you! (*Seizes one from Hampshire, and falls on Sam with the butt end; he shifts about to escape, and then exit.*)

TOM My dearest aunt, you put me up to it! Didn't you tell me I should lose the plantation, if I did not shoot the Captain?

ALICE Me! – I tell you to shoot the Captain? You dare to say, that I told you to commit murder! O, you graceless puppy – you good-for-nothing –! I tell you to commit murder? I–I – Oh! (*Faints, Hampshire supports her.*)

HAMPSHIRE O, law! O, law! – Poor Miss Alice! help, help! Mass Tom!

TOM (*In great agitation.*) Aunt! dear aunt! – dearest aunt! We are all safe. I never said so – the pistols won't go off – not a grain of powder in them! I beg your pardon – I didn't say so. (*Greatly confused.*)

HAMPSHIRE Top, top, Mass Tom – she draw she breat!

ALICE (*Recovering.*) Hampshire! where's my brother? (*To Tom*) You scape-grace! Your uncle shall know of your conduct. He shall prosecute you, sir, for scandalizing me! That he shall! [*Exit, leaning on Hampshire.*

TOM Out of one hobble into another! Why, what a pretty mess I've got into now? But marry Emily I will, in spite of the Devil and Doctor Faustus! [*Exit.*

SCENE IV – *An apartment in Captain Carlove's quarters. Carlove seated as if in thought – seems agitated; – rises and takes a turn across the stage.*

CARLOVE It cannot possibly be a crime to reverence virtue! to esteem merit! to admire beauty! He who is insensible to beauty will ever form false conceptions of virtue! No, charming Emily! though your beauty may have dazzled my eyes; may have misled my heart, it never, alone, could have won my affections! It is that inestimable union of tender sensibility and sweetness of disposition – of justness of feeling and purity of soul; – it is, in a word, those charms of your mind, more than those of your person, which I adore! – which have enslaved me!

Enter MAJOR CHIDER

CHIDER What, Carlove, ruminating on the charms of your fair enslaver! I see a thousand little Cupids flitting across the room, while one sly archer sits on your brow triumphing in the shaft with which he has pierced your heart.

CARLOVE Major, I was calling to mind the hospitality which has so recently been lavished on us.

CHIDER And, consequently, Miss Errington was a prominent feature in your reminiscence. But tell me, Carlove, has the magic smile gently sleeping in her dimpled cheek, estranged your thoughts from your father's house, and love altogether usurped the place of duty?

CARLOVE Fear not, Major, for the duty I owe my revered parent! He who fails where nature should have her surest sway, will never know how to love his mistress truly! and I hold it a sure maxim that an undutiful son can never make an affectionate husband! So now, tell me what think ye of the lady?

CHIDER Now to make him jealous. (*Aside.*) Why, Carlove, I am rather too far advanced in life to fall into raptures with a face however soft and lovely; – or a form, however fair and delicate; – but I own to you, that since seeing this charming girl, some emotions have revived in my heart that had long lain dormant there, and on this occasion, my own susceptibility palliates yours.

CARLOVE (*Aside.*) Revived emotions! his own susceptibility! sure I shall not find a rival in my Mentor? (*With emotion.*)

CHIDER But are you not precipitate in speaking of the affections of a husband? – Or, perhaps you are already affianced, contrary to the double promise you are under to your father and myself?

CARLOVE I have broken no pledge, Major, to either! for whatever my feelings may have involuntarily betrayed to the charming girl, my tongue has not falsified the pledge given to my parent or yourself!

CHIDER But then, you think the lady has caught the sympathies of your heart, and is ready to make a free exchange with you, whenever you shall condescend to propose it?

CARLOVE Not so vain or presumptuous; – nor do I think so lightly of the lady! – and indeed, Major, I apprehend some obstacles that threaten embarrassment to her, and vexation – if not disappointment, to myself!

CHIDER Aye, aye, he grows suspicious of me.— I'll rouse his fears. (*Aside.*) Carlove, I purpose extending my ride as far as *Hickford's* to pay my respects to the family. – I am sorry your duty of the day must prevent your accompanying me.

CARLOVE You avail yourself of an opportunity for this visit *mal à propos* to my convenience; and perhaps –

CHIDER There is design in it, you would say, – and in truth, my purpose is to go alone. Can I take any message for you? – or haply I may be the bearer of one to you!

CARLOVE I have no commission for you – nor have I reason to expect any communication from the family.

CHIDER I leave you then to your occupations, and take my leave. [*Exit.*

CARLOVE (*Solus.*) Chider, surely, has formed no pretensions inimical to my views? O, it were folly – madness! alike in him to meditate such treachery, as in me to fear it! – Away with the thought! And yet I chuckle in my heart at his disappointment in his ride, for the family all returned to town last might, as soon as we left. A pleasant journey to you, Major! – ha! ha! ha! (*Going, then returns.*) 'Tis but a maniac's laugh! I am embarrassed – perplexed – distressed alike by the slipperiness of hope, and the agonies of fear! – and yet, a few, but a few days more, and the packet now due, must bring me that parental sanction without which my union could not be blessed! – without which, not even with you, charming Emily, could I be happy!   [*Exit.*

[END OF THE SECOND ACT]

ACT III

SCENE I – *An apartment in Errington's house; a table, with drawing apparatus, music books, and Ladies' ornamental work; Emily seated, thoughtful and dejected. Rises and comes forward.*

EMILY I am surely blest with the kindest of fathers! – How then could I ever reconcile to myself to disappoint his wishes? – It must not be! – duty forbids it, and the consciousness of a right performance of our duty is ever attended with peace of mind! Yes, my father! your parental solicitude hath even supplied the loss of maternal tenderness! – Ah, alas! – that mother! – young as I was when deprived of her, I shall yet ever cherish her memory with gratitude and love! and it is my firm purpose to yield obedience to her last wishes – her dying request, no matter how great the sacrifice! Resignation is a duty! – but 'tis not happiness! Happiness! – alas! what happiness can I hope for with a man between whom and myself there is not one reciprocal sentiment, – one solitary feeling of a congenial mind! (*Sighs deeply.*)

Enter ERRINGTON *and* HAMPSHIRE.

JUDGE Emily! (*Kindly taking her by the hand.*) Emily! I shall never be at peace – shall never have comfort while racked with doubt and mistrust as to the fulfilment of that solemn pledge given your mother – in which we are *both* equally bound! Do not – oh! do not deceive me! If you have been estranged from your duty – if your heart has been ensnared from its allegiance, confess the fatal truth! Tell me – tell me truly! – has not Captain Carlove made a declaration of love to you?

EMILY By every hope of happiness – alas! not in this world! – (*aside*) – by every duty I owe my lost mother's memory! – by every obedience due to your parental affection! – he has never avowed by his lips, a sentiment that would justify my regarding him as a lover!

JUDGE Nor given you reason to suppose he had such pretensions?

EMILY It were an unworthy evasion to say he had not! – Yes, though his lips have been silent, he has spoken by an organ more eloquent than words! – his eyes indeed have avowed the sentiments of his heart!

JUDGE And yours have as feelingly responded! – Yet you would have me believe you are prepared to fulfil your solemn promise respecting Tom!

EMILY Most ready! — though it break my heart! (*Aside.*) All obedience to your will—though I sacrifice my peace, and destroy every hope! (*Aside.*)

JUDGE Believe me, my daughter, it only requires an exertion of the will to place your affections where your duty should guide them. Tom, it is true, is a wild, thoughtless boy; but his errors are of the head, not of the heart; and, by your good sense and tenderness, they may easily be eradicated!

EMILY It is a task a solemn promise has imposed on me, and I am ready to undertake it. Dispose of me when you please – my hand is ready — my heart, alas! never.(*Aside.*)

JUDGE Emily! the kindred tie already subsisting between you and Tom, will, when drawn closer by the sacred bond of marriage, ripen into tenderness and love. You must now prepare yourself for those duties. – The first step towards it will be to banish Captain Carlove from your mind; – the next, to meet Tom with conciliation, and treat him with kindness. (It is now that I must press her to the measure.) (*Aside.*) I will send him to you – remember my injunctions!   [*Exit*

HAMPSHIRE Oh! Missy Emily! – me heart bun for you! Nyung Missy – no bex with Hampshire! Keep heart! keep heart, nyung Missy! – Hampshire go do sunting for you yet!

EMILY (*Taking his hand.*) Bless you, my good man! Go, attend on my father! Be assured, Hampshire! I shall ever esteem you – thou good and worthy man!

(*Hampshire with great reverence kisses her hand; she offers him a purse: he presses it back upon her, then clasping his hands together in a great agony – Exit.*)

EMILY (*Sola.*) Oh! that my father should be so blind to his daughter's peace! – to his nephew's dissipated habits! But –

Enter TOM APPLEBURY.

TOM My dearest cousin. I come at my uncle's bidding – on the wings of love, to throw myself at your feet. (*Kneels.*)

EMILY Pray rise, sir – that is a posture to which I fear you seldom humble yourself, where it were most becoming you should. (*With dignity.*)

TOM. Law! – it isn't the fashion to kneel at Church. It is to you the adorable goddess of my affections, to whom I pay my devotions – and thus – and thus – (*seizing her hand and kissing it*) – vow eternal love!

EMILY Mr. Applebury, whatever regard you may affect to feel for me, I beg you will preserve more decorum in expressing it. (*With sternness.*)

TOM (*Rising discomfited*) My dear cousin, my aunt, and uncle have both accused me of neglecting you – of not paying you proper attention; and now that I am endeavouring to prove to you the warmth of my affection – how ardently I love you – how enraptured I am at the thought of our approaching union, you huff at me, and are as cross and ill-natured as though – but I'll have a kiss for all that! (*Seizes her round the waist and attempts to kiss her.*)

EMILY (*Shrieks.*) Oh! where is my mother's gentle spirit! – my father's tenderness and love! to rescue their unhappy daughter from the degrading embrace of a libertine! (*With great indignation and emotion.*)

TOM As to your calling names, Miss, there's no great politeness in that! (*Resentfully.*) If I wore a red coat and golden epaulets, you'd then find some kinder terms to apply to me. Yes, I should then be a charming fellow! – a dear sweet man! But stay – let me become your husband, and then – then bestow your insulting epithets! (*Menacingly.*)

EMILY Husband! (*With great agitation.*) Methinks I already feel the weight of his harsh resentment, and fierce indignation! But if it must be so – (*With emotion.*)

TOM Yes, and so it shall speedily be! Here comes one, who will settle that point with you – I'll warrant it she'll know how to manage you!

Enter MISS ALICE.

EMILY (*Greatly agitated.*) My aunt! – Oh! shield me – succour your poor unhappy – (*Throws herself in great agony upon her aunt's neck.*)

ALICE Emily! My dearest girl! why this agitation? – For Heaven's sake, say what has so affected you? – My dear niece! – Emily! (*With great anxiety and concern.*)

EMILY (*Deeply sighing, attempts to raise her head, then falls again on her aunt.*) Oh!

TOM O' she's got the 'tericks! – My aunt seems affected; I must get off. (*Aside.*) I'll run for some lavender.   [*Exit.*

ALICE Come, my dearest girl! – exert yourself! I hope there has been no dispute between you and your cousin? – Tom is too impetuous – but surely he has offered you no insult?

EMILY (*Recovering.*) Oh! If it be possible? – Is there no way? – must I be thus sacrificed? – Oh! my aunt, can I not? – Ah! blest spirit of my mother! Can I not be absolved from this fatal – (*Sighing deeply.*)

ALICE Yes! I knew it would come to this! Yes, I knew that all your fine promises and solemn vows, were mere words – as false as the winds! (*Disdainfully.*)

EMILY (*Exerting herself.*) I am greatly to blame! – And yet, O, my aunt! spurn me not from you! – my offence shall be expiated – and the will of my parents fulfilled! Yes, my aunt, you shall see with what firmness – with what constancy of mind, your niece can embrace the martyrdom of duty! (*With assumed firmness and dignity.*)

ALICE Martyrdom, indeed! I'd have you remember, that Tom is of the same family – the same flesh and blood as yourself! That it was *his* as well as *your* grandfather's-great-grandfather's-grandfather, old *General Fustick*, that was once *President of the Island!* – and if you mean to make this great martyrdom (or whatever you please to call it) let it be done at once, for your father, as well as myself, is anxious to have it settled; and he has desired me to make arrangements with you for the wedding. He sends you this order on his Town Agent for £300, that you may buy what finery you want for the occasion – (*presenting the order.*)

EMILY Thank my father for his liberality – but take it back to him. I need no finery; – I need no preparation! All that is necessary – all that is *possible* is already made in a sickened and distracted heart! (*Sighing deeply and dejected.*)

ALICE There are some articles in the drawing room come from the Emporium, that are very beautiful, and of the newest fashion – if you choose to look at them? (*Sneeringly, then in a softened tone of conciliation.*) Come, Emily, don't give way to such unkind feelings towards Tom! – remember, child, he is your cousin! You shall choose me a dress! – you know I always like your choice. Come, that's a good girl! (*Drawing Emily gently after her.*)   [*Exeunt.*

Enter JUDGE ERRINGTON, *his hand kindly resting on* HAMPSHIRE'S *shoulder, and as in conversation with him.*

JUDGE And how long, Hampshire, has this graceless nephew of mine been carrying on these intrigues?

HAMPSHIRE Ebba since, Massa! He been want fa ruin my poor pick'nee, too; and dat make me go hurry she marriage with Jack Ranger! – you memba I been beg you give'um leave, and you gee'um doubloon, too!

JUDGE Does my sister know any thing of this conduct of his?

HAMPSHIRE Yes, sir! – Miss Alice know all 'bout 'um. I been tell she about my poor child; and she make Mass Tom shame, and threaten for 'tell you; – so he let she 'lone, and—

JUDGE And this is the youth that my sister – that I – would have sacrificed my child, my beloved daughter, to! Oh! Eternal Power, how shall I express my gratitude! – my thanks for this timely rescue of my child! How, O, how can I sufficiently reward you, my faithful Hampshire? You have exhibited to me a scene of depravity that will ever disgrace the morals of our society! What and *my* nephew, too! Oh! I feel contaminated by such a foul consanguinity! – and my poor daughter! – Gracious Heavens! (*Greatly agitated starts as with horror.*)

HAMPSHIRE Don't fret, Massa! No bex! – lay we go to Miss Emily! she too grief fa tink she be going fa marry Mass Tom!

JUDGE When I reflect on the mean physiognomy of the wretch in whose embraces he has been revelling – her black and fuzzy poll – her squat nose – her murky greasy skin – her clumsy short figure – and the leading expression in her countenance of insolent boldness, I am driven almost to distraction. (*With emotion.*)

HAMPSHIRE Ah, no matter, Massa! Tho' we be black the same God who been make you – make we, too! (*With suppressed anger.*)

JUDGE. True, Hampshire! – forgive me! I have spoken under the impulse of irritated feelings, not with a malevolent heart! We are all children of one common parent; and if man be created in God's own image, he is not the less so, whether carved in ivory, ebony, or sandal wood. We will go, Hampshire, to my child. She must not, like Jephtha's daughter be sacrificed to a rash vow.

HAMPSHIRE O, Massa Judge! you make me too glad! Lau, lau! me heart begin fa dance aready! (*In ecstasy.*)   [*Exeunt*

SCENE II – *Scene changes to a room in Captain Carlove's quarters; Carlove with a pen in his hand, seated and thoughtful over military papers before him, rises as under great perplexity.*

CARLOVE 'Tis unaccountably strange! At the very time I am most anxious – most interested, to hear from my venerable parent that there should be no letter for me! – Surely there has been no treachery! – How else can I account for his silence? He would know – he would feel my anxiety! – that my peace – my happiness – my very being, depended, upon his will; and that I was waiting his mandate with a lover's fears and a son's obedience.

Enter MAJOR CHIDER.

CHIDER Carlove! I have committed a breach of one duty to perform another. I have left the garrison orders uncopied that I might the sooner place this original into your hands. (*Presenting him with a letter.*)

CARLOVE Major! (*With eagerness and anxiety turning the letter over.*) 'Tis from my father, – but directed to you! Shall I – may – may I read its contents? (*Reads with great agitation; then turns to Chider.*) Major! your friendship has ever demanded my warmest acknowledgements; but this instance of it! – the interest I find, by my father's letter, you have taken in promoting my happiness by inducing his concurrence to my union, lays me under an obligation never to be obliterated.

CHIDER Does he – does your father, by that letter, sanction your union? How have I read it – how have I understood it? (*Sarcastically.*)

CARLOVE Eh! – No, no, Major! – but he has done more! Relying on your discrimination and judgement – on your discretion and prudence, he has delegated the parental authority to you; and I have no misgivings – no distrust of your warm approval and ready sanction to my union.

CHIDER But suppose, Carlove, I have formed some pretensions to the lady's heart! you would not surely desire that I should be accessary to my own overthrow?

CARLOVE Eh. – No, oh, no! – why – yes! Well, ah! – (*Confused and agitated.*)

CHIDER Then as you have so warmly acknowledged my friendship to you in your pretensions to the lady – you will, I have no doubt, aid mine in the same pursuit! Therefore, I confide to you this letter, expecting you will deliver it immediately! (*Offers another letter.*)

CARLOVE Hem! – What, eh? – well! (*Hesitating and distrustful; looks astonished; then tremblingly receives the letter; turns it over in great agitation; but at length reads the superscription.*) 'To the Hon. Judge Errington; to be personally delivered by Captain Carlove.' – Do my eyes deceive me? 'Tis my father's writing! – Eh! Major! – Excuse me, Major! – Good morning! – Good morning! Major, adieu! – I pray you. – (*Exit in great agitation and hurry, but hastily returns.*) This letter is unsealed! – Were it not as well that I peruse its contents. Pray advise – what think you?

CHIDER It most probably was your father's purpose in leaving it unsealed, that you should – and I think –

CARLOVE That I may! – Yes, yes! (*Hurriedly and confused, with great agitation opens the letter, reads as to himself, and occasionally repeats aloud broken sentences and words.*) In obedience to an exacted promise – upon leaving me – delay a declaration of his – my concurrence – persuaded – her highly-cultivated – accomplished – chaste mind – influenced by religion – his admiration – and – (*he here betrays increased agitation*) – cordial sanction to his union! (*Kisses the letter; tremblingly folds it and places it in his bosom.*) Major! my dear Major! (*With exhausted feelings.*)

CHIDER It were as well, Carlove, that you be more collected, and soften down this phrenzy of your heart by the influence of your better reason, before you deliver that letter. Having never made a declaration of your passion, what grounds have you, (besides the enthusiasm of your imagination,) to expect that the lady entertains a reciprocity of sentiment; or that her parent will acquiesce in your views?

CARLOVE Eh! – I am bewildered! – Major, do you think that her heart is so insensibly cold as not to have caught one spark from the glowing flame she herself has kindled? – or, that it is possi-

ble, after all the courtesies of her father, that he has not pene-
trated my secret? Intoxicated with my passion, I have yet
waited this happy moment of my father's consent with the most
anxious forbearance; and now that the cup of joy is at my lips,
you would, Major, dash it from my hand!

CHIDER No, Carlove! I would rather assist to guide the cup with a
steady hand, lest in the intoxication of your heart you let it fall,
and all your hopes be dashed to the ground! Be more tranquil –
we will finish our official duties and then advise upon the course
most prudent to pursue.   [*Exeunt.*

SCENE III – *Drawing-room in Errington's house; Emily seated
on a sofa, her head resting dejectedly on the elbow of it; Miss
Alice in a chair near the opposite end of the sofa, with various
articles of finery on it, and band-boxes before her, from which
she occasionally draws other articles of female finery.*

ALICE 'Tis provoking! – Indeed, it is very unmannerly! – She will
neither give me an answer, nor even look at the things! (*Taking
up a fresh article and admiring it.*) Well! this is beautiful! – I
think I should look well in a dress of it – 'tis so genteel! – and
would just do for the occasion.

EMILY (*Drawing a deep and melancholy sigh.*) Ah!

Enter ERRINGTON *and* HAMPSHIRE. *The Judge approaches his
daughter with great tenderness – pauses, and looking agonised
at her, strikes his forehead; he is unperceived by her, and she
again sighs.*

JUDGE 'Tis but the wreck of my child! Alas! how altered! she trembles! – Emily! my child! my daughter! 'Tis your father speaks.
(*Tenderly placing his hand on her.*)

EMILY (*Gently raising her head, and recognising her father, hastily
rises from the chair, and throws herself on his bosom.*) Oh! my –

HAMPSHIRE Poor ting! – Take heart, take heart, nyung Missy! –
(*piteously.*)

JUDGE Away with all that frippery! – My child shall not be mocked with such trappings of folly and extravagance. – Emily! speak to your father! Be comforted, my child! There is no cause for this wretchedness and despair!

EMILY (*Raising herself.*) Is there no cause? Oh, is there not surely an excess of wretchedness in an unhappy marriage that transcends all other misery on earth.

JUDGE My daughter! no such marriage awaits you. Banish from your thoughts the unworthy object of your wretchedness. Confide in a father's love for restoring your peace – for securing your happiness!

EMILY O, my father! there is healing in thy words. Methinks I again live! or is it a dream? (*Clasps her hands, and hides her face, as if in great agitation and fear; then removing her hands, looks round with great vacancy.*) Who's that?

ALICE (*Rising and coming forward.*) Your aunt! 'Tis your aunt, Emily – don't you know me?

EMILY And Hampshire too! – My father! – Ha, ha, ha! (*Breaks into a strong hysterical laugh.*)

JUDGE Oh, my head swims! – my heart will burst! What pains of gout are equal to this agony of mind! – Be comforted, my child! – tranquilize yourself!

HAMPSHIRE (*Taking her hand diffidently, and with great tenderness.*) O, Miss Emily! no 'fraid, – you no going to marry Mass Tom – keep heart! – keep heart, nyung Missy!

JUDGE (*With great energy and indignation.*) Marry Mass Tom! – As soon may the young profligate stretch forth his hand to grasp the morning star, as to pluck this tender, fresh lily from its parent stem!

EMILY But how appease my mother's blest spirit for my broken pledge? – How satisfy high Heaven's justice for my perjured vow?

HAMPSHIRE No fraid, nyung Missy – no 'fraid, I tell you all about um.

JUDGE Hear, my Emily! hear what this good man has to say. There is honesty in his heart, and truth on his lips! In what he has already related to me, returning memory now bears its ample testimony.

EMILY O speak, Hampshire, speak! Say what it is thou knowest that can loose the fetters of mind!

ALICE Yes, speak out, Hampshire! 'Tis now no avail to dissemble! He knows the truth! He well remembers all.

HAMPSHIRE Tan! lay me tell you all about um. You memba dat time Misse go dead. When the parson been gone from she room, Miss Alice set 'pon de bed, so Misse lean 'pon she. Massa 'tan by de bed-post, like one tone, and lean upon um just like when he hab gout he lean upon he crutch! Miss Emily, ah! poor child! then little gal, no bigger dan so. She kneel down at de foot of the bed, and so bury she head in um – oh! she cry and cry as if she been bruck she heart! (*They all betray great emotion.*)

ALICE Law! Brother, send the man out of the room – he wants to give us all the hystericks.

HAMPSHIRE Dan'na, so Miss Alice interrupt we?

JUDGE Go on, Hampshire! – go on.

HAMPSHIRE Me, Hampshire, 'tan close by de poor child, keep me hand 'pon she fau comfort she! I watch eb'ry word Misse say – eb'ry breat she draw. Bun by, Misse say – 'George!' – no me call you George, Massa! – Misse say, 'George, when our dear Emily grows up–'

ALICE (*With impatience.*) Pshaw! the man's so tiresome! – My sister said that if Tom and Emily should form an attachment in their youth, encourage them to marry when they grow up. It would keep *Hickford's* in the family, and at the same time provide for my poor sister's orphan son. He is a wild boy, but may make a steady man! said she.

HAMPSHIRE Now wan else, I be going fau say? – Miss Alice too interruption!

JUDGE Hampshire, go on – tell your story your own way!

HAMPSHIRE Um no story, Massa! I tell you trut! Um's all true! Miss Alice know ums true?

ALICE But you are so tiresome.

EMILY Good Hampshire, go on.

HAMPSHIRE Misse been d'en most gone! – She take breat – then presently she say – Promise me, George! Emily, promise, me! You no peak! – you both 'tan, cry, cry! Misse den say – Wha you no grant my last dying wish? And she make one heaby sigh! Massa d'en, as if he been wake, say – 'Yes, my deary Fanny!' – (you know you been always call she Fanny) – I swear for do all you ask! Bun'by, Misse say – come near me, my Emily! Oh d'en the poor little ting, she get up off she knee, and I, me Hampshire, lift she round to she murrow! She heart beat – beat just as if um was going fau bruck! Misse say – Emily, promise me to marry your cousin – and she boice 'top. She been most gone! – and the poor child frighten – no know wha she say; so she say, – indeed, dearest mama! indeed, I promise! Misse den recover a little bit, she take breat; then she say – (*Hampshire here, with strong excitement, more immediately addresses the Judge*) – Now, Massa, look ye! – I swear, so help me, by dat christening the parson been gee me da' day at Church! – Misse, when this last time she go 'peak – she say – But, George, no ge me child to Tom fau marry, less he be worthy of she! – and she fall dead. (*A deep sigh breaks from them all.*)

JUDGE Oh, what an host of memory's tenderest offspring has crowded on my fancy throughout this sad – sad recital! Get me my crutch! (*Moves as in great pain.*)

ALICE O, Emily! I was in hopes you might have reclaimed him. It is true! true enough what Hampshire says!

EMILY Decide, my father! decide for your child!

HAMPSHIRE 'Top, 'top little! I see Mass Captain coming dis way! (*With anxiety.*)

JUDGE Hasten – hasten, Hampshire, to the door. Tell him we're engaged! – busy! – that we're from home! – tell him – (*agitated and confused.*)   [*Exit Hampshire.*

JUDGE (*In continuation.*) Receive, my Emily! My dearest daughter! receive this embrace! (*They embrace.*) The dark clouds of wretchedness which have of late overshadowed your peace, are now dispelling.

EMILY And a dawn of happiness breaks in upon me.

Enter HAMPSHIRE.

HAMPSHIRE Sir, I been carry de Captain in de parlour. I no been yerry wha you say go do – so I carry he in de parlour.

ALICE Art – Artful! (*With suppressed anger, aside.*)

JUDGE Well, well! I'll attend him. Retire, my child! compose yourself; – tranquilize your mind! (*Embraces her.*)

[*Exeunt severally, different sides.*

Enter TOM APPLEBURY *and* SAM SHADDOCK, *as slily coming from a back room.*

SAM Why, I say, Tom, you're dish't, eh, my boy?

TOM Well I know my uncle will do something for me! I'll ask him to get me a commission in the militia! Tut! What will be the profit of that? Aye! I have it! – I'll turn my thoughts to the church! – I'll study theology, and be a parson! (*With careless indifference.*)

SAM Eh? – a parson indeed? – Don't you know what a tight 'on you'll have to deal with? Why, if you could *say* all the Latin and *Dutch* in the world, he'd not make such a rum'un as you a parson! No, no, Tom! Take my advice, study *treeology* and become a planter!

TOM Zounds, Man! You've hit it – and the chances are ten to one, but I get a plantation of my own.

SAM True, true, my boy! and you may then live merrily!

TOM Live merrily! Aye! Heaven created us in gladness – cheerfulness therefore is a duty! and in order to live without care, I'll not even be careful to be happy – for that one care would be more injurious than all others.

SAM Dang it, man, is'nt that old Square Toes coming this way? We'd better be off –

TOM Off like a shot, or I may come in for one of his long yarns – and I'm damn' vexed with him already. (*With affected indifference.*)   [*Exeunt.*

SCENE IV – *Scene changes to the parlour in Errington's house – the Judge and Carlove seated as in earnest conversation – they rise and come forward; the Judge returns Captain Carlove an open letter*

JUDGE I perceive, sir, in all you say, the rectitude of an honest mind confident in its own integrity; and I value you the more for it.

CARLOVE To merit the confidence I ask of you shall be the undeviating study of my life. Believe me, sir, it is as much upon the deliberate conviction of my mind as upon the ardour of my passion, that I found my pretensions; and I dare believe that I am not altogether indifferent to your amiable and lovely daughter.

JUDGE I would almost willingly believe so, too; for nature, which has endowed you both with such reciprocal feelings of duty and obedience to your parents, may well have formed your hearts for mutual love!

CARLOVE O, Heaven's light dawns on my hopes – upon my love! – my heart is filled with tumultous joy! Permit me, sir, to fly. O, lead me, sir, to the presence of your lovely daughter – of this enchanting maid! – Sanction me to throw myself at her feet, that I may pour out my whole soul, and pay my homage to those virtues that have so long enslaved me.

JUDGE (*Dignified and deliberately.*) First consult your reason! – Consider well before you venture upon an interview! Remember that it is a matter on which rests the future peace and happiness – not of yourself alone – but of a sensitive, timorous and delicate female – of *my* daughter! (*With strong emphasis.*)

CARLOVE Oh! sir, it is no false and deceitful passion which agitates and influences me! It is that sentiment alone which ennobles, refines and raises us above ourselves! – that pure and hallowed *love* which base and vulgar minds can never feel, that controls and animates me.

JUDGE (*Dignified and deliberately.*) Captain Carlove, my daughter is in the drawing-room; you are at liberty to seek her there! – but let not the tumult of your mind overstep the gentleness and delicacy with which she must be approached! It is a confidence, sir, which I repose in you by permitting this interview, because I respect your merit; and I trust you will avoid that flattery and deceit which tend only to mislead the unsuspecting tenderness and sensibility of an artless heart!

CARLOVE A tear of joy trickles on my cheek! – a pleasing tranquility steals through my whole frame! Sir, this transcendant goodness – this sacred confidence – shall never – never be abused. (*Exit.*)(*The Judge pointing to the way.*)

Enter HAMPSHIRE *with a parchment deed.*

HAMPSHIRE (*Presenting the parchment.*) Sir, lawyer Mays send dis to you.

JUDGE (*Receiving it and turning it over.*) Aye! – This, Hampshire, is your manumission! To reward your fidelity and long services, I have given you freedom!

HAMPSHIRE (*Starts – strikes his breast.*) Gee me free! – Wha I want with free? If Massa lub Hampshire, he no trow he way upon the world! – You gee me free – who den gee me cloths – who gee me victuals – who gee me money? where I get house for live in – who take care of Hampshire when he sick? – who bury poor Hampshire when he dead Oh! Massa – Massa! if you will part wid Hampshire, gee he to Miss Emily! – gee he to Mass Captain! – No gee he free! (*Greatly agitated.*)

JUDGE No, no! my faithful Hampshire! – in giving you freedom, I have not treated you as a useless house dog whom we would turn into the streets to seek a precarious subsistence; but bearing in mind how faithfully you have served me, I have made good provision for your future comfort.

HAMPSHIRE But 'tan! – when you hab gout, who you get for wait 'pon you? Where's Hampshire fau gee you de tick? – who gee you de crutch? (*With kindness and anxiety.*)

JUDGE Hampshire still! – but he will then be a hired servant – no longer a slave! And now, Hampshire, that you are free, by the liberal spirit of our laws you are possessed of all the rights and privileges of a British subject, equally with myself.

HAMPSHIRE (*With amazement, examining his hands and opening his bosom.*) Hey! – I like you? Massa, you making you fun! – I tan like you? Ha, ha! (*With surprise and half-gratified feelings.*)

JUDGE No, Hampshire! – no human laws can counteract nature! – your condition in society is changed, but not your complexion; and though free and having rights and privileges conferred on you, you yet have *duties* to perform! By obedience to the laws, and conforming your mind to the principles of Christianity, you will learn how to fulfil the one, and value the other; for you must ever bear in mind that no society can exist without subordination, or its members be happy without religion!

HAMPSHIRE But, Massa, you no say I hab right and privilege fau do waugh I please?

JUDGE No, my good man! – They who do what they *please*, seldom do what they ought; and those who may do evil with impunity generally do it with licentiousness; – hence comes the necessity of laws to restrain and punish us; for men are least likely to offend, when they *dare not*!

HAMPSHIRE Well, Massa, I suppose ums good sun 'ting you gee me – na say Massa no gee! – But Hampshire no go – he still lib with Massa!

JUDGE So I would have you my good man! and we will settle your wages when I am more at leisure; but take this as an earnest of my future liberality. (*Gives him money.*)

HAMPSHIRE Massa do all dis good for Hampshire what he do for poor Mass Tom! – You no go trow he way?

JUDGE No, Hampshire, no! Tom after being buoyed up, through the weakness of family pride, with prospects that can never be realized, must not now be left by the ebb tide of his fortunes stranded in helpless dejection; – I shall take care to provide for him the means that may lead, through his own exertion and industry, to competency and ease. (*Goes up to the back of the stage—Hampshire following dances awkwardly after him—and singing.*)

> Rights and privilege – rights and privilege,
>> Dumpt tee didle dee, dumpt tee dee,
> Captain Carlove and Miss Emily –
>> Emily – Emily – didle de dee.

Enter CAPTAIN CARLOVE *and* EMILY, *as in conversation.*

CARLOVE Thy firmness – thy fancied duties, shall not resist my tenderness – my love – my agony! The voice that has so often touched thy heart, shall vanquish every obstacle!

EMILY My heart God sees! and in high Heaven hears the prayers I breathe for your happiness!

CARLOVE And yet you would withhold that very happiness which Heaven decrees you alone can give me. Your scruples, enchanting Emily, are those of a timorous mind, frightened at itself! you have been the mistress of my destiny from the moment of our first meeting – Cease, O, cease not to be so still!

EMILY Must then I confess my weakness! – that thou art dear to me! O, I blush at the temerity of my heart! but yet, my honor – my duty – my plighted vow! – Oh, my heart exhausted by the trial it has so lately undergone, is left in a state of weakness that palpitates at every emotion.

CARLOVE What do I hear! – she loves me! O, overpowering delight! lovely woman! – Never does beauty display its power so

magically as when struggling to conceal a conscious passion! –
yet why blush at a passion as innocent as yourself?

EMILY An insupportable burden oppresses my heart, and leaves
so deep an impression of sorrow, that I can hardly shake it off,
and yet, love in itself can never be a crime! It is ever the effect
of assiduity when united with distinguished merit!

JUDGE (*Coming forward.*) Why reproach yourself, my daughter!
Past evil should ever be effaced by present joy! Have you not
the power of rewarding a worthy man – a high spirited and generous youth – a gallant soldier and a dutiful son! – a man educated in the sentiments of virtue and honour! one every way
worthy of you!

EMILY O, my benefactor, my father! in giving myself up entirely to
your disposal, I only offer back the gift I have received at your
hands! – your daughter looks up to you as a ministering spirit
from the throne of grace to direct her conduct – to decide her
fate!

CARLOVE My full heart! my swelling bosom will burst! what is now
wanting to complete my happiness?

JUDGE Come hither my daughter! Goodness does not more certainly make us happy, than that happiness should make us good!
I would fain be a good man! I wish to do no ill; and strive to be
benevolent to all. I bear no animosity to any individual, but
would embrace all my countrymen as friends and breathren! I
would rebuke their vices, but yet promote their honour! and
bound by the ties of nature to the land of my birth, I ardently
wish it a long succession of internal peace and uninterrupted
prosperity! I know how to respect talent – and rejoice to reward
merit! and it is now that I enjoy one of the purest pleasures that
can warm a parent's bosom. Young soldier! take her! and cherish her in the inviolable sanctuary of your heart! and remember
that very helplessness, which is the attribute of her sex, should
ever be its greatest safeguard! O may the fates spin a rose
coloured thread of many joyous years to you both, and those
virtues which have united you, produce a rivalry of duty and
obedience among the sons and daughters of our isle that, while

it secures their own happiness, shall prove to their parents (as it has done to me) *The best cure for the gout.*   [*Exeunt.*
While the curtain drops, Hampshire dances about the stage in great glee, sings 'Rights and Privileges' &c. &c. &c.

[FINIS]

In both *Creoleana* and *The Fair Barbadian and Faithful Black*, the spelling and punctuation of the original have been followed, except for a few misprints which have been silently corrected. In accordance modern practice, single inverted comman have been used for dialogue with quotations instead of the double ones used in the original editions. Full details of works referred to in the notes by abbreviated titles will be found in the bibliography.

Dedication

Edward Geoffrey Smith Stanley (1799–1869) was known by the courtesy title of Lord Stanley from October 1834, when his father became Earl of Derby. As Secretary of State for the Colonies (1833–4), he was responsible for introducing into the British parliament (14 May 1833) the Bill which brought about the emanicipation of the slaves in the British colonies in the following year. He was Secretary of State for the Colonies again (1841–45) and later, having succeeded as 14th Earl of Derby (1851), was three times Prime Minister of the United Kingdom. The 'occasion' of his Lordship's condescension in 1833, to which Orderson refers, remains obscure.

p. 22

traductive events Those which are being or can be passed on (presumably here in the sense of from one generation to another).

William Wilberforce (1759–1833), for many years a member of the British parliament, was well known for his commitment to Evangelical Christianity and his opposition to the slave trade. He was one of the leading figures in the campaign which eventually secured the abolition of the British slave trade in 1807, and later campaigned against slavery itself in the British colonies, though he retired from parliament in 1825 and died a month before the Emancipation Bill was finally passed in August 1833.

There is no mention of Orderson in the five volume *Life of William Wilberforce* published by his sons in 1838. However, Orderson appears to allude to a passage in Wilberforce's *An Appeal to the Religion, Justice, and Humanity of the Inhabitants of the British Empire, in behalf of the Negro Slaves in the West Indies* (1823), in which Wilberforce refers in a footnote (pp. 21–2) to 'a passage in one of the many pamphlets published against the Registry Bill, in 1816, by a gentleman some time resident in Barbados' and says that the pamphlet's author 'speaks with real humanity of the free coloured people, and strongly recommends their being invested with civil and political rights.' Although Wilberforce nowhere mentions Orderson by name, this and other comments, such as the statement that the author of the pamphlet 'even suggests a plan, through the medium of the moral union of the sexes among the coloured people in the colonies, for the gradual emanicpation of the slaves' indicate that he refers to *Cursory remarks and plain facts connected with the question produced by the proposed Slave Registry Bill*, which is described on the title-page as 'By J. W. Orderson, late of Barbadoes'. Wilberforce went on to condemn the pamphlet's author for saying that intermarriage between whites and free coloureds was 'contrary to his idea of morals, religion, and polity' – this, and the earlier reference to 'the moral union of the sexes' are almost verbatim quotations from a passage in *Cursory remarks*, p. 22.

We may note that Orderson's version of the passage in Wilberforce (perhaps misquoted from memory) differs somewhat from the original.

William Hone (1780–1842) was an English writer, publisher and bookseller. His *Every-Day Book* (1826 and later editions) was a bulky collection of anecdotes and miscellaneous scraps of information. At Vol. I, col. 592 of the 1826 edition, in the course of a section on chimney-sweeps in Britain, Hone says that 'The "*Examiner*," some time ago, related an anecdote much to the purpose, from a pamphlet by Mr. J. W. Orderson, late of Barbadoes; it is a fine specimen of pure feeling.' Although he did not name the pamphlet, Hone went on to quote the following passage which appears as a footnote on pp. 7–8 of Orderson's *Cursory Remarks*:

About fourteen years ago, a Mrs. P. arrived at Bristol,from the West Indies, and brought with her a female Negro servant, mother of two or three children left in that country. A few days after their arrival, and they had gone into private lodgings, a sweep boy was sent for by the landlady to sweep the kitchen chimney. This woman being seated in the kitchen when little Soot entered, was struck with amazement at the spectacle he presented, and with great vehemence clapping her hands together, exclaimed, 'Wha dis me see! La, la, dat buckara piccaninny! So help me, nyung Misse, (addressing herself to the housemaid then present,) sooner dan see one o'mine picaninnies tan so, I drown he in de sea.' The progress of the poor child in sweeping the chimney closely engrosed [*sic*] her attention, and when she saw him return from his sooty incarceration, she addressed him with a feeling that did honour to her maternal tenderness, saying, 'Child! come yaw, child;' (and without waiting any reply, and putting a sixpence into his hand) 'Who you mammy? You hab daddy too? Wha dem be, da la you go no chimney for?' and moistening her finger at her lips, began to rub the poor child's cheek, to ascertain, what yet appeared doubtful to her, whether he was really a *buccara*. I saw this woman some time after in the West Indies; and it was a congratulation to her ever after, that 'her children were not born to be sweeps.'

Hone gives the passage in its entirety, with some minor variations in spelling and punctuation, including italicization of some of the non-standard features of the servant's speech, and adds 'white' in brackets as a gloss after the second appearance of 'buccara.'

As he says, Hone's source was *The Examiner*, a periodical edited by the well-known English essayist Leigh Hunt (1784–1859) and his brother John Hunt (1775–1848). The anecdote is given in *The Examiner*, IX, 456 (No. 447, issue for 21 July 1816); the full title of *Cursory Remarks* is given, and it is described as 'a pamphlet just published,' but no other comment is given. *The Examiner* was a radical paper, which was opposed to slavery, and during 1816 it referred on several occasions to the sufferings of chimney sweeps in Britain, small boys who were forced (often with shocking brutality) to climb up chimney flues in order to clean them. The Hunts also had a connection with Barbados: their grandfather was a clergyman there; while it seems unlikely that he was ever Rector of St Michael's, as Leigh Hunt said in his *Autobiography* (ed. Morpugo, p. 5), he is probably to be identified with the Brian Hunt who was Rector of St Joseph, 1731–1743 (Barbados Department of Archives, St Joseph Baptismal Register, RL1/30, pp. 7–22; see also Reece and Clark-Hunt, *Barbados Diocesan History*, pp. 95,97). Orderson's later reference to Lauder in *Creoleana* caught Leigh Hunt's eye: see note on p.75 below.

his publication on the *Education of the Poor of Barbados* was Orderson's *Leisure Hours at the Pier; or, a treatise on the poor of Barbados.* According to Handler (*Guide*, p.81) this was a 56-page pamphlet published in Liverpool, in 1827, in which Orderson 'argues for an effective program of vocational education for lower-class white children because he feels that Barbadian free coloreds are beginning to monopolize a variety of the island's trades and crafts.' Handler locates a copy in the Barbados Public Library: I endeavoured to consult this many years ago and was told it could not be produced for conservation reasons; more recently (1998) I found it had disappeared from the Library's card catalogue. I have been unable to trace another copy.

Shilstone, ('Orderson Family Records,' p. 156,) notes that on 2 October 1827 the Barbados House of Assembly passed a resolution thanking Orderson 'for his laudable and judicious pamphlet.'

p. 23

that lamentable catastrophe was the fire which started in High Street late on the night of 13 May 1766 (not 1776 as the first edition of *Creoleana* prints it) and burned till about nine the following morning, destroying over a thousand buildings and causing losses estimated at what was then the prodigious total of half a million pounds. For a description of the fire and the subsequent rebuilding, see Alleyne, *Historic Bridgetown*, pp. 63–4. See also Poyer, *History of Barbados*, pp. 342–3.

Lancaster is a port in the north-west of England, and the county town of Lancashire, though even in the time to which Orderson refers it was being eclipsed by Liverpool (in the same county) which had become an important slaving port and a significant centre of trade to the British Caribbean colonies by the middle of the eighteenth century (see pp. 38-9).

Belfast is a port in the north-east of Ireland (now the capital of Northern Ireland); it was already of considerable commercial importance by the beginning of the eighteenth century, though its development as a major centre of shipbuilding and textile industries did not begin until much later.

Codrington College Christopher Codrington (1668–1710), a Barbadian scholar, soldier and administrator, bequeathed two plantations in Barbados to the Society for the Propagation of the Gospel in Foreign Parts, a Church of England (Episcopalian) missionary society founded in 1701, with the intention that the plantations be used to support the establishment of a missionary college. However when, after many delays, the college finally opened its doors to students in 1745, it was as a grammar school for the education of young sons of the Barbadian elite. Only in 1829–30 did it become a theological college, intended mainly for the training of candidates for the Church of England ministry, a function which it has fulfilled ever since. It is now affiliated to the University of the West Indies.

p.25

grain, vegetables and ground provisions The 'grain' referred to probably included both guinea corn (i.e., millet, *Sorghum vulgare*) and Indian corn (maize, *Zea mais*), though it is worth noting that Barbadians of an older generation in the twentieth century (and perhaps earlier) used 'grain' to refer to peas or beans, particularly pigeon peas (*Cajanus cajan*). The 'ground provisions' would include yams (*Dioscorea var species*), eddoes (*Colocasia esculenta*) and tanias (*Xanthosoma sagittifolium*), as well as sweet potatoes (*Ipomoea batatas*).

Falernum Barbadian liqueur, the main ingredients of which are rum, lime juice and sugar. **Bub** was a drink made of fresh milk sweetened with sugar and flavoured with nutmeg, and perhaps with the addition of lime-juice and rum; in her *West Indian and Other Recipes* (1932), Mrs. H. Graham Yearwood gives the following recipe for 'Boiling House Bub':' 2 pints of milk, 6 beaten yolks of eggs, half pint of sweet liquor [i.e., cane juice boiled to just before the point at which it will crystallise], 4 wine glasses of rum, or more to taste, (both sweet and strong must be to taste). Beat the eggs with a spoonful of water, swizzle in the milk, liquor, and rum, and grate a little nutmeg on the top.' **Black-strap** refers, not to black-strap molasses, but to a drink for which the following recipe is given by Mrs. Yearwood: '1 pint cracked liquor [cane juice after its pre-liminary boiling], the juice of a large lime, and half gill of rum and nut-meg grated on the top.' There are many recipes for various types of rum punch; how exactly that to which Orderson refers here was 'improved' is a matter of conjecture.

place William Dickson, in a 'Glossary of Words peculiar to the West Indies, or taken in peculiar senses' in his *Mitigation of Slavery* (pp. 526–8) says 'The possessions of the Ten-acre-men, or small freeholders, in Barbadoes, are called Places, to distinguish them from the large sugar-plantations.' Note the distinction which Orderson makes here between 'place' and 'estate.'

"holing" his neighbours' fields Hiring out some of his slaves to neighbouring planters to dig cane-holes on their land. Sugar-cane was often grown from the cut stumps of the previous crop, but ratoons (as canes grown in this manner were called) produced less sugar. After a few years, the stumps would have to be dug up and fresh canes planted (these were grown from cane-tops or cut pieces of cane, not from seed). Canes were planted, not in furrows, but in square holes some two feet (60 cm) or more along each side which were dug out by men and women using hoes. Digging cane-holes was extremely hard work, and some planters were glad to hire other peoples' slaves (a 'jobbing gang') to do it in order to save the wear and tear on their own. Like the 'holing,' Mr. Fairfield's 'indefatigable industry' is a matter of getting other people – his slaves – to do the actual physical work.

However, while holing must have been a profitable business for the owners of the slaves hired out to do it, planters in the late eighteenth century who had to pay for holing lamented it was expensive. One attorney for an absentee owner ended a long list of complaints by saying, 'You cannot get an acre of land holed for less than four pounds ten shillings' – Seale Yearwood to Applewhaite Frere, Barbados, 26 April 1797, printed in Anon., 'Odd pages from old records,' *Journal of the Barbados Museum and Historical Society*, XVI, 113– 7 (May 1949), at p. 117.

p. 26

the mote in their brother's eye A paraphrase, rather than a direct quotation, of the Gospel according to St. Matthew (vii, 3–5) in the King James Version of the Bible (1611) ('And why beholdest thou the mote that is in thy brother's eye, but considerest not the beam that is in thine own eye? . . .'), or the similar passage in St. Luke (vi, 41–2).

'a certain Levite' Compare Judges xix, 1, in the King James Version of the Bible: 'And it came to pass in those days, when there was no king in Israel, that there was a certain Levite sojourning on the side of mount Ephraim, who took to him a concubine out of Bethlehem-Judah.'

to manumit his paramour Under a Barbados law of 1739, any owner wishing to free a slave was required to pay £50 island currency to the parish vestry (the body responsible for local government in each of the eleven parishes into which Barbados was divided). The interest earned by this money was used to provide an annuity of £4 to the freed slave so that there would be no risk of public funds having to be used to support them if they were unable to find any means of earning a living. This law was reinforced in 1783, but there were various ways of evading it, such as by having slaves manumitted in England rather than in Barbados: for details of manumission procedures, see Jerome Handler, *The Unappropriated People*, pp. 29–65, especially pp. 39–44.

Combined with the annuity required by law, the additional £6 per annum given to his cast-off mistress by Mr. Fairfield would have been enough to guarantee her a life of modest respectability. However, she did not live long to enjoy it: see p. 33.

The money referred to is Barbados currency, not pounds sterling. In the later eighteenth century, Barbados currency was normally at a discount of one-third in relation to sterling, or in other words, £133 6s 8d. Barbados currency was equivalent to £100 sterling. For further details, see the Notes on *Creoleana*, p. 27, on 'the price of some of the necessary articles of life'.

p. 27

the average crop did not exceed 7000 hogsheads A hogshead was a large wooden cask containing about 15 or 16 hundredweight of muscovado sugar (which would be exported to Britain and refined there); a quantity equivalent to approximately 762 or 812.8 kilogrammes. The 'borer' is *Diatraea saccharilis* (Fabricius), an important insect pest of the sugar-cane.

The figures provided by Noel Deerr in *The History of Sugar* (I, 193) for the sugar production of Barbados show a significant drop in the 1770s: production for 1778, for example, was less than a third of what it had been in 1768. Taking 15 hundredweight to the hogshead, Orderson's '7000 hogsheads' would be equivalent to 5,250 tons; Deerr's figures for the 1770s range from a high of 8,635 tons in 1770 to a low of 2,304 in 1778.

open hostility Armed conflict between Great Britain and her North American colonists broke out with the skirmishes at Lexington and Concord in Massachusetts, 19 April 1775. The war which followed eventually led to Britain formally acknowledging the independence of the United States of America in 1783. Since Barbados normally received a large proportion of its food and other supplies from North America, the disruption of trade caused by the war brought severe hardship to the is-

land. In his *History of Barbados*, John Poyer (1758–1807), who was an
eye-witness of this period, commented that 'The commerce of the country was almost annihilated by swarms of hostile cruizers, which infested
the ocean. The negroes were almost starving; and the business of sugar-
boiling was greatly impeded, for want of the necessary supplies of timber
and provisions from America' (p. 422). William Dickson, another eye-
witness, describes the distress caused by the non-arrival of provisions
from North America, and the failure of attempts to plant corn locally at
the wrong time of the year: 'The poor of the land, both black and white,
were dropping down in the streets, or silently pining and expiring in their
cottages' (*Mitigation of Slavery*, p. 309).

the price of some of the necessary articles of life In the eighteenth
century the British Caribbean colonies had no coins of their own and
generally used those of the Spanish American colonies. The dollar to
which Orderson refers was the Spanish silver dollar equal to eight *reales*
(the 'piece of eight' famous in pirate stories). However, the nominal
value of the dollar and other foreign coins in the British Caribbean
colonies was often greater than what would have been considered in
Britain to be the value of their precious metal content. This was a deliberate over-valuation, intended to discourage the export of scarce coin
from the colonies, and this is the origin of the difference between pounds
sterling and pounds currency (which varied not only over time, but from
one British colony to another).

In Barbados, from about 1740 until 1838, the dollar was reckoned as
equivalent to six shillings and three pence Barbados currency (just as in
Britain before the introduction of decimalization in 1971, twelve pence
made a shilling, and twenty shillings made a pound). In 1838, the British
government declared the dollar to be equal to four shillings and two
pence sterling, while at the same time it was revalued at six shillings and
six pence Barbados currency. In 1848, the system of pounds currency
was abolished, and all outstanding accounts in them were converted to
sterling at a rate of £156 currency to £100 sterling. By the mid-nine-
teenth century, the ordinary British sterling coins in pounds, shillings
and pence had ousted the old Spanish colonial coins as the normal circulating medium, but for most purposes the dollar (rated at four shillings
and two pence sterling, which conveniently made the penny equal to two
cents) continued to be the normal money of account, and banks issued

circulating notes in dollars. This situation lasted in Barbados until the introduction in 1955 of a decimal coinage in cents issued for the Eastern Group of the British Caribbean Territories.

In the eighteenth and early nineteenth centuries, there was an almost permanent shortage of small change. In an attempt to alleviate this, silver dollars were cut into smaller pieces, whose value was expressed in 'bits'. Uncut coins ('round money') smaller than a dollar were also given values in bits. Although the bit (or 'bitt') was originally supposed to be equivalent to the Spanish *real*, that is, one-eighth of a dollar, by the mid-eighteenth century in Barbados the bit had come to be regarded as one-tenth of a dollar; until 1838 this was reckoned as seven and a half pence Barbados currency, and thereafter as five pence sterling or ten cents. Although the bit as a piece of silver cut from a dollar went out of circulation about the time *Creoleana* appeared, and there was no coin of equivalent value until the introduction of the decimal coinage in 1955, the bit survived in popular speech as a unit of reckoning. The anonymous author of an article on 'Miscellaneous Words and Phrases in use in Barbados' published in the *Harrisonian* (the school magazine of Harrison College, Barbados) in April 1926 defined 'bit' as 'An imaginary coin worth 10 cents, universally used by hucksters. [*e.g.* Eggs sell at 3 for the bit, etc.]' (square brackets in original).

While it is difficult to give an accurate idea of the purchasing power of money in a previous era, it may be worth noting that, in Barbados in 1840 (not long after the end of slavery and about the time Orderson was writing *Creoleana*), an average day's wages for a male agricultural labourer were a shilling, or ten pence if he had a house on the plantation (see Claude Levy, *Emancipation, Sugar, and Federalism*, p. 79). While these rates were low in comparison with other British Caribbean colonies at the time (and they were often lower in the course of the succeeding century), they do suggest that the prices given by Orderson for foodstuffs in the 1770s were (if accurately reported) extremely high. Schomburgk, *History of Barbados*, p.183, gives a table of 'average prices' in the island in the early 1840s; the only one directly comparable with those given by Orderson is that for wheaten flour, which Schomburgk says averaged one pound ten shillings sterling for a barrel of 196 pounds weight in 1843, and one pound five shillings in 1844 and 1845. These prices were equivalent to seven dollars and twenty cents or six dollars, or (if we can assume the sizes of the barrels referred to were similar) as little as one eighth of the prices given by Orderson for the period of the American War of Independence. See also Watson, *Civilised Island*, p. 22, for a table of 'Market quotations in Barbados' which shows significant increases in the prices of some commodities between 1774–5 and 1776.

The period of high prices does not appear to have lasted; the author of an account of Barbados in 1789 said that meat was plentiful and cheap – see Gilmore, 'A 1798 Description of Barbados' at p. 137.

On coinage and currency in general in the period, see Ida Greaves, 'Money and Currency in Barbados,' *Journal of the Barbados Museum and Historical Society*, XIX, 164–9; XX, 3–19, 53–66 (August, November 1952, February 1953).

p. 28

Pharaoh's lean kine A reference to the biblical famine in Egypt (Genesis, xiii).

a plague of ants Poyer (*History of Barbados*, pp. 334–5) says that 'Afflicted by continued drought, and visited by tribes of vermin, more destructive than the locusts and caterpillars of old, Barbadoes was then reduced to a state of comparative poverty; her soil and her negroes had sunk fifty per cent. below their original value.' A species of ant which destroyed the sugar-canes was a serious problem from about 1760 until the time of the hurricane of 1780, which was credited with ridding the island of them (Schomburgk, *History of Barbados*, pp. 640–643).

one of the most severe and pitiless hurricanes An eye-witness account is given by Poyer (*History of Barbados*, pp. 446–456).

p. 29

Major General C— was Major-General James Cunninghame, Governor of Barbados, 1780–82, said by Poyer (who provides a detailed account of his period in office, pp. 410–528) to have been a 'tyrannical ruler' and the worst governor the island had ever had. A number of the details in Orderson's account echo those in Poyer.

The **Mole Head** was the breakwater and pier on the southern side of the entrance to the Careenage in Bridgetown. It was destroyed by the hurricane of 1780, but its reconstruction proved an extraordinarily prolonged process, since as Schomburgk (who describes its history at length,

History of Barbados, pp. 179–180) put it, 'A tonnage-duty for the repair of this work [. . .] raised considerable funds, which were frequently applied to purposes quite foreign to this object [. . .]' – such as buying gunpowder for salutes. See also Alleyne, *History of Bridgetown*, pp. 34–8.

had it run out Apparently in the sense of 'to mark off, define' (given by the *Oxford English Dictionary* as a North American usage, with quotations from the eighteenth century), or perhaps simply equivalent to 'surveyed'. The 'pie' is explained on p. 30.

'**asked in church**' Married by banns; it was considered more dignified to be married by licence, which removed the necessity for the publication of banns – compare the anecdote Orderson gives on pp.150–2. As there was no bishop resident in the British Caribbean colonies at this date, the issuing of marriage licences was included in the governor's functions.

p. 30

that frugal President Each British Caribbean colony had a Council, a small group of prominent local land-owners appointed to advise the governor, which functioned as the Upper House of the colonial legislature. Members of the Council were nominated and usually served for life, unlike members of the Lower House, the House of Assembly, who were elected – although the right to vote was based on an extremely restrictive property qualification; in addition, from 1721 to 1831 the law in Barbados also specified that voters had to be white. If a governor died in office or was recalled, the longest-serving member of the Council assumed the executive power until the arrival of a new governor. During this period, he was styled the President and exercised most of the functions of a governor. The 'frugal President' who 'ordered the discontinuance of the lamps usually lighted at Pilgrim gates' is identified by Poyer (*History of Barbados*, pp. 405–6) as John Dotin (d. 1783), who assumed office in 1779 on the death of Governor Edward Hay, and his order is described by Poyer as 'an act which was extolled as a noble proof of his generous regard for the interest of his country.'

'Pilgrim' is what is now known as Government House, about a mile to the east of the centre of Bridgetown. It was the official residence of the Governor of Barbados from 1703 (and, after Independence in 1966, of the Governor-General). Although altered and repaired at various times, it is substantially the same as it was in the mid-eighteenth century. When there was a President, he lived at Pilgrim during his term of office.

Little England A once-common nickname for Barbados. The earliest known example of its use is 1789; see Gilmore, 'A 1789 Description of Barbados'.

Montpellier is a town in southern France which was popular as a health resort.

p.31

the munificent donation The British Parliament voted £80,000 'to relieve and support' their 'unhappy fellow subjects in the island of Barbadoes' and further sums were raised for the same purpose by private contributions, including £20,000 from citizens of Dublin (Poyer, *History of Barbados*, p. 491).

p. 33

consumption Tuberculosis.

p. 34

Parson Hebson was the Rev. Joseph Hebson, who was ordained in England in 1768 with a title as assistant in the parish of St Philip, Barbados, but he was described as curate at St Michael's, Barbados, in a list dated December 1772 – he could have combined this position with teaching at Harrison's. By September 1788 he had moved to another Barbadian parish, St Andrew's, as Rector, and was still there in 1790, but he was appointed to St Philip's in 1792 and died as Rector of St Philip's in January 1793 – information from the Fulham Papers in the Lambeth Palace Library, American Colonial Section, XVI, 170, 175; XXVII, 120–9; Barbados Department of Archives, RB6/29 p. 14 (will of Rev. Dr. Thomas Wharton), RL1/25, p. 96 (St Philip Burial Register); and Reece and Clark-Hunt, ed. *Barbados Diocesan History*, p. 82.

p.35

'**Han't the pro'marshal broke up the Estates**' The provost marshal was the official responsible for enforcing judgements against debtors (the result of the suits in the Court of Chancery described below). Poyer

(*History of Barbados*, p. 335) describes the consequences of such suits when planters got into debt as a result of the various calamities which occurred around the time of the American War of Independence:

> A total failure of crops, instead of exciting commiseration, sharpened the avidity of the rapacious; and the wretched slaves of the unfortunate debtor were dragged in crowds to the market, and thence transported to cultivate and enrich by their labour those colonies which, at the conclusion of the war, passed into the hands of our enemies. At that season of calamity, the pernicious tendency of the law was made visible as the sun at noon day. The slaves were sold for less than half their value; the soil remained uncultivated; the original proprietors were ruined, and the junior creditors were defrauded of their just due, by the accumulation of expense, and the rapacity of the provost marshal.

moidore Anglicised name of a Portuguese gold coin (*moeda d'ouro*) whose value in Barbados was fixed in 1791 at one pound seventeen shillings and sixpence Barbados currency by a proclamation of Governor David Parry which regulated the values of the Spanish and Portuguese gold coins then current in the island. The proclamation is printed in Samuel Moore, *The Public Arts in Force, passed by the Legislature of Barbados, from May 11th 1762 to April 8th, 1800, inclusive* (London, 1801), pp. 278–80.

p. 36

O tempora! O mores! 'What times! What customs!' – a cliché ultimately derived from the famous Roman orator Marcus Tullius Cicero (106–43 BCE), who uses it in several of his speeches.

the merry dance Who, one wonders, played the 'violin, pipe and tabor'? it may have been members of the 'chance assembly' of (white) neighbours, but it is at least as likely that the music was provided by some of their slaves – perhaps we have here the protohistory of the Bajan tuk band.

p. 38

poan Cassava pone, for which Mrs. H. Graham Yearwood gives the following recipe (*West Indian and Other Recipes*, p. 87): '1/4 lb. of lard, 1/4 lb. of butter, 1 lb. of sugar, 1 large cocoanut grated, say 1/2 lb., 4 beaten eggs, and 1 lb. of cassava flour, throw the mixture into a dripping pan and bake.'

For 'bub', see Notes on *Creoleana*, p. 25. Roasted corn, that is, Indian corn (*Zea mais*) roasted on the cob, is still popular in Barbados.

gang, i.e., of slaves.

let concealment, like a worm in the bud [. . .] Shakespeare, *Twelfth Night*, Act II, Scene iv.

Dr. Seawick Not identified; possibly a fictitious name. There is nobody with a name resembling this in the list given in Anon., 'Barbadians who qualified as Doctors of Medicine at Edinburgh up to 1845,'*Journal of the Barbados Museum and Historical Society*, XXVIII, 149–152 (August 1961), nor is there anybody called Seawick in Brandow, *Genealogies of Barbados Families* or Oliver, *Monumental Inscriptions*.

p. 40

'screwed himself up to the very point of sentimentality' Untraced.

p. 42

'vasty deep' From Glendower's line in Shakespeare, *Henry IV*, Act III, Scene I: 'I can call spirits from the vasty deep.'

p. 43

Obi or obeah, a system of popular beliefs, often involving the use of charms and incantations to secure desired aims. While it survives to some extent today (almost certainly in a modified form), the vague descriptions offered by white writers of the eighteenth and nineteenth centuries function mainly as expressions of their own feelings of pious horror or racial superiority and offer little indication of what obeah actually meant to Afro-Caribbean people of the slavery period. However, it does seem clear that obeah was regarded as a sort of witchcraft, and that while those who believed in its power feared it, they regarded it as evil. At the same time, obeah was certainly not the whole of the slaves' belief-system; it can be safely assumed that enslaved Africans brought their religious beliefs and practices to Barbados and that at least some aspects of these survived among their descendants into the early nineteenth century or even later. While some present-day folk beliefs and practices have been traced to African origins, in Barbados (unlike some other parts of the Caribbean) evidence for any detailed description of the religious beliefs of the slaves in the later eighteenth century is extremely limited.

Orderson's suggestion that the slaves' commemoration of their dead was related to obeah is a misunderstanding. His description of 'drumming, dancing and riot', like his reference to 'orgies', merely indicates that he saw their behaviour as 'frenzied' and that he disapproved of it. 'Orgies' does not necessarily imply anything sexual, though his reference to something 'yet *more abominable*, of which we shudder to think' may hint at this, or perhaps be intended to suggest that Afro-Caribbean religion sometimes involved human sacrifice (an accusation which was often levelled at Haitian vodun by white writers).

'Christ's Church militant' In the Holy Communion service in the Anglican *Book of Common Prayer* (1662), the Priest says 'Let us pray for the whole state of Christ's Church militant here in earth.'

an Episcopal head In the eighteenth and early nineteenth centuries, the Anglican Church in the British Caribbean colonies was theoretically under the supervision of the Bishop of London. In 1824 two Anglican bishoprics were established in Barbados and Jamaica, which were funded by the British government as part of its plans for the 'amelioration' of the conditions of the slave population. The first Bishop of Barbados, William Hart Coleridge, arrived in the island in January 1825. In Barbados, unlike other islands, the Anglican Church had little competition from other denominations, and while its earlier attempts to convert the slaves had been very limited, Bishop Coleridge did rouse it to greater effort and was able to increase the number of both church-buildings and clergy. By the time he retired in 1842, most of the ex-slave population in Barbados were Christians at least in name (though some critics doubted how deep the process of conversion went), and most were Anglicans. See J. T. Gilmore, 'Episcopacy, Emancipation and Evangelization'.

p. 44

the venerable rector of St. George's Almost certainly a reference to the Rev. John Carter, who according to a marble tablet still visible in the church which was erected by the Vestry of the Parish (inscription printed in Reece and Clark-Hunt, ed., *Barbados Diocesan History*, p. 86), died in 1796 at the age of ninety after being Rector of St George's, Barbados, 'for almost half a century'. Orderson's 'venerable' suggests a reference to Carter's age; both of his successors, Anthony Keighly Thomas (Rector, 1797–1820) and William Lake Pinder (Rector, 1820–1841) held the

parish for much shorter periods and were much younger than Carter
(Thomas resigned when he was about fifty-one; Pinder died as Rector,
aged fifty-nine. (Information from Reece and Clark-Hunt, *loc. cit.*;
Oliver, *Monumental Inscriptions*, p. 191; Fulham Papers, XXVIII,
199–234; Barbados Department of Archives, RL1/52, p. 87 [St George's
Baptismal Register] and RL1/56, f. 87 v [St George's Burial Register];
entry on Thomas in Foster, *Alumni Oxonienses;* entry on Pinder in Venn
and Venn, *Alumni Cantabrigienses*).

However, if Carter is meant, it is clear that Orderson's chronology
(here, as elsewhere) is more than a little elastic. Joe Pollard is described
(p. 44) as being 'near forty years of age' at the time he begins to court
Lucy, which has to be placed about the early or middle years of the 1780s;
this is obviously inconsistent with the suggestion that he died at the age
of eighty-two while Carter was still alive.

p. 45

Dulcinea is the beloved of Don Quixote in the famous novel by Miguel
de Cervantes (first published in 1605). Orderson uses her name to suggest that Lucy was not as perfect as Joe thought her to be.

p. 47

Hibernian An Irishman.

p. 48

the carenage For Orderson's personal connection with the careenage
(as it is now usually spelt and pronounced in Barbados) and the Mole-
Head, see the Introduction.

the Emerald Isle Ireland.

p. 49

his father's town agentss They would have been responsible for shipping the senior Goldacre's sugar to a buyer in England, and importing the
supplies he needed for his plantation (see p. 23 above), probably being
paid on a commission basis. In his 'Glossary' (see the Note on 'place', p.
215), William Dickson says that *'Town-agents* receive on shore imported
plantation stores; often supply the planters with foreign articles, especially provisions; take charge of the produce, till shipped &c.'

p. 50

Mr. Cater Unidentified. 'Mr. Donohugh' is probably to be identified with the 'Mr. Thomas Donohue, teacher of the mathematics in Bridgetown' who calculated an Almanac published by Orderson's family firm in 1788 (advertisement in the *Barbados Mercury*, 5 December 1787, quoted in Shilstone, 'Orderson Family Records', p. 153). The name is Irish, and the dialogue Orderson gives to Donohugh may be intended as a representation of Irish English.

Cotton Coast The *Barbados Mercury*, 23 October 1787, advertised for sale or rent, '16 acres of good cotton land with a well-built dwelling house suitable for a genteel family situate at Cotton Coast, Christ Church about a mile from Bridgetown commanding view of the sea both windward and leeward of Needham's Fort', while on 9 December 1788, the paper advertised for sale 'An excellent cotton estate in a pleasant situation in Cotton Coast, Christ Church called Woodland, three miles from Bridgetown bounding on the sea and having an excellent bay thereto' (extracts in *Journal of the Barbados Museum and Historical Society*, XVII, 26, 175, November 1949 and August 1950).

p. 55

'**for better for worse**' In 'The Form of Solemnization of Matrimony' in the Anglican *Book of Common Prayer*, the bride and groom promise to take each other 'for better for worse, for richer for poorer, in sickness and in health, to love and to cherish, till death do us part'.

gay Lothario Orderson seems to use the expression here simply to refer to Mac Flashby in his rôle as Caroline's suitor, but there is certainly a suggestion that Mac Flashby is a libertine. The original 'gay Lothario' was a character in the play *The Fair Penitent* (1703) by Nicholas Rowe (1674–1718).

p. 56

the South Bridge In the later eighteenth century, there were two bridges in Bridgetown, just as there are today, but they were usually known as the East Bridge or Old Bridge (where the Charles Duncan O'Neal Bridge now is) and the West Bridge or New Bridge (where what is called the Chamberlain or Swing Bridge now is). The *Barbados*

Mercury, 4 December 1784, advertised that 'Rebecca Hill informs the public that she has taken the house near the New Bridge known as the British Coffee House which she has fitted up for the reception of company' (extract in *Journal of the Barbados Museum and Historical Society*, XVI, 213, August 1949).

p.57

Mistress Quickly is a character in several of Shakespeare's plays: in *1* and *2 Henry IV* (where she is hostess of the Boar's Head Tavern in Eastcheap), in *The Merry Wives of Windsor*, and in *Henry V*.

'**Literary Society**' Founded in 1777, it appears to have been wound up in the 1860s, and its books (which amounted to some 8,000 volumes) were presented in 1868 to the Public Library which had been established in 1847. However, the name of the street called Literary Row (running between Cheapside and Lake's Folly in Bridgetown) commemorates the site of the society's premises. See Alleyne, *Historic Bridgetown*, p. 18, and extracts from *The Times* (Barbados) for 25 November 1868 and 5 October 1870, printed in *Journal of the Barbados Museum and Historical Society*, XXXII, 207 (November 1968), and XXXIII, 196 (November 1970).

the recognised lover At this period, the expression merely means 'suitor' and does not imply any sexual relationship.

p. 58

quadrilles All the dances referred to, including the 'country dance' were of European origin and very different from the dances of the slave population which Orderson refers to in disparaging terms (p. 43).

'**wanton boy who delights in love's gambols**' If this is intended as a quotation, I have not been able to trace it, but 'wanton boy' was frequently used (as here) with reference to Cupid.

negus A drink made of port or madeira wine diluted with hot water, sweetened with sugar and flavoured with lemon and nutmeg or other spices.

p. 59

Prince William Henry (1765–1837) was King of Great Britain and Ireland from 1830 to 1837. His youth was spent in the Royal Navy, and he spent several years as a captain in the West Indies. One result of this was that he later defended the interests of the West Indian planters in the British House of Lords, and was strongly opposed to the emancipation of the slaves – which, ironically, became law during his reign.

During his naval service, he visited Barbados briefly in 1786 and 1789. Writing some half a century later, Orderson's memory appears to have telescoped the two visits into one, and one or two of the details he gives of the Prince's time in Barbados (referred to again, pp. 78–9) are demonstrably inaccurate – for example, while he refers to 'one of those balls given in honour of the Prince', implying that there were several, it appears that there was only one such ball. Other details, however, can be substantiated from other sources; see Neville Connell, 'Prince William Henry's visits to Barbados in 1786 & 1789,' *Journal of the Barbados Museum and Historical Society*, XXV, 157–164 (August 1958).

There is still a Prince William Henry Street in Bridgetown.

George III King of Great Britain and Ireland from 1760–1820 was 'unhappy' in the sense of 'unfortunate'; he suffered from a bout of insanity in 1788–9 (the news of which Prince William Henry learnt on his arrival in Barbados), and although he recovered, he went mad again in 1811 and remained incapacitated for the remainder of his life.

our late patriotic Baronet was Sir John Gay Alleyne (1724–1801), a member of one of the leading planter families in Barbados and for many years Speaker of the House of Assembly. Genealogical information about the Alleynes may be found in a series of articles by Louise R. Allen originally published in the *Journal of the Barbados Museum and Historical Society* and collected in Brandow, *Genealogies of Barbados Families*, pp. 3–107.

p. 61

Pollard's little "place" Compare the distinction between 'place' and 'estate' made on page 25.

p. 62

fair one This was a conventional expression for a female beloved in English literature of the period, and does not necessarily imply any reference to Lucy's complexion. She is of course of mixed race, while Joe Pollard is referred to as 'coloured' (pp. 44) which is probably intended by Orderson to mean mixed race rather than black.

p. 64

according to Sterne The father of the eponymous narrator in the novel *Tristram Shandy* (1760–67) by Laurence Sterne (1713–68) believed 'That there was a strange kind of magic bias, which good or bad names, as he called them, irresistably impressed upon our characters and conduct' (Wordsworth Classics edition, p. 37).

Orderson's point appears to be one which depends on a knowledge of the Bible. In the Book of Judges (ch. iv and v) Deborah is a prophetess who is responsible for the defeat and death of the Canaanite general Sisera (though it is actually Jael who kills Sisera). In the apocryphal Book of Judith, Judith tricks the Assyrian general Holofernes into drinking 'much more wine than he had drunk at any time in one day since he was born' and cuts his head off. The jocular suggestion seems to be that the names of Deborah and Judith Chrichton might have been enough to frighten any man off, rather than anything to do with the marital status of their biblical namesakes: in the Bible, Deborah is 'the wife of Lapidoth' while Judith is described as a widow.

a young Cockney A native of the City of London.

p. 65

on the *qui vive* On the alert (French).

p. 66

daring exploits The account which the 'person in military costume' gives of his 'daring exploits' is a tissue of geographical and historical nonsense which does, however, have some very vague connections to real events of the Seven Years' War (1756–63; known in North America as 'the French and Indian War') which was fought between the British and the French and their respective allies in Europe, India and the Americas. 'General Gage' is probably intended for Thomas Gage (1721–1787) governor of Montreal, 1759–60 and British commander-in-chief in America, 1763–72; 'nabob' (ultimately from Hindi, *Nawab*, a deputy, in the sense of a high official representing the Mughal Emperor) was used by British writers to refer to any Indian prince or high-ranking official; the 'Moro-Castle' may refer to the British capture of Havana in 1762; 'the Queen of Hungary' is the Empress Maria Theresa (1717–80; Queen of Hungary from 1740), whose territorial disputes with Frederick the Great (1712–86; King of Prussia from 1740) were a leading cause of the Seven Years' War.

The Count D'Grasse was François Joseph Paul, Comte de Grasse and Marquis de Grasse-Tilly (1722–88), a French sailor who commanded in several battles in the Caribbean during the American War of Independence, before being defeated by the British admiral, George Brydges Rodney (1719–92), at the Battle of the Saints (fought to the north of Dominica) in 1782.

p.67

their reading had not extended . . . *The Whole Duty of Man* was a popular devotional work first published in 1658 and perhaps written by Richard Allestree (1619–81). *The Pilgrim's Progress, from this World to that which is to come*, a famous allegorical narrative by John Bunyan (1628–88), was first published 1678–84. *Sir Charles Grandison* (first published 1754) and *Pamela, or Virtue Rewarded* (first published 1740–41) are both novels by Samuel Richardson (1689–1761).

Desdemona A character in Shakespeare's *The Tragedy of Othello, the Moor of Venice*.

bastard son of Mars A pretended soldier (Mars was the Roman god of War). Soldiers are referred to as 'sons of Mars' below (pp. 69, 71). Most British soldiers at this period (and for long after) wore red coats, whence the reference to 'rascals in red'.

p. 68

cow-skin A whip made of plaited leather-thongs; used by plantation overseers and drivers to whip their slaves, it was almost their badge of office. As a former book-keeper (assistant manager on a sugar-plantation) Crosier would never have been considered a suitable match for a plantation-owner like Miss Judy; had he really been a British army officer as he pretended to be, things might have been different.

The Pool is still the name of a plantation in the Barbadian parish of St John.

taches Also spelt 'teaches' and 'tayches' (this last gives the best idea of the pronunciation), these were a series of progressively smaller open vessels of copper or iron in which the juice which had been expressed from the sugar-canes in the mill was boiled. When the juice in the smallest tayche had reached the point at which it was judged it would crystallize properly without further boiling, it was transferred to a 'cooler', which was a large wooden or copper container. After cooling, but still in the state of a thick liquid, the sugar would be transferred to pots or wooden casks in which it was 'cured': the sugar would finally crystallize and the surplus molasses would drain off, to be collected and distilled into rum.

A detailed contemporary description of eighteenth-century methods of planting and sugar-making is provided by Samuel Martin, *An Essay upon Plantership*, which was first printed in Antigua in 1750.

p. 69

Demerara Now part of Guyana, Demerara was a Dutch colony until it was captured by the British during the Napoleonic Wars. It was finally ceded to Britain in 1814.

'**Animal Flower Cave**' Still a tourist attraction. The name derives from a kind of sea-anemone. Orderson quotes (with slight variations) from the description given in the Rev. Griffith Hughes, *The Natural History of Barbados*, pp.293–8. The bet to which he refers seems to have been based on a real one: the *Barbados Mercury*, 14 March 1789, reported under 'Sporting Intelligence' that 'Mr. Cage bets Mr. Moe 50 guineas that he does not take a horse down the Cave of the Animal Flowers with the assistance of six hours labour on the road down the cave' (extract in *Journal of the Barbados Museum and Historical Society*, XVII, 178, August 1950).

p.70

a spacious barrack Long demolished, this was a building some 300 feet long which was constructed in 1783 to the west of what is now Queen's Park House (Alleyne and Sheppard, *The Barbados Garrison and its Buildings*,p. 11).

The *Barbados Mercury*, 5 April 1788, noted that 'The 49th regiment being intended to garrison in this island, the same was yesterday disembarked and marched to the barracks in Constitution Hill' (extract in *Journal of the Barbados Museum and Historical Society*, XVII, 108, February, May 1950).

Major W —— of Buenos Ayres notoriety Probably John Whitelock or Whitelocke (1757–1833), a British army officer who was a major from 1788 and served in the Caribbean in this period – he was in Barbados in 1796 (see monumental inscription to his infant son in Oliver, *Monumental Inscriptions*, p. 29). He later rose to the rank of lieutenant-general, and in this capacity commanded a spectacularly unsuccessful attempt to capture Buenos Aires in 1807. As a result of this, he was cashiered by court martial in 1808.

p. 71

'**Rachael's**' This is the first mention of Rachael Pringle and the 'Royal Naval Hotel,' described at greater length below, pp. 75–9 (see note on that passage). Orderson consistently refers to her as 'Rachael', though she is often called 'Rachel' by other writers.

'**What duel?**' A number of these were reported in the local press, e.g., *Barbados Mercury*, 13 November 1784 (extract in *Journal of the Barbados Museum and Historical Society*, XVI, 213, August 1949).

freeholders' feast The freeholders were white men whose ownership of ten or more acres of land gave them the right to vote in the election of the two members of the House of Assembly for their parish. Candidates for election to the House can be found advertizing, soliciting for votes and inviting electors to dinner or 'a cold repast' in the *Barbados Mercury*,

6 September 1783 (extract in *Journal of the Barbados Museum and Historical Society*, XVI, 72, November 1948/February 1949).

'**more honoured in the breach than in the observance**' A cliché adapted from Shakespeare, *The Tragedy of Hamlet, Prince of Denmark*, Act I, Scene iv.

p.72

'**merry, merry dance**' Perhaps ultimately from the line 'Strike up Piper a merry merry dance' spoken by the First Beggar in *A Joviall Crew, or, The Merry Beggars*, by Richard Brome (c. 1590–1652/3), first produced 1641 and often revived, being frequently performed and printed in the eighteenth century. See Ann Haaker, ed., *Richard Brome : A Jovial Crew* (London 1968), pp. 1968; xii, 30.

Lieutenant C—— was Lieutenant John Cage of the 49th Regiment, who was killed in a duel by a Mr. Forte on 18 July 1789. He was probably the same as the Mr. Cage who was involved in a bet about sending the horse down into the Animal Flower Cave (see note on the passage on p. 69). Forte is clearly Orderson's 'Mr.F—', and in this edition 'F—' has been given in the passage on p. 73, 'F—, conscious of no premeditated insult...', where the original edition has 'H—', which is clearly an error. When *Creoleana* first appeared, some of the other persons referred to in this passage by initials and dashes could perhaps have been recognized by Orderson's older readers, but identification would no longer appear to be possible.

The 'Hermitage' referred to on p. 73 was still identifiable in the early twentieth century as a building in what is now Whitepark Road, Bridgetown. 'Dead as Cage' became a proverbial expression in Barbados, especially referring to cases of sudden or accidental death, though it appeared to be dying out by the early 1940s. See Anon., 'As Dead as Cage,' *Journal of the Barbados Museum and Historical Society*, IX, 51–3 (November 1941).

p.73

Quakers' Meeting-street A name sometimes given to Tudor Street in Bridgetown, because a meeting house of the Quakers (Society of Friends) stood there until it was destroyed in the hurricane of 1780 (see Alleyne, *Historic Bridgetown*, p. 20).

St. Michael's church Then the only Anglican place of worship in Bridgetown. A church has stood on the site since the 1660s, but the present building (since 1825 St Michael's Cathedral) dates from after the 1780 hurricane.

King's House The building now known as Queen's Park House. Constructed in 1783 to replace an earlier building destroyed in the 1780 hurricane, it was the residence of the officer commanding the British garrison in Barbados.

p. 75

'**mufti**' Civilian clothes; of obscure origin, this was originally a slang term current among British military men in India.

'**Gilpin**' A reference the once very popular poem 'The Diverting History of John Gilpin' by William Cowper (1731–1800), which was first published in 1782. The point is that Gilpin was unable to control his horse. See Sambrook, ed., *William Cowper: The Task and Selected Other Poems*, pp. 278–87.

Rachael Polgreen Also known as Rachael Pringle or Rachael Pringle Polgreen (c. 1753–1791), she was probably the first freedwoman to keep a hotel or tavern in Bridgetown. Her reputed father, William Lauder, was a Scotsman who achieved considerable notoriety by claiming, in a series of publications between 1747 and 1750, that the celebrated English poet John Milton (1608–74) had plagiarised significant portions of his most famous work, *Paradise Lost*, from a large number of modern writers of Latin verse. However, it was demonstrated that Lauder had falsified his evidence by including extracts from a Latin translation of *Paradise Lost* in the passages he gave as examples of Milton's plagiarism, and he left Britain in disgrace. The famous English poet, critic and lexicographer Samuel Johnson (1709–84) was originally persuaded by Lauder's arguments and did, as Orderson says, write a preface (and a postscript) for his main work on the subject, but when Lauder was later exposed, dictated a letter for him for publication, 'acknowledging his fraud in terms of suitable contrition' – see R.W. Chapman, ed., *James Boswell: Life of Johnson*, pp. 163–4.

Lauder went to Barbados, where in 1754 he was appointed Master of the Free School in St. Michael (the institution later known as Harrison College), but he was dismissed in 1762 when the trustees found 'to their great concern and surprise that though he had been appointed to that office for above eight years he never taught a single Scholar on the foundation . . .' (This may have meant, not that Lauder had done no teaching at all, but that he had devoted himself to private pupils whom he could charge fees, to the neglect of the scholars whom he was supposed to teach in return for his salary.) Lauder died in Barbados in 1771. Documents relating to Lauder's time in Barbados were preserved by Nathan Lucas (1761–1828), a member of the Council of Barbados and an indefatigable student of the island's history, and these were printed in *The Harrisonian* for December 1923 (pp. 2–5) by a later Barbadian antiquary, E. M. Shilstone. Lucas questioned the story of Lauder's parentage of Rachael Pringle, saying that

> It has been said, without the least authority however, that Rachael Lauder, a free woman, the foundress of Hotels in Bridgetown, and who was uncommonly useful to the Navy during the American Revolutionary War, was either his child or servant. Her master came from Windward, was indicted or punished for stealing a cow, and she continued to reside in Bridgetown. The late Attorney General (Beckles) gave me this information from report and not from his own knowledge.

The Attorney General of Barbados referred to was John Beckles (1751–1823). 'Windward' in the context means from one of the parishes on the east coast of Barbados, perhaps specifically from St Philip (as opposed to Leeward, which referred to the St James and St Peter area).

The English essayist Leigh Hunt (see note on p. 22 above) claimed in his *Autobiography* (ed. Morpurgo, pp. 5–6) that it had been his grandfather who had 'recommended the famous Lauder to the mastership of the free school there [i.e., in Barbados]; influenced, no doubt, partly by his pretended repentance, and partly by sympathy with his Toryism.' In a footnote added later, Hunt noticed the passage in *Creoleana* referring to Lauder and Rachael Pringle, and gave a brief summary of it. The *Autobiography* first appeared in 1850 and was revised by Hunt in 1859, though the new edition did not appear until after his death in that year.

A certain R. Reece – possibly to be identified with the Robert Reece who published a work entitled *Hints to young Barbados planters* in 1857 (see Handler, *Guide*, p. 97) published an article on 'An unpublished page in the life of Lauder' in *Notes and Queries*, Fourth Series, V, 83–5 (22 January 1870). This gives an account of Lauder's time in Barbados, refers to him as the parent of Rachael Pringle, and describes the episode of Prince William Henry's visit, all taken more or less verbatim, but without acknowledgement, from *Creoleana*. Apart from the date of Lauder's death, the one detail which is not taken from Orderson, and which may represent independent information, is that Rachael's second 'protector,' who is called by Orderson 'a gentleman of the name of Polgreen', is referred to by Reece as 'the Deputy-Provost-Marshal Palgreen' [sic]. Reece's article was in turn drawn upon by Sidney Lee in his article on Lauder in the *Dictionary of National Biography*. See also [P. F. Campbell], *Paintings and Prints of Barbados in the Barbados Museum*, which includes a discussion of the well-known print 'Rachel Pringle of Barbadoes' which was etched by Thomas Rowlandson (p. 10) and a biographical note by Warren Alleyne on 'Rachel Pringle Polgreen' pp. 11–2); Handler, *Unappropriated People*, pp. 134–5.

Neville Connell, in his article on 'Prince William Henry's visits to Barbados in 1786 & 1789' (see note on p. 59 above), argued that the episode of the Prince's visit to Rachael Pringle's hotel probably took place on his second visit in 1789. Orderson is our only source for this famous story, which has been much repeated, especially since Rachael Pringle was elevated into a sort of patron saint of the Barbados tourist industry in the later twentieth century. However, the Prince's 'wild frolics and pranks' were remembered by other Barbadians: Poyer (*History of Barbados* p. 577) referred to 'some princely frolics, the remembrance of which often contributes to promote the hilarity of the festive board,' while in 1842 the editor of the *Barbadian*, referring to the recent publication of *Creoleana* and speaking of Rachael Pringle, said

> We perfectly recollect this immense mass of flesh (she was nearly as big as a sugar hogshead) walking with the Prince, actually leaning on the Royal Arm, and accompanied by other Naval officers, and a host of mulatto women, as His Royal Highness promenaded the crowded streets, for three nights that the town was brilliantly illuminated, the balconies crowded with ladies, waving their handkerchiefs to the mad Prince and the shouts of the populace deafening the ears [quoted by Connell].

The editor of the *Barbadian* was Abel Clinckett (1775 1854), who would have been about fourteen at the time of the Prince's second visit (see Schomburgk, *History of Barbados*, p. 125 and Oliver, *Monumental Inscriptions*, p. 78).

Although Orderson is silent on the point, one of the attractions of Bridgetown hotels and taverns in the late eighteenth and early nineteenth centuries was that the free coloured women who were their owners staffed them with attractive female slaves who were allowed or indeed encouraged to sell sexual favours to the almost exclusively white male clientele of these establishments (see Handler, *Unappropriated People*, pp. 133–8). Stories of Prince William Henry's interest in black women in the Caribbean reached England, and were made the subject of a caricature by the well-known English artist James Gillray, published 23 January 1788 (see p. 17 above).

p. 76

the Roebuck Roebuck Street, still an important centre of commercial activity in Bridgetown.

the "Jumper" A professional whipper of slaves. On the 'cowskin' mentioned below, see note on p. 68 above.

'**the accursed thing**' In the King James Version of the Bible (Joshua, vi, vii) it is said of Jericho that 'the city shall be accursed, even it and all that are therein, to the Lord.' However, because Achan had taken for his own use some of the loot from Jericho which was supposed to 'come into the treasury of the Lord,' God punished the Israelites by causing them to be defeated by the men of Ai. When it was discovered that Achan had taken of 'the accursed thing,' that is, that which had been 'consecrated unto the Lord,' the Israelites purged themselves of what they regarded as their collective guilt by putting Achan and his entire family to death.

Orderson's frequent biblical allusions, and his mention of 'Christian principle' a few lines later, suggest he may have had this story in mind, even though the phrase 'the accursed thing' was used by many eighteenth- and nineteenth-century writers in different senses, often with no reference to the biblical narrative. However, Orderson may also have been influenced here by the English poet Robert Southey (1774–1843), whose work was widely read in his own time: in his *A Tale of Paraguay* (first published 1825), Canto III, stanzas 7–10, Southey uses 'The accursed thing' to refer specifically to slavery, as something for which 'England' (presumably he meant Britain) as a nation is guilty. See Maurice H. Fitzgerald, ed. *Poems of Robert Southey*, (Oxford, 1909), p. 679.

'**do unto others . . .**' A variation of the well-known 'Golden Rule'; compare Christ's statement in the Bible: 'And as ye would that men should do to you, do ye also to them likewise' (Luke, vi, 31, in the King James Version).

p. 77

'tar' Here and on p. 79, 'tar' is used as a common expression for a sailor in the Royal Navy.

Captain Pringle of the Centaur Warren Alleyne (in [Campbell] *Paintings and Prints of Barbados*, pp. 11–12) has established that there was a British naval officer in this period called Thomas Pringle, who eventually reached the rank of Vice-Admiral, but points out that he did not become a Captain until 1776, five years after Lauder's death. While Orderson's account thus appears to be inaccurate in at least some of its details, there clearly was a connection between Pringle and Rachael – when she died in 1791 she left him a third of the residue of her estate, which was not inconsiderable, as she owned ten properties in Canary Street, Bridgetown (the present St George Street), besides her hotel, as well as nineteen slaves (Alleyne, *loc. cit.* Handler, *Unappropriated People*, p. 135).

p. 78

as Moore says in his almanack Francis Moore (1657–1715?) was an English astrologer who published an almanac which was continued under his name after his death and which still appears as *Old Moore's Almanac*. I have not found 'now about' but a late eighteenth-century example qualifies its prophecies of the weather and other events with phrases like 'About this Time', 'or near unto this very Time' – *Vox Stellarum: or a Loyal Almanack For the Year of Human Redemption, MDCCLXXX [---] By Francis Moore* (London, 1780). 'Given those symptoms of *en bon point*' means she was beginning to get fat: from a French expression, sometimes seen as embonpoint.

p. 79

Firebrace & Co. Probably a real name: 'Odwin & Firebrace' are among a list of individuals and mercantile firms or partnerships who signed an advertisement in the *Barbados Mercury*, 23 February 1788, pledging to receive all dollars and half and quarter dollars in payment at a fixed rate (extract in *Journal of the Barbados Museum and Historical Society*, XVII, 107, February, May 1950).

p. 80

petit-souper Light meal taken in the evening (French).

p. 81

'**Irish Giant**' This probably refers to Patrick Cotter (1761?–1806) who exhibited himself in Britain under the name Patrick O'Brien, 1779–1804; he was sometimes claimed to be more than eight feet tall. Another possibility is Charles Byrne (1761–83), another Irish giant of the period – the two were often confused.

Littledale and Marwell's The firm has previously been referred to (p. 49) as Littledale and Makewell; the discrepancy may be due to a compositor's problem with Orderson's handwriting, rather than to any inconsistency on the author's part.

p. 82

sans ceremonie 'Without any formality' (French).

p. 84

his confidential man Orderson does not actually say so, but it appears clear that Musso was Mr. Fairfield's slave.

p. 85

'**great doctor**' As Orderson explains later, the 'great doctor' was the white, European-trained physician or surgeon (as opposed to the black 'doctor' or 'doctoress' who treated ailments by the use of 'bush' and other remedies derived from a mainly African tradition).

p. 86

fortunately frustrated his purpose Had Joe Pollard killed, or even merely injured, Mac Flashby he would almost certainly have ended up facing the death penalty. Although Pollard was free, he would have been tried by an all-white jury which would have been unlikely to have considered that Mac Flashby's seduction of Lucy counted as extenuating circumstances for the killing of a white man by a black one. Compare the case of Joseph Denny, a free mulatto who in 1796 shot and killed his neighbour in Speightstown, a white man: Denny claimed he had mistaken the victim for a thief and had only been defending his property, but he was convicted of murder. The case (described at length by Poyer,

History of Barbados, pp. 632–44) caused a great sensation, and there was 'uproar and confusion' among the white population of Bridgetown, when it became known that the governor had decided Denny should be transported from the island instead of being executed, and some of them resorted to armed opposition in an unsuccessful attempt to prevent this. The Governor's decision was attributed by some to the influence of his coloured mistress.

p. 87

that maxim of the wise king The 'wise king' is Solomon, to whom several books of the Bible were attributed. Orderson's first quotation is from the apocryphal Wisdom of Solomon, iv, 1, 6, and his second is adapted from the third verse of the same chapter: 'But the multiplying brood of the ungodly shall not thrive, nor take deep rooting from bastard slips, nor lay any fast foundation' (King James Version).

'sangaree' A drink similar to negus (see the note to the passage on p. 58 above), but made cold. Funerals in eighteenth-century Barbados (including those of whites) were often occasions for drunken excess. A writer in 1710 claimed that

> there is always carried to the Church 10 or 12 Gallons of burnt wine or a Pail full or 2 of Rum-punch to refresh the people (for a funeral sermon makes them squeamish) where as soon as the Corps are interr'd they sit round the Liquor in the Church porch drinke to the obsequies of the defunct, smoke drink untill they are as drunk as Tinckers, and never think of the dead afterwards [. . .]

(See Walduck, 'T. Walduck's Letters from Barbados,' p. 45.) In 1743, the catechist on the Codrington estates desired a modest funeral, with 'no burnt wines, nor pipes nor tobacco two glasses of sack to each person' (Will of Sampson Smirk, 27 October 1743, Barbados Department of Archives, RB6/34, p. 376) while in 1801 Sir John Gay Alleyne bequeathed 'all the Madeira and Port wine that may not be required for my funeral' (codicil to his will, 22 May 1801, printed in Brandow, *Genealogies of Barbados Families*, p. 45).

p. 88

'when titty Lucy . . .' 'When little Lucy heard Uncle Musso tell you about him, she sat up in her bed in order to listen to what he was saying . . .'

p. 89

'**crop time**' That is, the period of the sugar-cane harvest – roughly speaking, from January to June.

'**where'er the merry dance was trip't among**' Untraced.

p. 91

'**calling out**' Challenging him to a duel.

p. 92

the Gold Coast In West Africa, in the region of modern Ghana.

'**in backara country**' In the white people's country.

p. 95

Mrs. Parry Wife of Major David Parry, who arrived in Barbados as governor, 8 January 1783, but was not accompanied by his wife, who did not come to the island until 15 April. The governor went to England on leave, 6 July 1789, but his departure 'had been preceded by that of his lady about fifteen months', which must have been around April 1788, and she died soon after her return to England, while her husband came back to Barbados in June 1790 and continued as governor until his final departure in July 1793 (Poyer, *History of Barbados*, p. 540, 586, 589, 598–9, noting corrections required by the errata leaf).

Some of Orderson's account can be substantiated from a contemporary source. What appears to have been the first balloon experiment in Barbados was reported by the *Barbados Mercury*, 15 May 1784, to have taken place 'on Monday last,' i.e., 10 May, when

An air balloon of 6 ft. diameter [. . .] was filled in 2 hours at the house of Mr Erasmus Brown in James Street. At 10 o'clock it went away in n.w. direction. The consternation of many of the inhabitants of the north part of the town who saw it in progress over them cannot be described. The crew and passengers of a Speights boat [that is, one of the small vessels which travelled regularly along the coast of Barbados between Bridgetown and the island's second town, Speightstown] suffered equal perturbation; they saw it descending and after many rebounds floating on the water. They touched and examined it but with no knowledge of what it was they brought it to Bridgetown.

The same issue of the *Mercury* noted that 'This day [i.e., 15 May] at 12 o'clock an air balloon 7 ft in diameter was let off from Mr. Brown's house. Mrs Parry (the Governor's lady) cutting the string' (extracts in *Journal of the Barbados Museum and Historical Society*, XVI, 148, May 1949).

The 15 May experiment would appear to be the one referred to by Orderson in *Creoleana*, and we may note it was very early in the history of ballooning. The first experiment with a hot-air balloon, invented by the Montgolfier brothers, took place in France in June 1783, while the first using a hydrogen balloon (the type used in Barbados, as is shown by Orderson's reference to 'steel filings and vitriolic acid') was in August 1783, also in France, as was the first human ascent in a balloon, later the same year. The first balloon experiment in Britain was on 25 November 1783, while the first in the New World took place in the French colony of St-Domingue on 31 March 1784, and there were several other balloon experiments in St-Domingue in the 1780s (see McClellan, *Colonialism and Science*, pp. 168–171). The first Barbados experiment thus took place less than six weeks after the first such experiment in the New World, and more than eight years earlier than the first balloon flight in the United States, which took place in Philadelphia, 9 January 1793.

Orderson's description places the balloon's ascent as being approximately from the area now occupied by the Central Police Station in Bridgetown. The 'Mr. Jordan, (an eminent lawyer of that day)' is identifiable from the account in the *Barbados Mercury* as Gibbes Walker Jordan (d. 1823) who was at one point a member of the island's legislature (Schomburgk does not say whether the Council or the Assembly) before becoming the Colonial Agent for Barbados in England, a position he had held for some years at the time of his death. He was a bencher of the Inner Temple and a Fellow of the Royal Society (Schomburgk, *History of Barbados*, pp. 415–6: Brandow, *Genealogies of Barbados Families*, p. 447).

I cannot identify the 'Mr. Græm' who may or may not be the same as the 'Colonel Græm' of the Ned Crosier episode (above, p. 69). Besides Jordan, the *Mercury* named Robert Ewing, James Hendy and a Mr. Cruickshanks as the organisers of the two experiments.

The enthusiasm was not maintained. The *Barbados Mercury* informed 'the Curious and Lovers of Natural Philosophy' on 22 May 1784 that 'A subscription is open at the printing office of John Orderson & Son for the purpose of constructing an air balloon large enough to carry up two men as soon as a sum of money may be raised to pay the expenses.' However, on 19 June the paper announced that 'Subscribers to the expenses of the air balloon which was advertised several weeks ago are desired to send for their subscription money and it will be returned, the sum received being so small a proportion of what is necessary as to give no encouragement to the undertaking' (extracts in *Journal of the Barbados Museum and Historical Society*, XVI, 149, 209, May/August 1949).

p. 98

'like one forlorn, crazied with care, or crossed in hopeless love!' Quoted, not quite accurately, from the *Elegy written in a country churchyard* by Thomas Gray (1716–71), first published 1751 and possibly the best known English poem of the eighteenth century. The original has 'like one forlorn,/Or craz'd with care, or cross'd in hopeless love.' (See Lonsdale, ed., *Thomas Gray and William Collins: Poetical Works*, p. 39.)

p. 102

'the sear and yellow leaf' A cliché derived from Shakespeare, *The Tragedy of Macbeth*, V, iii: 'my way of life/Is fall'n into the sear, the yellow leaf [. . .]'

p. 103

'punch and mandram' The punch is rum-punch, or possibly brandy-punch, whilst mandram is described by Nathaniel Weekes in a footnote to his *Barbados: A Poem* (1754, p. 48) as 'A Composition of minc'd Cucumber, Onion, Lemon Juice, Kyan Pepper, Salt, Water, and madera Wine. A Glass of it, is generally drunk about an Hour before Dinner, to quicken the Appetite, It is not at first relish'd by Strangers; but on Practice it soon becomes Agreeable'.

p. 104

ignis fatuus A will o' the wisp (Latin), an imaginary delusion (originally a light seen moving about in marshy land, which led unwary travellers to their doom, perhaps caused by spontaneous combustion of decaying vegetable matter).

p. 106

'**I wait, Sir, fau yerry whau Missee say**' 'I am waiting, Sir, to hear what the Mistress says.'

p. 107

'**the dew of Hermon**' Compare Psalm cxxxiii in the *Book of Common Prayer*: 'Behold, how good and joyful a thing it is: brethren, to dwell together in unity! [. . .] Like as the dew of Hermon: which fell upon the hill of Sion.'

p. 109

the old militia law Theoretically, the law in Barbados encouraged plantation owners to lease small-holdings to poor white men in return for their being obliged to serve in the island's militia. Planters were supposed to keep a specified number of white servants in relation to the number of slaves they owned, but two tenants were to be regarded as equivalent to three servants. The law was intended to keep up the numbers of the white population in general, by providing a livelihood for poor whites, and to maintain the strength of the militia as a defence against slave rebellion or external invasion. In practice, it was not very effective: see Jill Sheppard, *The "Redlegs" of Barbados: Their Origins and History* (Millwood, New York, 1977).

p. 110

'**the two elderly ladies**' The 1842 edition has 'the too elderly ladies', which is an obvious misprint.

p. 114

'**The king of France [. . .]**' A variant of the better known rhyme. 'The Grand Old Duke of York,/He had ten thousand men,/He marched them up to the top of the hill,/And marched them down again' which was applied to Frederick Augustus, Duke of York (1763–1827), second son of George III, as a result of his sometimes less than effective generalship during the French Revolutionary Wars.

p. 115

'**turned down**' Used here in the sense of 'chosen, selected.' A relic or variation of this usage can still be heard in Barbados in a set phrase: a convicted murderer sentenced to death is said to be 'turned down to hang.'

climacteric Turning-point in life.

p. 116

The Rev. Mr. Sair This is probably the Rev. Richard Saer, who was Rector of St Peter's at the time of his death in 1787, and who may have been a relative of the Rev. David Saer, who died as Rector of Christ Church in 1772 (Barbados Department of Archives: note on inside of fly-leaf of St Peter Register, RL1/39; Christ Church Burial Register, RL1/22, p. 145).

The 'desk service' probably means the Order for Morning Prayer from the *Book of Common Prayer*. Anglican churches in this period often had a reading-desk (distinct from the pulpit, used only for the delivery of sermons) from which the clergyman would read the service, while the parish clerk would read the responses from a desk of his own. Sometimes the pulpit, the clergyman's desk, and the clerk's desk were one on top of each other, forming a 'three-decker pulpit.' The 'desk service' would be opposed to the 'altar service', the less frequent celebration of Holy Communion.

The Rev. Thomas Wharton was Rector of St Michael from 1767 until his death in 1790 (Barbados Department of Archives: St Michael Register, RL1/4, p. 362; will, dated 3 April 1790 and proved 17 August 1790, in will-book, RB6/19, p. 274; see also Reece and Clark-Hunt, ed., *Barbados Diocesan History*, pp. 76–7). While the *Barbados Diocesan History* credits him with the degree of Doctor of Divinity and the *Barbados Mercury*, 14 February 1789 referred to him as the 'Rev. Dr. Thos. Wharton D.D.' (extract in *Journal of the Barbados Museum and Historical Society*, XVII, 176, August 1950), I have been unable to trace this degree, which was apparently not an Oxford or Cambridge one. He is perhaps to be identified with a Thomas Wharton who graduated MA from Queen's College, Oxford, in 1724, though this would make him very old at the time of his death.

The biblical text is from Proverbs, xxix, 2 (King James Version).

'**as pure as the consecrated snow . . .**' Adapted from Shakespeare, *The Life of Timon of Athens*, Act IV, Scene iii:

> Thou ever young, fresh, lov'd, and delicate wooer,
> Whose blush doth thaw the consecrated snow
> That lies on Dian's lap!

p. 118

mode of appointing the chief justice An Act of the Barbados Legislature in 1708 established a Court of Grand Sessions of Oyer and Terminer, and General Sessions of the Peace, and empowered the Governor to preside as Chief Justice or to appoint a Chief-Justice with the consent of his Council. As Schomburgk (*History of Barbados*, p. 203) put it

> The impropriety of the Governor's presiding over this court rendered it necessary that the power of Chief-Justice should be delegated to some other individual, and since this came into operation, it has been until recently the practice of succeeding Governors to delegate this authority to a member of the Council, or to a Judge of the Common Pleas, who in the majority of cases did not possess any legal ability or forensic skill.

What Schomburgk called 'this absurd practice, which subjected the accused to the ignorance of the presiding judge in legal matters,' lasted until 1841 when Sir Robert Bowcher Clarke took office as the first Chief Justice of Barbados to be both professionally trained as a lawyer and appointed on a permanent basis (*op. cit.*, pp. 491–2).

p. 119

'**bub**' See the Note on p. 25 above.

p. 120

'**Hope told a flattering tale**' Listed by Leigh Hunt in his *Autobiography* (ed. Morpurgo, p. 42) among 'The once popular English songs and duets' of the late eighteenth century.

p. 126

Mr. Grassett and Mr. Barrow, of Saint Philip's parish In the sessions
of 1802–3 and 1803–4, the members of the House of Assembly for St
Philip were Joshua Gittens and Elliot Grasett [sic] (extracts from records
of the House of Assembly in *Journal of the Barbados Museum and
Historical Society*, XVII, 15, November 1949). 'Mr. Barrow' is perhaps
the George Barrow who owned Mount Pleasant in St Philip in 1790
(Oliver, *Monumental Inscriptions*, p. 11), or the Hon. John Barrow who
owned Sunbury in St Philip in 1816 ([Barbados House of Assembly], *The
Report from a Select Committee of the House of Assembly, appointed to
inquire into the Origin, Causes, and Progress of the late Insurrection*, p.
59); the title of 'Honourable' indicates he was a member of the island's
Council).

Complaining about the state of the roads in Barbados was (and is) a
traditional pastime; compare Poyer, *History of Barbados*, p. 573–4.

p. 127

'When a tender maid [. . .]' The first of two stanzas of a song from Act
II, Scene ii, of *The Duenna*, by the Irish dramatist and politician Richard
Brinsley Sheridan (1751–1816). Orderson misquotes slightly: the original has no 'with' in the penultimate line, and the final line is 'Her heart
avows her fright.' See Cecil Price, ed., *Sheridan's Plays* (Oxford, 1975),
p. 134. Although not now as well-remembered as Sheridan's *The Rivals*
and *The School for Scandal*, *The Duenna*, first performed in 1775, was a
success in its time.

p. 128

'That glance that took [. . .]' Adapted from *Lara: A Tale* (1814) by the
English poet George Gordon, Lord Byron (1788–1824), Canto the First,
V, 11. 71 2. Orderson is perhaps misquoting from memory; the original
has '[. . .] a glance that took/Their thoughts from others by a single look
[. . .]'; see Frederick Page, ed., *Byron: Poetical Works* (3rd. ed. corrected
by John Jump, Oxford, 1970), p. 304.

p. 129

the simple squire is Sancho Panza, while the 'redoubtable knight' is
Don Quixote.

p. 134

amende honorable Apology (French).

p. 138

Rev. William Duke was Rector of St Thomas, Barbados, from 1758 until his death in 1786 (Barbados Department of Archives, St Thomas Register, RL1/49, pp. 133, 238). The Dukes were a prominent planter family who supplied Barbados with several Anglican clergy in the eighteenth and early nineteenth centuries; this William Duke was the author of *A Course of plain and familiar Lectures on the Articles of the Christian Faith, and on the Two Sacraments, Baptism and the Lord's Supper* (2nd ed. Gloucester, 1790), which was originally delivered to a congregation of slaves in St Thomas' Church.

There is still a district called Duke's in the parish of St Thomas.

the ancient vault of the family Planter families in Barbados often buried their dead in private burying grounds on their own plantations, usually in vaults which were substantial structures built of the local coral stone, similar to those found in the island's older churchyards. Some of these plantation vaults are still in existence; a few continued in use into the early twentieth century, even though since about the 1830s nearly all Barbadians have been buried in churchyards or public cemeteries (unlike some other Caribbean islands, where the practice of burial in private land is still relatively common).

p. 138

'**dogs of war**' Another cliché derived from Shakespeare, this time from *Julius Cæsar*, Act III, Scene i: 'And Cæsar's spirit, ranging for revenge,/[. . .] Shall [. . .]/Cry 'Havoc!' and let slip the dogs of war'.

Orderson refers to the French Revolution of 1789 and, more particularly to the events following the execution of King Louis XVI on 21 January 1793, which led to war between France and most of the rest of Europe. France declared war against Britain on 1 February 1793. The 'Imperial eagle' is the Emperor Napoleon I, ultimately exiled by the British to the 'Solitary rock' of St Helena in 1815.

The expedition of Admiral Gardner and General Bruce from Barbados to Martinique, which Orderson describes later, took place in June 1793 (Poyer, *History of Barbados*, p. 598).

p. 139

Sir Charles Grey (1729–1827), British general (later 1st Earl Grey) and **Sir John Jervis** (1735–1823), British admiral (later Earl St. Vincent), were appointed to command an expedition against the French Caribbean colonies, which left England in November 1793 and reached Barbados in January 1794. Martinique was reduced in March 1794, and St. Lucia and Guadeloupe followed in April.

President Bishop William Bishop (c. 1752–1801) was President from the departure of Governor Parry in July 1793 until the arrival of Governor George Poyntz Ricketts in June 1794, and again from Ricketts' departure in February 1800 until the arrival of Lord Seaforth as governor in March 1801. Bishop's attempts to support the British expedition against the French in the Caribbean were favourably noted in Britain, and he 'expected to have been confirmed in the government of the is-land' but was disappointed, 'the policy of the British court not allowing the appointment of a native to that situation' (Poyer, *History of Barbados*, pp. 598–9, 606–7, 651–2, 658; see also Oliver, *Monumental Inscriptions*, p. 147).

Lieut. Col. B——m, D. Q., B. M. G. The individual is unidentified, but the initials probably stood for 'Deputy Quartermaster and Barrack-Master General.' Schomburgk (*History of Barbados*, p. 191) mentions 'a barrackmaster and quartermaster-general with the rank of colonel' among the staff of the island's militia in 1841.

for the information of the public Poyer (*History of Barbados*, p. 602–7) indicates that relations between Grey and Jervis and President Bishop were not always as cordial as Orderson here suggests. The general and admiral had intended their reports for the president's personal information, and 'were not well pleased' to see them published. The 'official paper of the day' was the *Barbados Mercury*.

p.140

His Royal Highness Prince Edward (1767–1820), fourth son of George III, was a career soldier who held the rank of Major-General from November 1793. He later became a Field Marshal in 1805. He had a reputation as a strict disciplinarian. He was the younger brother of Prince William Henry (for whom see the Note on p. 59 above), referred to below as 'our old royal sailor-friend.' Prince Edward was created Duke of Kent and Strathearn in 1799. 'His illustrious daughter' was Victoria (Queen of Great Britain and Ireland, 1837–1901).

Prince Edward arrived in Martinique, 4 March 1794. He was mentioned in dispatches and thanked by the British Parliament for his part in the Martinique campaign.

The open roadstead of Carlisle Bay, on which Bridgetown stands, was the main port of arrival for shipping in Barbados until the opening of the Deep Water Harbour in 1961.

Halifax in Nova Scotia, Canada, was an important British naval station at this period.

p. 141

'**Hethersal's**' Hothersal Plantation in the parish of St. John. That this was known as 'Hogstye Plantation' in the late eighteenth century is mentioned by E. M. Shilstone in an article on its owners, the Pinder family (Brandow, *Genealogies of Barbados Families*, p. 447).

'**fortiter in re**' 'firmness in action'; from the proverbial Latin expression, *suaviter in modo, fortiter in re* ('gently in manner, but with firmness in action,' or, in other words, 'an iron hand in a velvet glove'), and here implying that the Prince lacked the gentleness of manner.

'**shearing the hog' 'hunting the boar'** There was a proverbial expression 'A great cry and little wool, quoth the Devil when he sheard the hog,' quoted by the *Oxford English Dictionary* under Hog, V, 11. The Prince also appears to be using 'hunting the boar' as an expression for wasting time, but I have not found this sense elsewhere.

p. 142

Fort Royal is what is now known as Fort de France, capital of Martinique. 'General Rochembeau' is a mis-spelt reference to Jean Baptiste Donatien de Vimeur, Comte de Rochambeau (1725–1807), a French general who had previously distinguished himself against the British in the American War of Independence.

p. 146

'**best double distilled**' Probably bay rum.

p.147

the great Duke Arthur Wellesley (1769–1852), 1st Duke of Wellington, Irish–born British military commander and victor over the Emperor Napoleon. The 'famed city' is Paris.

p. 150

compos mentis Of sound mind (Latin).

Sitting At this date, and for long afterwards in Barbados, members of the élite had fixed and regular seats in their local parish church, for which they paid an annual rent.

p. 151

to say the catechism properly The catechism in the *Book of Common Prayer*, where it is described as 'An instruction to be learned of every person, before he be brought to be confirmed by the bishop.' It is a summary of Christianity as understood by the Church of England, and even though there was then no bishop in Barbados to administer confirmation, it would appear that Caroline was teaching the tenants' daughters (almost certainly, the daughters of militia tenants, for whom see the Note on 'the old militia law' on p. 109) to say the catechism by heart as the basis of their religious education. Together with being taught to read sufficiently to read their Bible, it was probably as much education as the tenants' daughters were ever likely to receive.

'True as the dial to the sun' Adapted from *Hudibras* (1662–77) a long satirical poem by the English writer Samuel Butler (1613–80), which enjoyed considerable popularity well into the nineteenth century. *Hudibras: The Third and Last Part* (first published 1677), Canto II, 11. 175–6, reads

True as a Dyal to the Sun,
Although it be not shin'd upon.

(Italics in the original.) See John Wilder, ed., *Samuel Butler: Hudibras* (Oxford, 1967) p. 239.

p. 152

'glorious golden opportunity' Perhaps derived, at first hand or otherwise, from the mock-epic by the English parodist John Hookham Frere

(1769–1846), *Prospectus and Specimen of an intended National Work, by William and Robert Whistlecraft, of Stow-Market, in Suffolk, Harness and Collar-Makers. Intended to comprise the most interesting particulars relating to King Arthur and his Round Table*. Originally published in two parts (London, 1817 and 1818), this has the phrase 'glorious, golden opportunity' in Canto III, Stanza VI (p. 4 of the 1818 volume). Frere's poem was one of the sources of inspiration for the stanza-form and mock-heroic style of Byron's *Beppo* and *Don Juan*.

'**putting the hazard on the die**' Perhaps a reminiscence of Shakespeare, *The Tragedy of Richard III*, Act V, Scene iv: '[. . .] I have set my life upon a cast,/And I will stand the hazard of the die.'

p. 153

'**where my heart is [. . .]**' An inversion of the Biblical 'where your treasure is, there will your heart be also' (Matthew vi, 21; Luke xii, 34, King James Version).

'**e'en to touch the nerve where agony was born**' Apparently a variation of a passage in *The Brothers: A Tragedy* (1753), by the English poet Edward Young (1683–1765), Act V, Scene I:

> As love alone can exquisitely bless,
> Love only feels the marvellous of pain;
> Opens new veins of torture in the soul,
> And wakes the nerve where agonies are born.

See [James Nichols, ed.], *The Complete Works, Poetry and prose, of the Rev. Edward Young* [...], II, 301.

p. 155

pomme rose or rose apple – scientific name *Syzygium jambos* (L.) – is a cultivated species belonging to the same family (Myrtaceae) as the guava. Although it is mentioned by Gooding et al., (*Flora of Barbados*, p. 314) it is not (at least nowadays) common in the island.

'**Sweet as noyeau, and as mustard tart [. . .]**' Unidentified.

The names of the speakers in the play have been given in large and small capitals, instead of the italics used in the original edition, and a few contractions have been expanded. The positioning of stage directions follow the original edition, in which comment an how a passage should be spoken often follow, rather than precede, the passage referred to. Although notes on a few points of detail are given below, I have not provided translations of Hampshire's speeches. While they will be easier for those with some acquaintance with Bajan speech, most readers should find them intelligible, particularly if read aloud.

p. 159

he exclaims with Father Paul, *"Esta perpetua"* The quotation appears to be a misprint for '*Esto perpetua*,' which would be Latin for 'May it be everlasting,' but I have been unable to identify 'father Paul' or the source (it is not the Vulgate version of the Bible, and it would appear that it is not St Paul who is meant).

p. 164

Massa nago This expression, which appears in several of Hampshire's speeches, appears to be equivalent to 'Massa no go' in the sense of 'Don't be absurd.'

p.167

the King's House See note on *Creoleana*, p. 73 above.

p. 167–8

Bond Street . . . Bow Street In London; then as now, Bond Street was a fashionable shopping area, while Bow Street was the location of a magistrates' court, and appears to be mentioned here by Sam Shadock to suggest that Tom is the sort of person who is likely to get himself in trouble with the law.

p.168

Surplice Comical name for a clergyman (from item of ecclesiastical costume). On marriage licences, see note on *Creoleana*, p. 29 above. 'In souce' means 'all of a sudden; in one fell swoop.'

'**reticule**' A small bag, usually of woven material, used by ladies for the same purposes as a modern handbag.

p.169

God Almighty . . . He no love ugly 'God don't love ugly' is still a prover-bial expression in Barbados, meaning that God will not tolerate wicked or immoral behaviour.

p. 173

by your military law The judge does not exaggerate; punishment in the British armed forces in this period could be extremely brutal. On the com-paratively short campaign against the French Caribbean colonies in 1794 three soldiers were hanged for plunder (one of them without any form of trial), two others were sentenced to four hundred lashes each for being ab-sent without leave, and another was sentenced to eight hundred lashes for desertion, but was pardoned; see Cooper Willyams, *An Account of the Campaign in the West Indies in the year 1794*, (London, 1796) pp. 28, 42, and Appendix, pp. 10–12, 23–4.

p. 178

Squire Schanco Either a misprint or a malapropism for 'Sancho'; Alice ap-pears to be casting Hampshire, the 'Faithful Black' in the rôle of Sancho Panza, and comparing Chider and Carlove to Don Quixote. 'Knights of St. Ann's' alludes to St Ann's Castle, headquarters of the British garrison in Barbados, as well as to Quixote, the knight whom Sancho Panza served as squire in Cervantes' novel.

p.179

Distant sound of negro music In the absence of further description, one can only speculate as to what Orderson intended here – drums? a tuk band?

p.180

'**Negroes pass to and fro [. . .] on the back of the stage** Were these black actors? Who played Hampshire? It is possible they were white actors 'blacked up', as seems to have been the custom with the not insignificant number of black characters appearing in plays on the British stage in the eighteenth and early nineteenth centuries, but it is difficult to be certain, in the absence of explicit evidence.

p. 181

Aldermanbury Place in London, location of the headquarters of the Anti-Slavery Society.

p. 184

'**love our enemies**' Compare Luke, vi, 27, in the King James Version of the Bible: 'Love your enemies, do good to them which hate you.'

p. 185

to make love to you This does not have its usual modern meaning: Alice is accusing Emily only of encouraging Captain Carlove to be her suitor.

p. 186

call him out See note on *Creoleana*, p. 91 above.

the treadmill A device for the punishment of prisoners, much used in the British Caribbean during the Apprenticeship period (1834–38).

pink that red breasted robin A pun based on the red uniform of Carlove as a British soldier, and the meaning of 'pink' in the sense of 'to wound'.

p. 195

the 'tericks Hysterics.

p. 196

President of the Island See note on *Creoleana*, p. 30 above.

Town Agent See note on *Creoleana*, p. 49 above.

doubloon A Spanish gold coin, officially valued at four pounds ten shillings Barbados currency by Governor Parry's proclamation of 1791 (see the Note on page 35 of *Creoleana*,) though in 1816 the merchants of Bridgetown agreed to raise its value to 100 shillings, or five pounds currency (see Greaves, 'Money and Currency in Barbados,' XX, 14).

p. 197

whether carved in ivory [. . .] There is possibly an allusion here to the English churchman and miscellaneous writer Thomas Fuller (1608–1661) who, in his description of the character of 'The good Sea-Captain' in *The Holy State* (Cambridge, 1642, p. 129), said that 'our Captain counts the image of God nevertheless his image cut in ebony as if done in ivory'. In his 'Imperfect Sympathies', first published in 1821 and reprinted in his *Essays of Elia*, which were popular throughout the nineteenth century, the English essayist Charles Lamb (1775–1834) paraphrases Fuller, claiming 'I love what Fuller beautifully calls – these "images of God cut in ebony". But I should not like to associate with them, to share my meals and my good-nights with them – because they are black.' See Thomas Hutchinson, ed., *The Works in Prose and Verse of Charles and Mary Lamb* (2 vols., Oxford, n. d.), I, 549.

A similar reference, probably derived from Lamb, appears in Frieda Cassin's *With Silent Tread: A West Indian Novel*, printed in Antigua in the 1890s – (see the edition by Evelyn O' Callaghan in the Macmillan Caribbean Classics series).

Jephtha's daughter In the biblical account (Judges, xi),

> Jephthah vowed a vow unto the Lord, and said, If thou shalt without fail deliver the children of Ammon into mine hands; Then it shall be, that whatsoever cometh forth of the doors of my house to meet me, when I return in peace from the children of Ammon, shall surely be the Lord's, and I will offer it up for a burnt offering.

Jephthah was horrified when it turned out to be his daughter who came to meet him, but he nevertheless killed her as a sacrifice to God.

The Barbadian poet Matthew James Chapman (1796–1865) treated this subject in his *Jephtha's Daughter: A dramatic poem* (London, 1834).

p. 203

she murrow 'Her mother'. This pronunciation is still remembered in Barbados, though it is now seldom heard, having been more or less ousted by 'mudda'.

p. 204

I been carry de Captain in de parlour A perfect example of the still common Bajan use of 'carry' to mean 'take, conduct'.

treeology Jokes on *-ology* are still popular in Barbados. Bajan readers will recall, for example, the Merrymen's 'big-rockology.'

BIBLIOGRAPHY

(a) Manuscript sources:

Barbados Department of Archives
  Parochial registers of the Anglican Church
  Will of Sampson Smirk, 27 October 1743, recopied will-book, RB6/34, p. 376.
  Will of Rev. Dr. Thomas Wharton, 3 April 1790, recopied will-book, RB6/19, p. 274.
  Shilstone Notebook No. 2: original letter of I[saac] W[illiamson] Orderson to William Reid, Governor of Barbados, [Bridgetown], 8 July 1847.

Cambridge University Library
  J. T. Gilmore, "Episcopacy, Emancipation and Evangelization: Aspects of the History of the Church of England in the British West Indies" (Ph.D. thesis, 1984).

Lambeth Palace Library, London
  Fulham Papers, American Colonial Section (these include documents relating to Anglican clergy in Barbados in the eighteenth century; a calendar is provided in Manross, *Fulham Papers*, for which see below).

(b) Printed works:

Alleyne, Warren, *Historic Bridgetown* (Barbados, 1978).
Alleyne, Warren, and Jill Sheppard, *The Barbados Garrison and its Buildings* (London and Basingstoke, 1990).
Allsopp, Richard, *Dictionary of Caribbean English Usage* (Oxford, 1996).
Anon., *Hamel, The Obeah Man* (2 vols., London, 1827).
Anon., "Miscellaneous Words and Phrases in use in Barbados," *The Harrisonian* (April 1926), pp. 8–10.
Anon., "As Dead as Cage," *Journal of the Barbados Museum and Historical Society*, IX, 51–3 (November 1941).
Anon., "Odd pages from old records," *Journal of the Barbados Museum and Historical Society*, XVI, 113–7 (May 1949).

Anon., "Barbadians who qualified as Doctors of Medicine at Edinburgh up to 1845," *Journal of the Barbados Museum and Historical Society*, XXVIII, 149–152 (August 1961).

[Barbados House of Assembly], *The Report from a Select Committee of the House of Assembly, appointed to inquire into the Origin, Causes and Progress of the late Insurrection* (Barbados, n.d. [1818]; facsimile reprint by Barbados Museum and Historical Society, Barbados, n.d.).

Beckles, Hilary, *A History of Barbados: From Amerindian settlement to nation-state* (Cambridge, 1990).

Brandow, James C., comp., *Genealogies of Barbados Families* (Baltimore, 1983).

Brathwaite, Edward [Kamau], *The Development of Creole Society in Jamaica, 1770–1820* (Oxford, 1971).

[Campbell, P. F.], *Paintings and Prints of Barbados in the Barbados Museum* (Barbados, 1981).

Cassin, Frieda, *With Silent Tread: A West Indian Novel* (Antigua, n.d. [c. 1890]).

Chapman, R. W., ed., *James Boswell: Life of Johnson* (Oxford, 1980: World's Classics ed., intro. by Pat Rogers, repr. 1989).

Collymore, Frank A., *Notes for a Glossary of Words and Phrases of Barbadian Dialect* (5th ed., Barbados, n.d.).

Connell, Neville, "Prince William Henry's visits to Barbados in 1786 & 1789," *Journal of the Barbados Museum and Historical Society*, XXV, 157–64 (August 1958).

Cruden, Alexander, *A Complete Concordance to the Old and New Testament or a Dictionary and Alphabetical Index to the Bible* (reprint of edition by William Youngman, London and New York, n.d.).

Deerr, Noel, *The History of Sugar* (2 vols., London, 1949–50).

Dickson, William, *Mitigation of Slavery, in two parts [...]* (London, 1814, facsimile reprint, Miami, 1969).

Drabble, Margaret, ed., *The Oxford Companion to English Literature* (5th ed., revised; Oxford and New York, 1995).

Edwards, Bryan, *The History, Civil and Commercial, of the British West Indies* (5th ed., 5 vols., London, 1819).

Encylopaedia Britannica, 11th edition (29 vols., Cambridge, 1910–11).

Fitzgerald, Maurice H., ed., *Poems of Robert Southey* (Oxford, 1909).

Foster, Joseph, *Alumni Oxonienses: The Members of the University of Oxford, 1500–1714* [and 1715–1886] (8 vols., Oxford, 1888, 1891–92.)

Fraser, Henry, and Sean Carrington, Addinton Forde, John Gilmore, *A-Z of Barbadian Heritage* (Kingston, Jamaica, 1990).

Frere, John Hookham, *Prospectus and Specimen of an intended National Work, by William and Robert Whistlecraft, of Stow-Market, in Suffolk, Harness and Collar-Makers. Intended to comprise the most interesting particulars relating to King Arthur and his Round Table.* (London, 1817 and 1818; facsimile reprint in one volume, with new intro. by Donald H. Reiman, New York and London, 1978).

Fuller, Thomas, *The Holy State* (with *The Profane State*) (Cambridge, 1642).

Gilmore, John, "A 1789 Description of Barbados", *Journal of the Barbados Museum and Historical Society*, Vol. XLIII (1996/1997 [in fact, 1998]), pp. 125–142.

——, *Faces of the Caribbean* (London, 2000).

——, *The Poetics of Empire: A Study of James Grainger's* The Sugar-Cane (London, 2000).

Gooding, E. G. B., and A. R. Loveless, G. R. Proctor, *Flora of Barbados* (London, 1965).

Greaves, Ida, "Money and Currency in Barbados," *Journal of the Barbados Museum and Historical Society*, XIX, 164–9; XX, 3–19, 53–66 (August, November 1952, February 1953).

Haaker, Ann, ed., *Richard Brome: A Jovial Crew* (London, 1968).

Handler, Jerome S., *A Guide to Source Materials for the Study of Barbados History, 1627–1834* (Carbondale, Illinois, 1971).

——, *The Unappropriated People: Freedmen in the Slave Society of Barbados* (Baltimore and London, 1974).

——, *Supplement to A Guide to Source Materials for the Study of Barbados History, 1627–1834* (Providence, RI, 1991).

Hone, William, *The Every Day-Book; or, Everlasting Calendar of popular amusements, sports, pastimes, ceremonies, manners, customs, and events, incident to each of the Three Hundred and Sixty-Five Days, in past and present times; forming a complete history of the year, months and seasons, and a perpetual key to the Almanack; …* (2 vols., London, 1826).

Hughes, Griffith, *The Natural History of Barbados* (London, 1750; facsimile reprint, New York, 1972).

[Hunt, John, and Leigh Hunt, ed.], *The Examiner*, vol. IX (London, 1816; facsimile reprint, London, 1997).

Hutchinson, Thomas, ed., *The Works in Prose and Verse of Charles and Mary Lamb* (2 vols., Oxford, n.d.),

Levy, Claude, *Emancipation, Sugar, and Federalism: Barbados and the West Indies, 1833–1876* (Gainesville, 1980).

Lonsdale, Roger, ed., *Thomas Gray and William Collins: Poetical Works* (Oxford, 1977; repr. 1985; Oxford Standard Authors series.)

McClellan, James E., III, *Colonialism and Science: Saint Domingue in the Old Regime* (Baltimore and London, 1992).

Manross, William Wilson, *The Fulham Papers in the Lambeth Palace Library: American Colonial Section, Calendar and Indexes* (Oxford, 1965).

Martin, Samuel, *An Essay upon Plantership [...]* (4th ed., Antigua printed, London reprinted, 1765).

Moore, Samuel, ed., *The Public Acts in Force, passed by the Legislature of Barbados, from May 11th 1762 to April 8th, 1800, inclusive* (London, 1801).

Morpurgo, John, ed., *The Autobiography of Leigh Hunt* (London, 1949).

[Nichols, James, ed.], *The Complete Works, Poetry and Prose, of the Rev. Edward Young, LL. D., formerly Rector of Welwyn, Hertfordshire, &c. revised and collated with the earliest editions. To which is prefixed, A Life of the Author, by John Doran, LL. D.* (2 vols., London, 1854; facsimile reprint, Hildesheim, 1968).

Oliver, Vere Langford, *The Monumental Inscriptions in the Churches and Churchyards of the Island of Barbados, British West Indies* (London, 1915).

Orderson, J. W., *Cursory remarks and plain facts connected with the question produced by the proposed Slave Registry Bill* (London, 1816).

——, *The Fair Barbadian and Faithful Black; or, A Cure for the Gout. A Comedy in Three Acts* (Liverpool, 1835).

——, *Creoleana: or, Social and Domestic Scenes and Incidents in Barbados in Days of Yore* (London, 1842).

Page, Frederick, ed., *Byron: Poetical Works* (3rd ed., corrected by John Jump; Oxford, 1970).

Partington, Angela, ed., *Oxford Dictionary of Quotations* (revised 4th ed., Oxford, 1996).

Philip, Maxwell, *Emmanuel Appadoca; or, Blighted Life: A Tale of the Boucaneers* (new edition, edited with an afterword by Selwyn

R. Cudjoe, introduction and annotations by William E. Cain; Amherst, MA, 1997).

Poyer, John, *The History of Barbados, from the first discovery of the Island, in the year 1605, till the accession of Lord Seaforth, 1801* (London, 1808; facsimile reprint, London, 1971).

Price, Cecil, ed., *Sheridan's Plays* (Oxford, 1975).

Reece, J. E., and Clark-Hunt, C. G., ed., *Barbados Diocesan History* (London, n.d. [c. 1927]).

Reece, R., "An unpublished page in the life of Lauder," *Notes and Queries*, Fourth Series, V, 83–85 (22 January 1870).

Sambrook, James, ed., *William Cowper: The Task and Selected Other Poems* (London and New York, 1994; Longman Annotated Texts).

Schomburgk, Sir Robert Hermann, *The History of Barbados; comprising a geographical and statistical description of the island; a sketch of the historical events since the settlement; and an account of its geology and natural production* (London, 1848, facsimile reprint, London, 1971).

[Shakespeare, William], *The Riverside Shakespeare* (Boston, 1974).

Sheppard, Jill, *The "Redlegs" of Barbados: Their Origins and History* (Millwood, New York, 1977).

Shilstone, E. M., "Orderson Family Records," *Journal of the Barbados Museum and Historical Society*, XXV, 152–7 (August 1958); reprinted in Brandow, *Genealogies of Barbados Families*, pp. 427–432.

Spevack, Marvin, *The Harvard Concordance to Shakespeare* (Cambridge, Mass., 1973).

Starkey, Otis P., *The Economic Geography of Barbados: A study of the relationships between environmental variations and economic development* (New York, 1939; facsimile reprint, Westport, CT, 1971).

Sterne, Laurence, *The Life and Opinions of Tristram Shandy, Gentleman* (Wordsworth Classics edition, Ware, Hertfordshire, 1996)

Stephen, Leslie, and Sidney Lee, ed., *The Dictionary of National Biography* (63 vols., London, 1885–1900, with later editions and supplements).

Venn, John, and J. A. Venn, *Alumni Cantabrigienses: A biographical list of all known students, graduates and holders of office at the university of Cambridge, from the earliest times to 1900* (10 vols., Cambridge, 1922–54).

264   BIBLIOGRAPHY

Vox Stellarum: or, A Loyal Almanack For the Year of Human Redemption, MDCCLXXX [...] By Francis Moore (London, 1780).

Walduck, T., "T. Walduck's Letters from Barbados, 1710–11", *Journal of the Barbados Museum and Historical Society*, XV, 27–51, 84–88, 137–149 (November 1947, February, May 1948).

Watson, Karl, *The Civilised Island, Barbados: A Social History 1750–1816* (Barbados, 1979).

Weekes, Nathaniel, *Barbados: A Poem* (London, 1754).

Wilberforce, Robert Isaac, and Samuel Wilberforce, *Life of William Wilberforce* (5 vols., London, 1838).

Wilberforce, William, *An Appeal to the Religion, Justice, and Humanity of the Inhabitants of the British Empire, in behalf of the Negro Slaves in the West Indies* (London, 1823).

Wilder, John, ed., *Samuel Butler: Hudibras* (Oxford, 1967).

Willyams, Cooper, *An Account of the Campaign in the West Indies in the year 1794* (London, 1796).

Yearwood, Mrs. H. Graham, *West Indian and Other Recipes* (n. p. [Barbados], 1932).